ERAMUS
OF
HARES
END

GUILLAUME F. CHARRON

WARRINGTON
PUBLISHING

DANBURY, CONNECTICUT

Eramus of Hares End
Copyright © 2025 by Guillaume F. Charron

Published by Warrington Publishing
Danbury, CT
www.warringtonpublishing.com

Printed in the United States of America

First Edition

ISBN: 978-1-944972-54-7 (paperback)
        978-1-944972-53-0 (hardcover)
        978-1-944972-52-3 (ebook)

Cover designed by GetCovers

Edited by Mike Waitz at Sticks & Stones

To all those who have suffered psychological trauma and have become "forever changed". I admire your courage, fighting hard every day to live a semblance of a normal life. I have seen that kind of suffering firsthand and know the toll it takes. Move forward, ever forward, one foot in front of the other. Never despair and never give up because there is always hope.

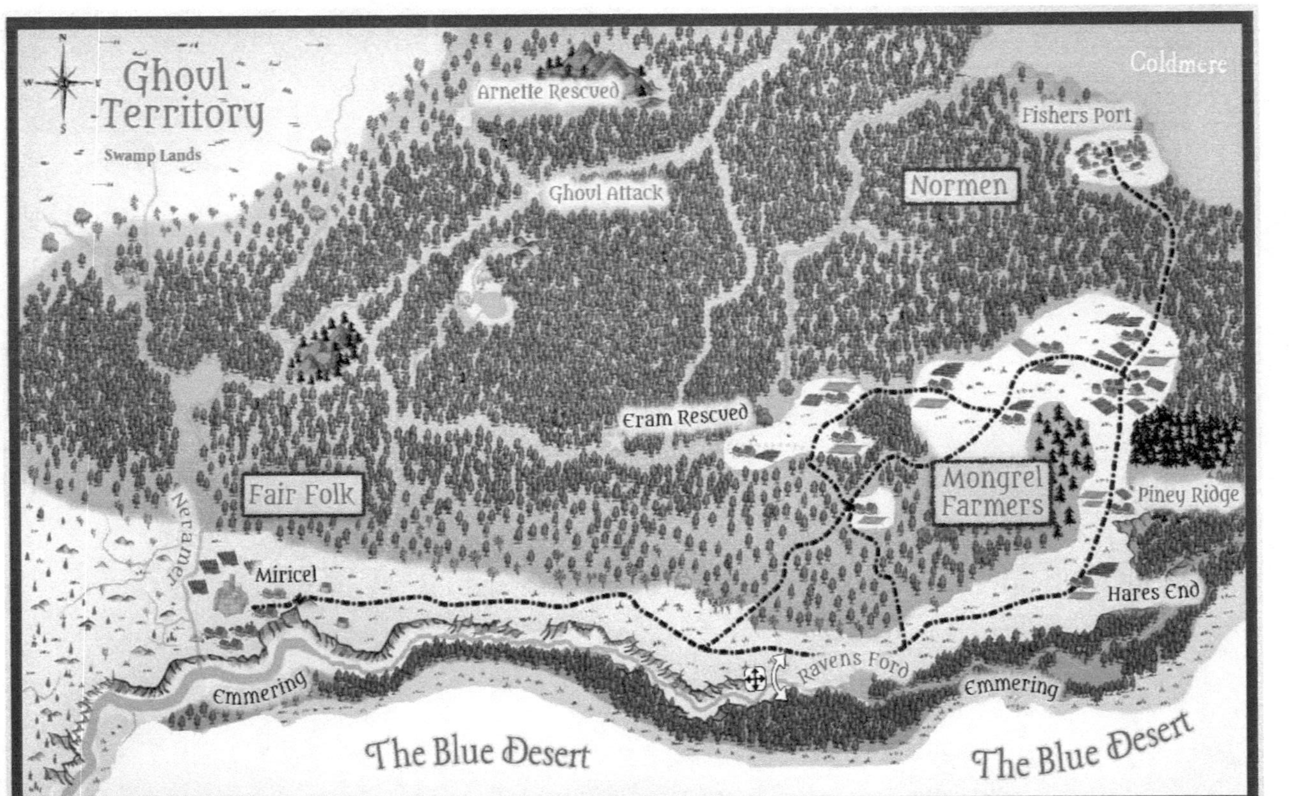

Ghoul Territory
Swamp Lands
Arnette Rescued
Ghoul Attack
Normen
Coldmere
Fishers Port
Eram Rescued
Mongrel Farmers
Piney Ridge
Fair Folk
Neramer
Miricel
Hares End
Ravens Ford
Emmering
Emmering
The Blue Desert
The Blue Desert

PROLOGUE

The young woman pulled a chair alongside the bed where the scrawny, grizzled man lay. She took his hand and he turned to regard her. Smiling lovingly, she pushed back the remaining hairs on his head out of his face and kissed his forehead.

"How are you feeling today?" she gently queried.

"Tired. Just like yesterday and the day before."

"Do you feel up to continuing?"

"Where is your mother? I haven't seen her in days."

The woman did not answer immediately. Her mother had been gone for years, and it saddened her to know he was experiencing periods of mental infirmity with increasing regularity. She was deeply concerned for him, but also for her present task to capture his personal history. It was something she had determined to accomplish on her own. No one asked her to do it, but she felt a compelling need to record everything about this man who had changed their entire society.

"She is not here presently, but Sheralutra will be back later today. Will that please you?"

The old man's face screwed up slightly and his brow furrowed, but he made no response.

"Can we talk about your life some more? I am deeply interested in hearing about all the things you have done and all the places you have been."

His face relaxed somewhat, and he responded, "Sure, Minushua. Where did we leave off?"

"Tell me more about Hares End."

FARMER

"Eramus's maternal grandparents were merchants and traveled extensively. As a girl, while traveling with her parents, his mother heard the name and fell in love with it. She decided in her early years to give that name to her first son."

– Minushua's notebook

Eramus wandered through his village's field. The corn was barely as tall as him and the ears were small and only partially full. Many of the stalks had only one full ear, only a few bore two, and he found none with the expected three. Frowning, he wiped the sweat off his brow as the sun beat down upon him. *Another failed season of crops*, he thought. This year, drought, the year before, it was too wet, and the corn blighted. A bad season could be expected occasionally, but this was the third in a row, and the surplus gathered in the good years was gone.

The village needed this year's crop to be a success to get them through to the next. A bad crop was always unwelcome news, but especially so for Eramus, for he was a farmer. It was his responsibility to plan the village's plantings, diversify the crops, and offset the fickle effects of nature. He had failed, though not for a lack of trying. Nature conspired against him and now the village elders were sure to blame him. Blame, however, seemed trivial with starvation looming on the horizon.

And it wasn't just the corn. Hoppers had devastated the beans, the hot, dry weather sent the kerrits to seed, and maggots ruined the cabbage and turnips. Even the apple orchards barely produced this year. Eramus stooped to put his rough, callused hand into the scorched earth. It was dry and dusty, and everywhere, deep cracks split the ground open. He used a stick to pry deep into the soil — no sign of moisture. Standing, he clapped the dust off his hands and using them to shade his brown eyes, searched the sky for any sign of rain. But the skies held none.

He hadn't checked the parsnips yet, but the scraggly plants that should have been full and leafy didn't bode well. Eramus was encouraged this spring by a particularly good turnout of the peas and leafy greens that provided much-needed relief from the skimpy rations of this last winter. But they could not compensate for the summer's drought.

Last winter was bad; the village even killed a larger than usual share of hares to make ends meet. But the hares were scarce this year and were surely not going to meet the village's food needs.

Such was the agricultural plight of Hares End, so named because of the once-plentiful rabbit population in the outlying grassy plains extending all around the village. Eramus frowned because tonight, he would have to make his report to the Ruling Hand. At least this wasn't going to be a big surprise for them, but it was Eramus's responsibility to come up with an alternate survival plan for the village, and right now, nothing was coming to mind.

Noise filled the lodge. All around, Eramus could hear men talking in worried tones. Sherman, the spokesman for the Ruling Hand, stood upon the earthen dais and called for quiet. The din subsided to a low rumble.

"Quiet, I said, quiet in here!" the spokesman barked out, his voice straining. But though his voice was old, his piercing, deep brown eyes commanded respect. This time, a real hush fell upon the lodge. Behind the spokesman, the other four members of the Ruling Hand fidgeted on the long bench that supported them. The spokesman looked around sternly, eyeballing the few remaining men who were whispering. When he was satisfied that he had everyone's attention, he addressed the Hares End assembly.

Sherman pushed the few remaining hairs on his head off to one side and began, "It is Summer's End Day, where night has caught an' now overtakes the day, an' according ta our wisdom, it is time ta report on the crops an' the 'spected harvest. Eram, our chief farmer, will come forward an' give us his report."

This was the moment Eramus had been dreading all day. Making his way through the men sitting on the lodge floor, he looked straight ahead, trying to forget every eye was on him. Climbing the short incline to the platform where the Ruling Hand sat, he raised his right hand, fingers spread wide as was the custom to acknowledge the village leadership. They all nodded in response to Eramus's hand gesture. He took position and faced the village's men.

He was not an imposing figure, but he stood tall, his shoulders squared. His lean, but well-muscled arms hung loosely at his sides. Eramus caught himself clenching his fists; he took a deep breath and forced himself to relax as he looked quickly at the twenty-six men who represented their families in village affairs.

He glanced at the spot where he sat the very first time he attended a council meeting. Having turned eighteen and becoming a husband earned him that seat. It was a night to be remembered — his father nominated him to be the next lead farmer under his tutelage. The Ruling Hand and everyone present assented cheerfully. His father was on the dais smiling at him proudly that day. He only wished he could feel that proud and confident now.

Eramus then pushed back his sandy brown hair with his hand and cleared his throat.

"It is Summer's End Day an' according ta the wisdom a the Ruling Hand, it is time ta judge our harvest outlook fer the comin' season." This was the easy part, as the words never varied year to year. Eramus could remember his father standing in this very spot making his report. He couldn't recall him ever having to bear bad news. More was the pity; he could have used some inspiring words just now. Drawing another deep breath, he steadied himself.

"Corn was hurt by the dry weather…I think it will only meet half of our needs till next harvest."

Heads were collectively shaking, and a low murmur rose from the floor. Unfortunately, half did not equate to simple hunger — it meant a serious threat to the survival of the families in Hares End, for it represented half of the minimum to keep them alive. It meant some would starve. Eramus waited a moment before he continued.

"The drought has 'fected the other crops an' the orchards. Cause of no rain, most of the root crop has done poorly. Kerrits: only a third of what we hoped fer. Parsnips, only half. Hoppers have eaten most of the beans. I think only a few pounds will be harvested. Worms got the turnips an' cabbages an' we lost a third of those."

The noise from the floor grew louder with every bit of unwelcome news. Behind him, Eramus could hear the elders talking amongst themselves. He sighed to himself and then spoke loudly.

"But that's not all." Eramus paused to allow the talking to subside. "The stores from last year was used up gettin' us through last winter. I fear we face a very hard season ta come."

The spokesman rose and placed his hand on Eramus's shoulder and motioned for him to step aside.

"What word, hunters?" he called out. The assembly quieted in anticipation of some good news. Lance stood up to represent the hunters.

"Game is scarce, the grasslands is too dry. We've spotted few hares, an' the large game has moved ta find better feed. We'll 'ave ta look farther ta find what we need. Some of us are worried about crossing over inta the other villages' huntin' grounds. An' ya know what that means." The burly man took his seat quickly.

"What word, Fishers?" the spokesman queried.

"Nuttin good 'ere, spring run weren't very large. We 'ave some smoky fish, but not 'nough to make up fer a bad crop."

The mood in the lodge was palpably grim. Each man was talking to his neighbor. Everyone was asking the same question, and everyone was giving the same reply: What will we do? I don't know.

Sherman said, "We must find food ta hold us till next spring, or some a us will starve. There's no food here so we must look elsewhere." He turned to face Eramus. "Can yer men handle bringin' in the rest a this year's crop?"

"With so little ta harvest, it won't take hardly many men at all," Eramus said, shaking his head.

Sherman continued, "Well, then, it falls upon ya ta find us more food." He turned back to face the villagers and announced loudly, "We'll send Eram ta the neighboring villages ta bargain fer whatever they can spare."

The blood ran from Eramus's face. He had resigned himself to taking the blame, but he had not anticipated this! He had never traveled far from Hares End — there was never a need. The idea of going out alone to strange villages on such a desperate mission made his stomach knot.

A moment later, another disturbing thought occurred to Eramus. Maybe this was a polite way of asking him to leave and never come back. He tried to push that unpleasant idea out of his mind. The reaction from the men gathered there was not one of overwhelming confidence. Everyone here knew that if Hares End did poorly, the other villages were probably no better off than they.

A tall, lanky man, Carmac, one of the hunters, stood to speak. "Supposin' they do have some extras, what will we barter with?" A fresh wave of whispering rippled across the floor of the lodge. The spokesman looked back to the other members of the village council. They leaned close to each other and exchanged words for a few moments. Finally, they all nodded in agreement. Alma's head sagged to lean on his hands, covering his face.

Ed, the man who would probably be the next spokesman after Sherman's passing, spoke in a hushed voice. "As we agreed."

The spokesman paused and looked at each of the men on the bench.

"Jes' do it," Ed asserted, his old, dry voice cracking.

The spokesman faced the tense crowd. Eramus could see there was a lot of emotion bottled up in the Ruling Hand. Ed was staring at the wall, away from the other men. Eramus could see a tear running down one of Alma's arms. The other two men sat there, a scowl on their faces. Eramus wondered what terrible news was going to be revealed. Sherman took a deep breath.

"We'll marry off our daughters in trade."

Eramus's eyebrows shot up in surprise as the room exploded with angry shouts.

"No! Not my daughters! How could you!" Orson, one of the hunters, was on his feet protesting loudly.

"I know this is a hard thing, son, it breaks ma heart. They're ma granddaughters, too. I love 'em very much. But I'm not gonna watch 'em, or anyone else's children starve! An' I don't have ta remind any of ya that two of the men behind me have daughters, too."

Ed and Alma's reaction now made sense. They both had a daughter late in their lives, and they treasured those young girls more than life itself. Those girls were what probably kept them going at their extreme age. Both men were over fifty years old. They might have only another five summers left before they passed on. Losing the joy of their old age would certainly lessen that expectancy.

"Now listen, we have four marrying age daughters an' only one young man. Three of them would have left sooner or later. If they go to a village that's better off, at least they won't starve, an' our food will go that much further."

"Who'll stay an' who'll go, then?" asked Orson, standing defiantly with his arms folded.

"It's up ta Artur," Sherman said firmly.

Sitting near the front, a sixteen-year-old boy with sandy blond hair turned bright red. "Poor Artur," Eramus muttered to himself. He felt bad for his nephew. Choosing from the four girls would be hard enough without any kind of pressure from their parents. To date, the boy hadn't shown any real preference. He was struggling to help his mother care for their family after his father died last year. Eramus wasn't even sure the lad was ready to marry yet. Eramus decided to step forward and speak up. "Listen, this is a big decision. I'm sure the Ruling Hand didn't come by it easy-like. We's in a bad spot an' that calls fer hard choices, let's not make it worse." Orson glared at him. He could almost feel the anger.

"Well, if ya had done yer job right, we wouldn't a come ta this," Orson spat vehemently, pointing an accusing finger at Eramus.

The other farmers leaped to their feet and angry words began to fly back and forth across the room. The farmers were adamantly defending Eramus (and themselves). While the gatherers accused the growers of being lazy, the volume rose significantly.

"Enough," bellowed Sherman. His tone of voice hushed them immediately. Orson stood there, his face red with anger. "All o'ya sit down an' shut up!" Sherman concluded.

Orson complied but gave his father a look of disgust before doing so.

"Eram is right, this is hard — but blamin' each other won't make our problems go away. If we want ta survive, we hav'ta work together. No more arguin'. The Ruling Hand has decided." He thrust his open hand into the air. The other members of the council raised theirs, as did Eramus. The rest of the men were silent. The men began to extend their hands to acknowledge the Ruling Hand's decision, Orson's hand being the last to go up.

Looking around the room, the spokesman found the support to be unanimous. Dropping his hand, he continued. "Eram'll set off as soon as he can. Council meetin' is over!" The men began to stand up and file out.

Eramus moved quickly to the front of the platform and added loudly, "Look..." The men all paused and turned toward him. "I'll only use the marriage barter if I has ta. I'll see what I can do ta make other trades. But if I have ta give yer daughters away, I'll make sure they get good husbands an', if I can, try ta get them the right ta choose fer themselves."

Some of the men nodded in agreement, but not Orson, he just left. It wasn't much, but it was all Eramus could offer them. The other members of the council approached.

"Thankee, Eram, I know you'll do yer best." Ed gently put his fist on his shoulder and gave him several firm thumps.

"We don't blame ya, Eram. Ya worked as hard as any man here, maybe harder, just bad luck that's all. But we know you'll give it ya best. That's why we're sendin' ya. We're sendin' ya out alone, not as punishment, but so there will be just one man bargainin'. Ya is right fer the job, ya know the worth of grains an' foodstuffs. Ya is our best hope." Charlie was speaking but the other members of the council all nodded in agreement.

"Thankee," Eramus answered.

"How soon can ya go, Eram?" Sherman inquired.

"A day or so, just long enough ta set the chores fer the others an'...uh...pack."

"Good, good! Well, let's all git home," Sherman offered.

Charlie grabbed the last torch from its sconce and the six men left the lodge. Just outside, Orson was waiting. He stepped up to his father and speaking as quietly as he could manage given his anger, he said, "I raised ma hand an', I'll go along with this. But you can break the news ta ma wife. I ain't doin' yer dirty work fer ya!" He turned and left without waiting for a reply.

"Jes give 'im a lil' time, Sherman." Vince put his hand on the old man's shoulder. Sherman just sighed. He suddenly looked much older, more weighed down.

Eramus didn't feel much like going home. His empty hut seemed more like a cage than a place of comfort. Comfort. *When did I last know comfort,* he wondered. The last few years seemed to be one struggle after another beginning when Miriam and his son died. Tonight, he ached for the comfort of her arms, her gentle reassuring words that might have given him the strength and courage to embark on this journey. A journey about which he had serious doubts of being successful. The weight of responsibility for the welfare of the entire village burdened him mercilessly.

He wandered to the slopes east of the village and found a fair spot in the field of wild grasses and late-flowering plants. He sat down, hugged his knees, and rested his chin on them. The fields sloped downward for many hundreds of yards into a stand of young trees. Beyond them were the steep banks leading down to the Emmering River. He listened carefully, trying to hear its churning waters, but the gentle night breezes stirred the grasses and drowned out any sound from below.

Looking now into the night sky, he stared at the pinpricks of light in the deep blue. They shimmered near the horizon. Sighing, he leaned back carefully until he lay flat on his back. Above him, the stars stared down. He looked deep into the starlit tapestry of the night until he felt like it was going to engulf him. The feeling was almost like he was moving toward them. The grass around him blocked out all else, even the wind. *What are they? How far away are they?* he wondered. The stars drew him in toward infinity while the wind sang a soft lullaby. Slowly, he slipped off to sleep, hypnotized by the night.

DREAMER

A small child was crying, lost, and alone in the dark. Her small, pitiful cries drew him to her. He felt compassion for the child and wiped away her tears. Taking hold of her little hand, he led her away, and together they searched. At length, she found what she had lost: a little wreath of flowers. Kneeling before her, Eramus placed it upon her head as she smiled back at him. Then the flowers began to move, to spin as it were, about their centers. Slowly at first, then they rapidly gained speed until they became blinding points of light. Eramus sat back on his heels, surprised and frightened by this unusual transformation.

She reached out to Eramus with her right hand and placed her fingers upon his forehead. She fixed his gaze with hers. Her eyes were dark, bottomless pools that reflected naught but infinity. Eramus gasped as he felt himself being swallowed up by those eyes. Suddenly, she transfigured before him, no longer a child, but a mature woman full of serene grace and wisdom. Her noble qualities emanated like the warming rays of the sun and all of

Eramus's apprehension dissolved into a peaceful calm. Smiling, she spoke to him and as she did, he felt an astonishing sensation. A pleasant, tingling shock penetrated his entire being. She spoke unto him but a single word: *Cerusmet.*

Eramus sat bolt upright and blinked in the bright, early morning sun. His sudden motion sent several rabbits scurrying to their warrens. He looked around for a moment gathering his wits. Finding himself once again at Hares End, he laughed aloud, "Wild hares and wild dreams!" Rising from his grassy bed, he brushed away the bits of seeds, stems, and leaves from his clothes. Giving his short sandy hair a quick toss, he turned to face the village. The mirth dissolved from his face, and the grim affairs of the night before returned to rest like a great weight upon his shoulders. Inhaling deeply first, he let a long, slow sigh escape his lips. Unhurriedly, he walked back into the little circle of homes.

Eramus gathered what little food he could take on his journey and placed it in his backpack. Some dried kerrits, a few red, sun-dried tomas, and some dried hare-jerky. He looked through the rest of his pantry, where he found a few pounds of ground corn and a small crock of honey. He would have liked to take the honey but there was no way to keep it from making a mess in his backpack. Honey was Eramus's weakness. Great on cornbread, or over porridge. He even had a special recipe for fresh kerrits with butter and honey, his all-time favorite dish. Rearranging his backpack, he moved the bag of corn to the bottom and distributed its weight evenly.

Examining the other makeshift shelves, he found some goat cheese wrapped in cloth. It was getting hard, so he gave it a sniff. It was still good, but he knew he should finish it soon before it became completely inedible. He found his wooden bowl and a small, sturdy metal pot for cooking. The other cooking utensils were too cumbersome to cart around in a backpack.

He looked around, wondering where he had put his eating utensils. He found the wooden fork and spoon on the windowsill. He had carved them himself from a good piece of birch; two spoons and two three-tined forks. He had given them to Miriam as a gift when they were married long ago. His memory couldn't or wouldn't recall where the other set was.

Under a bench in the corner was his root storage. He lifted the lid and ran his hands through the damp, loose sand, searching for any root crop stored there. As he moved his hand through it systematically, his efforts yielded two small kerrits. Dusting them off, he let the lid drop, making a dull thump. Arranging the latest items carefully in his backpack, he stowed all but one of the two roots. He walked over to a water pot and rinsed the kerrit off.

Holding the kerrit in his teeth, he went back to the cupboard and took the crock of honey to the table. He uncovered the crock, took the kerrit, dipped it in the honey, and noisily munched his meal.

Mentally reviewing his instructions to the other farmers from this morning, he sorted through all the details to make sure he hadn't forgotten anything. Dipping his meal into the honey before every bite, he slowly crunched his way to the top. After eating all that was good to eat, he licked the last of the honey off the stub and set it on the table. With his forearms resting on the table, he stared blankly into the air. Finally, after a few minutes, he picked up the root top, walked over to the window, and tossed the stub onto the compost pile.

He looked one last time around his dingy little hut and its meager contents. *Not much of a home anymore*, he thought. Miriam had used flowers and dried herbs to brighten and give it a sweet fragrance. Her bright eyes, smile, and laughter alone turned this simple abode into something of a palace where Eramus felt himself a king. Now dusty, quiet, and cold, it had become a prison of painful memories. He put the honey pot away and went to shutter the windows.

He rolled up his blanket, and then stooping through the short entrance, he exited his cottage and closed the door behind him. Sheron, his lanky sister-in-law, was waiting just outside, Little Miriam holding her hand. Sheron had her long hair partially tied back with a bit of string, the rest of it shooting out as it saw fit, a jumbled mixture of brown and gray. Wearing a simple smock that was once green, but now faded and ragged at the hem, she smiled generously at Eramus.

"Hello, Sheron! I was comin' ta see ya afore I left, but I see ya saved me the trip." Eramus finished securing the door behind him, stepped over to her, and gave Miriam's older sister a warm embrace. He squatted to be on Little Miriam's level. Taking her free hand and kissing it, he teased her saying, "How's the prettiest girl in the village doin' today?" She giggled and buried her face in her mother's skirt. Eramus smiled.

After her sister died, Sheron bore another child late in life and gave her the name of her lost sister. The love between the two sisters was strong. Miriam's mother was sickly, and Sheron had practically raised Miriam herself, and so her grief was double — she had lost both a sister and a daughter. But Little Miriam was the balm that healed Sheron's grieving soul and filled the painful void with love. Although the little girl was a joy to all, within him, Eramus's soul was still a gloomy cavern of emptiness.

"I made sumpin' fer ya — fer ya trip, Eram." She handed him a small package wrapped in a small piece of cloth. The mouth-watering aroma of freshly baked bread brought a smile to his face.

"Mmmm, it smells wonderful. Thankee, Sheron, but won't ya need this more 'n me?" Eramus said as he offered it back to her.

Sheron refused, saying, "No, Eram, ya must. If ya don't ..." She looked down, biting her lip. She couldn't finish. The weight of Eramus's task became a little heavier. He put his hands upon her arms.

"Are ya goin' ta Piney Grove?" she asked after composing herself.

"Acourse. I'm goin' there first."

"Please look in on me son an' his family."

"Ya bet I will. Someone has ta keep an eye on that young rascal."

"Would ya give this ta 'im? It's just a little gift ta let 'im know I love an' miss 'im." She handed Eramus a small, hand-sized bundle. From the smell, he could tell it was medicinal herbs. He opened his backpack and placed the bread and herbs carefully on top of his other supplies. He slung the backpack over one shoulder.

"Look after me place while I'm gone, will ya, Sheron?"

"Acourse."

Breaking away, he started toward the orchard, but after only a few steps, he halted and returned to Sheron. He took her by the hands and stared deeply into her blue eyes. He felt like he was abandoning her. She was the only family he had left. Sheron had lost her husband last year and even though her son Artur was strong and able, he worried about her family's welfare. Artur was nearly of marrying age and soon he would have a family of his own to care for, leaving Sheron to care for Little Miriam by herself. He spoke seriously to her.

"If I'm not back by the first snow, take what ya can use from me stuff, an' give the rest ta the others. Artur can start his family here. I hope he makes better use of the place than I did," he said, nodding toward his hut.

"You'll be back," she answered confidently.

"I hope yer right," he said with a smile and gave her a final long embrace.

Eramus started back down the well-worn path leading to the orchard. Along the way, he picked some flowers and began to work them into a wreath. He wandered off into the long prairie grasses to find enough to finish his little project. Satisfied that he had plenty, he hopped across the weeds and grass back onto the path. He moved up into the orchard and turned left to walk along the far edge.

He made his way to a small spot under the shade of a great elm. He looked around and found the grave where his son and wife were interred. Nothing marked the spot except a slight rise in the ground and a few dry leaves from a small patch of white-bulb spring-bloomers he had planted at the head of their grave. Kneeling, he began to fashion the rest of the flowers he had picked into a wreath.

Memories of Miriam coursed through his mind. He had buried her together with his son. He put them together with her arm around his little body to protect him. That was four springs ago, but the images were still vivid, and though diminished, the pain was still deep.

It was here under the shade of this tree that he courted her. Where he offered, and she accepted, the wreath of flowers that signified she would have him to be her husband. They would retire here after a long, hot summer day's work to frolic in the cool grass and watch the stars appear.

It was a favorite game of hers to tease him then run away, daring him to catch her. Of course, she never had a chance, as his long powerful legs could easily outrun hers. Half the time, he suspected she didn't really try. He recalled her lying there in the grass, her long, light brown hair splayed about, sparkling blue eyes, her arms extended and inviting him into her embrace. Oh, how he loved her smile and the dimples it made and how she loved to run her fingers through his wavy hair.

It was there they talked about their dreams for the future and the family they planned to raise. This was her favorite spot above anywhere else in the entire world, as far as their little world extended anyway. She had told him that many times, lying in his arms beneath this great, old tree.

"Miriam, I hope ya can hear me. I have missed ya so much. Things is bad here, crops been poor last few years an' now I'm off ta find food ta save the village. I know ya wouldn't approve of me naysayin', but I don't feel very hopeful about the whole thin'. I just wanted ta say goodbye in case I never make it back ta our heaven-spot. I love ya. I'll be thinkin' of ya always. Bye, love."

Eramus tenderly placed the flower wreath on the mound. Standing up, he dried his eyes and looked around. A gentle breeze rustled the leaves. He strode off back toward the orchard. He decided to cut through the field and adjacent woods rather than walk back through the village. The undergrowth wasn't very heavy here and he weaved his way through it to the old path that connected the other villages.

Eramus stopped just briefly to adjust his straps for comfort. He looked back toward Hares End and thought for a moment about all the people who were counting on him for survival this winter.

"Here ya go, old boy," he muttered to himself and started down the path that led around the corner into the woods north of Hares End.

GUILLAUME F. CHARRON

PINEY GROVE

"The farming village folk were not a sophisticated lot. They simply looked about and named the towns and villages after whatever was there. If a lake was nearby, then Lake Town, a hill — Hillsdale, a stream — Brookville. They never used a person's name. Survival was so preeminent, being remembered for something was too far into the future to merit any serious thought."

– Minushua's notebook

As Eramus came into sight of the first few structures of Piney Grove, dusty, barefoot children came running from everywhere. They surrounded him, keeping pace with him. Mostly it was the younger ones. The older children were probably working. A little girl was running alongside him, struggling to keep up with the rest. She was tugging at his tunic, trying to get his attention as Eramus was bombarded with a series of questions.

"Where did ya come from?"

"Hares End."

"Is it far?"

"Not really."

"What's yer name?"

"Eram."

"Are ya goin' ta stay?"

"Just a little while."

"Are ya stayin' the night?"

"Maybe."

"What's in yer backpack?"

"My things."

"How long ya been travelin'?"

"Just today."

"Did ya see any wolves?"

"No."

"Did ya see any bears?"

"Hmmm. No."

"Did ya see any monsters?!" It was the littlest one tugging his tunic who asked the last question. She was almost out of breath, but her squeaky, excited voice rose above the others. Eramus laughed out loud. He reached down and picked her up, carrying her with one arm. "No. No monsters."

The other children had gleaned enough information and ran ahead to announce his arrival, a much disorganized, chaotic, chorus of town criers. The little one in his arms fidgeted and he put her down. She ran after the others shouting, "Wait fer me-ee!" It made Eramus happy to see all these children — it was a sign of a healthy, growing village. But it hadn't escaped him how thin they were, not a chubby cheek in the bunch. He feared conditions here were much the same as at Hares End.

Two women and an elderly man appeared in the village commons with the children leading the way. They waited for Eramus to approach, giving the children hand signs and shushing them to be quiet. The elderly man stepped forward and greeted him with outstretched hands.

"Welcome ta Piney Grove, traveler."

"Hullo, I'm Eram from Hares End," he responded and loosely hugged the old man, and they clapped each other on the back as was customary among the small farming villages.

He motioned for the women to leave. They herded the children in front of them, talking quietly among themselves. The old man took Eramus's elbow for support, and they slowly made their way toward the community lodge.

"What news from Hares End, Eram?"

He knew what the old man was asking, and Eramus answered, "I've been sent ta talk with the elders about—" and he almost said food, but he paused for half a breath and said, "—the drought."

The old man shook his head in acknowledgment.

"Yea-up," he drawled, "bin dry here, too." The old man looked him in the eye when he spoke.

Eramus knew the answer to his question. Asking the village elders would now be a mere formality.

"Are ya just passin' through?" The old man's dry voice cracked slightly as he spoke.

"Yep."

"Next village is a long day's trip. Stay here tonight an' ya can tell us what's new at Hares End."

"Thankee, I'd like that." Eramus was glad he was invited to stay. The rest of his visit could be spent pleasantly now. The old man was probably one of the Ruling Hand and he could have just as easily said, "Ya got a long way ta go, best be on yer way." This trip was going to be hard enough. It would be easier if he could spend part of it as a welcome guest.

Of all the villages, this one was the most closely tied to Hares End. Colleen, one of Piney Groves's daughters, married Jimmy, a young farmer from Hares End. His nephew, Erin, moved here and married five years ago. News from the two villages was exchanged during their mutual visits and usually shared publicly if it was good, or amusing. It was a time looked forward to by everyone in these small villages.

"What is that rascal, my nephew, Erin up ta? I have sumpin' fer him from his mother."

"Let's go see." The old man led him through the central village commons out toward the fields. After a short walk, the old man pointed out Erin working in one of the fields, then took his leave and returned to the village.

It had been a long time since Eramus had seen his nephew, and he almost didn't recognize the boy who had grown into a man. Farming was hard, demanding work, and Eramus could see the years on his nephew's brow like the furrows a farmer worked year after year. His arms and neck were browned deeply where the sun had baked them unmercifully. His wife, Lavender, was working beside him, an infant strapped to her back, another sitting close by. Together the couple worked a row of vegetables, removing weeds, loosening the soil, and mounding it around the base of the plants. Occasionally, he would see Lavender pluck a diseased leaf or crush a leaf miner as she moved along the row.

"Well, that's a real nice family ya has there, Erin."

Erin looked up and wiped the sweat from his face with the back of his hand.

"Uncle Eram! Hullo! Lav, this is ma uncle from Hares End." Lavender stood up; her hand pressed hard against her back. Eramus could see now she was expecting another child soon, her distended belly no longer hidden by her clothing. She smiled and moved to her husband's side. Erin put his arm around her waist, and she leaned heavily on him.

"Good geese! I ain't seen ya in years! What brings ya ta Piney Grove?"

"It's a long story. We can talk 'bout it afta dinner."

"Ah, good idea! We need ta finish up here, then we can start fixin' some food."

"Why don't ya send Lav an' the children on ahead an' I'll help ya finish up."

"An even better idea! Lav, go on an' start home. Uncle Eram an' I can knock out the rest a this easily, then we'll be along shortly." He kissed her on the brow and gave her a gentle pat on the bottom as she started home. She turned her head and gave him a disapproving look.

"See if ya can teach him some manners while yer at it, Uncle Eram. He's in sore need!"

"I'll give it a try, but don't get yer hopes too high — me manners ain't much better!" Lavender laughed and waved them goodbye, then taking the older child's hand, she made her way back to the village.

"So, Erin, how's yer crop doin?"

"It's bin really dry, Uncle." Erin looked over the fields pensively, and then turned to Eramus and asked, "Hoe or weed?"

"I'll hoe. Yer younger than me. You do the bendin'," Eramus replied as he took the hoe from him. The two men started back to work. After a few minutes of silence, Erin spoke without even looking up. "An' how are the crops at Hares End this year?"

"Bad, Erin. Really bad. That's why I'm here. The Ruling Hand has sent me ta find food. If we can't get some, not everyone's goin' ta make it till spring." Erin paused momentarily and then resumed work, but he remained silent.

"I can tell the drought has hurt yer crops, too. I really didn't 'spect anythin' from Piney Grove. It took all a one minute ta figure that out from the elder that greeted me."

"Yep, it's gonna be a pinch for us this winter, but we has enough, just no extras."

"That's good. I wanted to send your family away while we talked about this. No need ta upset them, too. I want'cha ta look after yer mother an' sister at Hares End. Maybe ya should invite them ta winter over with ya. Your mom's not so young, ya know, an' it's a lot fer her ta take care of Little Miriam. Besides, she would probably give her share ta Miriam an' Artur, even if it meant she'd starve."

"What 'bout Artur?"

"He can handle hisself, he's young an' strong. Besides, he'll be starting his own family soon an' ya know what that means. Just take care a yer mom an' yer sister; everythin' else will sort itself out."

"I have ta get the Rulin' Hand's permission, ya know. They're not goin' ta take well ta more mouths ta feed."

"She'll be able ta bring her portion with her, plus she's a widder with a little child, ya can use that ta convince 'em. It won't be like they have ta support them totally. Another thin', yer mom's good with herbs — is there room at Piney Grove fer a good healer?"

"Ah, that there is!"

"See, ya can make it work! Be a good son an' see ta it."

"I will, Uncle. Ya can let me mum know."

Eramus grew silent, his jaw clenching as he pondered his next words. "You'll have ta tell her yerself. I'll not be going back ta Hares End. At least not fer some time, if I make it back, that is."

Erin looked up at him, squinting against the sinking sun, his expression one of concern.

"Oh, don't give me that look, I'm serious. If I don't find some grain, there'll be no reason ta go back. I'm not goin' back just ta watch 'em starve ta death." Erin still seemed unconvinced. Eramus paused, leaning on the hoe while he caught his nephew's eye. "OK, here's some proof, but ya can't tell a soul, not even Lav."

"All right then, what is it?"

"I've bin given leave ta trade off some of our daughters fer food!"

Erin's mouth dropped open and he cocked his head to the side as if he hadn't heard clearly. "Yer just makin' that up," he finally managed.

"No, it's true! From the mouth of the Rulin' Hand an' approved by the villagers. I was there when it happened, an' let me tell ya, there were a bit of an uproar over that!"

Erin returned to the row and Eramus put the hoe to task again. The two men had nearly finished while they were speaking. When they finished, Erin got up, arched backward to stretch his spine, and shook himself off. Eramus tossed him the hoe and Erin slung it over his shoulder. Together they walked to the edge of the garden, where Eramus picked up his backpack.

"Well now, Uncle, are ya ready ta eat?"

"Yep! More than ready. In fact, I has a fresh loaf of bread made by yer mother, given ta me just this mornin' afore I left. We'll all have a bit with dinner. I'm dyin' ta taste it, the smell's bin makin' me crazy all day!"

"That'll be a real treat! Maybe in the next couple of days, Lav can make some cornbread, too!"

"I won't be stayin' that long. I need ta press on ta the next village. Be leavin' first thing tomorrow morning. I know it's a bit soon, but winter's comin' an' I think I might have ta travel quite a distance ta find what I'm lookin' fer. I'll just need some directions, then I'll be off. Now, remember, ya promised ta take care of yer mother and sister, right."

"Don't fret, I'll be sure they's taken care of."

The men walked along the well-worn path back to Erin's little cottage. There they dined and spent the night talking about old times and updated each other with the latest news and gossip. Eramus brought out Sheron's little gift and presented it to Lavender, who received it graciously. Then he held Erin's first-born child and tickled her until her mom interceded and put her to bed. The adults retired to the outside and watched the day fade into the night. Eramus sat back and sighed while Lavender made herself comfortable in Erin's arms.

Tomorrow would bring another day of traveling and Eramus could already feel the effects of today's journey in his legs. But the day was drawing to a close. A good day and a good start to his errand.

One of the village elders approached them and said, "We's gonna meet in the lodge if'n ya wants ta share some news."

Eramus responded, "Sure, I'd be glad ta'."

Lav got up and kissed her husband, saying, "I'll clean up an' stay with the children, ya go on ahead, ya kin fill me in after." Erin nodded and got up, and the three men ambled to the lodge.

Eramus was mildly surprised at the turnout — the floor was full of men, women, and children. He thought it would be only the leadership, but now there was a sizeable audience making him just a little uncomfortable. The old man who greeted Eramus when he arrived earlier that day, stood and motioned him to join the Ruling Hand on a rickety-looking platform just two feet above the earthen floor. Putting his arm around Eramus's shoulder, he guided him to the front, saying, "This be Eram a' Hares End. He's gonna tell us the news from his village."

After clearing his throat, Eramus began, "Well..." He started by naming the men that comprised the Ruling Hand and the current state of the village, how bad the crops were and the Ruling Hand's decision to send him out to look for food. He started talking about the families at Hares End, relating some important and sometimes humorous affairs of the village. There were a handful of folks there who knew of or had kin in his village, and he answered their questions to the best of his recollection.

When it was all over, Eramus thanked the village elders for their hospitality and wished them well. Then he and Erin walked silently back to the cottage. They found Lav outside enjoying the cool breeze. Getting up, she let Erin sit, then took up a comfortable position in his arms.

Soon they retired inside, where Eramus found a spot in the loft to sleep. He spread out his blanket over the straw bedding and lay quietly on his back in the cozy cottage. His eyelids became suddenly heavy, and he closed them and quickly fell into a deep, dreamless sleep.

The days and weeks passed without success for Eramus. Wandering from village to village, he found the circumstances of each to be similar to Hares End. The effect of the drought was widespread, but its severity seemed to lessen as he traveled farther north. He came to realize how small and desperate his village was compared to the other farming communities. Many of the ones he had visited were at least four or five times as large as his. One, Farmsdale, was easily ten times the population of Hares End.

So many of the other villages had so much more diversity. Most residents were farmers, of course, but some had men who specialized solely in trades like working metal and wood. Some had seamstresses and millers. One even had a place just for travelers called an inn, though Eramus was too poor to stay there. He was amazed that some had turned their commons into long rows of buildings that touched end to end with a long wide path running between the two rows of structures. There were stores where farmers traded their produce for goods. Still, despite their prosperity, none were interested in helping Hares End. His pleas for help fell upon deaf ears in their councils.

But he would get offers from individuals, often farmers who, although they had little, offered to share what they had. But their offers would only scratch the surface of Hares End's problem. So, he politely refused them for the time being, adding that if he returned this way, he would collect the donations on the way home.

Fortunately for Eramus, lodging was never a problem. He was always welcome to stay with those men who worked the soil. There was an unbreakable bond among those who eked out their existence from the earth by their sweat and toil. Thanks to their generosity, Eramus was able to continue his search with an occasional bit of bread, a piece of cheese, or some corn meal, and always their encouragement and best wishes for his success.

Unlike Hares End, the larger villages or towns, as they called themselves, did not seem to work as a unit. Individual families seemed to survive independently of each other. This had a surprising effect. In some towns, some were well-fed and well-dressed, living alongside those who were hungry and ragged. In Hares End, the status of every family was the same. If the village was prosperous, all shared in that prosperity. If they were not, they would find themselves as they did today.

ERAMUS OF HARES END

Eramus's experiences gave him much to ponder while traveling the long distances between villages and towns. The faces of those he met would linger in his memory when he sat around campfires on cool evenings, making his journey seem less lonely. There were many good people out there and if circumstances were different at Hares End, he probably would have invited them to come to live among them.

The day was pleasant, and the sun was warm for autumn. He busied himself with his impressions of the many towns he had traveled through and the folks he met. The trail was easy to follow, and he gave it little thought, expecting to find another farm, town, or village at every turn. Thus far, he had not discovered any real help for Hares End. He pushed that worry far from his mind, telling himself the very help he needed might be just around the bend.

Eramus's reflections were suddenly interrupted. The trail he traveled had come to a fork. He didn't remember any advice about which way he should go next, and he wondered if it even mattered. Scratching his head, he tried to think it out. Finally, he decided he should go to the closest village, but which way? Both trails seemed equally worn. He pondered for another long moment, hands on his hips, gazing up into the trees towering above him. Looking around the area, he spied a large pine with lower branches within his reach.

"Well, let's jes' go take a look-see," he said aloud to himself. He removed the backpack and set it at the base of the great tree. He spat into his hands and leaped up to grasp the lowest branch. He swung his body and hooked a leg over a neighboring branch and pried himself up between the two limbs. From here, the rest was an easy climb. When he was a youth, the orchard behind Hares End was one of his favorite spots. He must have climbed every one of those trees, including the great elm. He remembered seeing into the distance from its top, clinging to the springy branches, letting the wind sway him gently back and forth. And that was what he planned to do now, take a good look around from this lofty tree.

He congratulated himself on being so clever, and still in good enough shape to climb. It was exhilarating to work his way up through the branches. As he neared the top, he stepped back on the limb beneath him to see how much farther he had to go. Holding onto the next limb, he leaned back, shading his eyes from the sun with his free hand.

But a pine tree is not an elm, and Eramus was not the light, young boy he had once been. The brittle branch he held snapped with a sharp crack and backward he fell through the feathery greenery. He tumbled out of control, plummeting through the branches. His upper thighs caught a branch, and it spun him before splintering into sharp shards that gouged his lower left leg deeply.

He had lost his orientation; everything was a green blur. Another branch caught him in the ribs and spun him in the opposite direction. The limb didn't break but Eramus thought he heard something crack. Finally, he came to a sudden stop, landing flat on his back, a great *Oooof!* escaping his lungs. The wind was knocked clean out of him, and he lay there staring up into the great tree, unable to breathe. Around him fell a gentle rain of needles, showering him with their pleasant fragrance.

After a long moment, he finally managed to gasp a breath of air. Slowly, he recovered his wind and began to breathe evenly again. His leg throbbed and his ribs burned, making breathing laborious. When he tried to sit up and look at his leg, the pain from his ribs shot through him like a red-hot knife. He gasped at the suddenness of the sensation and the frightening way it slapped him back onto the ground. Falling helplessly onto his back, he wondered out loud, "Oh, no. What 'ave I done?"

The last two days, or was it three, he wasn't quite sure, had become a nightmarish blur. The fever that started in his injured leg spread to his whole body and muddled his thinking. Eramus pulled himself along the ground and set himself with his back to a tree. His bulky backpack prevented him from getting closer. Suddenly, he couldn't recall how he got his backpack on. This and many other details were a confusing puzzle, like rope tangled around his feet. His poor, dazed mind kept tripping over the facts, but was unable to make any sense of it all. His ribs throbbed and burned. His injured leg was oozing a trail of pus and blood, leading the wolves right to him.

Ahh, the wolves! How long had they been trailing him? More knots in his tangled mind. He struggled to remember. Since the stream? One day or two days ago? He vaguely recalled one chilly night when the howling woke him. Hour by hour, they drew closer. Since then, his sleep had been fitful at best. He was weakened. No food in days and the hand that held the small scythe he used to defend himself trembled. In the distance, he could hear the snuffling wolves closing in on his scent.

"This is it, old boy," he muttered, and he looked around to see if he had chosen a good place to die. Yellow eyes appeared in the corner of his vision, and he agonizingly pulled his legs up as close to himself as he could to keep the wolves from pulling him away from his last place of defense. They circled slowly inward, their noses working the air and their mouths drooling over the prospect of a meal. Eramus pushed up against the tree and swung the scythe from side to side in hopes the wolves would not approach. The leader came in close for a good look but stayed just out of Eramus's reach.

Eramus cleared his throat and yelled in an attempt to frighten him off. The lanky wolf hopped away a couple of paces, only to return just as quickly. Others came in closer, and they were beginning to snarl at each other and grow bolder. One tried to snap at Eramus's leg but ducked out of the scythe's way. Eramus swung again but one of the wolves caught the scythe in its teeth. In shock, he yelled loudly, but as he did, another wolf seized Eramus's wounded leg in his jaws and shook it violently. Eramus's lungs seemed to burst as he cried out in anguish. His cries echoed through the woods. The wolf released the leg but now he was bleeding profusely, and the throbbing pain further clouded his mind. He feebly swung the scythe before him, but his vision was beginning to blur. He blinked hard to regain focus, but nothing changed.

A realization came to him, *I'm going to die*. An odd sort of peace filled him, and his pain began to fade into a warm numbness. Still waving the scythe feebly about, he felt wonderfully comfortable and sleepy. *This isn't so bad,* he thought. Any fears he had about death passed away and he allowed himself to relax. The very last thing he saw before passing out was a beautiful woman standing over him. Her hair was long and her face very fair. *An angel,* he mused before slipping through the haze into unconsciousness.

ENTER THE ANGEL

"Once, as a child, I found a young sinnimurus. It was injured and I pitied it, bringing it home to care for until it healed. Though my father disapproved, my mother interceded, fostering my kind nature. She told me that compassion for others was a sublime grace that should be promoted. She also told me that small deeds of compassion can bring forth great and unimaginable changes in people's lives."

– Lewatollma's memoirs

Eramus came out of the blackness into a strange place. He saw Miriam in the distance. She was calling him, but he couldn't hear what she was saying. "Miriam, come closer," he called out weakly to her. "What is it?" She floated closer to him. He could see her face clearly. There was lavender braided into her hair and she was in a flowing light blue smock. Eramus smiled. He had forgotten how lovely she was. She came close, her face well within arm's length. He tried to reach out to her, but his limbs were frozen. "Miriam," he cried out, "help me!"

"Eram," she said softly, in a sound that was somewhere between a whisper and the burbling of a brook, "wake up."

Wake up? Eramus was confused. Miriam faded into the blackness.

"Wake up," a different voice called from close by. *I must be asleep*, he thought. Eramus tried to pry his eyes open but could not.

"Wake up," the voice boomed louder and Eramus felt his ribs catch fire. Instantly, his eyelids flew open and he screamed out in pain, his parched voice cracking. He saw flames all around and a cloaked figure looming just above him, the face hooded and dark. Fear seized Eramus's heart. *Am I dead?* he wondered.

"Drink," the voice said and Eramus felt water splash about his mouth. A few drops made it inside and he swallowed painfully. His leg hurt, but the water helped bring his senses into focus. He felt more liquid in his mouth, and he drank, gulping it hastily.

"Carefully now, go easy," the voice gently warned.

It slowly dawned on Eramus that a hand was supporting his head and neck. He swallowed two more small mouthfuls from the waterskin that trickled cool refreshment into his mouth. The hand gently lowered his head. He blinked hard twice to try to focus on his surroundings. The hooded figure moved down toward his leg. He felt cool water dribble over his fiery wounds and the pain subsided somewhat in his leg.

He licked his dry lips and managed a hoarse, "Who?"

"Silence. Do not talk. Save your strength, you are severely injured," the voice chided.

The figure pulled an amulet from beneath her robe. A small, red gem shone from a simple, silvery chain. The figure grasped the gem in her fist and held it to her chest, just below the throat. She slowly lowered her head to Eramus's leg, nearly bringing her forehead in contact with the wound, lingering there for just a moment, during which Eramus felt a brief tingling sensation in his leg. Quickly, the figure placed the charm back into its place of hiding. His benefactor carefully inspected the injury and then replaced the bandages.

Eramus watched, but it all seemed so unreal. He tried to stop them, but his treacherous eyelids slid shut and he slipped once again into the dream-like haze that enveloped him. Eramus passed in and out of consciousness repeatedly that night. He was disoriented, to say the least, and his strength was gone. At one point, he awoke to feel a chill running through his entire body.

His senses were coming back, and he realized it was a woman's voice talking to him, but the words made no sense. He could hear a fire crackling and it must have been a large one, for he could feel its heat on his side, and it felt good. Cracking his eyes open for a moment, he saw a hooded figure hovering over his leg. He closed his eyes and rested while his leg was being treated. The figure finished attending to his wound and moved away to crouch with her back to him. His thirst was tremendous, and it nagged him awake.

Eramus opened his eyes again and with inordinate effort, managed to say, "More...water."

She turned to look at him and set down her work, came close to him, lifted him by the shoulders, and put the waterskin to his mouth. She let him draw water by himself this time. Eramus drank four small mouthfuls and then turned away from the skin, signaling he had had enough.

"Cold," said Eramus, shivering.

The woman stood and fiddled with her cloak's clasp near her throat. She removed her hood and Eramus saw long, mahogany brown hair fall all around her face. She shook it back to reveal a fair complexion, bright, soft brown eyes, and pointed ears. *Pointed ears*!! This was something Eramus was not prepared for, and he experienced a piercing cold shock that ran through his whole body.

The firelight danced off her features, casting strange, haunting shadows. His mind was still fevered and the sight of her caused memories of childhood stories to surface. Tales about pointy-eared demons that wandered the deep woods at night, stealing children and the souls of fools who wandered out alone. Fear seized his heart. As she moved closer, he shut his eyes tightly, turned away, and wailed in a small, frightened voice, "Nooooo!"

Placing her hand on his forehead, she sighed, "Still feverish and sweating profusely." She finished removing her cloak and placed it around him. Getting behind him, she moved him closer to the fire. He groaned loudly when his ribs were moved. He was so weak that he couldn't even raise a single finger to resist her.

"Does that hurt?" she inquired, giving his sides a gentle squeeze. Eramus answered with a sharp intake of breath. His mind was fighting to connect with reality but gaining no real ground. *Why is she torturing me?* he wondered. She gently put her hand under his shirt.

"Your clothes are saturated with perspiration; little wonder you are cold. I know it hurts to move about, but this garment must come off." She worked it and his arm to remove the shirt and jacket with the least amount of movement. Still, he occasionally complained with a groan or a sharp whistle of in-drawn breath.

My clothes, why is she taking off my clothes? His fevered mind puzzled and then aimlessly wandered into a dream-like distortion of reality. He imagined he had donkey legs and a man's torso while she danced with him around the fire. Feebly, he shook his head to chase the scene from his mind. She held him about the waist, pulling him slowly toward her. Crazy eyes reflected tongues of flame in the soaring fire. He was burning up. He imagined that his skin was fire-red.

After getting his shirt off, she gently ran her fingers back and forth across each rib. Eramus jumped slightly as she passed over the broken ones. His eyes opened again. Her hands were upon him, he was certain he could feel them, and the fire burned brightly before him. So hot! And so thirsty! His tongue seemed stuck to the roof of his mouth, and he couldn't speak.

"Hmm. Three broken ribs. After you are rested and less chilled, I will bandage those ribs and it will be considerably less problematic to move around." His fevered mind interpreted that she said, "Yum! Smoky ribs served roasted and chilled!" *Is she going to eat me?* His mind puzzled in the short moments before he slipped back into a distorted, dream-like state.

She arranged him so he was partially propped up facing the fire, using her lap to support his head and upper back, her legs positioned on either side of him.

She pulled him closer, and the pain jerked him rudely back to the here and now. Eramus stared into the fire for a few moments.

He closed his eyes and moaned audibly. The woman shifted slightly to make herself more comfortable.

Summoning all his energy, Eramus croaked, "Please don't eat..."

"Hush. Sleep now," she replied in a voice both gentle and soothing. *A demon's seductive siren call?* he wondered. "Relax. Be calm. Do not struggle. I have you." *You have me?!* Fear and suspicion tried to urge him to fight off that velvety voice, but his strength was gone.

Will I awaken tomorrow transformed into a braying ass? With a collar around my neck and led about on a chain? he wondered. The idea energized him and summoning all his will, he tried to break free, but her strong arms pulled him closer. He was lost to her! His mouth fell open to cry, but no sound escaped, and only a single tear rolled from the corner of his eye. The dancing flames began to work their hypnotic magic and finally, he resigned himself to his fate. His eyelids grew impossibly heavy, exhaustion overtook him, and he drifted away into black, dreamless, sleep.

Birds were chirping noisily in the tree branches above. Eramus tried to ignore them and go back to sleep, but they were too boisterous to allow it. He opened his eyes to a bright sun shining through the pines. The brightness caused him to blink, then he groaned and covered his eyes with his forearm, resting it across his face.

His senses were clearer now, and he wondered how much of what he remembered was a dream and how much was real. He smelled smoke but could not hear a fire. If one was still burning, it must be just a small one, for he could not hear it above the birds' chatter. Suddenly, their chirping ceased, and an eerie silence ensued. With a sudden beating of wings and a few final notes, they all flocked elsewhere. Footsteps approached, crunching softly through the ancient needle bed of the forest floor.

The demon-woman? he wondered, and apprehension began to fill him. The sounds grew closer and stopped, followed by a sudden crash of wood dropped at the base of a nearby tree. Eramus's arm flew away instinctively from his face. She stood there sweeping needles and bits of bark from the sleeves of her shirt.

"Ah, awake, are you? You had a nice long nap. It is quite late in the day," she noted.

Eramus watched her finish cleaning up. She didn't seem as menacing in broad daylight, but her ears were still pointed. That much of his recollection was accurate at least. He wasn't sure what to make of his rescuer just yet, but he didn't feel quite as threatened. His head was still foggy and concentrating proved difficult.

Dropping onto one knee, she inspected his injured leg.

"How exactly did you injure this?" she inquired.

"I think I fell outa tree," he answered groggily.

"Well, that certainly explains your rib injuries, but this leg..." she said and shook her head before continuing, "How long ago did this happen?"

Eramus screwed up his face, thinking hard. "Not sure."

"How does that feel?" she asked, lifting the leg slightly. Eramus looked down and was relieved to see it was a human leg.

"Okay," Eramus mumbled.

"How about that?" she said, twisting the limb slightly to one side.

"Okay," Eramus repeated.

"Does this cause any pain?" She put the leg through a short series of motions, carefully avoiding the bandaged area. Eramus just shook his head side to side.

"Good. It did not seem to be broken, but I had to be certain. Those wolves did it no favors; they made quite a mess of it. But I tended to it as well as I could. It should be mended well enough to allow you to use it in a week or so." Removing the bandages, she examined the wounds.

"I don't think..." Eramus began weakly but suddenly stopped. Where there had been deep gashes, only bright pink scars remained. *How long have I been unconscious?* he wondered. Eramus watched as she produced a little amulet and repeated her ritual of closing her eyes, clutching the gem, and bringing her forehead to his leg. Once again, he felt a brief tingling, not painful, just an odd sensation. He wondered what it was she did that caused such a feeling.

"What's that?" Eramus asked.

"To what do you refer?" she responded, looking up.

"That charm."

Holding it up for him to see, she said, "It is called an Onnum."

"Is it magic?"

"It may be said it is magic in that we do not know how it works. It aids me in channeling certain abilities."

"So, it helps ya do magic, like healin' me leg?"

She smiled, saying, "In that you are not able to comprehend what is happening, yes, it helps me perform magic." She returned the Onnum inside her shirt.

She stood up after attending to his leg and moved to the fire. Taking a stick, she poked the embers, stirring up live coals. She grabbed a small handful of dry needles and sprinkled them on top. Then holding her hair back from the fire, she blew gently several times until thick gray smoke started to billow from the pit. The woman continued to gently encourage the embers until the familiar crackling of fire consuming pitch-laden needles replaced the dense smoke. She laid a few small twigs on top of the fledgling blaze, watching it carefully. Slowly, she fed the infant fire larger sustenance until the flames began to flicker above the edge of the pit. She laid a few medium pieces of wood across it and pushed herself away. She brushed off her leggings and sat down facing Eramus cross-armed, cross-legged.

Eramus just stared at her for a while, watching the red glow of the fire dance off her face. The daylight was dwindling, hastened by clouds that had crept in silently. He noted she was quite beautiful as weariness suddenly swept over him. He sighed a long sigh, then turned his head from her and closed his eyes. He heard her quietly "Humph!" just once, then she got up and made herself busy in the little camp. He drifted back to sleep to the sound of her unseen activities.

After completing a few tasks around the camp, the woman leaned against a tree and studied him carefully. A laborer certainly. His bronzed arms and brown neck confirmed he spent much of his time outdoors. Not a bit of fat on him and he was solidly built with strong arms, shoulders, and back. All the hallmarks of a man accustomed to manual labor. She recalled having trouble restraining him. Despite his poor condition, he nearly escaped her grasp. She sensed there was a strength of spirit in him as well.

She guessed his age to be about thirty — the same as hers — but the wear and tear of a hard life took its toll on his body. Unlike many of the men she had encountered in this part of the world, he appeared to have no facial hair. In the brief time that she had been around him, there was no stubble or shadow. It gave him a youthful look. He could be older or younger than she guessed.

Still, she was disappointed but not surprised that he fell back to sleep. Having been out here three days alone, she was becoming desperate for human interaction.

"Who are you?" she wondered aloud. "And what circumstances brought you here?" Sitting down, she rested her elbows on her knees, folded her hands together, and propped her chin atop them. Shaking her head, she continued, "How did your leg get so gravely injured? This cannot be solely attributed to a wolf attack; your leg was already seriously infected when I found you. So, I brought you here and patched you up.

"What? My remedies seem somewhat crude?

"I do apologize, but my medical supplies are quite limited. I did not have sufficient bandages to dress all your wounds and I had to resort to using the materials at hand. I do hope you can forgive me for using your shirt.

"It was dirty, you say?

"I noticed that. Calling it 'dirty,' however, is a gross understatement. It seems you had been wearing it for quite some time, but fear not, I boiled it twice before using it."

The woman sat up and folded her arms across her chest. "It was a miracle I found you when I did," she whispered to herself. Looking up, she studied the sky and estimated it would be dark in an hour.

Sighing, she finished her monologue, "Well, it was lovely chatting with you, but I have work to do, so you rest, and we will speak later." Rising, she grabbed a pot, and went to fetch water. As she walked off into the wilderness, she cried out in frustration "...and I am talking to myself again!"

It was completely dark when Eramus's eyes next snapped open. A delightful smell filled the air and his limbs found strength in the aroma. Carefully, he pushed himself up to a sitting position and leaned back against a log. He drew a sharp intake of air when he moved his tender ribs too quickly. He was stiff from having lain so long on the ground, and it felt good to move. He stretched and the cloak that had covered him slipped off.

His chest was wrapped snugly with long strips of cloth. He no longer felt cold, so he carefully folded the cloak and set it to one side. His jacket was within reach, but his shirt was nowhere in sight. Feeling a little self-conscious, he put his jacket over his shoulders. He looked around, but his rescuer was not in sight.

"Hullo, are ya still here?" he called out into the night.

"Right behind you," a soft voice answered from over his shoulder. He turned quickly, wincing from the pain, to see her leaning against a tree, cleaning her teeth with a bit of stick. Flicking the stick into the fire, she moved around to sit on a log across from him. "Feeling stronger, I see, but those ribs are still quite tender, are they not?"

"Yep. It hurts if I move 'em too sudden like. An' I feel much better, except I'm..." He paused momentarily to wonder if he was being rude, then continued, "I'm a wee bit hungry."

"Drink some water first. I saved you some food." She got up and plucked a waterskin from a low branch, extended it to him by the straps, and moved over to the fire's edge.

"I has a bowl in me backpack. Where's me backpack? Somewhere, I guess," he mumbled as he unstopped the skin and drank without touching the spout to his mouth.

"No need to get more things dirty. You can just eat from the pot tonight." She moved toward him holding the pot, using the edge of her cloak to protect her hand. "Be careful, it is still hot."

He accepted the pot gingerly. His callused hands allowed him to hold it, but it was hot enough that he had to shift it back and forth between his hands every couple of seconds. He blew on the hot mixture and brought the pot to his mouth when he heard the woman clear her throat. He looked up at her. She was extending a small spoon to him.

"Oh, uh...thankee," he said, taking the spoon from her hand. He dove into the meal, his first in many days, eagerly consuming the delicious food.

The woman watched in amazement as he ate noisily. "Finish it if you like, I've already eaten," she added, almost too late. Eramus chased the last morsel around the bottom several times, then finally upended the pot and tipped the last of it into his gaping mouth. He then licked the spoon clean and handed the spoon and pot back to the woman.

"Oh, that were good!" he said at last, then drank some more water. He grunted and shifted himself into a little more comfortable position against the log. Drawing a deep breath, he heaved a great sigh of contentment. The woman rinsed the pot and spoon with a little water from the skin, then hung them from a branch.

He studied her while she worked. She seemed young, barely eighteen, he guessed. *What is she doing out here alone?* he wondered. "Yer not a demon, are ya?" Eramus ventured to ask.

The woman looked up from her cleaning, laughed, and said, "What would make you think I was a demon?"

"Yer ears are pointed and ya does magic."

"So? All my people have pointed ears, and as I said before, it is not magic. It only seems like magic because you do not understand how it works."

"Well, accordin' ta old tales, demons has pointy ears."

"In your tales, do demons rescue people, dress their wounds, help them heal, feed and care for them?"

"Uh, no. They's usually bad an' not very nice." Eramus silently pondered this contradiction before continuing, "So, if ya isn't a demon, what are ya?"

"We are a race from a distant land, so it is not surprising that you might confuse us with strange creatures from folk tales. Among my people, we call ourselves the Emallinawima. But it is perfectly fine to just refer to us as Nawima."

"So, I's suppost ta call ya Nawiman?" Eramus inquired.

"That is fine, but if you wish, you may call me by my given name, Lewatollma."

"Lewatollma. Lewatollma." Eramus repeated it several times to familiarize himself, then offered, "My name is Eramus, but I thinks Eramus is too much, an' I like just plain, ole Eram."

Lewatollma moved to sit on the log across from Eramus before continuing, "Eramus. That is a curious name. What does it mean?"

"A name hasta mean sumpin'?" Eramus replied quizzically.

"In certain cultures, a name can have a special origin or meaning. For example, my name means 'New Star.'"

"You don't look like a new star, except yer eyes do twinkle."

Suppressing a smile, she explained, "My mother chose this name, and she told me many times it is a metaphor for a brilliant, new beginning of something wondrous and special, meaning I was wondrous and special to her."

"That's very nice." After a thoughtful pause, he looked her in the eye and continued, "I could see the love ya had fer yer mother when ya spoke of her."

Her features softened and her eyes seemed to focus far away as she replied, "I do love my mother. Dearly." Snapping back to the present, she added, "Enough of me. Tell me about yourself, Eramus. Where do you come from?"

"Hares End."

"I am not familiar with Hares End. Where is it located?"

"South of here, north a the Emmerin', an' there be nuttin' but forest east a that."

"Hmm. You are far from Hares End. What's the significance of the name Hares End?"

"Well, when they first come there, the hills above the Emmerin' was just full of rabbits. An' I guess End because the river is difficult to cross, so no one goes any further. Besides, the only thing south of the Emmerin' is the Blue Desert. Supposed ta be very dangerous."

"Hmm. Interesting. What brings you so far from home — alone no less — in the Norman wilds?"

"Well, yes, that's a story ta be sure. I uh, I..." Eramus trailed off and looked down at the ground while the recollection of what he was supposed to be doing came suddenly back to him.

"I'm tryin' ta save me village," he finally mumbled, staring into the fire.

"Save it from what?"

"Starvin'," he said tersely. She grew quiet, furrowed her brow, and looked genuinely puzzled.

Shaking her head, she asked, "How could this happen?"

"Crops failed three years in a row. Blight, hoppers an' now drought." He studied her puzzled face. "Hares End's a small place. It's harder when yer small like that."

"Can you get food from somewhere else?"

"That's what I'm tryin' ta do. Not much luck yet. The other villages are bad off too cause a the drought. I was movin' north hopin' ta find some corn ta trade."

"Trade? Why do they not give it to you if you need it?"

It was his turn to look incredulous.

"Give it away? Are ya daft? Within the village, yeah, we all share what there is, but outside athat, each village stands on its own."

"Well, what do you have to trade?" she replied.

He looked at her hard and long before answering. "The only thing we have to trade is our daughters."

She gasped. Eramus looked back into the fire, her expression too much for him to bear. Her revulsion made him suddenly uncomfortable.

"It's not like we're selling them. Just marrying them off," he explained.

"But in exchange for food, correct?"

"In exchange fer stayin' alive," he countered.

"I do not perceive a great distinction between trading and selling."

"Have ya ever seen anyone starve ta death?"

"No."

"Neither 'ave I an' I don't want ta, either. If nothing else, some a our kids may survive the winter. If we're lucky, some a the village may still be alive come spring an' we'll try again. Maybe nature will be kinder ta us next year."

"It all seems so wrong, dealing in human life like it is a commodity." She suddenly grew sullen. "It must be terrible to be torn from your family. It is not something I could do."

"No one's tearin' anyone away from anyone." Eramus's tone grew defensive. "These girls all agreed ta help. No one is happy about this! Do ya think we have no feelings fer our own flesh an' blood? Do ya think there were no tears?"

"What do you mean? They agreed to this?"

"They said they would do whatever was needed ta help the village." She stared at him, shaking her head, signifying she did not understand. "Wouldn't you help if it meant savin' the lives of yer family an' friends?" She looked away and grew quiet for a few seconds.

"A tremendous burden for anyone to bear. They are very brave. How old are they?"

"Two are seventeen, one is fifteen, an' one is sixteen."

Lewatollma's mouth fell open and her eyes bulged. "They are only children! How could they possibly comprehend the ramifications, or be expected to assume such responsibility? How appalling!" Lewatollma responded with her voice full of harsh judgment.

"Yes, despicable indeed!" a new voice from outside the camp added disdainfully. The voice took Eramus by surprise and he turned quickly toward its source, wincing as he did. A tall, hooded figure moved out from the shadows. Long, dark hair extended from beneath her hood. Bright, hazel eyes regarded Eramus cautiously as she addressed Lewatollma in a strange language.

"Me?! Where have you been?!" Lewatollma responded exasperatedly. "And he is not a pet! He was injured. I just provided some assistance."

"Yes. Well, how humane of you. I hope you do not intend to keep it like you did that sinnimurus."

"Oh, Nesneratha, of course not," Lewatollma angrily replied.

"Good. Because of the two," she said and paused to regard Eramus critically, "the sinnimurus is by far the better looking." She sat down beside Lewatollma and pulled back her hood.

Eramus looked carefully at the two women. There were a lot of similarities between them. They wore identical brown hooded cloaks. Both were about the same height, just a hair shorter than him. The mahogany brown hair they sported was fine and silky. Lewatollma's hair was a bit lighter than Nesneratha's and her eyes were soft brown and kind.

Lewatollma's face was roundish with just a trace amount of baby fat, giving her a very pleasing appearance. On the other hand, Nesneratha's features were sharp as if chiseled from stone.

After carefully pondering, he asked, "Sisters?"

"No!" Lewatollma quickly replied.

"No relation," Nesneratha confirmed.

"But ya look so much alike an' ya argue like sisters, too," he continued.

Nesneratha threw back her head and laughed heartily while Lewatollma simply scowled. "We are just traveling companions," Nesneratha offered, putting her arm around Lewatollma's shoulders. "My name is Nesneratha. Have you a name, stranger?"

"Eramus or Eram. I prefer Eram."

"Tell me, Eramus, how did you come into the company of my misguided, albeit benevolent, friend Lewatollma?"

"Well, there was these wolves an' —"

"I will tell you later, Nesneratha. Right now, we should all retire," Lewatollma added quickly, cutting off Eramus mid-sentence. "Eramus, lie down and sleep. You need your rest. Nesneratha, help me gather more wood for the fire."

"Of course," Nesneratha answered while rising from her seat. Pointing at Eramus, she ordered, "Lie down! Sleep! Good boy!"

Lewatollma glared at her.

"What?" Nesneratha asked with an impish grin on her face. Lewatollma motioned with her head for Nesneratha to join her. The two women wandered off, talking in hushed whispers.

Eramus slid to the ground and made himself comfortable. *Two Nawimans,* he marveled to himself as he curled up near the fire, *and both women ta boot! But what,* he wondered, *is a sinnimurus?*

Eramus decided Nesneratha didn't approve of him. His first impression of her was less than favorable as well, insulting him like that! Oh, well, at least Lewatollma was nice enough. Maybe they were demons. One good and one evil like some sort of magical balance of power. He then remembered what his father had told him about jumping to conclusions.

"Don't call the soup spoiled afore it's cooked," he muttered softly. Tomorrow was another day. Perhaps she would be more civil after a good night's rest. He yawned and felt the fire's warmth. Between the fire and a full belly, he began to doze off. His last thought was, *Where's my shirt?*

TRAVELING COMPANIONS

"The name Nesneratha is the ancient tongue for bloom (amid) thorns — a metaphor for joy can only be known by experiencing sorrow, or that something desirable cannot be obtained without cost or sacrifice."

– Emallinawiman Genealogy, volume XI

Eramus awoke to the sound of the two women talking or arguing, he couldn't be sure — they were speaking in a strange language. But whatever it was, they were both adamant about something. He sat up and looked around. The discussion suddenly stopped. Probably about him, he assumed. Maybe he was causing problems between the two and he should just thank Lewatollma and leave.

Wondering if his leg would support his weight, he tried to stand. Although his ribs hurt, he could deal with that pain. But he was still very weak, and it was all he could do to stand and lean heavily against the tree. His leg was very sore and sharp pains shot through his calf when he put weight on it.

"Please sit down, Eramus! Your leg is still mending, and it is too soon to be walking about," Lewatollma scolded.

"I should leave. I've bin too much trouble already. Thankee for savin' me an' tendin' ta ma wounds an' feedin' me. Ya bin very kind. Where's me backpack an' shirt?"

"Here, allow me to get your things," Nesneratha added cheerfully.

"No! He cannot travel in his condition! Just look at him," Lewatollma countered.

"See there, Lewatollma, he is up and about and doing well enough," Nesneratha said as she handed Eramus his small backpack. The weight of his backpack unbalanced Eramus and when he tried to counter by using his injured leg, it crumpled, and he fell crashing to the ground.

"Well, maybe not," Nesneratha said resignedly.

Lewatollma placed her hands on her hips and looked at Nesneratha. "Help him back to the fire. I will prepare some food," she said testily.

Nesneratha reached out her hand to Eramus and said, "Give me your hand and I will help you up."

Eramus was holding himself perfectly still, and trying not to breathe as he answered, "As soon as it stops hurtin'."

Nesneratha pursed her lips and pondered for a moment, then shaking her head, she replied, "That could take days. I do not think Lewatollma will wait that long." Taking Eramus under the arms, she pulled him quickly upright.

"No! Wait! Aargh!!!" he bellowed out in agony.

She put her arm around Eramus's chest and threw his other arm across her shoulder. "Let us get this over with." Supporting his weight, she quickly moved him over to the log. Eramus hopped on his one good leg. Groaning, he set his teeth and let the pain flood over him. She let him down roughly onto the log.

He looked up at her and saw her grinning. "Ya was a little rough, don'tcha think," Eramus growled.

"Nonsense. No matter what I did, it was going to cause pain. I just completed the operation most expeditiously and efficiently, thereby minimizing your discomfort," she answered in a mockingly cheerful tone. After a brief pause, she placed her hands on her hips and added, "In fact, you should thank me!"

Eramus hmphed. "Thankee so much, Nesneratha. I don't know what I'da done without cha," he answered coldly. He was beginning to think the good demon-bad demon concept was correct after all.

"You are very welcome, Eramus. Now just sit there and relax," she replied mock-sweetly. Then patting him on the head, she added, "Good boy," and walked away.

Lewatollma was kneeling as she went through the contents of her backpack. Nesneratha's last remark caused her to freeze for a moment. Closing her eyes and setting her teeth, she let the anger and embarrassment pass. She shook her head slightly and sighed deeply before continuing. She would have another talk with Nesneratha later.

Eramus's leg improved slowly, and it was another three days before he had strength enough to stand on it. Still, he was unable to take more than a few steps. So, they remained at their little camp and rested. Lewatollma and Nesneratha must have reached some sort of agreement, because she never overtly vexed him again. In fact, on the fifth day, Nesneratha presented him with a hand-carved walking stick, complete with ornamentation. She had even carved his name into it. Lewatollma took the time to explain it to Eramus since he couldn't read.

Lewatollma seemed genuinely pleased about the gift and she showered Nesneratha with compliments. They seemed now to be the best of friends whose petty disagreement was put behind them and forgotten completely. The three of them spent their days puttering around the camp. The two women did most of the work. Eramus assisted when he could. Lewatollma watched over him, making sure his wounds healed properly. Nesneratha would walk him around, encouraging him to do more each day, gradually increasing his stamina and strength.

In the evening, they would talk. Eramus learned the two were in school together and had traveled with others to the lands north of Hares End to explore and meet the inhabitants. He also learned that their homeland was quite distant. They had traveled across the great lake that was the Norman eastern border and the source of the Emmering.

Lewatollma had a brother two years younger. Nesneratha had no siblings, which explained much in Eramus's mind.

Eramus related to them all he knew about farming and life in Hares End.

Two weeks had passed and Nesneratha grew increasingly restless. Eramus could walk well enough, although he was not as spry as when he started. He sensed the time to part company was at hand. Even though he did not want to admit it, he enjoyed their companionship.

"Lewatollma, is it not time we moved on?" Nesneratha prodded.

"Yes, you are right. Thank you for your patience, dear. I hope I can return the favor someday. I suppose I am keeping Eramus from his task, as well. What a sad burden he must carry. I wish I could help."

"You have helped, Lewatollma. You saved his life and nursed him back to health. Now he can continue. Without you, he would have failed long ago."

"I cannot help but think of the children in his village, the sacrifice they must make, just to survive. Could we not get some supplies for Hares End? I am sure we could spare something from Fishers Port."

"No, and you know why!" Nesneratha said sternly as she stared down Lewatollma.

"I am sorry. My heart goes out to them." Lewatollma looked down.

Nesneratha hugged her. "Ah, dear Lewatollma, you are compassionate to a fault. But it is time we were about our own business. We should move north and west from here, for there is still much territory to cover."

"Of course." Lewatollma sighed and returned the hug. "Let us tell Eramus."

"Tell me what?" he asked as he walked over to the pair with only the slightest hint of a limp.

"It is time for us to move on, Eramus," Nesneratha explained.

"Yes, time for all a us, I suppose," he agreed.

"Which direction will you take, Eramus?" Lewatollma inquired.

"I has ta find food for the village. I was workin' ma way north ta the next village. I guess I'll try the westward fork first," he answered.

Lewatollma looked at Nesneratha, her eyes pleading. Nesneratha sighed and smiled slightly. "Well, we are going northwest as well. Shall we travel together as far as our journey will permit?"

"Are ya sure?" Eramus asked cautiously.

"Of course, you are welcome to join us. Besides, we cannot have you feeding the wolves, can we, Lewatollma?"

"I am forced to agree with Nesneratha. It would be cruel to make the wolves suffer digesting such a disagreeable meal," Lewatollma deadpanned. The three of them laughed.

"Well, then it's settled. When do we leave? First thing tomorrow?" Eramus suggested.

The two women nodded in agreement.

"Rest well tonight, young maidens. Tomorrow, we stretch our legs!"

The day dawned bright and beautiful and the three started side by side with Eramus using his walking stick. For several days, they moved along the old road. The brush crowded in from the sides and small trees had taken root in the center. Eramus began to wonder if this was a viable choice; an overgrown road meant no traffic, calling into question the existence of nearby villages. Yet there were fresh hoofmarks visible, so Eramus kept his thoughts to himself and hoped for the best.

On the morning of the fourth day, the sun shone brightly, and the day grew warm. They came to a place on the road where there had been recent activity. Hoofmarks were everywhere, and the brush had been trampled, with branches broken off nearby trees.

"Somebody were busy here," Eramus remarked.

"The tracks lead off into the woods," Lewatollma added.

Nesneratha walked on ahead and observed, "There are no tracks up here. They must have left the road and gone west for some reason."

Eramus squatted to examine the marks, and something caught his eye. The grass seemed oddly flattened in this spot. He put his head down low to the ground and looked across the road to the east. From the lower angle, he could see that something had been dragged off into the bushes. He followed the drag marks to the edge of the bushes. Then he spotted something disturbing. "Blood!" he called out. "There's blood over here! Lots of it!"

The women joined his side as Eramus moved into the dense brush. Up ahead, there was a faint buzzing sound. Curious, he pressed forward. The sound grew louder, and the breeze wafted a putrid stench, confirming what he suspected: death. Flies swarmed over the rotting carcass of a horse, or at least part of one. Eramus covered his nose with his sleeve to block the smell. Behind him, he could hear the women uttering complaints about the disturbing odor.

"I am going back to see what else I can find. Besides, if I stay here, I am going to be sick," Nesneratha said, pinching her nose shut. Her footsteps crunched off into the distance.

He looked at the remains, trying to reassemble the pieces in his mind. He concluded that the rear quarters were missing. He muttered to himself, "Where be the rest? Why drag half a horse inta the bushes?"

Lewatollma stepped beside Eramus, her mouth and nose covered with a fold of her cloak. "What happened?" she asked, the sound muffled by her cloak.

"I don't know," Eramus said. "But this don't make no sense. Where's the rest of the animal?"

"Ughh! Poor beast! Let us get away from here."

Eramus and Lewatollma turned and made their way back to the road. Nesneratha was nowhere in sight. But before Lewatollma could call out her name, a short, piercing scream rang out from the woods.

"Nesneratha!" they called out together.

"Over here!" a distant, distressed voice answered.

Eramus charged into the underbrush in her direction. "Where are ya? Keep talkin' so I can find ya!"

"Over here!" she called out, followed by the sound of retching.

Eramus found her on all fours puking her guts out. "What happened?" he anxiously cried. "Are ya all right?"

"Do I look all right?" she answered weakly while retaining her keen sarcasm. She heaved again, producing nothing but a little bile. Salivating profusely, she let her mouth hang open so it could run out onto the ground. The bitter taste in her mouth caused her entire frame to shudder. She pointed a shaky finger behind her. "There. Back there."

Eramus carefully made his way in that direction. Just as before, the buzz of flies and an overpowering stench guided him straight to the source. He supposed he might find the other half of the horse, but he found so much more. Even Eramus, a farmer well acquainted with death, was not prepared for what he saw.

In the distance, he could hear Lewatollma calling their names, the pitch of her voice belying much anxiety. Eramus's stomach began to convulse. Covering his mouth, he ran back to Nesneratha. She was still on her hands and knees. He grabbed her about the waist and lifted her onto her feet. "Let's get back ta Lewatollma," he managed to say.

Coming out of the bushes onto the road, they found Lewatollma wringing her hands. She assaulted them with a barrage of questions. Eramus responded by holding up a single finger. He bent over and put his hands on his knees. He took long, deep breaths until the nausea passed. Nesneratha found the waterskin and rinsed out her mouth, then tried to drink a little. Shuddering from the aftertaste, she spat out the water.

"Eramus?" Lewatollma asked quietly. He stood to face her. "Eramus, your face is almost white!" she exclaimed. "What did you see?"

"Men. Horses. Butchered. Awful!" he summarized. He looked at Nesneratha, whose face was pale, and her hair was disheveled with bits of food caught in the ends.

"We must get away from here fast," Nesneratha said. "They cannot have been dead for more than two days. Some of them looked even more recently dismembered than that." Looking anxiously about, she continued, "Whoever did this may still be nearby. I recommend we go back, as up ahead is too great an unknown." She began to tremble, then started to whimper, "Oh, Eramus, why did they do that to their eyes?"

Lewatollma's anxiety began to transition to fear. The condition of her companions unnerved her. But the situation called for action, and right now, she was the only one in any condition to act. But she couldn't do this, controlled by fear.

Lewatollma grasped her Onnum with her right hand. *Stability, focus, clarity*, she repeated inside her head. She closed her eyes and found a place outside of her emotions to think objectively. There, she carefully analyzed their current situation. Her eyes snapped open a fraction of a second later. She ran and grabbed their backpacks. "Let us go," she said quietly and started urging them back down the road from the direction they just arrived. "Quickly, now," she whispered as she looked over her shoulder. "No more talking."

Lewatollma drove them as hard and as long as she believed they could endure. An hour passed in silence except for footfalls and breathing. Lewatollma stopped them for a rest when she noticed Eramus's limp becoming more pronounced. She ushered them off into the brush, out of sight of the main road, and made them lie down. She wrapped her cloak around her, squatted, and balanced herself on the balls of her feet. Facing the road, she sat there motionless. She slowed her breathing so she could quickly pick out approaching sounds.

The woods were unusually quiet. Too quiet, she thought. She closed her eyes to better take in the ambient sounds. The gentle rustle of leaves by a faint breeze, and far away, a cicada droned. Now a bird twittered nervously, then another. Slowly, the sounds of nature going about her business resounded all about them. Lewatollma opened her eyes and breathed a sigh. She attenuated herself to the background noise. Any change now would trigger her awareness like an alarm.

She reached to her left side and touched the hilt of her blade. Its presence reassured her. It was there if she needed it. If. Her hand rested gently there, while the rest of her body crouched like a tightly coiled spring.

Behind her, Eramus lay on his back looking up through the leafy canopy. Eramus turned to look at Nesneratha. Although she was facing him, her gaze was far away. Sighing, she changed her focus to him.

"How many horses did you see, Eramus?" Nesneratha whispered.

"At least eight," he whispered back.

"I counted eight also. How many humans?"

"Five, I think."

"What does this tell you, Eramus?"

He contemplated the numbers for a moment then answered, "Maybe three of 'em got away?"

"Or perhaps there are three prisoners," she replied.

"I'd 'spose that if anyone got away, we woulda run across 'em by now, huh?" Eramus added.

"Most likely. This scenario would indicate three prisoners."

"Who do ya think did this?" Eramus asked her.

"I do not know, but we should find out."

"An' ya think we should go after 'em?"

"Yes."

"You be nuts!" Eramus hissed. "What chance do ya think the three a us would 'ave if they did that ta eight men on horseback?"

"We may have the advantage of surprise. Maybe we will not have to engage them directly. If we could free their prisoners, our numbers would be doubled. There are so many factors that could tip the scales in our favor!"

"Or against us. Like maybe them surprising us. It's crazy, Nesneratha."

Lewatollma turned and gave them both a stern look. "Eramus is right. It is foolish. Now silence, both of you!"

"I cannot believe that you, of all people, would not go to the aid of someone in distress, Lewatollma! How could you leave someone in the clutches of such violent and murderous villains?" Nesneratha inquired. "That could have been us. I know that if I were taken prisoner and someone came along, I would be grateful to be rescued."

When Lewatollma did not respond, Nesneratha looked her in the eye and saw doubt lingering there. Smirking, Nesneratha got to her feet and firmly asserted, "Well, I have made up my mind. I am going after the captives. Let us go, Eramus."

Eramus got up as well, extended his hand to her, and said, "Goodbye, missy, an' good luck."

"You are not coming with me?"

"Are ya crazy?! Have ya already forgotten whatcha just seen? Maybe ya should loosen yer cloak, girl — I think ya cut off the blood ta yer head!"

Nesneratha turned to Lewatollma and began to open her mouth. Lewatollma cut her off. "No, absolutely not!" Lewatollma answered before she could ask. "It is needlessly reckless and irresponsible!"

Nesneratha looked at both in turn. Flipping her cloak back, she pulled her blade halfway out, looked at it momentarily, then smartly snapped it back into place. Picking up her backpack, she strode off to the road without a word.

"Nesneratha!" Lewatollma hissed. A moment later, she hissed more loudly, "Nesneratha!" But there was no reply. Lewatollma muttered something under her breath that Eramus didn't understand. By her tone, he assumed it wasn't complimentary. Lewatollma angrily grabbed her backpack and started after her.

"Where is ya goin'?" Eramus asked incredulously.

"I cannot let her go off alone. Besides, maybe I can talk her out of it," Lewatollma answered in a dejected tone as she disappeared into the underbrush.

"An' if ya can't?" Eramus called after her.

"Then I will bury what is left of her!" Lewatollma answered.

"Great!" Eramus muttered to himself, standing there with his hands on his hips. He didn't fancy the idea of tracking down brutal killers. The odds were stacked so unfavorably against them. Besides, he was on a mission of his own, one vital to Hares End. But his conscience began to feed on the fact that he just let two young women wander off by themselves into a dangerous situation.

"Oh, hare droppings!" he cursed, stamping his foot. "This be so stupid!"

He picked up his backpack and started after them. Walking briskly, he caught up to them. If only there were some way to convince Nesneratha to abandon her quest. But he had already learned that she was headstrong and wouldn't listen to reason. *Maybe we can force her to stop,* Eramus wondered to himself. As he walked, he contemplated diverse ways to subdue Nesneratha. *A blow to the head? Hmmm. Tempting. Very tempting. Should I use a thick branch or a large stone? Or I could choke her until she just loses consciousness!* Eramus savored the idea for a moment.

He sighed and shook his head. No, he was sure Lewatollma would object to either of those plans. It looked like they would have to do it the old-fashioned way and tie her up. But maybe tie her up really tight and gag her. *Oh, that's a nice touch!* he thought. Bound and gagged may not have been as easy as his first two ideas, but it was not without virtues of its own. He imagined himself lecturing her on how he actually was helping her, concluding with, *in fact, you should thank me!* Oh, how sweet that would be! Eramus grinned like an idiot at Nesneratha.

"What?" she asked, regarding him through suspicious eyes.

"Nuttin," he replied and smiled even broader. His little fantasy, though somewhat perverse, distracted him from the very real possibility that they were en route to a grisly and painful death.

IN PURSUIT

"How dearly she paid for her choices! If only she were more cautious. Alas, it was not in Nesneratha's nature."

– Lewatollma

They returned to the site of the ambush and picked up the westward trail. Nesneratha was a skilled tracker, but skill was not really required due to the gross signs left by the marauding band. Several indications of a scuffle were evident along the way, but no more bodies or blood. Nesneratha viewed this as a good sign that the prisoners were still alive. It was also obvious where they stopped to rest because they cleared an area, and numerous branches were hewn from nearby trees and piled together, but not for fuel. Never was there a sign of a fire, and that puzzled Eramus — why would they cut branches, but not build a fire? And always they cut green branches with leaves still intact, usually pine boughs.

The track led west for a day then turned northwest. Nesneratha encouraged her companions to make haste, driving them from dawn to dusk each day. Always in the lead, she was attentive and wary. They decided against a cooking fire at night, so they consumed only water and dried food.

Late on the second day, the forest gave way to open grassland. Nesneratha held back and stayed in the shelter of the woodland canopy. She did not dare enter open spaces where they might be easily detected. She stared silently into the grassy fields for a few minutes and then retraced her steps into the forest. Looking around, she found a tall tree.

"This will do nicely. I am going up for a look." She dropped her backpack and removed her cloak. Folding it carefully, she placed it across the top of her backpack. Crouching, she sprang upward a surprising distance to the lowest branch. She deftly swung her legs up over an adjacent branch and rapidly disappeared. Eramus was surprised at her agility and speed. He tried hard to listen for noise from her ascent, but he could detect none. He recalled his own experience in the trees and unconsciously put his arms around his ribs, instinctively protecting them.

Lewatollma's eyes carefully surveyed their surroundings. She automatically assumed guard duty in her partner's absence. Eramus studied her and he marveled at how she stood perfectly still, listening and looking for any sign of danger. It reminded him of a deer he had seen once standing frozen at the edge of the orchard taking in everything around it using all the senses it possessed.

Nesneratha dropped noiselessly from the tree. "Well?" Eramus inquired.

"The tracks lead straight across the field to the woods on the other side."

"Is we goin' ta follow 'em?" Eramus asked.

"Yes."

"We run a serious risk of exposing ourselves if we cross in broad daylight," Lewatollma commented.

"Agreed," Nesneratha replied. "We will rest here and cross under the concealment of darkness."

Eramus was having trouble with some of the words they used. He had no clue as to their meaning, but he followed them the best he could. Not understanding the conversation made him feel left out and frankly, more than a little stupid. "How close is we ta catchin' up with 'em, Nesneratha?" Eramus asked.

"Soon, Eramus. They are not moving fast. Perhaps their prisoners delay them. I do not know for certain. But whatever their circumstances, for the last two days of our travel, we have discovered three of their encampments. We may overtake them tomorrow or the next day, I hope."

"An 'ave ya given any thought ta what we'll do when we find 'em?" Eramus continued.

"From what I have observed at their encampments, the prisoners are bound to trees while they sleep. You may have noticed the marks made by the legs and heels of the captives in the soil near the base of the trees. This information also confirms there are three captives. Determining the number of the opposing host is still problematic. I believe our best option is to sneak in, release the prisoners, and spirit them away while their captors are asleep."

"Ya sound so sure of yerself, Nesneratha! What if they be guarded?" Eramus countered.

"If I am not mistaken — and I seldom make mistakes — there will be no guard."

Cocking her head slightly, Lewatollma gave Nesneratha a hard, searching stare and asked, "What have you not told us yet, Nesneratha? Do not withhold anything from us!"

"Yeah, spit it out! If we's goin' ta follow ya inta this mess, the least ya can do is keep us in the know!" Eramus added, folding his arms.

Nesneratha regarded her companions, trying to gauge their receptiveness to what she was about to share. "Sit," she said softly as she deposited herself cross-legged on the forest floor. "There is a Norman song that goes as follows —" She cleared her throat and sang:

"Far from the green and living wood,
Far from the laughing waters good,
Where no trace of man is found
And cursed and rotten is the ground,
There is a bane in the northern wilds,
That every man, and every child,
Should fear the ghouls!
Now hear of ghouls!
Stay clear of ghouls!

In the shadow of night's dark cloak,
There live a vile and loathsome folk
Men-beasts who find upon the road
Some hapless soul with a heavy load,
Who fall into their evil clutch,

Woe unto that miserable wretch
Who meets the ghouls!
Entreats the ghouls!
Fresh meat for ghouls!

From the ancient rotting bogs
Come they forth in hidden fogs,
Always at night, and never sun,
Their deeds in dark are ever done,
They cannot bear the light of day,
In barrow hidden, they sleep away,
Light-hating ghouls!
Fell, pale-eyed ghouls!
Night wandering ghouls!
Beware of ghouls!"

Eramus was taken aback to hear Nesneratha sing so melodiously. Without thinking, he blurted out, "What a beautiful voice!"

Lewatollma smiled and Nesneratha blushed ever so slightly. An awkward silence ensued.

"Too bad about the rest of yer personality," he added, giving Lewatollma a quick wink.

Nesneratha smiled that sarcastic smile Eramus had come to know so well, then retorted, "Thank you for the compliment, Eramus. I do my utmost to be a gracious example to the undereducated and uncivilized. Now, before we go any further astray, I would like to explain my theory. I believe that these butchers we are pursuing are ghouls, and if this song has any truth to it, they do not like the sun and our greatest advantage will be to sneak in and grab the prisoners during the day."

Lewatollma countered, "You are basing your assumption on a Norman song, which, may I remind you, is probably for entertainment or even worse, frightening strangers with fanciful exaggeration, and not based on any fact whatsoever."

"Perhaps, but there is more," Nesneratha added. "I have spoken with many of the Normen who travel these parts, especially the hunters, and they all agree that the Westwood should be religiously avoided because of ghouls. One such hunter, Fantroth, has come upon the remains of a man who was killed by ghouls, and his description is terribly similar to our discovery upon the West Road. Moreover, they say there has been an increase in ghoul activity as of late."

"Well, what does we do now?" Eramus asked.

"For now, we rest. We will continue our journey tonight for a brief period to compensate for the time we lost. We have only a couple of hours of daylight left, so we should take advantage."

At sunset, they made themselves ready and when the last light left the sky, they slowly and carefully made their way across the grassy field. Nesneratha led the way, cautiously picking the path. Their progress was slow because Nesneratha insisted they go on their hands and knees to preclude any chance of being seen.

Halfway across, Nesneratha suddenly froze.

"What?" Eramus started to ask in a half-whisper.

"Silence! Listen!" Nesneratha hissed.

At first, Eramus heard nothing except the night's breezes rustling through crisp grasses and an occasional insect singing. But then a sound came floating over the grassy plain: chanting. Eramus listened carefully, but the words were indistinguishable.

Their language was nothing like Eramus had heard before, a guttural grunting. Guhm-dar! Guhm-dar! Rhythmic drumming also accompanied the words. It could have been the stamping of feet, or a sound made by striking the body. The sound grew louder by degrees and the tempo gradually increased.

A piercing cry of someone in pain cut through the night. He was moaning loudly, but as his suffering increased, so did the frequency of his outbursts until finally, he was wailing out one unending song of anguish punctuated only by irregular, ragged breaths. The man's torment went on for several minutes.

When Eramus had imagined he could bear no more, a woman's voice joined in, crying and pleading for them to stop, calling out a man's name. All the while, the unseen host grew louder, and the drumming and grunting reached a frantic pace.

Guhm-DAR! Guhm-DAR! Guhm-DAR! Guhm-DAR!

The night was filled with sounds that seemed to close in from every direction. It had a terrible effect on Eramus's mind. His heart became filled with overpowering dread, and he had to fight back the instinct to run blindly away. Gritting his teeth, he fixed his gaze on the ground. He turned to look behind him to see if Lewatollma was still there. She was huddled upon the ground, her hands over her ears, shaking her head back and forth as if expressing disbelief.

Suddenly, the horrific, shrieking ended in a final chilling, shrill outcry of exquisite pain that rang out, then died suddenly upon the chilly night air. The fell host bellowed a triumphant "DAR!" and the chanting and drumming ended, leaving only a woman's bitter sobbing floating up unto the heavens.

Nesneratha turned to face Eramus. She drew close and whispered, "Are you willing to continue?"

Eramus was deeply shaken, yet somehow, he managed to say, "Ya."

Nesneratha crawled to Lewatollma, who with her eyes tightly closed, still had her hands over her ears and was softly mumbling, "No. No. No."

"Lewatollma," Nesneratha quietly called to her. But Lewatollma continued as before. Nesneratha placed her hands on the woman's shoulders and shook her gently, calling her name again.

Lewatollma dropped her hands, looked into her friends eyes, and started to softly cry. Nesneratha pulled Lewatollma's head into her shoulder to muffle the crying. "Please stop, Lewatollma. Pull yourself together — our collective safety depends upon it."

Lewatollma stopped crying instantly at Nesneratha's command. Nesneratha pushed her upright and brushed away the tears from Lewatollma's cheek with her thumbs.

"Are you willing to continue?" Nesneratha asked at length.

A terrible fear was in Lewatollma's eyes as she shook her head in the negative.

"Very well. Eramus and I will go on and try to free the prisoners."

"Pardon me fer askin', Nesneratha, but why don't we wait fer dawn?" Eramus asked.

"Come dawn, there may be no more prisoners, I fear," Nesneratha grimly replied.

"Lewatollma, be prepared for a hasty retreat. If things go badly for Eramus and me, fly, Lewatollma! Make great haste to Fishers Port! Do not look back or stop. Can you promise me that?"

Lewatollma shook her head in the affirmative then embraced Nesneratha and whispered, "I am sorry!"

Eramus leaned over to Lewatollma and kissed her on top of the head, saying, "Thankee fer all yer kindness. I hope ta return an' thankee again, but if I can't, ya should follow yer friend's good advice."

Nesneratha removed her cloak and backpack and handed them to Lewatollma. She took her long hair and pulled it together, giving it several gentle twists to form a single braid. Then she wrapped it around her neck and secured it with a simple knot. As she checked her blade, she turned to Eramus and whispered, "Ready?"

Eramus nodded, removed his backpack, and quietly pulled the small hand-scythe from it. They crept off silently into the tall grass, leaving Lewatollma alone. She retrieved her Onnum and clutched it tightly to her breast, looking for courage.

Working their way carefully down the grassy slope, Eramus and Nesneratha came at last to the edge of the woods. They were able to quickly home in on the ghoul party, led by their grunting and noisy eating. To Eramus's surprise, the ghouls had a small fire burning. Carefully, they circled, sizing up the number of ghouls and the location of the prisoners.

The two remaining prisoners had their backs to a great tree, their arms extended backward around the trunk and tied behind it. They sat with their heads bent over. In front, their feet were hobbled with a short piece of cord, securely tied, long enough to allow walking, but not running. From the swelling and bruising around their ankles, it was apparent their hosts did not have great concern for their captives' welfare. They looked tired and weak, and it was doubtful that they had been fed.

Squatting around the grisly feast, eleven creatures gorged themselves on human flesh. They wore only simple loin skins, their thin, ragged hair was lopped off unevenly at shoulder length, and patches of their pale scalp were visible. Out of their heads, they regarded the world through small, watery eyes. There was practically no nose at all, only two holes in their flat faces to breathe through. But their teeth were jagged and sharp. Loose, pale flesh hung off their large frames in folds about their waist and upper breast. Large through the chest, their bodies seemed barrel-like, and they looked malformed on the short, scrawny legs that carried them. Their long arms ended in claw-like hands tipped with grimy, black nails. For weapons, they had crude knives set with rough wooden handles that hung from their waist belts.

The ghouls grunted contentedly among themselves, cutting off pieces of flesh and consuming them like wild animals around a kill. It was a stomach-wrenching sight.

Eramus and Nesneratha withdrew to take final counsel.

"Well, what do ya think?" Eramus whispered.

"I think I shall be ill," she said dejectedly. "Oh, Eramus, I thought we could help these people, but now it seems impossible to do anything except throw our own lives away as well."

Eramus shared his observation. "I think the brush will provide enough cover fer us ta sneak in close enough ta cut loose the one facing away from the ghouls an' at least make some distance afore we be discovered. But it would take a miracle ta reach the other one. Do we try ta save just one?"

Nesneratha took one more long look at the prisoners. Her face contorted with conflicted feelings, she turned to Eramus and whispered, "Are you willing to continue?"

"Like ya said, that coulda been us, so yeah."

"Saving one is better than none. Yes, we shall execute your plan. I will creep in and liberate the man. You watch the ghouls and warn me if I am discovered," Nesneratha concluded.

Eramus nodded in agreement. They split up, Nesneratha noiselessly disappearing into the underbrush. Eramus circled to the left, moving into a position where he could watch both the ghouls and their captives. He crept in as close as he dared, using the brush for cover.

Nesneratha crawled in on her belly until she was within arm's length of the one captive. Using a stick, she gently poked the sole of the man's foot. Slowly, he looked up and his eyes widened in surprise to see Nesneratha signaling to him to be quiet. He looked quickly about and then nodded in agreement. Nesneratha's knife flashed out, severing the cords that bound his feet with a single lightning stroke, and just as quickly, disappeared back into the undergrowth. She paused for a long moment, listening carefully before rising and peering cautiously around the edge of the tree. Quickly she sliced the rope holding his hands fast and turned to see a pair of black eyes staring maliciously at her from a colorless face.

The ghoul started to draw breath to sound an alarm but was never able to utter a sound. From behind, Eramus covered its mouth and nose with his hand, and pulling it backward, split open its neck with his scythe. The blood spilled down the creature's front as its eyes rolled back into its head, its knees gave way, and it slid twitching noiselessly to the ground. Eramus disappeared back into the bushes, dragging the ghoul with him out of sight.

Nesneratha grabbed the now-free man by his shirt front and yanked him erect. Bringing her mouth close to his ear, she hissed, "Run!" through clenched teeth and pushed him roughly toward the dark woods, guiding him from behind.

A second ghoul appeared and grunted in surprise. He bared his gory teeth and raised his knife, aiming at Nesneratha's back. Eramus burst from the underbrush screaming a fierce battle cry. Nesneratha glanced over her shoulder as Eramus plowed into the other ghoul, nearly hacking off its knife hand with the razor-sharp scythe. In his left hand, Eramus wielded a recently liberated ghoul knife, which he plunged into its guts. The ghoul fell backward, howling in anguish among its kin.

Nesneratha then quickly disappeared with the man into the bushes, guiding him back toward the field's edge. She could tell he had difficulty walking and once he almost stumbled, but she supported his weight by gripping his arm tightly, keeping him on his feet.

"What about Milady?" the stranger managed at length. "I can't leave her behind."

"I am sorry, but all that can be done has been done." The man tried to turn back, but Nesneratha grabbed him by the shirt front and pulled his face near hers. "It would be certain death to return now. Our only hope is to press forward without delay and at our greatest speed," Nesneratha whispered. Behind them, the woods were filled with chaotic noise. Nesneratha continued, "You are in no condition to fight, you can barely walk! We must go now," and she pushed him forward.

Lewatollma intercepted the pair midway down the hill. Drawing close to Nesneratha, she asked, "What of Eramus?" in an anxious whisper.

"I cannot be certain of his fate. Here, help this one ahead and I shall find out," she said, pushing the man into her arms.

"No! Do not leave me again, Nesneratha! This has been a most horrific night. You could not imagine the dread of waiting here alone! Let us keep together as we ought," Lewatollma pleaded.

"Very well, but I am grieved to leave Eramus behind, for without his aid, my escape would have not been possible. Now he is left to his own devices," Nesneratha answered sadly. Looking over her shoulder quickly, just once, she uttered a quiet prayer aloud, "Geahuffus protect him!" Turning to Lewatollma, she urged, "Let us get back into the woods. Quickly now!" Once at the top and under the cover of the woods, Nesneratha picked up her items, donned her cloak, and shouldered her backpack. Pointing to the trail that brought them there, she motioned to Lewatollma to begin their retreat.

After killing his second ghoul, Eramus rolled his eyes back into his head and menacingly shaking his weapons, let go a terrible laugh-shriek as he charged the remaining ghouls. The pale ghouls wailed in fright and scattered, tripping over each other trying to escape Eramus's wild slashing.

A moment later, Eramus found himself alone, two more ghouls dead or dying at his feet. He turned to the remaining captive, who stared open-mouthed, her face filled with shocked terror at the sight she had just witnessed.

He brought his blade down swiftly between her ankles and split the cruel bonds in half. Ducking behind the tree, he cut the final rope and slipped the ghoul knife into his belt. Grabbing her by one arm, he dragged her away into the underbrush, running toward what he desperately hoped was safety. The young woman Eramus had just freed was struggling to keep her feet and she tripped, sending them both crashing to the earth. Eramus rose and tried to pull her up.

"I can't...go on. Just leave me," she pleaded as she gasped for air.

In the distance, Eramus could hear angry grunts and snarls and he knew that soon the ghouls would overcome the initial shock, regroup, and begin hotly pursuing them. He secured the scythe under his belt to free his other hand.

"What's yer name?" he asked.

"Why?" she asked despondently.

"Well, Wye, forgive me if'n I'm a little ungentlemanly, but it be time ta go," he answered. Grabbing her around the thighs, he tossed her headfirst over his shoulder. Grunting, he pushed himself upright and ran. He searched anxiously for the path leading across the open grassland. Above him, in the distance, he saw three shadows disappear into the tree line. Finally, he found the break in the grass that marked the way back up the hill.

Eramus strained under his burden. His legs pumped and his muscles burned as he propelled himself up the incline toward the woods. The leg he had recently injured was beginning to send shooting pain and he was forced to slow down to keep his feet. Suddenly, he realized he didn't know which way his friends were headed.

"Lewatollma! Nesneratha!" he called out as loudly as he dared. "Wait!"

Nesneratha halted and looked back toward the field.

"What is it?" Lewatollma inquired.

"I am uncertain. Wait here while I investigate."

Nesneratha sprang back to the grass's edge and searched for signs of pursuit. In the middle of the path, a large dark shape emerged moving slowly. It was too large to be a ghoul, and

Nesneratha gave a sigh of relief and smiled knowing Eramus was still alive. Speeding downhill, she joined him. Together they situated the woman between them and quickly ascended the remainder of the hill. Silently, they moved out of sight into the tree line and joined Lewatollma and the man.

"Milady!" the man exclaimed. "Is she alive?"

"Yup, quite," answered Eramus between labored pants.

Nesneratha quickly organized the group. "Lewatollma, you will assist the woman and take the lead. Eramus, you stay with the man. I shall take the rear."

"My feet," the young woman complained weakly.

Lewatollma dropped to inspect them. They were swollen and bruised where the remainder of the cord cut into her ankles. Drawing her blade, she nimbly cut the rest of the cord away. Then gently, she massaged her ankles to stimulate circulation. As she did, the girl whimpered softly in pain.

"There, that should help." Lewatollma turned to the man and cut his remaining bonds away as well.

All heads snapped to look behind them when an angry and fierce "Guhnd-Gee!" reverberated through the night air. Everyone was on edge, and they all unconsciously held their breath in dread anticipation. Nesneratha swallowed her fear and using the faintest of breath, uttered the chilling command, "Fly!"

The little band pressed urgently into the night, their hearts pounding. The thought of falling into the hands of the ghouls spurred them on past their natural limits. Periodically, Nesneratha would drop behind and listen carefully for signs of pursuit. Upon returning, she would encourage them to move faster and be quiet. The freed prisoners slowed them considerably. During a short break, Lewatollma gave them water and a small piece of waybread to give them strength. She examined them for other wounds. Besides bruises and general deprivation, they were surprisingly sound.

Dawn arrived bright and most welcome. Not until the sun was well above the horizon did Nesneratha allow them to stop. The young woman slumped immediately to the ground. For the first time, they had a real chance to see each other. The man was a yellow-haired soldier in his late twenties. His uniform was severely damaged, and he bore fresh scars about his head and shoulder. His pants were ripped and dirty, and his green shirt was torn and missing several brass buttons. An orange epaulet hung limply from his right shoulder and the left collar was half torn off.

The woman was but a young maiden, not yet twenty. Her clothes too, were in tatters. From the knees down, her breeches were soiled and rent, exposing her shins. The dark earth on her legs made it hard to discern where the clothing ended and the human began. What must have been a white smock was rumpled, filthy, and stained yellow with sweat below the armpits. One sleeve was half torn from the bodice, exposing her left upper arm, revealing bruises, scrapes, and scratches. Her long, brown hair was tangled and part of it hung forward, partially covering her gaunt, pale face.

Lewatollma made a brief introduction.

"I am Lewatollma. This," she said as she pointed to her companion, "is Nesneratha. We are travelers scouting out the land. Our friend is Eramus of Hares End."

The girl did not respond because she had already passed into a deep sleep.

"I am Sergeant Emil Aster, and this is Arnette Donatina, daughter of Lord and Lady Donatina. We are both from Miricel. Thank you for saving us from those, those ..." Emil waved his hand in the air as he searched for a word.

"Ghouls," Eramus injected.

"Yes. Whatever they were, ghouls certainly fit them well. But how did you find us?"

"This is not the time to tell tales. We must rest presently and be well underway before sunset. All night, they have been at our heels. But I have questions that need answers before you can sleep," Nesneratha insisted.

"Ask away," Emil replied.

"Do they travel at all by day?"

"No! They hate the light! They don't even set a guard while they sleep. They're just all huddled together covered by branches and leaves. And they don't rise until it's completely dark," Emil answered.

"If they hate light so much, why'd they 'ave a fire?" Eramus inquired.

"That's a part of their abominable ritual. But it was the only fire they made while we were their prisoners," Emil answered sternly, but a shadow fell upon him, and he suddenly looked old and careworn.

"Enough for now. Sleep." Nesneratha's voice was uncharacteristically gentle.

Emil nodded, then removed his vest and laid it gently over Arnette. He positioned himself nearby and covered his eyes with his forearm. Eramus yawned too and lay down upon the ground. But he could not close his eyes.

Nesneratha and Lewatollma huddled.

"Rest, Nesneratha. I will stand watch first," Lewatollma offered.

"No, you rest now and take the later watch. We will switch positions tonight. I will lead in addition to assisting Arnette and you will guard our rear. We will need your sharp eyes and ears. I suspect that in their aggravated state, the ghouls may brave some daylight to gain an advantage over us. We must be cautious," Nesneratha warned.

"I am sorry I was not braver last night. But fear overwhelmed me," Lewatollma apologized.

Nesneratha gently hugged her, then she tenderly pushed a length of hair back behind Lewatollma's ear. Smiling, she said, "I am sorry for placing you in such dreadful circumstances. I can still see the torment on your brow. Bless you, Lewatollma, for trying. I am sure you tested your courage to the limits, yet you did not fail. A friend cannot ask, nor expect more. Sleep, if you can, or if not, rest well. I will call upon you in a few hours."

Eramus was shaken out of his sleep by a crow flying overhead noisily complaining. He sat upright and looked around anxiously. Other than the raucous crow, all was still. Around him, the others slept. Lewatollma was perched on the balls of her feet looking intently westward in her watch position. The sun was beginning to move toward the horizon and Eramus assumed they would soon break camp and depart.

He rose slowly and stretched all the tired, aching muscles in his body. He moved behind Lewatollma, leaned over, and whispered.

"Are we safe?"

"Yes. You should sleep while you can."

"There'll be no more sleeping fer me today. I'm afraid if I do, there'll be no wakin' up. Do ya mind if I sit with ya?"

"As long as you are quiet," she replied in a whisper.

"Well, never mind then, I just wanted ta talk ta someone. A lot happened, an' I wanted ta talk it out."

"A burden shared is half as heavy," Lewatollma added. "That is a saying among our people. I would be glad to talk to you but now is not appropriate. I must be vigilant."

Only understanding her general intent, Eramus sighed, returned to his backpack, and sat down. Digging through his pack, he inventoried its contents. The food was nearly gone and now they had two additional mouths to feed. He contemplated wandering about for wild fruit, but even the slightest chance of running into ghouls ended any desire to go. Eramus sat staring up into the forest roof above him. Some of the walnut trees' leaves were turning yellow. Summer was at its end. He had left Hares End several weeks ago and he still had no food for his village. Just then, his mind was filled with an image of Hares End with everyone in the lodge, all staring at him, lean and hungry. Up front were Sheron and Little Miriam. He could see Little Miriam tugging on her mother's skirt tearfully pleading, "I'm hungry, Mommy" and Sheron bravely replying, "Don'tcha cry, Miriam, yer uncle will save us."

He wondered, what am I doing here, running for my life in the company of strangers? Should I have let Nesneratha and Lewatollma go off on their own to rescue those two? No, he reasoned, it would be wrong and cowardly to abandon them, especially after Lewatollma saved his life and healed him. Yet, his entire purpose was to take care of Hares End. If I survive this, he thought, I must get back on track—too many people are depending on me.

He looked at Lewatollma to take his mind off his overwhelming responsibility. How beautiful and graceful she was. Kind, caring, and smart. It was a shame he only understood half the words she used. He then felt the spark of love begin to burn in his sorrowing heart. He began to imagine a life together with her and finding happiness.

"Oh, quit dreamin', ya fool," he said out loud. His words awakened Nesneratha, who stirred, sat up, looked at the sun's position, and lay back down. He took a cue from Nesneratha, stopped tormenting himself, settled against a tree, closed his eyes, and fell back to sleep.

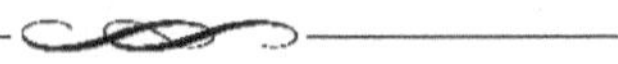

"Wake up! We must leave!" Lewatollma hissed, shaking Eramus's shoulder. His eyes snapped open, and he looked intently about him. It was light still, but the sun had gone. From the south, dark clouds moved swiftly in. He got up and made himself ready.

Nesneratha was tending to the others, encouraging them to arise and get prepared to depart. She passed out more waybread and water. Soon the little band was on the move. Eramus walked up beside Emil. He pulled the ghoul blade from his belt and handed it to the sergeant.

"Here. In case we has ta fight our way outa this," Eramus said.

"Thanks. I hope not, though, as I'm still a bit weak. They're devilishly strong once they get their hands on you."

"Would ya like some more food? I've one last bite a cheese if ya'd like."

"That would be most generous!"

Eramus swung his backpack off his shoulder and pulled out the last piece of cheese. He handed it to Emil, who broke it in half.

"M'Lady," he said, passing half to her.

She shook her head from side to side.

"Please, you must eat, M'Lady," Emil insisted.

She sighed and took it from him, and only then did he eat his half. They walked on in silence. Periodically, Eramus would hear Lewatollma running up fast from behind catching up to them. It set his nerves on edge every time she did, but he sighed in relief when she had nothing to report. The clouds moved in black and solid, sending an early night descending upon the travelers. They walked on into the night at a brisk pace, but not running. Hours passed in near silence.

The sound of Lewatollma's footsteps grew loud behind Eramus, but much faster than before. He turned to see her speeding full-bore toward them.

"Flee! Flee! They are upon us!" she cried in a shrill, frightened voice that set the hair on Eramus's neck on end.

Eramus and Emil drew their weapons. Peering into the dark, Eramus could see nothing, but the sound of footfalls and heavy breathing was becoming more distinct. Like a group of frightened deer, the group broke into a run. Nesneratha firmly grasped Arnette's wrist and sped away as they bolted into the forest. Nesneratha's sharp eyes kept them on the trail, but she was so intent on her flight that she did not notice two figures lurking behind the trees just ahead of her.

A huge ax blade arced through the air and bit into the ground just a few feet in front of Nesneratha. The blade's inscription was familiar, and she smiled a wry little smile. Using its handle as a step, she sprang over the great ax.

Turning to face the ax's unseen owner, she whispered, "Five humans. Ghouls behind." She then disappeared, pulling Arnette along behind her into the night. The ax snapped back into the shadows behind the tree. Eramus, Emil, and Lewatollma passed by in rapid succession. Lewatollma slowed to get a glance at the shadowy figures and then raced to catch Eramus and Emil.

"That be five," a voice whispered in the dark.

"Ya shouldn't tease Nessie like that, she'll —" another voice whispered back.

"Hush, 'em ghouls is acomin'!" the voice answered, cutting off the other.

The two figures slid farther back into the shadows as the ghouls closed in. The horde rushed past the trees, taking no notice of them.

"Be prepared to turn and fight," Lewatollma said to her companions. She glanced back over her shoulder. "Now!" she yelled.

Emil and Eramus slid to a halt and turned to face the ghouls. Lewatollma positioned herself behind them. Her heart pounded like a frightened animal in flight, but her hand was firmly around her blade's handle. The advancing footsteps and grunting grew menacingly louder.

"Wait for the Normen," Lewatollma hastily added.

"What?!" Eramus and Emil said simultaneously.

It was at that moment the Normen fell upon the ghouls from the rear, their axes hissing as they sliced through the air. Two of the ghouls went crashing down, their spines severed by sharp, heavy steel. Eramus and Emil leaped into the fray with a cry. Noises of all sorts filled the night. Men yelled. Ghouls shrieked. Steel sang. The Normen cut through the pale host like soft butter. Eramus and Emil had only to keep them from fleeing. The Norman attack was swift and savage. Three more ghouls were hewn down in a blur of flying steel. Two ghouls broke free, pushing their way past Emil, and fled into the woods. The Normen ran after them, cursing and yelling.

"Git back 'ere, ya bloodsuckers!" one of them yelled and crashed noisily into the forest in pursuit.

"Save one fer me, Hammie," the other Norman laugh-hooted, following close on his heels. The ghouls split up to try to elude them, but after a brief pursuit, the cursing and yelling turned to shrieks of pain and the sickly sound of metal hacking flesh into pieces. Suddenly, the night was eerily quiet, as if the forest were holding its breath in dreadful anticipation.

The five gathered as two broad-shouldered and barrel-chested men strode casually out of the woods, their axes resting easily on their shoulders. Lewatollma and Nesneratha smiled broadly.

"Who be they?" Eramus asked Lewatollma.

"Allow me to introduce Hamlin and Gorim. Two of my favorite Normen," Lewatollma replied grandly.

"At yer service!" Gorim bowed deeply.

"Miss us, loves?" Hamlin asked while stroking his bushy, tangled beard, his green eyes twinkling.

ITINERARY

Nesneratha: "It was generally well-known that the Normen who inhabited the wooded areas north of the farming communities were chiefly hunters, dwelling in lodges constructed of great logs. They were poorly educated and socially primitive, but expert woodsmen and gifted craftsmen in the art of woodworking — which was a matter of pride with them."

Minushua: "Proud of their expertise in woodworking, as woodsmen or (laughing) being uneducated and socially primitive?"

Nesneratha: "Actually (after a thoughtful pause) all of those things."

— Interview with Nesneratha

The Normen strutted confidently up to Nesneratha and Lewatollma, sporting cocky grins. Half a head taller than the women, they both sported thick, bushy beards. Gorim's hair was chestnut brown and Hamlin's was dark copper.

"So, what be ya doing out here in ghoul-land, girls?" Gorim asked. "An' who be yer friends?" he continued, nodding toward the rest of the party.

"We were rescuing these people," Nesneratha said and gestured to Emil and Arnette, "from those marauding fiends. This other man—" and she pointed to Eramus, "—is Eramus, a simple farmer. Lewatollma found him alone, lost, and wounded. She patched him up and adopted him as a pet," she said matter-of-factly.

Lewatollma shook her head imperceptibly from side to side. She looked apologetically at Eramus, who merely frowned.

"We permitted him to tag along out of sympathy," Nesneratha sighed and exaggeratedly shook her head. "Frankly, I do not understand her affection for homely creatures."

Looking aside at Emil, Eramus asked, "Is she makin' fun o' me?" Emil shrugged rather than delve into the details.

"Ya almost got caught as well," Hamlin cut in. "It's a good thing we spotted that mess on the West Road an' came a lookin' fer us selves. Seems we rescued ya, an' got 'ere in da nick a' time, too."

Strutting over to Nesneratha he began appealing to her saying, "Maybe now ya will show me some kindness, eh, Nessie-girl? Having saved you from 'em ghouls an' all." He tried to put his arm around her shoulder, but she deftly slapped it off and stepped away from him.

"Oaf! Keep your hands to yourself! Even if you shaved and bathed, something I doubt you have ever done in your life, I would never consent to your advances. Besides, we would have escaped without your help."

The Normen roared with laughter.

"See, Gorim! That's why I fancy 'er so much! She be spirited!"

"Even so, 'Ammie, ya best keep away from her. I don't think she cares fer ya much," Gorim warned. He stroked his beard then gently jabbed Hamlin in the ribs with his elbow.

"Besides, why would ya want her? She's skinny an' too small in the hips. She'd probably die bearin' ya children. An' even if she survived the birthin', yer children would starve she ain't got no chest ta speak of! You'd be way better off finding a *real* woman," he said in mock disdain.

Nesneratha stared at them, her mouth agape, momentarily stunned and at a loss for words.

"Aye, you're right, cousin. She ain't much ta look at. But ya knows I can't resist the fiery ones!" Hamlin gave her a wink. "Rrrr-ruff," he barked in her direction.

Nesneratha's countenance darkened, and she clenched her jaw as her right hand grasped her blade's handle. Lewatollma wrapped her arms around Nesneratha from behind, pinning her arms.

"Well, I for one am glad to see you," Lewatollma said brightly. "And I appreciate your assistance. Certainly, you made our night less traumatic, and we can rest much easier now. We are grateful for your timely arrival and the efficient way in which you dispatched those nasty ghouls! Right, Nesneratha?" Lewatollma smiled and squeezed her partner. Nesneratha struggled to free her knife arm, but Lewatollma held her fast.

"Come now, Nesneratha, say thank you to our friends. They did help us out of a very awkward situation," Lewatollma said, smiling and giving another, firmer squeeze.

Nesneratha glared at Hamlin, who just stroked his beard and smiled gleefully back at her. Lewatollma saw that Nesneratha was still tightly gripping her blade, so she kicked her in the ankle.

"Ow," Nesneratha cried and shot an angry look at Lewatollma.

"It is most ungracious to threaten your friends with a knife," Lewatollma whispered so only Nesneratha would hear.

"They made the most ungracious remarks about my person," she whispered back through gritted teeth.

"Rise above it, Nesneratha. They meant no harm," Lewatollma answered. "Come now, show a little magnanimity," she chided. "Please?" Nesneratha took a deep breath and exhaled it slowly before releasing her grip on the blade.

"Thank you," Nesneratha muttered through her still-clenched teeth as she glared back at the two Normen.

"There now, all is well," Lewatollma cheerfully added as she released her grip on Nesneratha but as a precaution, retained a firm grip on her right arm, using both hands and giving the appearance she was lovingly attached to the arm of a dear, old friend.

Emil stepped forward, extending his hand. "Yes, thank you. I feared the worst when the ghouls came upon us, but you truly saved the day. You have both my and Lady Donatina's," and he motioned to the sullen Arnette standing near the women, "... heartfelt gratitude." He gripped the two Normen at the forearm and placed his hand upon their shoulders.

"Ya's lucky ta be alive. We saw what happened ta yer party back on the road. How'd they kill so many a ya?" Gorim inquired.

"They snuck up and killed our watchman, then attacked us while we were asleep. Most of the men didn't even get a chance to fight back against those savages! They tied them up and tortured them to death. They killed Arnette's brother the same way then ate him right in front of her. I only wish I could have avenged my brothers-in-arms myself, but I thank you for sending them back to Hell."

"Yes...thankee. I've already fought 'em ghouls once an' ta be honest, I wasn't looking forward ta another fight," Eramus added as he stepped forward.

"Ya fought ghouls, eh? Jya kill any of 'em?" Gorim asked, suddenly interested.

"Uh...four I think," Eramus added, unsure of himself.

"Really! Four! With just that thar farmin' tewl?" Gorim asked incredulously, pointing to Eramus's scythe.

"Yep. Oh, an' a blade I took from 'em," Eramus answered.

Pointing to the scythe, Hamlin asked, "Howdya kill a ghoul wit dat puny thing?"

"Yes, Eramus," Nesneratha inquired, joining the discussion, "you dispatched that first ghoul very efficiently. Where did you learn to do that, knowing to go for the throat?"

"Just same as butcherin'. That be the fastest way; ta slit the throat. They die quick-like." The Normen both nodded in agreement. "Ain't ya ever killed farm stock, Nesneratha?"

"You do that to poor innocent animals?" she asked in disbelief.

"Acourse, how do yer kind do it?"

Shuddering at the thought, Nesneratha spat out, "Barbaric," in disgust and walked away.

Eramus and the Normen shrugged off Nesneratha's disparaging remark. "Well, that be fine enough killin' fer a farmer," Gorim continued as he and Hamlin nodded their approval.

"I killed four meself an Hammie here, he got three," Gorim added proudly.

"No, ya got it switched about. I got four an' you got three," Hamlin corrected.

"No, I got four! I'm sure of it," Gorim answered.

"Not so, cousin! Ya left one back there only wounded. I was the one that kilt 'im, not you," Hamlin retorted, poking his finger into Gorim's chest.

"Well, he wasn't going ta git very fer with only one leg! He was as good as dead," Gorim shot back, putting his hands on his hips and wagging his head slightly. The two Normen eye-balled each other critically for a moment.

"All right. Three an' a half each, then," Hamlin concluded.

"Fair enough," Gorim conceded with a nod.

Eramus and Emil chuckled softly at the absurd compromise.

Arnette walked up behind Emil and spoke to him in a weary voice. "Can we leave this awful place? I'm cold. A fire would be welcome, but I want to be far away from these..." A mixture of vile emotions swept in rapid succession over her face before she continued, "…things first."

"Of course, Milady," Emil replied, taking on the air of a servant.

"And stop calling me that," she added mournfully.

Lewatollma seized the opportunity to get the group moving again and jumped in. "Nesneratha, take Arnette and Emil with you in the lead, and I will take the rear. Eramus, Gorim, and Hamlin will stay back with me in case I need them."

Nesneratha nodded her agreement then shot Hamlin one last threatening look through narrowed eyes. Lewatollma released Nesneratha, stepped over to Arnette, and put her arm around her as she walked her toward Nesneratha.

"Just tell Nesneratha when you are ready to stop. If you do not, she will travel all night long." Arnette did not respond. Lewatollma sensed her distress and tried to reassure her. "Do not worry, you are safe now! You will see tomorrow that everything will be quite right again."

Arnette turned her head suddenly toward Lewatollma. Her eyes flashed angrily, and her face was set sternly. "No! Things will not be right! They will never be right again," she lashed out in a harsh and bitter voice. Arnette forcibly shook herself free of Lewatollma's grip and strode abruptly past Nesneratha.

Lewatollma and Nesneratha exchanged concerned glances. Lewatollma gestured with her head to go on ahead. Nesneratha turned, took long, sure strides, caught up, and passed Arnette. Emil walked to Lewatollma's side and watched Arnette leave.

"Will she be all right?" Lewatollma quietly asked Emil.

"It was a hard blow to lose her brother last night. They were very close," he explained with a sigh, his voice a bare whisper.

"Alas, the poor, bereft child," Lewatollma intoned sadly. She let her head drop slightly out of respect for her loss.

"Well said and true. It is sad enough to lose your kin, but there is more," Emil replied, pausing momentarily.

Lewatollma raised her head and gazed into the man's exhausted face.

"Her brother wanted to go farther east, then turn north through the farming villages. But instead, we took that cursed West Road..." Emil stopped as if he was not quite sure which words to use. A pained look fell upon his features as he sighed, "...because Arnette insisted."

"What was your original destination?"

"We were escorting Arnette to Auroradale. She was supposed to spend a month up there to meet a suitor and his family. She didn't want to go and resented the idea of an arranged marriage. She felt like her parents were forcing her. It embarrassed her and she didn't want to be paraded through all the villages. From the start, she argued with her brother Izaiah, and he relented to appease her. He felt going through the mongrel farming villages was better even if it took longer. There were more towns to stop at and resupply if needed. None of us knew the ghouls were active again."

Emil left without another word and joined Arnette to keep guard at her side. Lewatollma studied the girl anew as she plodded along behind Nesneratha. It was now clear to Lewatollma why her back was bent, her shoulders slumped, and her eyes downcast. Her burden was almost palpable.

Lewatollma turned to face Eramus and the two burly Normen. She breathed a slight sigh, gave a sweeping gesture with her arm toward the others, and said, "We leave now."

Nesneratha moved noiselessly into the night, keeping true to the path that led them back to the West Road. She let several hours pass before halting the little band of travelers. She selected a small clearing, suitable for sleeping with ample space for a fire. Turning to Arnette, she asked, "Is this far enough? Can we stop and make camp, Milady?"

Arnette answered by dropping to the ground. Grabbing a nearby stick, she began digging a pit for the fire. Nesneratha stood over her watching as Lewatollma and the others walked up. Eramus and Emil gathered stones and surrounded the pit with them while the Normen began searching for firewood.

Lewatollma pulled Nesneratha aside and spoke in hushed whispers to her partner, to which she only nodded.

"Sergeant Aster, get a fire started, please," Arnette requested.

"Yes, Milady," he replied and foraged for tinder. He returned and carefully arranged the sticks, leaves, and dry grass into a small pile. He reached into his pocket and produced a flint and steel. He struck them together, producing several bright flashes that briefly illuminated the party around the fire pit. The shower of sparks ignited the tinder, and it began to smolder. Soon the flames surged skyward, and fuel was added until a good-sized blaze began to crackle merrily.

Arnette sat silently staring into the fire as the Normen piled dry wood between two small trees.

"Thar be 'nuff for t'nite," Gorim concluded, clapping his hands, scattering bits of dirt and dust everywhere. Eramus was hungry, but he knew better than to mention it aloud. So, he made a spot for himself near the fire, placed his backpack beneath his head, and drifted off to sleep.

The next morning, he awoke before the others. He shook off the cool morning air and tossed some more wood on the remaining embers. Looking around, he saw his companions spread around, asleep in various positions and combinations. The two Nawimans were curled up together covered completely by their cloaks. The Normen were propped up against a fallen log, their chests rising rhythmically with their breathing, dew drops shimmering in their beards. Arnette was curled up near the fire and Emil was nearby using his arm as a pillow.

Eramus wandered off into the gray dawn in search of something that might be edible. This late in the year, he didn't expect to find much in the wild. A half-hour of searching yielded some mushrooms, three chestnuts, and four small bunches of sour, wild grapes. For himself, this would have been enough to scrape by for two days, but for the seven of them, it was sadly insufficient. Discouraged, Eramus returned to the fire.

Arnette looked anxiously at Eramus when he walked back into the clearing. He placed his finding on top of Emil's jacket, where Arnette quickly looked over the meager offering. She looked up at Eramus, an unspoken question in her eyes.

"Give me a minute to warm my hands and I'll see what else I can find," he said quietly. Placing his palms toward the small blaze, he let the heat drive off the damp chill. Behind him, he heard the women stirring. Arnette began dividing the food into seven, more or less equal piles. Eramus looked at her efforts and sighed — it looked to be about two small mouthfuls each.

Breakfast was brief, unceremonious, and wholly unsatisfying. The Normen began to grumble about hospitality and gratitude, but a single, icy look from Arnette silenced them. Nesneratha glanced at Lewatollma, who nodded in silent agreement.

"We should press on and return to the West Road by the same way we arrived. From there, we can decide the best course for all concerned," Nesneratha advised. When she heard no dissenting voice, she added, "Lewatollma will take the lead. Let us depart." The group filed quietly into the woods, picking up the original trail. They traveled that day in silence. The sky was gray and bleak, adding to the somber mood. They stopped only for brief rest breaks and forged steadily forward, driven from the rear by Nesneratha and coaxed from the front by Lewatollma. Thanks to their persistence, they made the West Road by late afternoon.

The stench that was merely nauseating before was beyond description when the party returned to the location of the ambush. Lewatollma gave the site a wide berth and they made camp nearby, well out of olfactory range.

Emil, Eramus, Hamlin, and Gorim gathered all the supplies that were still useful, doing so via brief, but numerous trips. Emil recovered some personal items that he and Arnette would need for their journey. Much of the foodstuffs had been plundered by four-legged forest thieves and not ghouls. Still, some food stored in heavy leather pouches survived the determined attacks of bird and beast, affording the travelers a meager serving each of steaming corn mush. Amazingly enough, a small crock of honey survived along with some hardtack and crackers, which were enjoyed as well.

Arnette remained sullen throughout the meal, but the others were somewhat lifted in their spirits by a warm meal and a cheery fire. No one noticed Arnette except for Lewatollma, who finally dared to venture past her stony silence.

"What is bothering you, Milady?" she asked gently and compassionately, which was Lewatollma's special gift.

"We have to bury our friends," she replied after sighing deeply.

Each man looked at the next with anxious glances.

"Milady," Emil began, "I knew all those men and I hold the deepest respect for them and their kin, but—"

"But now it's above you to see that their remains are properly interred?"

"It's not above me to honor my fallen comrades," he replied sharply, cutting her off from further accusation. "It's that we have no tools to dig with."

"Aye, an we be deep in da forest, is naught but root an stone beneath ya'. It could take a long spell ta dig graves fer six men. Ya' should just make a pyre, then bury the ashes. Besides, I'm not sure what belongs to who, them bein' hacked up an all," Hamlin prattled, saying much more than he ought.

"Dare we make a big fire?" Eramus injected. "I mean, ain't we still in ghoul country?"

"I hate to agree with Eramus, but a funeral pyre does sound like a bad idea," Nesneratha added. "This may not have been the only ghoul raiding party. Besides, what if some ghouls find their slaughtered friends? Will they pursue us looking for revenge or worse? More importantly, others should be warned. Therefore, we should tarry here no longer than absolutely required."

"Look, Milady, the Grandames can send an armed party back with wagons and coffins to collect our friends. That way, their families can have them buried along with their kin," Emil offered.

"And what of *my* kin?" she began angrily. "Who will collect my brother's remains deep in ghoul land?" She tried to fight back the tears but was losing the will to deny herself much longer.

"I will," Emil replied confidently. "If the Grandames allow us to perform an armed expedition, I will lead them and recover your brother. I promise."

Arnette Donatina sat silently. Her jaw was set hard, and her eyes brimmed with tears, but they did not spill. She stared into the little campfire until she found resolve.

"Sergeant Aster, I will hold you to your promise and," she said, and taking in a deep breath, continued, "I accept your judgment in this matter. Let's return without delay to Miricel."

"As you wish, Milady," he responded.

Hamlin nudged Gorim in the ribs. "An' we'll see ya safely there, lass...er...Milady," Gorim added, then stood and executed a bow to cover his blunder.

Nesneratha and Lewatollma looked at each other without saying a word. Nesneratha was fingering the tiny jewel around her neck. Eramus had not noticed it before, but it was red, just like Lewatollma's. Grasping the gem tightly in her fist, she leaned close to Lewatollma. For the briefest instant, they shut their eyes and touched their foreheads. All this happened while Gorim fumbled about. Eramus was the only one aware of the young women's silent communion. Nesneratha slid her gem back out of sight and announced that she and Lewatollma would also be escorting Lady Donatina back to Miricel.

All eyes turned to Eramus.

"Do ya think they might have some food ta spare in Miricel an' men lookin' fer a wife? I really is beginnin' ta worry 'bout ma village. So fer I's got nuttin'," Eramus fretted aloud.

"I'm sure something can be arranged, as there is no lack of food in Miricel. I can't speak to the need for wives. Why is that important, Eramus?" Emil asked.

Lewatollma jumped into the conversation on behalf of Eramus. "That is all they have to trade in exchange for supplies: their daughters' hands in marriage. It is a desperate situation. They are not looking for *extra* food — if they do not obtain supplies, many in his village will perish this winter."

Arnette broke her silence. "Traded like livestock," she scoffed. "Almost as bad as my family," she muttered as she walked away.

"Eramus," Nesneratha began, "I think Miricel is your best choice at this time. It is pointless and dangerous to go back north, and you have already traveled to the east without success. You should stay with us. It is safer for all of us if we travel together. If what Emil says is true, Miricel may be the best hope for your village."

"Nesneratha is right, Eramus," Lewatollma added. "This is your best option." Noticing the doubt on his face, she approached him and took his hand in hers. "If you wandered off by yourself, I would be worried about you. Please stay with us."

With just one look at her kindly face and those pleading brown eyes, Eramus's doubts vanished. "If ya think so, then sure, I'll go wit ya."

Lewatollma embraced him and whispered, "Thank you," in his ear.

The group held another brief discussion to decide who would stand the watches that night. Eramus drew the first watch, so he collected some dry wood to keep the fire going and listened attentively to the night's sounds. He paced quietly about the little camp to keep himself alert. Lewatollma arose sometime later and relieved him.

"Sleep now, Eramus," she whispered to him.

"With ya on watch, I'll sleep like a babe!"

She smiled at this compliment but said nothing. She moved to the edge of the camp, wrapped herself securely in her cloak, and faced west. Eramus lay down with his back to a log and put his sack under his head. He watched Lewatollma standing there rock-still deeply attuned to the night's every sound. As he drifted off to sleep, he wondered if Miricel had grain they were willing to trade.

The next morning, Hamlin rousted them with rude kicks to the bottom of their feet. The sky was cold and gray once again. After consuming a hasty breakfast consisting of some hardtack recovered from the site of the attack, they divided the supplies among themselves.

Emil suggested that they follow the West Road south, and then turn west toward Miricel as they neared the Emmering. This route, Emil guessed, would take four days on foot to reach Miricel. Emil noted that there were no towns or villages between here and

Miricel, nor were they likely to meet anyone on the road this time of year until they had almost arrived. The supplies would have to be used sparingly to last the whole trip.

So, they started at a brisk pace. The road was clear and solid underfoot, allowing them to make substantial progress. At first, Emil kept beside Arnette, but she refused his company, so he spent most of his time trading stories with Hamlin and Gorim. Emil, Gorim, and 'Ammie — as his cousin called him — took the lead, three abreast. Eramus walked alongside Lewatollma and Nesneratha guarded the rear.

"She's a moody one, eh?" Eramus finally whispered to Lewatollma, motioning to the girl in front of them.

"She is grieving for her lost brother, Eramus. But her grief is compounded by the guilt she has laid upon herself for his death, something which she ought not have done. It was not her fault."

"Why don'tcha talk ta her 'bout it?"

"She has not been receptive to my counsel." Lewatollma frowned.

"Why not?"

Lewatollma could only shrug.

"Well, I guess I ought ta give it a try."

"Eramus," Lewatollma cautioned, "be sensitive," and as if to illustrate her point, she laid her hand softly upon his forearm. "And be gentle," she added, her eyes meeting his as her voice softened.

Eramus nodded matter-of-factly and then jogged to Arnette Donatina's side. "How are ya today, Milady?" Eramus started.

"Please don't call me that. Just call me Arnette," she sighed.

"Okay, Arnette it is. Are ya feelin' better? Are ya feet doin' good?"

She turned slightly to look at him from the corner of her eye. "Why do you care?" she asked critically.

"Well, since that night I rescued ya, we haven't had much chance ta talk, bein' in a rush an' all. Ya know, ghouls hot on our tracks an' all. I didn't want ya ta think I had forgotten all about ya. I'm not the kind ta just rescue people an' then ignore 'em, ya' know!"

"Unfortunately, I am going to survive, thank you very much. But I wish I hadn't. I wish I had died alongside my brother."

"Oh, ya can't mean that!"

"Oh, but I do! Besides, what would you know about how I feel?" she answered with vehemence.

Eramus drew back in surprise at her fervor, and he felt a surge of anger because the pain he felt for the loss of his wife and son was dismissed by this youngster. His features turned stern, and he fired a volley right back at her.

"What a saucy tongue ya have! Do ya think yer t'only one ta'ever lost kin?" Eramus snorted indignantly. "I lost both me wife an' son within days of each other! That smarts, I'll tell ya! Took the will ta live right outa' me! So there, I do know how ya feel, you brassy bitch!"

Her mouth fell open and she stared at him, shocked and speechless, but her shock turned to indignation and she responded with, "How dare you—"

Eramus cut her off, and drawing himself up to his full stature, he jabbed his finger in her face. "How dare ya, yerself! Have ya no respect fer yer elders or them that risk their lives ta save ya? Yer just a selfish, little brat! I've a good mind ta cut a switch an' whip some respect inta ya'! Thinkin' only a yerself, 'boo-hoo, poor me!' What about yer parents? How do ya think they'd feel if they lost both you an' yer brother? Pretty darn poorly, I'll wager. I know what it feels like ta be left alone ta grieve. It's grim fer sure and I'd wish it on no one."

"But it's my fault he's dead," she finally blurted out.

"Oh, really?" Eramus asked skeptically, his hands upon his hips. "How old was yer brother?"

"What?" she asked, suddenly confused.

"How old was yer brother?" Eramus reiterated.

"Thirty-one," she replied, somewhat puzzled.

"What? Thirty-one and not enough sense ta stay out of dangerous lands? Pah, he deserved ta die," Eramus scoffed.

Suddenly, Arnette's face screwed up, the pain exploding to the surface from the depths of her very soul. She launched herself at Eramus with a feral yell and began pelting him with her fists. His arms flew up instinctively to protect himself from her furious, but ineffectual blows.

"You bastard! He didn't know there were ghouls there!" she screamed. And then the tears began to flow in earnest. "I didn't know! He didn't know! None of us knew!" She continued her attack as the others looked cautiously on.

Emil Aster went to intervene, but Hamlin blocked the way with his arm, advising, "Let it be, lad."

Soon her rage was spent and her strength with it. Eramus seized her by the forearms as she started to fall, and he pulled her up, so they met face to face. "We didn't know! We didn't know!" the words tumbled repeatedly from her tear-streaked face.

When her ranting ceased and she paused to draw a breath, Eramus looked her in the eye and said softly, apologetically, "Then it were no one's fault, were it?"

She looked up blankly into his face as the truth of it sank deep into her heart. "It's not my fault?" she asked one final time.

Eramus shook his head no, then pulled her to his chest and patted her gently on the back. "It wasn't yer fault, so let it go now. Go ahead an' cry fer him." She buried her face in his chest and although he could not hear anything, he could feel her body shaking as she wept bitterly.

"Well, then, let us take a short rest," Nesneratha announced mock-cheerfully.

Eramus escorted Arnette to a nearby rock and sat her down, stroking her hair gently just once. He walked over to Lewatollma.

"That was gentle and sensitive?" she whispered low.

Eramus just shrugged. "Can I get a drink from yer skin? Mine's empty." She shook her head, smiled oddly, and handed him the waterskin.

When they resumed their journey, Eramus accompanied Arnette and they spoke at length of life and death.

Stopping early that day, they left the road for a sheltered spot behind a small cluster of firs. In the distance, they could hear the sound of water splashing merrily.

"Arnette, help me gather up the waterskins. There be a stream nearby, we can fill 'em while the others make camp." She sighed, nodded, and got the Nawimans' waterskins while Eramus collected the rest. Together they wandered into the forest in the direction of the stream.

Upon reaching it, they found a good-sized brook with a deep, clear pool near the base of small falls. At the far end, the water ran swiftly through a narrow outlet.

Eramus pulled off his boots, rolled up his leggings, and waded in near the edge of the falls. "Dump out ta stale an' toss me 'em skins. One at a time, acourse."

She unstopped each skin, dumped their contents, and handed them to Eramus to fill them with fresh water.

"What kept you going after your wife and son died?"

Eramus drew a deep breath and let it out before starting. "Other people needed me. I couldn't let 'em down, even if me own life didn't seem ta have a purpose. The longer ya live, the more ya realize we're all in this together. Each one affects the other." Then Eramus laughed. "Sounds pretty stupid, don't it?"

"No, it doesn't. I guess my family will need me. But I don't know how to tell them how my brother died, Eramus."

"Don't tell them," he said, looking her in the eye. "Let Emil do it. He's a soldier an' that's soldier's work — ta report what happened on the field a battle. Let him tell yer father then let yer father break it ta yer mother. Ya don't have ta carry that burden alone."

As he mindlessly filled the waterskins, he gazed deep into the pool, where he spied a large fish swimming lazily about.

"Arnette?"

"Yes?"

"Would ya like ta have fish fer dinner?"

"Absolutely! Anything besides peasant's mush again!"

"Good! Take off yer clothes."

"What!" she exclaimed, giving him an incredulous look.

"Not all yer clothes, just yer boots an' outers. Ya don't want ta get 'em wet."

"Why?" she asked suspiciously.

"If ya can chase that fish toward me, I'm pretty sure I can spear him. But you'll have ta get in the pool, 'cause I don't think he'll pay ya much heed from the bank."

After the last skin was filled, Eramus returned to the rocky bank and found a thin, sturdy piece of wood. Using his blade, he removed all the small branches and carefully sharpened one end.

Arnette stripped down to her undergarments. Feeling slightly self-conscious, she waited with her arms folded across her chest. Eramus removed most of his clothes without hesitation and waded into the distant neck of the pool, where it narrowed near the outlet. He spread his legs and positioned his crude spear, so he was looking straight down into the water.

"Yeah, it's cold! Come on now, send 'im this way — but slow an' easy!"

Arnette eased herself into the opposite end of the pool and started slowly toward the fish. It took her several tries, but she finally managed to urge it toward Eramus. He held his breath as it swam closer. Arnette jumped as Eramus's spear thrust suddenly and violently downward.

"Did you g-get him?" she chattered.

Eramus held the crude spear firmly to the brook's rocky bottom, staring intently past its quivering shaft into the now-cloudy water. Then he reached down slowly, sliding both hands along the pole. His head disappeared below the surface for a moment, then emerged with a broad grin and a huge, twitching fish hooked firmly through the mouth and gill with his thumb and forefinger.

"Oh, real food for dinner," she sighed in relief.

"Yep. Let's get outa these clothes an' hang 'em ta dry." Exchanging their wet clothes for the dry ones, they returned excitedly to camp.

Hamlin watched in despair as Emil and Nesneratha argued about how much of their rations they should use for their dinner. Hamlin's appetite demanded at least twice the sum that each proposed.

"Maybe we could 'ave just a wee bit more," he begged, gesturing with his thumb and forefinger held apart.

Emil and Nesneratha glared at him like he was an idiot. He looked at Lewatollma for support, but she just stared into the small fire from her seat on a nearby log. Her gaze was very distant as she sat with her arms folded and her cloak wrapped about to ward off the rapidly cooling evening air.

"Care to join this discussion, Lewatollma? Do you have nothing to contribute regarding your even-meal?" Nesneratha inquired impatiently.

Without gazing up from the fire, Lewatollma answered, "Others' metabolism may have greater requirements than ours, Nesneratha. One serving quantity may not suit everyone's needs. Nor should you forget that Emil and Arnette have endured deprivation and must restore their strength. They should receive larger portions. The rest..." and looking squarely at Hamlin, she added, "...will have to endure until we reach Miricel."

Hamlin was nearly in tears. "But aren't ya hungry, lass? We done a good bit a travelin'. Surely, ya must be hungry?"

"Oh, yes, I am indeed hungry. But it will be better to endure a little hunger now than to consume all our supplies at once and faint before we complete our journey. Surely, you must see the wisdom in that?"

"Me head sees it all right, but me belly disagrees!" Hamlin whimpered.

Sergeant Aster started to object to special treatment for him when Arnette and Eramus stepped into camp shivering and smiling sheepishly.

Her face was full of curiosity as Nesneratha asked, "What have you two been up to?"

"Eramus, why is your hair wet?" Lewatollma asked.

"Milady, you're shivering! I say, what is going on here?!" Emil demanded.

Eramus and Arnette smiled knowingly at each other.

"We have a surprise announcement to make," Arnette said, smiling. Emil's face paled, Lewatollma's eyes widened, Nesneratha raised an eyebrow, and Hamlin grinned devilishly.

"What? What? Say what?" Gorim added, suddenly interested.

"We're having fish for dinner," Eramus and Arnette announced in unison as they produced the pole supporting the waterskins and their grand catch.

Lewatollma jumped up and clapped her hands in joy. "Oh, fresh fish!" she blurted out. Her face lit up with excitement and she hopped up and down, unable to contain herself. Everyone stood open-mouthed, transfixed by the sight of a real meal.

"Well, somebody needs ta clean it, an' cook it, acourse," Eramus hinted when no one moved to take the fish from him.

"Ere, lad, I'll gut an' fillet that thar fish fer ya'." Hamlin smiled, giving Eramus a wink.

"We will need some good coals for the cooking fire, so Emil and Gorim, please see to that. Lewatollma and I will cook it," Nesneratha added.

"Oh, and there's some salt in my backpack," Emil mentioned before he turned away.

"Wipe that ridiculous grin off your face and help me," Nesneratha whispered to Lewatollma as she walked past her.

"And I'm freezing!" Arnette muttered as she rushed toward the fire to warm herself.

Eramus moved close to the flames as well, turning his backside to the heat. "Ah, now that's better!" he sighed. "Are ya still cold, Arnette?" he asked.

"Y-y-yes," she answered through chattering teeth.

"Here," Lewatollma said and provided her cloak, which she wrapped around both their shoulders. "Just relax and warm yourselves while dinner is prepared. You have done enough for tonight. Well done, both of you!" she added with a smile.

Eramus put his arm around Arnette, and she leaned into him.

"What about our wet clothes?" she whispered.

"I'll go back fer 'em afta dinner," he answered quietly.

Dinner was prepared with much anticipation. In addition to savory fish, Lewatollma baked the residue of the corn meal and honey into cakes. These she reserved for future meals on the road.

A spirit of gaiety filled the camp and for the first time since their acquaintance, Arnette smiled and laughed.

Everyone praised Arnette and Eramus for the fine meal they enjoyed. Lewatollma was especially grateful, and it filled Eramus with a special kind of satisfaction to please her. Eramus laughed and enjoyed his meal until about halfway through, when he remembered something that he said to Arnette: "We're all connected." Suddenly, the hungry faces of Hares End flooded into his mind and just as quickly, his appetite fled; he could barely swallow what was still in his mouth.

"Does anyone want the rest a ma food?" he suddenly asked. "I'm full." He extended the rest of his meal to Arnette, Emil, then Lewatollma, who all shook their heads no. Hamlin eagerly snatched it from Eramus and split it with his cousin. Eramus stood and excused himself saying, "I'm going fer a little walk down ta the brook an' clean up." He gave Arnette a curt nod and disappeared into the trees.

Lewatollma looked after him suspiciously but did not follow. Shortly afterward, he returned. The camp began to settle for the night. Nesneratha, Emil, and Lewatollma decided there would be no need to post guard. This way, all could get a good night's rest and be fresh for tomorrow. One by one, they all settled in as the fire burned low.

Lewatollma woke to Eramus tossing and turning. She looked over in time to see him sit up.

"What is wrong?" she asked softly.

"Nuttin'," he lied. They locked their eyes for a moment then Eramus said, "Go back ta sleep," and looked away into the night.

Lewatollma lay back down and closed her eyes. But she heard him get up and leave. She made a quick note of the position of the stars in the sky and then settled back into a peaceful slumber.

Sometime later, Lewatollma heard a sound in the night, perhaps from some creature or the rustling of a tree or bush, and she opened her eyes. From the motion of the stars, she estimated that an hour had passed since speaking to Eramus. She turned to check on him, but he wasn't there. She half sat up and surveyed the camp. He was nowhere to be found among the travelers scattered around the smoldering fire. Normally, she wouldn't have been concerned, but Eramus had been acting peculiar since dinner.

She reached down and slid on her boots, then wrapped her cloak around her shoulders against the damp and chill night air. Tracing his tracks, she followed Eramus out of the campsite down toward the brook. As she rounded a copse of fir trees that blocked the brook from the view of the camp, she found him sitting on a fallen tree staring into the dark rippling waters.

She approached casually, deliberately creating a little noise to make her presence known, but he didn't say anything or even turn to look to see who it was. Lewatollma positioned herself next to him on the log. She looked forward into the waters, without making eye contact. She sat there in silence for a quarter of an hour. Finally, Lewatollma spoke.

"Tomorrow will be another long day on the road. You really should get some rest. I cannot believe you are not exhausted after all we have been through."

"Why aren't you asleep?" Eramus mumbled.

"I was until I discovered you had been gone for over an hour, so naturally, I came to look for you."

"Well, ya found me an' I'm all right. Go back ta sleep."

"You say you are well, but your actions say quite the opposite, Eramus of Hares End."

Eramus sighed a long sigh then offered, "Sometimes me heart won't let me sleep."

"I do not understand. Why would your heart interfere with your sleep?"

"There's a shadow there an' in that shadow sleeps a memory. When that memory is awake...I 'ave trouble sleeping."

"What kind of memory would do that?"

"Have ya never had a shadow o'er yer heart?"

She shook her head from side to side.

He looked at her incredulously. "Have ya ever experienced grief, had someone ya loved die?"

"No."

"Have ya ever been so lonely it hurt?"

"No."

"Been desperately hungry?"

"No."

"Been sick?"

"No." For some odd reason, she was beginning to feel guilty.

"What a beautiful, perfect life ya live! I envy ya, I really do. But ma life ain't bin so carefree. I've lived a hard life an' with that have come some hard times. I can't change them. If I could, I would, but the past is, well...gone. I just has ta live with them memories. With time they've grown dimmer, but they've never gone completely away."

Taking his arm, she coaxed, "Come back to the camp. It is chilly here by the water. You really must try to sleep now." She tugged at his arm, and he yielded. Leading him back to the fire, she asked, "Are you cold? If so, you can use my cloak. I can manage for the rest of the night."

"No. No thankee." Eramus grabbed a few pieces of wood and put them on the fire, then lay down and turned his back to her. Shutting his eyes, he feigned sleep so she wouldn't fret. Lewatollma lay there listening to him. She waited until she heard him begin the long, slow relaxed breathing indicative of sound sleep. She lay there watching Eramus for a few minutes, then she arose, took her bedding, and positioned herself next to him. Scooting as close as she could without disturbing him, she took her cloak and covered them both with it. Eramus was lying on his side facing her, fast asleep. Using her finger, Lewatollma gently pushed a lock of hair out of his face, moving it behind his ear.

In a soft voice, less than a whisper, she confessed, "I do not understand your struggles, but I am drawn to you, Eramus. My heart longs to comfort you and lift some of the burdens you carry. My experience offers no solution on how to help you, except to be your friend and to love you for who you are. Perhaps one day, you will open your heart and let me in."

Lewatollma kissed the tip of her finger, then gently touched his cheek with it. "Sleep. I will know if you stir, and I will be right here for you." Looking into the sky, she ascertained that she could slip in a few hours of sleep before anyone else would get up, so she could move back to her original spot undetected. She did not want to give the Normen anything to tease her about, nor provoke a lecture from Nesneratha. Her feelings were a very private matter for her, and she guarded them jealously.

The company awoke the next day refreshed and eager to be underway. The day was cool, and some high clouds began to move in from the west. The road was relatively clear and easy to travel. With a decent meal in their bellies, they found new strength and were able to put many miles behind them.

Eramus pondered the events of the day before. He reflected on the conversation he had with Lewatollma by the brook. How could life be that simple? Even as a child, his life was hard. The only beautiful bright spot in his life had been Miriam. While they were together, he really couldn't remember anything bad. But now he had no one to buoy his heart when times were hard. In this present situation, he missed her desperately.

As she looked at Eramus with his head hanging, Lewatollma's brow furrowed slightly with concern for the man and her eyes softened with compassion. Moving to join him, she reached out and took his arm. He looked at her and she smiled generously at him.

"How are you today, Eramus?" she kindly and gently inquired. He did not respond so she continued, "I have been reflecting on our discussion last night. I am sorry I cannot empathize with your plight; my experiences are so different from yours. I have never had to save anyone from starving, let alone an entire village. Wandering from town to town and finding nothing but disappointment instead of food must be weighing heavy on your mind. Yes?"

Eramus still did not respond. After a few seconds, she began again, "But that is not all, is it?" She paused for a moment before beginning, "Yesterday, I overheard you telling Arnette that you lost your wife and son within days of each other. You spoke of shadows on your heart last night. Are these the things that kept you awake? Your weighty responsibilities and the devastating loss of your young family?"

Eramus struggled for just a moment before he decided he could share his feelings openly with her. "When I remembered I was 'sposed ta be findin' food, it hit me hard. There I were stuffin' ma face with food, laughin', an' carefree while twenty-six families at Hares End were goin' hungry. I saw their faces in me mind an' sudden like I felt shame. Me feastin' an' them skimpin' an' cuttin' back on all their food worryin' if they're gonna make it through the winter. I couldn't eat 'nother bite."

Looking at his pained expression, she momentarily frowned then nodding to acknowledge she understood, Lewatollma sympathetically remarked, "I understand now why you forfeited the remainder of your dinner. I sorrow for you, Eramus. This is a tremendous responsibility to have the lives of so many depending on you." She sighed and then gave his arm a gentle squeeze. "I would like to point out that you hurt because you care for others more than yourself. This tells me that you have a good heart, and you risked your life to save Arnette, which tells me you also possess courage and character."

She turned to look at him and waited until he looked back at her before she said, "It is rewarding to know I saved someone of such rare qualities. Eramus of Hares End, it is my privilege to know you and count you as a friend. I believe you will make a difference for the better wherever you go."

She let him ponder her words for a few minutes as she continued to hold his arm tenderly.

"Tell me about your wife, Eramus. What was she like?"

Eramus sighed and then laid out the entire tale of how he and Miriam became friends, then partners. Their dreams, the joy she brought to him. The tender and beautiful experience of having a son. When he came to how he lost them both, he couldn't help but get emotional. Lewatollma listened silently and patiently, leaning against him to provide what comfort she could.

It took Eramus several miles to recover before he could speak again. "Ya remind me of her, ya know. Yer smile, yer kindness, how full of life ya are. An' ya look like her, too. Well, not 'xactly, but ya have a beautiful spirit aboutcha that just warms me heart. Ya is just someone I want ta be around. An' yes, ya be very pretty, too. When ya rescued me, I thought ya was a beautiful angel."

"Well, you were delirious at the time. That may have had something to do with it," she replied, smiling at him.

"Well, I'm not delirious now, an' ya still look like an angel ta me. An' now that I knows ya, yer even more beautiful. Yer a beautiful, gentle soul."

Lewatollma found herself blushing. Recovering, she said, "Thank you, Eramus. No one has ever said that to me before. That was truly kind of you."

About that time, Nesneratha began clearing her throat quite loudly from the rear. Turning, Lewatollma noticed her friend tossing her head, indicating she wanted her to fall back with her.

"I must go see what Nesneratha wants." Giving him a one arm hug she caught his eye and counseled, "Be happy, Eramus, you are a good man." She then halted to allow Nesneratha to catch up with her. "Do you want me to take the rear for a while?" she asked when they were side by side again.

"No. I want you to quit fawning over Eramus," Nesneratha informed her.

"I was not fawning; I was being kind and compassionate."

"I know you mean well, but I do not think Eramus knows the difference. You should be careful with your words and physical tokens of affection. There are significant differences between our cultures. What may seem kind and compassionate to you may be tantamount to betrothal for Eramus," Nesneratha warned sternly.

"Well, if he proposes, I will tell him he has to get your approval first. Does that set your mind at ease?" Lewatollma laughed.

"I am concerned you are not taking this seriously. Look at all the grief I suffer because of Hamlin's infatuation, and I did nothing to encourage his attention. If Eramus gets too attached to you, there could be dire consequences."

"Like what, Nesneratha?" Lewatollma asked glibly.

Nesneratha shook her finger at Lewatollma, saying, "Do not say I never warned you."

"I will give your warning the same amount of consideration that you give mine; in one pointy ear and out the other. I am going to check on Arnette. Please let me know if I am fawning too much."

Two more days passed before finally, they came to the junction of a road running east-west.

New to this area, Eramus pointed to the road leading east and asked Emil, "Where do that road go?"

"That will take you to Ravens Ford."

"What be at Ravens Ford?" Eramus queried.

"A graveyard for any Soulander foolish enough to try to invade."

"Who be da Soulanders?"

Frowning, Emil replied, "Barbarians who live south of the Blue Desert. The last time they tried to invade was many decades ago. I remember my grandfather telling me about battles he was in as a young man. They were savage, fierce fighters and they would fight to the death rather than yield any ground they gained, and..." Emil paused to take a deep breath before continuing. "They take no prisoners."

"I ain't never knowed about any battles," Eramus puzzled out loud.

"It has fallen to the Fair Folk to keep the Soulanders in check. And we have for hundreds of years. There's lots of bad blood between our peoples," Emil concluded.

Soon, the first farm appeared. "Ah, civilization at last," Arnette announced with visible relief. "We are nearly there! If we hurry, we won't have to spend another night sleeping on the ground!"

The tree-lined road began to climb slightly. Increased signs of human habitation appeared alongside the road, mainly small farms. Vineyards and orchards also dotted the fields and hillsides they passed. The odd little company drew more than one curious stare as they traveled toward Miricel. Everyone took on a more relaxed, almost cheerful air with all certainty of danger behind them.

Late in the afternoon, they rounded a large, grassy hill and the road began to descend.

"Oh, I know this place! Everyone, come see! Oh, you must see," Arnette exclaimed. She left the road, cutting through the dry grasses up the side of the adjacent hill. The others followed except Emil, who having been here before, took his time ascending the hilltop. Arnette reached the crest first and stood transfixed looking westward. Turning back, she beckoned the others to hurry.

There in the valley below spread an immense, walled city. Within its center, an alabaster edifice sporting six white spires pointed high into the sky. The late afternoon sun tinged them with gold. The travelers stood transfixed by the view. The city itself was enormous, encompassing many square miles.

The wall was twelve times the height of an average man. Outside the city, structures of every description sprawled, interconnected by a network of roads and narrow alleys. Beyond them, great fields stretched to the forest edge, where they intermingled with orchards and vineyards. Some were in the process of being harvested. Shocks of corn stalks dotted some of the fields at regular intervals. Others already sported a short green covering of next year's wheat. Wagons moved back and forth from the field to the city filled with golden ears of dried corn and bushels of colorful fruit.

To the west of the city, a wide chasm cut deep into the land, and beyond it lay sparsely forested hill country, connected only by a single narrow suspension bridge.

Eramus was overwhelmed by the grandeur of it, causing him to exclaim aloud...

O MIRICEL!

The road descended via a series of switchbacks, eventually leading to the edge of town. Onlookers regarded the odd collection of travelers with curiosity but dared not speak. Leading the way, Emil and Arnette walked briskly toward the great citadel. Eramus and the Nawiman women followed them closely with the two Normen bringing up the rear. Eramus's eyes wandered everywhere — the sights and sounds of this bustling city amazed him. A thousand questions filled his mind, but Emil and Arnette seemed somber, and he dared not interrupt them. More cautious and reserved, Lewatollma and Nesneratha kept their eyes forward and concealed their faces with their hoods.

As they approached the citadel, the city wall towered before them. Its surface was nearly vertical, smooth, and seemingly impenetrable. High above the ground, Eramus observed portals where on occasion, a silent guard's face could be seen staring out into the distance. Soon, they entered the shadow of the great citadel along a broad and well-maintained road as they approached the eastern gate. Several dozen armed soldiers were posted outside, forming a barrier to the entrance of the city.

Emil walked up to one of the soldiers.

"Sergeant Emil Aster with Lady Arnette Donatina. We seek immediate entrance on official business."

The guard looked them over disapprovingly.

"You should make yourselves more presentable before entering the Holy City. Go clean yourselves; you stink," he answered with unmasked disdain.

"How dare you," Arnette began loudly, her voice brimming with indignation.

"What's the problem down there?" someone called from above.

"Sergeant Emil Aster with Lady Arnette Donatina, sir," Emil repeated to the officer above. "We were attacked along the West Road and fled on foot. Forgive our appearance, but we have urgent news and seek immediate entrance."

The officer in charge held a brief discussion with the man beside him and then called down, "Let them enter!"

The soldier stepped aside, allowing Emil and Arnette to pass, but Eramus found a spear blocking his way when he tried to follow.

"Uhhh, Arnette?" he called out timidly. Arnette turned and pushed past the guards. Taking Eramus by the arm, she shot the guard a stern glance. "He is with me!"

The guard looked up for confirmation before allowing them to pass. From above, his commander called down, "Who else is with you, and what exactly is their business in Miricel?"

"This man saved me and is my guest. He is from Hares End and has business with the Grandames! These others were instrumental in our escape and are our friends."

"No Normen and no strangers outside of the mongrel farms are allowed entrance without the Grandames' invitation. Your friends will have to wait for you outside, but the farmer can enter. Let him pass."

Leaning closer to Lewatollma, Nesneratha whispered, "Not an overwhelmingly friendly place, is it?"

Hamlin had spied something of great interest to him down a side street and pointed it out to his cousin. Gorim hefted his little money bag and nodded approvingly. "We can wait out here till ye be done, laddie," Gorim said to Eramus. "Look fer us in that thar inn, the one wit ta mug hangin' o'er it." And he gestured with his finger down the street at a two-story structure with a sign in the shape of a mug suspended from a pole above its door.

Nesneratha looked down the alley at the sign over the inn. "The Sudsy Tankard," she read aloud, shaking her head disapprovingly. Then she added in a sardonic tone, "How charming." Gorim and Hamlin beamed.

Eramus looked at Lewatollma.

"We will meet you there, Eramus. It is all right. I am sure we will be safe with Hamlin and Gorim. Come as soon as you are able."

Arnette pulled Eramus away before he could answer and together, they crossed through the gate into Miricel.

ERAMUS OF HARES END

The entrance to Miricel was a long tunnel that penetrated the thick walls of the citadel. The outer doors were heavy oaken timbers fastened together with iron straps ornately decorated. The wood itself was polished and smooth. On the inside, there was a massive stone interior door, as thick as a man was tall, suspended above the entrance. A chill swept over Eramus when he realized it was precariously balanced so it could be dropped into place at a moment's notice. He quickly scurried to position himself beside Emil and Arnett, seeking the safety of distance from such an intimidating mass.

Smooth stones paved the streets of Miricel and along the inside of the citadel's high wall, buildings were neatly arrayed. Just inside the gate were quarters for the guards and a large stable set into the wall itself. From inside the stony stalls, the sound of horses stamping and whinnying spilled into the street. Outside the stables, five saddled horses stood tethered to a railing. They were white as snow except for the very end of their muzzles and hooves.

"Everything in here is white," Eramus mumbled aloud.

"This is the Holy City, Eramus. The color white is symbolic of purity," Arnette explained.

As Arnette led them to her home, another thing became apparent to Eramus, which surprised and puzzled him — there were no markets, no stores or shops anywhere to be seen. Just homes built in stone and covered with white-washed mortar, and it was eerily quiet. How strangely different from the other towns he had seen in his travels, filled with the hustle and bustle of commerce. As he progressed, he noticed the residents, most of whom were clad in simple white gowns tied at the waist. Eramus found himself growing self-conscious and he realized now why the guard objected to their appearance. He felt as if he were a black spot on a white potato: an unwholesome blight.

Their pace was brisk and Eramus was unsure whether Arnette and Emil were simply anxious to return home or to get out of sight as quickly as possible. Even though they were dirty and road-weary, Arnette and Sergeant Aster held their heads high and walked with certainty and purpose. The passersby gave them only a casual glance, and Eramus noted that no one seemed to disapprove or regard them with disdain.

Suddenly, Arnette slowed down and heaved an audible sigh. Her eyes were fixed on an open doorway of a house on the left of the street. She picked up the hem of her gown and ran through it. Eramus took Emil's lead and followed him inside. The two men entered in time to see Arnette remove her second shoe and cry out for her mother before disappearing through another interior door. Emil sat on a bench provided in the little chamber and began removing his footgear as well.

"Off with your boots, Eramus. It's customary here to take off your shoes inside someone's home."

Eramus sat down and as he did, he noticed there were many pairs of shoes of all sizes and styles in the anteroom, most belonging to children. Excited voices began to sound from within. The shrill giddy cries of little girls seemed to burst out of the doorway as Arnette greeted her siblings. The sound was a welcome relief to Eramus's ears; the odd silence of Miricel gave him the impression it was a tomb, not a city, but the gleeful greetings warmed his heart.

Following Emil's lead, Eramus stepped into the next room, where he found Arnette on her knees surrounded by six girls younger than her of varying ages. She was administering hugs and affectionate kisses to each of them in turn. Her face was split wide open with a beautiful smile and a tear trickled down her cheek. One of the girls dabbed it away with a fold of her dress.

"Oh, I am so happy to see all of my little darlings again," she said, and then in a more somber tone, Arnette asked, "Where are ma-ma and pa-pa?"

"In the garden! In the garden," the gaggle replied.

"Go fetch them and stay outside so I may be alone with them, do you understand?"

A series of disappointing sounds escaped them, but they were quickly ushered out the door by the second-eldest girl, who shot a questioning look at Arnette as she herded the children outside.

Emil drew himself up and took on the air of an official, bringing his heels together and dropping his arms straight to the sides. Arnette stood up as well, but her hands fumbled nervously with her dress and Eramus could perceive a slight trembling in her frame. The room, so recently filled with gaiety and tender emotion, now became still, foreboding, and cold, causing Eramus to shudder.

Her mother, a woman of middle age whose face was not unlike Arnette's, save that her hair was touched here and there by the silvery threads of time, came quickly into the room followed closely by her husband, both their faces anxious. Lord Donatina was tall and thin-faced; his hair was short and completely gray.

"Arnette," Lady Donatina half asked, half exclaimed, "why are you here and what happened to your clothes?"

No longer able to contain herself, Arnette threw herself into her mother's arms and wept like a babe, crying out her mother's name.

Lord Donatina cast a questioning glance at Emil and Eramus.

"Sir," Emil stiffened as he addressed Lord Donatina, "a word, please," and he motioned with a curt toss of his head for Lord Donatina to join him in the anteroom. Clenching his jaw slightly, the lord moved to join Sergeant Aster. Hushed words were exchanged between the two men and Eramus saw the lord's face pale slightly as he nodded in agreement with Emil's suggestion. Lord Donatina went quickly to his wife and daughter and embraced them both in his long arms. He placed a loving kiss upon Arnette's head and stroked his wife's hair.

"I am going with Sergeant Aster to hear his full report to his commander. I shall return as soon as possible. Wait here for me."

Turning, he sped through the door where Emil had already exited to don his footwear and prepare to depart.

"Where is your brother Izaiah, Arnette? Why have you returned?" her mother asked.

Arnette looked pleadingly at Eramus, who instantly regretted not staying with Emil and his Lordship. Lady Donatina locked her eyes with his and he knew his fate was inescapable. His shoulders dropped slightly. He puzzled for a moment, wondering what he should say and how he should say it.

"Sergeant Aster an' yer daughter here, they be all, uh, that we found," he said, and he added after a brief pause, seeing in the woman's face she did not comprehend, "alive. They was the only ones still alive. We was too late fer the others." Eram's stomach began to knot and he added a clumsy, muted, "Sorry."

Lady Donatina's legs failed her, and she slumped to the floor, joined by Arnette attempting to support her. Her Ladyship's eyes started to fill with tears as she shook her head in denial. A weak "No" was all she could manage to utter.

"I'm very sorry, Milady," Eramus added, looking away, unable to meet her eyes any longer. He backed away into a corner, leaving Arnette to console her mother.

Down the street, the two Normen boldly strode, as if they were conquering heroes entitled to the world's praise and admiration. Their faces sported haughty smiles as they strutted into the Sudsy Tankard. Lewatollma peeked cautiously inside the tavern before entering. Nesneratha gave her back a gentle push, forcing her through the door.

"Relax, Lewatollma, I will protect you from what little danger we shall find here."

"Hmph," Lewatollma snorted. "You would dance with danger if it asked you. One day, you shall realize peril has many disguises — some most appealing." Wrinkling her nose, she took in the environs with a single long glance. "Ugghh! It stinks in here! Too much smoke, too little circulation! Let us wait outside!"

Nesneratha grabbed her elbow and pulled Lewatollma beside her onto a bench at a table. "Just sit and watch. Why do you not try to be more like me?"

"I live in mortal fear of becoming like you, Nesneratha!"

Nesneratha threw her head back and laughed.

The Normen were busy striking up a conversation with the innkeeper, who while pretending to be engrossed in the substance of their tale, was in truth far more interested in the contents of their purse. Unable to convince the proprietor to allow them to sample his wares before parting with their money, they passed their coin in trade for two large tankards of ale. Making their way back to Nesneratha and Lewatollma, they sat on the bench across from the two women. Gingerly, they set their mugs on the table and smacked their lips.

"Now lassies, this 'ere is fine ale," Hamlin began. "Now we woodsmen fancy ourselves ta be good brewers, but this here be high art!"

"It stinks," Lewatollma said, "like something that should have been discarded."

The Normen stared at her as if she were insane. Gorim stood up stiffly. His face displayed the very essence of indignation as if his entire religion had been summarily condemned. He spoke with unmasked disdain. "'Ammie, I thinks we's should find more apree-shee-tive company."

"Well, maybe Nessie here would like ta join us. What say ye, Nessie-girl?" Hamlin said with eyes twinkling.

Nesneratha leaned forward slightly and daintily sniffed one of the mugs. She shook her head as one side of her mouth curled up and her nose wrinkled in repugnance. "I am afraid I must concur with Lewatollma; it smells off to me, too."

Hamlin frowned, stroked his whiskers once slowly, then stood up and ambled sadly away with Gorim to a nearby table occupied by like-minded men.

Lord Donatina returned home alone. He sat down heavily outside. He had accompanied Sergeant Aster to his commander's office and listened as he made his report to his superiors, then they all presented themselves to the Grandames. Miricel's ruling council consisted of seven matriarchs: one among them his wife's mother. He met his mother-in-law's eyes just once during the audience. How old she seemed today, how old he felt now. The Grandames listened patiently as the story was again related. Then the council whispered among themselves before asking a few questions of

Aster and the commanding officers. They decided an armed party would go and retrieve the bodies of those who were slain, Izaiah included.

Izaiah. His elder son. His pride and joy. A young man of sterling character and unshakeable faith, who now lay moldering in the wilderness. Carrion for scavengers and worms. It was a bitter image to embrace, this new and terrible reality.

But the burden of the loss of his son was not half as heavy as what he must yet do — inform Izaiah's wife, a young woman with small children. He groaned inwardly. If all he had to do was console his wife and children, he felt he might have had the strength to get up and go inside, but not now. The reality of the news and its far-reaching effect left him powerless. But his family wasn't the only one; others too would be mourning tonight as word of this tragedy spread throughout Miricel. He dropped his head in prayer and petitioned for strength. A calming warmth filled him like a reassuring hand on his shoulder, allowing him to raise his head and wipe away the tears that had begun to flow. He slipped off his shoes, straightened himself, and walked inside.

Inside, he found them all gathered. Little faces were puffy and red, but most of the tears had subsided and Lady Donatina had them all in her arms giving them courage. He smiled at her through newly sprung tears, and she smiled back.

"Where is Eramus?" he asked.

"Here, uh…sir, uh…yer Lordship," Eramus answered from the corner where he had been standing all this time helplessly watching the family.

Lord Donatina embraced Eramus. "Thank you for saving my daughter. You are forever welcome in the Donatina home."

Lady Donatina looked at Arnette and asked, "Is this true? Why didn't you tell us?"

"I was overcome with the loss of my brother, but yes, it's true. Were it not for Eramus, you would be mourning for me, too."

Lady Donatina rose and wrapped her arms around Eram's neck and expressed her gratitude silently. As if on cue, all the children gathered around Eramus and surrounded him in a giant hug and a chorus of tender "thank-yous."

"Where are you staying tonight, Eramus?" Lord Donatina inquired.

"I don't know, we came straight here. But me friends is waitin' outside the gate an' I guess we'll be staying outside somewhere like we always do." He saw the appalled look on Lady Donatina's face and quickly added with a smile, "Or perhaps in some stable or barn."

"I think not!" Lady Donatina stated indignantly. She left the room and upon returning, thrust a generous handful of gold coins at Eramus. "You take these and stay at the inn. You and all your friends. I insist!"

"Yes, Eramus, we insist." Lord Donatina added, "Normally, we would make you our guest here, but we will be in mourning, and

I'll not have a guest while there is sorrow under my roof. Stay at the inn and send word to the East Gate watchmen where we may find you. Tell them I am expecting them to notify me; they will understand. I will contact you in three days and take you to see the Grandames. Sergeant Aster said a woman named Nesteraster was instrumental in saving his life — she too should accompany us to the High Seat.

"Nesneratha," Eramus corrected.

Lord Donatina took his wife's hand and squeezed it firmly. "We must go to Izaiah's home and inform Sarai. In fact, we shall all go. Children! Your shoes and coats! Make ready! We must go and comfort Sarai and your cousins!" As the children made for the antechamber, Lord Donatina turned to Eramus. "We will see you to the East Gate since we must pass that way. I will send for you in several days, after we are finished mourning."

They walked in silence through the gathering dusk to the East Gate, where another round of embraces and verbal expressions of thanks were bestowed upon Eramus. Last of all, Arnette hugged him tightly, sighed a thank-you in his ear, and left a kiss on his cheek. Eramus turned and slowly made his way to the Sudsy Tankard.

Lewatollma and Nesneratha sat quietly at their corner table, maintaining a low profile for quite some time. "Did you say something, Nesneratha?" asked Lewatollma.

"No, but my stomach did!" she sighed. While they waited for Eramus to return, the inn filled with its evening clientele. The Normen roared with laughter as they entertained themselves by exchanging stories with the local townsfolk. The proprietor put on an evening meal and the savory smell filled the hall.

"I am going to get some food!" Nesneratha declared as she stood.

"And how do you intend to pay for it?" Lewatollma responded cautiously.

"We will dance for it," Nesneratha confidently replied.

"We?" Lewatollma asked suspiciously.

"Yes. We shall perform the Dance of the Knives. With any luck, some of these knaves will open their purses and we shall obtain sufficient pecuniary means to secure us a meal, and perhaps a clean bed as well. Come."

"Are you sure this is wise?" Lewatollma asked as Nesneratha tugged her along by the sleeve.

Nesneratha leaned across the bar and obtained permission from the owner to perform in his establishment. He consented with a shrug but sternly warned them not to break anything. "Only their hearts," Nesneratha assured him with a charming smile.

"Lewatollma, make a space clear while I introduce us." Lewatollma began moving chairs and tables out of the way as Nesneratha leaped nimbly atop a table.

"Gentle sirs and travelers from distant lands, Ladies, Lords, children, and guests of the Sudsy Tankard!" Nesneratha grandly announced, gaining a measure of quiet and catching the eye of everyone except the most inebriated. "It is my pleasure to introduce myself, Nesneratha, and my partner, Lewatollma." She pulled off her cloak and flung it dramatically to Lewatollma. "We are travelers from a distant and mysterious land..." She paused and with a toss of her head shook back her dark hair to expose her unique ears, exacting a few gasps from the audience. "...to present to you this evening a singular display of skill: the Emallinawiman Dance of the Knives!

"Watch closely as we square off and display every move and countermove used in the ancient art of knife combat. We ask only that you maintain silence so as not to disturb our concentration." Nesneratha strutted slowly up and down the tabletop, her hands proudly upon her hips as she spoke. "And if we please you with our performance, then perchance you will grace us with a few coins as a token of your sincere and humble appreciation!" Nesneratha bowed deeply, the back of her hand brushing the top of the table. She then sprang from the table with a backward flip, landing knife in hand, facing Lewatollma, one foot forward and the other back, her left arm extended to the rear for counterbalance.

"Anaha imunam Emallinawima!" Nesneratha shouted.

"Anaha infamenhem Emallinawima!" Lewatollma replied, tossing her cloak aside and drawing her blade.

Nesneratha dove at Lewatollma in a blinding flash, her blade a silvery blur. Lewatollma countered perfectly, deflecting the thrust, and spun about to deliver a counterstroke, which Nesneratha intercepted behind her back. She sprang off the floor, executing a back flip over Lewatollma's head. Back and forth the two women went: attack, defense, counterattack, counter-counterattack. Each move was more advanced than the previous one. They traded places several times, circling dramatically, their eyes locked on each other as if they were mortal foes.

The finale was a complex combination of thrusts and parries executed with blinding speed and a final headlong charge toward each other. They stepped into the air, kicking off the sole of each other's foot in performing another backflip and landing in an attack stance, their blades tip-to-tip held in place using only the open palms of their hands placed against the butt of the knife handle. They slowly circled so all could see this extreme display of balance and precision. Using the opposite hand, they simultaneously snatched their blades by the handle and held them high overhead, crying out, "Immortallem Emallinawima!"

They sheathed their blades and bowed deeply as the hall erupted in applause, whistles, and cheering. A copper coin landed near their feet, then another. A small silver piece joined them. Nesneratha's ear picked out the mellow sound of a gold piece that hit the wooden floor. She caught it before it could bounce a second time and raised her eyes to see her benefactor was none other than Eramus of Hares End.

Lewatollma turned to face Nesneratha. Both were breathing deeply, their cheeks rosy from the exertion. "You were a trifle slow on the eleventh cycle, Nesneratha. I felt you brush my hair!" Lewatollma whispered.

"Not as slow as you, dear Lewatollma." Nesneratha smiled impishly and held out a short length of Lewatollma's hair between her thumb and forefinger.

Lewatollma quickly reached back to touch her hair and indeed found a patch missing. Her eyes flashed angrily. "Meshanetta!" she hissed.

Nesneratha's eyes widened. "Oh! And I thought you were a lady! What would your mother say!" she said as she let the hair fall to the floor. "Oh, quit pouting and pick up the rest of the coins, Lewatollma."

"Get them yourself," she replied coldly as she retrieved her cloak. "And bring my dinner." Nesneratha started to open her mouth, but Lewatollma cut her off, "Also, I want a clean bed and a hot bath. Now be about it. I am hungry."

Nesneratha gaped in shock.

Eramus added, "I want some dinner, too," as they retired to a corner table.

From the corner of her eye, Nesneratha glimpsed a hand inching toward one of the coins on the floor. Bringing her foot down quickly on the fool's fingers, she curtly informed him, "Excuse me, that is mine."

After Nesneratha and the Normen joined them at the table and enjoyed dinner, Eramus related the happenings of the afternoon and produced the handful of gold coins gifted to them by Lord and Lady Donatina.

"They said we was ta stay at the inn," Eramus stated.

Hamlin and Gorim eyed the coins, mesmerized by what their experience amounted to as a small fortune. "We should split it even. Then we's can pick fer us-selves were ta stay an' what ta eat," Gorim suggested.

Eramus looked around at everyone else and saw no objections. So, he divided the coins into five piles, leaving three extra coins, and pushed the individual piles to each of the travelers.

"What about 'em three?" Hamlin asked.

"It's fer gettin' back home."

"Who's gonna keep 'em?" Hamlin asked.

"Lewatollma," Eramus replied, sliding the three extra coins to her.

Stroking their beards pensively, the Normen considered the arrangement. "That be fair," Hamlin finally said. Nodding in agreement, Gorim swept his pile into his hand and headed straight to the proprietor. Hamlin looked at Nesneratha for a moment, struggling as if he wanted to ask her something but abandoned the quest, swept up his coins, and joined his cousin.

"We can share a room, Lewatollma. What about you, Eramus?" Nesneratha asked.

"I think I should get ma own room, but thankee fer offerin'," Eramus replied.

Nesneratha rolled her eyes, but Lewatollma started giggling, and after a few moments lost control and broke out laughing. Pointing to Nesneratha, she managed to say, "He thought you..." and she started laughing again. Lewatollma swept her pile of coins into her hand and pocketed them inside her cloak. Wiping the tears away, she got up still laughing softly, and made her way to the proprietor to rent a room.

"What were so funny?" Eramus asked.

Nesneratha sighed, "She is very tired. We all are very tired." She swept her coins into her pocket as well. Standing, she wished Eramus goodnight and joined Lewatollma.

Shortly thereafter, the Normen returned to the table with tankards of ale, grinning from ear to ear.

"Well, where are ya stayin' tonight? The inn?" Eramus inquired.

Laughing, Gorim said, "No point in wastin' good coin on a room when there's a fine stable, eh, 'Ammie?" Hamlin nodded in agreement as he began gulping his drink.

The towels were little more than rags, but the large porcelain tub filled with hot water was a wonder to behold. "I cannot wait to get out of this miskinir and into that tub," Nesneratha moaned as she removed her clothes.

"Too late," Lewatollma teased as she slid into the tub. Sighing deeply, she cooed, "Oh, this reminds me of home. I had almost forgotten the sublime joy of a nice hot soak." Sliding beneath the water, she immersed her hair and then surfaced again, sighing, "I have found paradise, Nesneratha."

Standing with her arms folded, Nesneratha waited in her miskinir, a two-piece close-fitting garment that covered her form from wrist to ankle. Solid black, it served as a hygienically protective undergarment.

"Well, do not muck it up too much before I get in there. This bath costs almost as much as the room. We cannot afford another."

Perfectly content, Lewatollma hummed a tune as she washed. Sitting up, she dunked her head one last time and pulled her wet hair back over her head, wringing out as much water as possible.

"Towel, please," she requested of Nesneratha. Lewatollma stepped out daintily and took the towel from her friend. "All yours, dear." She smiled.

Nesneratha removed her miskinir and climbed in. Lewatollma dried herself, wrapped her hair in the towel, and secured her cloak around herself for warmth.

"Lewatollma, I think you were right. This is paradise. I almost feel human again," Nesneratha sighed as she put her feet up on the end of the tub and reclined leisurely, letting herself float.

Lewatollma joined her, sitting beside her on the floor. Resting her arms on the tub's edge, she queried, "How are we going to utilize our time while you and Eramus wait for your audience with the Grandames?"

"I do not care. Take leisurely walks. Explore the town. Socialize with the natives. Nap in the sun. Does it matter all that much, Lewatollma?"

"I think Eramus is expecting us to be with him, and I am a little concerned that he has become attached to us."

Giving her an incredulous look, Nesneratha scoffed, "Us?! Who are you kidding? He is attached to you, not to me...and you only have yourself to blame for *that* inconvenience." Lewatollma flinched and looked away from Nesneratha's damning glare. Shaking her head, Nesneratha continued, "But fear not —I n a few days, we shall part company and that will be the end of it. You and I shall return to Fishers Port with two pungent Normen in tow. We shall report our adventures, resume normal duties, sleep in our comfortable beds, and live happily ever after."

"Well, I am going to make a list of things I want to accomplish with or without you. I cannot spend my time idly; it is not in my nature to just sit around and relax."

"As you wish, my dear."

"Well, I am returning to our room. Do not forget to rinse out our miskinir and let the proprietor's daughter know we are finished here."

"Uh-huh," Nesneratha responded in a blissful, distant tone of voice.

Turning to leave, Lewatollma paused as an impish smile began to spread across her face. Moving to stand behind her, she lovingly shared, "Nesneratha, I would like to apologize for what I said to you earlier today. I momentarily lost my temper. It was crude, patently untrue, and totally uncalled for. Can you find it in your heart to forgive me?"

"Of course," she mumbled and waved her hand grandly as if bestowing a royal pardon.

"Thank you. You are most gracious. Now that we have sealed that breach, I wish to return to the subject of my hair." Bending near to whisper in her ear, she warned, "Never do that again." With both hands, she then pushed Nesneratha's head under the water. Nesneratha's legs slipped out of the tub and shot up into the air at the far end. Arms thrashing madly, spurting water, coughing, and gasping for air, she regained a sitting position. Nesneratha pushed her hair out of her face and shot an angry look in Lewatollma's direction.

Standing regally, her hand held high in the air, Lewatollma declared, "My hair is avenged!"

"That was childish, Lewatollma," she finally managed to say.

"As was cutting my hair." Smiling, Lewatollma concluded, "See you upstairs, dear."

Aaron was Lord Donatina's younger and now only son. His sandy hair was neat and cropped close to his head as was the fashion of men in military service. He had enlisted on his nineteenth birthday and four months later was guarding the citadel, assigned to stand the watches on the city gates. He felt it was work that didn't suit his high-born stature well. A lord's son, a gatekeeper. He often wondered why his father's position in the city hadn't afforded him an officer's rank instead. He resented that and he strongly suspected it was his father's doing to teach him character.

His jaw was tightly clenched, and he chafed at the fact he was now an escort. Bad enough he had to go into one of the beer-swilling pig troughs they dared to call an inn, but he was even more embarrassed that he had in tow a ragged farmer and some pointy-eared, evil-looking woman who shrouded herself in a cloak, secreting her identity away like a craven spy or assassin.

He brushed off his uniform sleeves as if trying to distance himself from the soil that accompanying these two had tainted him with. Again, it was his father's doing, requesting that he escort Eramus and Nesneratha — even her name sounded evil, like a curse from a serpent's mouth — to their home. His home. "Honored guests," Father had said. He shuddered thinking of the first time he laid eyes on her — her beauty was striking, unnaturally pure as was her companion. Those ears shocked and revolted him. She seemed to be a demon spawn; evil packaged in a pleasant disguise and nothing more. Yet they had rescued his sister from certain death, but for what purpose? His gratitude was diminished significantly by his distrust.

He rounded the corner near his father's home and saw his younger sisters standing watch outside. They recognized him and ran inside, like little geese squawking and honking out the news.

He couldn't help but smile to himself, thinking of them dancing all around his parents. He forced the smile from his face and assumed the well-trained emotionless demeanor of a soldier.

Exiting his home, Lord Donatina stood just outside his door as they approached. "Greetings, Nesneratha and Eramus, welcome to our home!" Lord Donatina said. He kissed Nesneratha's hand after she bowed, and he embraced Eramus. "Please come in," he said and motioned to the entrance. Eramus had warned Nesneratha about wearing shoes inside, and they sat down to remove their footwear.

Lord Donatina approached his son and embraced him. But Aaron returned no embrace.

"I will be leaving now, Father. You will accompany them to the Grandames, I assume."

"Yes, of course," Lord Donatina replied. Then he looked at his son's face with new concern. "Why so stern, Aaron? You should be happy. We all should be happy. The time for mourning is past."

"I'm not mourning. I don't trust them, pa-pa. They are outsiders," he said in a whisper.

"Someday you will learn, Aaron. Without trust and faith, we are nothing. Go, return to duty now, and we will speak later."

Aaron nodded, turned on his heel, and marched away.

Inside the Donatina residence, joyous greetings rang out. Nesneratha was instantly charmed and overwhelmed by all the

Donatina children. Lady Donatina insisted Nesneratha change into more appropriate clothes for her appearance in front of the Grandames, and she brought out one of her dresses for her to wear. Lady Donatina called for her sewing basket. They adjusted the sleeves, hem, and waist to suit Nesneratha's frame. The activity was like the hum of a beehive. She and her older daughters made quick work of the alterations while two of the younger children adorned her hair with matching ribbons. Finally, they all stood back to applaud how wonderful Nesneratha looked. Never once did they breathe a word about her ears. Even Nesneratha was impressed with what she saw in the mirror, and she lavished praise and kisses on them all.

Next, they outfitted Eramus, who started to protest but was overwhelmed by superior numbers. A pair of Aaron's old pants were pressed into service, but Eramus's chest was much too large for the young man's shirts and one of Lord Donatina's had to be used instead. At last, all was in preparation for their audience.

Lord and Lady Donatina with their daughter Arnette accompanied them to the Grandames' meeting chambers. On the way, Eramus kept giving sidelong glances at Nesneratha.

"What troubles you, Eramus?" she finally asked.

His face bore a puzzled expression. "I can't believe it's you! Ya look so, so..." and he struggled to find the right word, "...nice!" he finally said.

Nesneratha smiled beautifully and executed a small curtsy. "Thank you, Eramus. If you think I look out of character, you need only find a mirror," she quipped.

Eramus smiled back and gave a short laugh. She was right. He had never known such fine clothing. If he walked into Hares End right now, no one would recognize him.

After a short wait, they found themselves ushered before the Grandames. The chamber had a vaulted ceiling and was well-lit by tall, narrow windows. The Grandames consisted of seven matriarchs behind a V-shaped table built upon a raised platform. The construction was of finely polished wood and the front was enclosed, providing a barrier between the matriarchs and their audience. To the side of the platform, a woman nearer to Lady Donatina's age sat at a separate table, a large open book, a quill, and an inkwell before her.

The eldest matriarch occupied the highest and centermost seat, where the tables joined. She sat there quietly, with her hands folded delicately before her, barely even moving. She was a study in white; her hair, her robes, and even her skin seemed blanched.

Eramus was inwardly shocked. He had never seen anyone of such an advanced age, nor so many. To his surprise, although they all looked frail, they were bright-eyed and alert. He could sense them absorbing every detail around them, but mostly, their interest was focused on Nesneratha.

Bowing deeply, Lord Donatina addressed the Grandames, extending his greeting and appreciation for granting them an audience, and that led to yet another telling of the rescue. As he concluded, he introduced Eramus — who remembered to bow — and Nesneratha, asking the matriarchs to welcome and bless them.

The senior matriarch rose and drew a breath. "Lord and Lady Donatina, your petition is heard. Eramus of Hares End and Nesneratha, come forward." Her voice was strong and clear with only the slightest hint of age.

Eramus shuffled forward, Nesneratha at his side. She discreetly poked him in the ribs, reminding him to join her in rendering a respectful bow.

"I am Ariel, presiding Matriarch of the Grand Council of Matriarchs. What I say, I say for all. You have our deepest gratitude for returning unto us our children at the peril of your own lives. We regret that your other companions are not here as well to receive our thanks, but this is the Holy City, and we must limit access to only those found most deserving. You two, having openly risked your lives against dangerous enemies, merit such an honor. May God bless you both! We are in your debt." Then she bowed to them, and the rest of the matriarchs rose to their feet applauding, joined by the Donatinas.

After the chamber quieted, she continued by saying, "Is there anything else we can do to show our gratitude?"

Nesneratha gave Eramus a hard glance and motioned for him to speak. Eramus was painfully aware of his ignorance after having been in the company of people so far above his intellectual level. He feared revealing his ignorance and that fear momentarily surpassed his concerns for Hares End. "Thankee, but no, your graces," he said, fumbling the words.

Nesneratha groaned to herself and stepped in to save him. "Great matriarchs and wise counselors of this fair city, Eramus is but a humble farmer and not a man of great words. It is because of his simple, selfless nature he will not burden you with his petition. However, I desire to speak on his behalf."

Ariel nodded her approval.

Nesneratha bowed and continued. "You have heard only of the rescue, but not of the circumstances that brought this company together. My companion, Lewatollma, and I are explorers seeking knowledge of these regions, but Eramus is on a vital errand. Alone and on foot, he has been sent to ensure his village's survival. You know of the drought that has fallen upon the region's roundabout, but you may not be aware that upon Hares End, it has been especially severe. Their crops have failed for several consecutive seasons. This year's drought is their latest setback. If they do not obtain provisions for the coming winter, many will not live to see the spring."

Nesneratha took a small step forward and lowered her voice. "So desperate is their need, they have empowered Eramus to trade their daughters' hands in marriage to procure the needed supplies to ensure their survival. If we have found any grace in your sight, grant this man's village a measure of your surplus grain," Nesneratha concluded, curtsying slowly, going to one knee. The room fell silent except for the quiet scratching of the quill against the paper.

Ariel broke the silence. "Arise, Nesneratha." She then turned her attention to Eramus. "Is this true, Eramus of Hares End?"

"Uh, yep. Our crops has failed three years in a row. Our supplies is gone. But our daughters are fine girls an' I'm sure..."

Ariel raised her hand to stop him. "No, keep your daughters. It is our privilege to grant you your desire. Scribe, prepare an order for the steward of the keep. Direct him to provide Eramus with any supplies he desires and the means to transport them."

Eramus stammered a shocked thank-you. Suddenly, his burden was lifted, and he felt real hope for his village. This was an amazing change in fortune and his head swam trying to take it all in.

Ariel's gaze returned to Nesneratha. "Child of the Emallinawima, we desire to know why your people have returned to our land." Her tone was politely inquisitive, but Nesneratha's eyebrows rose slightly at the mention of her people's name, heretofore unspoken in this present company.

"Do not be surprised," Ariel continued, "that we know of you and your people. This is not your first visit. According to our records, twelve of your people arrived over forty-three years ago. They lived among us for several seasons, gleaning a great deal of knowledge concerning our language and customs. That knowledge they have, in turn, bestowed upon you and your fellow travelers. I am most impressed! Your command of our language is impeccable, and your graceful execution of protocol is nearly flawless. You must have been preparing for a long time. You have returned in greater numbers as well if the rumors from the North are to be believed. The Normen are prone to exaggeration, but I seem to recall stories of a ship — your ship — arriving three years ago with a crew of nearly one hundred twenty. Is this correct, child?"

Nesneratha smiled and said, "One hundred and seventeen, great lady. We arrived by vessel upon the great waters of the North, known by the Normen as Coldmere. We have come to further explore these lands and learn more about the people and their culture. Presently we are limiting our studies to the lands north of the Emmering, the lands southward being of no interest to us."

"I see," Ariel answered cautiously. "Rumor also has it you are collecting samples of plants, animals, and minerals."

"It is our way, great lady," Nesneratha answered carefully.

"Yes. We are familiar with this way. There is a word for this; it stems from an ancient word meaning 'to know' and those disciplined in such a way were called scientists. Are you a scientist, Nesneratha, come to study us? We are concerned, of course, about what you and your kind will do with that knowledge. Can you answer us plainly regarding your motives?"

"I can assure you we mean you no harm. We do not desire your lands — we have lands of our own and they are fair and supply our every need and want. We do not seek to dominate, enslave, or influence other cultures. We are content with our society. We will be here for only a brief time, after which we shall return home, likely to never return." Nesneratha answered from her heart, speaking with tenderness and conviction. "We have attained much as a society and all that remains is for us to explore, to fill the void of our existence."

The Grandames whispered to themselves for a moment. Ariel then announced, "We are pleased to hear you say as much, young one. We sense no guile in you and extend this greeting: Welcome back to Miricel and go in peace!"

Nesneratha bowed again. "Great council, on behalf of my fellow travelers, I accept your heartfelt welcome and reciprocate with the greetings of my people. May we all sojourn in peace all the days of our lives." Nesneratha again bowed. She paused slightly before continuing, "If I may be so bold, I would also beg a kindness of you. It would greatly assist my companion and me if we had a pair of riding horses to help us on our journey."

Ariel motioned to the scribe. "And two horses for the Emallinawiman ladies." She turned to Eramus. "What about you, Eramus? Is there nothing you desire? Surely, your deeds merit a reward. All you need to do is ask."

Eramus pondered for a moment, but nothing came to mind except for something they had not the power to grant. Sighing slightly, he, at last, answered, "No. As Nesneratha said, I'm just a simple farmer. My village is saved an' that's more than I could've ever hoped fer. Thankee."

The audience swiftly concluded, and they returned to the Donatina's to exchange their clothes and enjoy a simple, but satisfying lunch prepared in their absence. Lord Donatina made it clear to Eramus that he would always be a welcome guest in his home, and he hoped Eramus would return one day and visit longer with them.

Arnette presented Eramus with a parting gift. Taking his hand, she placed a length of her hair tied in a friendship knot. Embracing him tenderly, she whispered, "I will never forget you, Eramus. Do not forget me. Thank you for saving my life and helping me put my heart aright."

The afternoon passed swiftly, and the evening began to envelop Miricel in shadow. The entire family, save Aaron, escorted them to the city gate. Eramus waved farewell to the Donatinas as he and Nesneratha exited the great gate of the citadel.

In his pocket was a lock of Arnette's hair. In his hand was the writ from the Grandames granting him grain for Hares End. He reflected on the events of today. As he thought about his exchange with the Grandame, he realized if it hadn't been for Nesneratha, there would be no writ in his hand and the plight of Hares End would be unchanged.

"Nesneratha, I want ta thank ya fer whatcha did fer me back there. Speakin' up an' tellin' 'em 'bout Hares End. If ya hadn't, I'd still be...well, in a pickle. Ya saved me an' ya saved ma village. I didn't think ya cared a hoot fer me. Why'd ja do it?"

"Well, that is a good question, Eramus. First off, I do care for you. I know that I can be rude, sarcastic, and downright prickly at times, but I admire your courage and determination in the face of the difficult situation that your village faced. I do not think I could bear such a burden; it would crush my spirit.

"Second, I owe you a debt I cannot repay. Were it not for you, I would be rotting away in the woods with a ghoul blade in my back right now. And your brazen attack on the ghouls gave us the precious time we needed to escape. I believe we all owe our lives to you, Eramus. So, I humbly thank you for all you have done for me, and please forgive me for not saying so sooner.

"Now do not repeat this, because I will vehemently deny I ever said it. But when I saw you struggling up the hill with Arnette on your back, I was grateful and overjoyed that you were still alive." Nesneratha sniffled and wiped a tear from her face. "Now see what you have done? You have made me cry." It took a few moments for her to get back under control but then she continued, saying, "Speaking on your behalf was the least I could do in return. But I wonder, why did you not say something yourself? Surely, you had not forgotten about Hares End, so tell me, what stopped you?"

Eramus sighed deeply then confessed, "Cause I were afraid I would say sumpin' wrong an' I was 'shamed ta speak. Bein' around ya an' Lewatollma, I feel so stupid like I were only a two-year-old. I don't even know what yer talkin' about atimes an' I were too 'shamed ta ask ya 'bout words I never knowed."

"There is no need to feel shame because you do not know or understand something. Our experience is there to teach us, but unless you ask the question, you will never know the answer. Please do not hesitate to ask me about anything."

His mind turned back to Lewatollma and what it would take to win her. By his admission, he was a simple farmer, but not so simple that the exchange between the Grandames and Nesneratha was lost on him. Lewatollma would leave soon and never return.

He thought hard before asking because this was a very private feeling he was exposing. But she had just shared some of her feelings, which really surprised him, and she had said "anything," so he took her at her word. "Do you think I should court Lewatollma?"

"No," she answered without hesitation.

"Why not?" he asked somewhat defensively.

"Let us just say it is not in the stars for the two of you." She threw back her head and laughed mirthfully. "Eramus, we are just visiting here and when we finish, we shall return to our lands and people. Both Lewatollma and I have obligations to fulfill to which we are bound for many years yet to come. It is not a time for courtship or other such romantic notions, but for fulfilling our duty to our society.

"You are a fine man, Eramus, and any woman would be fortunate to be courted by you. Given your newfound fame, I think you could choose whomever you want — anyone except Lewatollma, or me, or any other of my kind. Put it out of your mind, Eramus. Lewatollma is a rare, delicate flower; you saw how deeply shaken she was the night we rescued Arnette and Emil. Though it does not always show, I love Lewatollma dearly and if you did anything to make her unhappy—" She drew a long, deep breath before continuing, "—I would have to kill you."

Eramus turned, expecting to see her usual sarcastic smile, but instead, he found cold, steely resolve. The discussion ended and they walked the rest of the way to the inn in silence.

INN TROUBLE

"It is a widespread practice among the residents to allow various fruit juices and grain slurries to ferment, yielding ethanol drinks for use in public gatherings. While not inherently dangerous, unless ethanol consumption is moderated, it can adversely alter one's behavioral norms."

– excerpt from Lewatollma's trip report

At the inn, Nesneratha and Eramus joined Lewatollma. "I am thirsty," Nesneratha declared. "What have you been drinking, Lewatollma?"

She held up her waterskin.

"Well, mine is empty." Turning, she looked at the proprietor leaning heavily on the bar. Leaving them, she approached the bar. "I would like some water, please." The innkeeper rolled his eyes and pointed to a wooden barrel in the corner of the room where a dog was noisily lapping up water. Frowning, she continued, "Hmm, what do you have that is fruity?"

"Apple cider," he replied without looking up.

Putting on her most charming smile, she said, "I have never tasted apple cider before. Will you allow me to try a little sip?"

The innkeeper sighed and shook his head, muttering something to himself. He then grabbed a shot glass and poured her about a tablespoon full. Nesneratha sniffed it carefully, then drank it.

Smacking her lips, she remarked, "Not bad. It has a delightful zing to it. I will take a large mug, if you please." She slid some coins onto the bar. Raising his eyebrow in surprise, he shrugged and poured her a large porcelain mug full of apple cider and took three of her copper coins. Taking the mug in both hands, she gave him a benevolent smile and joined Eramus and Lewatollma.

As Nesneratha sat down, Eramus brought up his favorite subject: "I'm hungry. Hows 'bout a lil' supper?" They all agreed and enjoyed a simple dinner. Eramus watched in silence while Nesneratha sipped her cider and related all the events of the day. Eramus did not follow the conversation but was deep in his thoughts. He was suddenly brought back to the present when Nesneratha elbowed him in the ribs, laughing while Lewatollma smiled pleasantly at him, shaking her head — obviously the brunt of some insult concocted by Nesneratha. The feelings he was having for Lewatollma and Nesneratha's stern warning left him feeling hopelessly confused.

"I am going to join some of the local citizens in an exchange of idle conversation," Nesneratha suddenly announced, pushing away from the table.

"I wish you would not wander off so," Lewatollma replied in her usual disapproving manner.

"Join me, Lewatollma," she invited, swinging her arms outward, sloshing a small amount of cider onto the floor. "Oopsie!" she giggled.

"I think not, and I advise you to sit down with us, where we can ensure your wellbeing," Lewatollma answered.

"I can care for my own being well," she sloppily replied. Then she spun about, spilling more cider, and strode away to join a group of townsfolk at a table near the far end of the room.

"I am at a loss on how to control her, Eramus. The extent of her cavalier attitude and reckless bravado are seemingly boundless. Do you have any suggestions?"

Eramus took a deep breath, then answered, "I'm not really sure of half those words, but I understood control an' I'm thinkin' yer best bet would be a leash or chain. Maybe a hobble."

Lewatollma laugh-snorted at the idea, even though it had merit. "Well, enough about her." Turning to Eramus, she smiled. "You must be excited, Eramus, now that you have accomplished your original mission. Within a few days, you can be on your way with enough food to keep Hares End through the winter and well into next year. I imagine they will be so pleased to see you arrive with their salvation, and none of their daughters will have to leave either," Lewatollma beamed brightly and seemed genuinely happy for him. "You will get a hero's welcome," she teased playfully.

Eramus just looked at her and reflected on her charm and grace. What a wonder she was to him. How he longed to share his life with her. The idea caused him pain.

Lewatollma picked up on Eramus's sorrow instantly.

"What is wrong? You should be celebrating."

Eramus only sighed. Lewatollma tried to engage him but gave up after a while and just sat silently with him. After forty minutes or so, Eramus spoke up, "What be yer plans, Lewatollma? How soon afore you an' Nesneratha be leaving?"

"We need to get back north soon. We are expected to be back well before winter settles in. I am sure that Nesneratha intends to leave immediately since she requested horses for us. I do not know what Hamlin and Gorim are planning. That is most likely tied to how long their money will supply them with libations."

"Would ya 'ave enough time ta come ta Hares End an' meet ma people?"

Lewatollma thought deeply. "That was not something I had considered, although I am very curious about your village. It would depend upon Nesneratha agreeing to delay our return."

The room was growing noisy. A bawdy song was starting at the table Nesneratha had joined, and Eramus had to lean forward so Lewatollma could hear him above the din.

"Then I guess ya won't be goin' with me given how Nesneratha feels about me."

"Oh, Nesneratha likes you well enough, she just has a hard edge to her personality."

"She likes me?!" he scoffed. "I wouldn't want ta see how she'd treat me if she hated me!"

The noise rose even higher as people began to pound their mugs against the table in rhythm to the song. Several other tables had now joined in and the whole room seemed to be caught up in the gaiety.

Lewatollma frowned at the increasing din of the music and her mouth was set in one of her tolerant, but disapproving frowns.

"What is all this racket about, Eramus? Perhaps they are celebrating your good fortune," Lewatollma offered cheerfully. "After all..." she began as she looked over her shoulder, but her cheer changed instantly to horror and her sentence ended in a sharp gasp. Lewatollma leaped from her seat and ran to where Nesneratha was dancing on top of a table surrounded by cheering patrons.

"Eramus! I need your help," Lewatollma shrieked above the din.

Nesneratha opened her bleary eyes to a blindingly bright and seemingly hostile world. "Oh, my head," she moaned weakly.

"Good morning, dearest Nesneratha!" Lewatollma said, loud and clear with mock sweetness in her voice.

"Shhh! Please, Lewatollma, not so loud!" she replied in a whisper.

"Oh, am I too loud for you?" Lewatollma turned to face Nesneratha with her hands on her hips. "How odd! You did not seem to care about how loud you were last night. Moaning, talking, and thrashing about in your sleep the entire night. It was difficult to find any peace for myself, yet you expect me to extend you the courtesy of peace and quiet?"

"If you were a true friend, you would speak quietly, if at all," Nesneratha mumbled and punctuated her remark with a noisy belch. "Oh, I think I am going to be sick," she whimpered.

"Imagine that!" Lewatollma added sarcastically.

"Help me, Lewatollma! I fear I shall die," she said and started to cry softly into the bed linen.

"Death is not likely, Nesneratha, but you are going to endure some discomfort until the deleterious effects of your careless ingestion of excess libation have subsided. It was suggested by the Normen that canine fur possesses antidotal properties. I doubt there is any substance to that claim. It is probably just a Norman prank. But by all means, if you wish to try..."

"I have to vomit," Nesneratha urgently announced.

"Not in our bed," Lewatollma sternly warned her.

"Help me! Please," her friend begged.

Lewatollma snorted and came to her side. She grabbed her by the shoulders and helped her to sit up. Nesneratha's face seemed paler than usual, and her hair looked like a carelessly made bird's nest. Nesneratha belched again and quickly covered her mouth with her hand, fighting back surging nausea.

Her vile exhalations reached Lewatollma, and she wrinkled her nose. "Oh, that is disgusting! Quickly now, get to the wash bowl before you befoul our sleeping area," she ordered, pulling her out of bed and giving her a push toward the corner, where a wash bowl and pitcher of water rested upon a small stand.

Nesneratha stumbled across the floor, the bed linen wrapped around her. Pausing momentarily at the wall, she rested her forehead against it, eyes closed. Suddenly, her face jerked up, her eyes wild with alarm. She bolted to the stand followed immediately by the disturbing sounds of stomach contents forcefully ejected.

"What a delightful sound you are making, Nesneratha! I hope you confined your revelry to the bowl, for I shall not be cleaning up after you."

Nesneratha's song of penance echoed noisily in the wash bowl. After she finished the fourth chorus, a paler and shakier Nesneratha turned to cling desperately to the wall. Slowly, she slid to the floor and rested her face upon the cool, wooden planks.

"Never had I imagined how soothing a cold floor could feel upon a fevered cheek!" she bemoaned. She lay there silently for a few moments, then turned the opposite cheek for its chance to be refreshed. Lewatollma looked on disapprovingly.

"What a lamentable manifestation of human degradation! It is fortunate Captain Emunihus is not here to witness your downfall. Without a doubt, he would never allow you out of his sight again," Lewatollma scolded harshly.

Nesneratha's eyes widened. "Do not report this to him, my dear friend Lewatollma! I beg of you! I am already under his scrutiny for past infractions. Surely, he would tie me to a post like an errant dog!"

"Do not 'dear friend' me! For your misdeeds, you deserve to be incarcerated! It will be my duty — and pleasure — to make a full and unabridged report."

Nesneratha's countenance fell, and she appealed to Lewatollma's compassionate nature with her eyes. Lewatollma looked away through the window to the village outside. Her face was stern, and her arms folded rigidly.

"When did you become cruel and callous, Lewatollma? Surely, your mother would disapprove."

"Attempting to influence me through references to my mother would be inadvisable at this time. Get dressed, I wish to break fast."

Nesneratha frowned and sat up and began to unwrap the sheets from her body. Finding herself wearing only her miskinir bottom, she asked, "Lewatollma, where are my clothes?"

"On the chair beside the bed."

"Why did you undress me?" she asked testily.

"Hmph! I did no such thing! That is exactly how you were dressed when Eramus and I carried you upstairs," Lewatollma said coldly and looked her companion straight in the eye to affirm the truth of it. Lewatollma thought it was impossible, but when Nesneratha fully realized the implication, she grew even paler.

"You let Eramus see me like this?" she asked, verging on hysteria.

"No. I wrapped you in my cloak before he came to my assistance."

Sighing in relief, Nesneratha continued, "Thank you for preserving my dignity. You are a devoted friend," after which she again belched loudly.

"You should be aware that Eramus was probably the only one who did not see your drunken antics last night."

"The Normen?" she asked aghast.

"Yes, front-row seats."

Nesneratha moaned and wrapped the sheets around her tightly. "I remember telling stories, singing, and laughing with everyone, but nothing after that. How shamefully did I behave?"

"Just a titillating dance atop the table. Thankfully, I got to you before you removed the rest of your miskinir." Lewatollma threw her clothes at her, saying, "Come now, get dressed. I am hungry."

"It keeps getting worse! Please do not tell me anything else I did. I would cry, but it only makes my head hurt worse! Maybe you should go without me. I dare not show my face. Would you bring something back for me to eat?"

"No. You are an adult. Deal with the consequences of your actions. Come along, Eramus is probably fretting over our absence."

Nesneratha got dressed and stumbled toward Lewatollma. Donning her cloak, she muttered, "I may need your help getting down the stairs."

"No doubt," Lewatollma surmised.

Eramus was patiently waiting at a corner table for his friends. His stomach was in eager anticipation of breakfast, but he wanted to make sure the women were all right first. Finally, they arrived, Nesneratha clinging to Lewatollma and moaning. Nesneratha dropped into her seat, folded her arms, and rested her head upon them.

Leaning toward Lewatollma, Eramus quietly asked, "How's she feelin'?"

"You should ask her yourself," Lewatollma responded indifferently.

After looking at her carefully for several seconds, he finally decided to take a chance and poke the bear. "Nesneratha, how be ya this morning?" Eramus inquired cautiously.

Raising her head and staring at him through bloodshot eyes, she belched loudly and quietly said, "Death would be a tender mercy." Her head then returned to the table cradled in her arms.

Lewatollma motioned for the proprietor's daughter to come to their table. "What do you have for this morning's meal?" Lewatollma politely inquired.

"Eggs, bread, some ham an' corn grits," she responded cheerfully.

"I would like to try the corn grits, please. Eramus, what would you like?"

"Two eggs fried, a piece a bread an' a slice a ham sound good to me, an' bring some butter an' honey fer ma friend's grits. Nesneratha? Do ya want anythin'?"

Nesneratha grunted without moving.

Lewatollma frowned, then asked, "Do you have a remedy for my friend? She seems to have overindulged last night on cider."

The girl smiled and quietly remarked, "So I've heard," in a barely audible voice. Then she continued speaking clearly, "Sure do, miss. Anythin' else?"

"No, thank you. That will be all," Lewatollma answered, smiling.

The young woman returned behind the bar and began making their breakfast. While Eram's eggs were cooking, she brought out a tall glass of water with white powder in the bottom and a spoon. She stirred it briskly, then putting her hand on Nesneratha's back, quietly said, "Miss, drink this down quick-like. It's not very tasty, but it will help ya. If ya start feelin' better, I'll fix ya some breakfast."

Nesneratha raised her head, grasped the glass with both hands, and downed the mixture quickly. She shuddered at the aftertaste, laid her head down on her arms, and belched once again.

Breakfast was delivered soon thereafter. Eramus and Lewatollma enjoyed their meal silently. They then began talking about their day. Eramus needed to take his writ to the storehouse and obtain the promised grain. Lewatollma was going to purchase supplies for the return trip and investigate the town. After a cursory discussion, they agreed to meet back at the inn for lunch. Getting up, they paid for their meals and bid each other farewell, leaving Nesneratha snoring loudly at the table.

Eramus located the storehouse and found himself in his natural element — among farmers. Approaching the chief steward, he produced the writ and asked, "Can ya help me wit this?"

The steward quickly looked over the paper and gave a surprised smile. "From the Grandames themselves! Ya must be someone special to get this here writ."

"I just saved Lord Donatina's daughter Arnette from ghouls."

"Just?" the steward laughed. "Well, I guess I'm not surprised. After all, the high matriarch Ariel is Arnette's grandma. She'd a probably given ya half of Miricel if ya asked for it."

Eramus looked at the steward in shock. "No one said anythin' 'bout it!"

"Well, how much do ya need?"

"There's twenty-six families an' thirty-one grown-ups an' thirty children."

"I guess ya got hit hard by the drought, eh?"

"Third year in a row, we's down to scraps."

"Well, let's give you a year's worth for each person. That should get ya back on yer feet." Grabbing a piece of paper and a pencil, the steward bent over his desk and began calculating. "Hmm, that's one-hundred-fifty pounds for each adult and seventy-five for each child." He scratched furiously with the pencil, then looked at Eramus, asking, "How do you want it, wheat, corn, or a mix?"

"We mostly eat corn so mostly corn an' the rest wheat."

Getting up, the steward went to the edge of the dock and called out, "Tim! Fetch me a big wagon and a pair of strong horses. Lookin' like three and a half tons. And we'll need a good tarp, too!"

Moving to the door of the granary, the steward yelled out over the din, "Don! Hey, Don! Yeah, I need forty-five hundredweight of corn sacked and twenty-four hundredweight of wheat. Tim's pullin' the wagon over to the dock now. What? Yeah, sack the wheat, too. Where's Manny? Well, tell him to forget that for now and get this order filled. What? No, forty-five corn and twenty-four wheat. You got that? OK, see to it then!"

Walking back over to Eramus, the steward smiled, saying, "It will take them a bit to get that sacked and loaded for ya. So, tell me, where ya from and what brings ya to Miricel?"

The workers carefully filled burlap bags and stitched them shut while Eramus chatted with his fellow brothers of the soil. He learned some new things about raising corn and the chief steward gave him a small sack of seed corn. Once everything was loaded, the wagon was covered with a heavy tarp. A pair of strong workhorses was brought out of the stables and hitched to the wagon. Waving farewell, Eramus drove back to the inn and parked his wagon just outside the stable. He unhitched the horses and led them into the stable behind the inn. Tossing the stable boy a copper, he said, "Keep an eye on me wagon, please."

Much to his delight, he ran into Lewatollma as he was exiting. She was leading in a pair of horses provided by the Grandames. Fine steeds indeed — sleek, strong, and beautiful, fitted with the finest tack Miricel could offer. He waited for her and offered his arm to join her inside for lunch.

Over lunch, they both remarked on the abundantly manifest gratitude of the Grandames. Nothing they received was second-rate and everyone they interacted with was genuinely cheerful and helpful, often going out of their way to assist. They finished quickly and Lewatollma excused herself to go to check on Nesneratha.

After lunch, Eramus wandered the town on his own, investigating every shop. Finding some useful tools and small things that would make life easier in Hares End, he purchased them. Though he didn't start with the intent to get everyone something, he found his money went far, and soon he had so many things, it didn't make sense to not purchase everyone a gift.

Upon returning, he looked in on his wagon and horses, then retired to his room for a nap. Later that evening, he came downstairs in hopes of finding his friends. Lewatollma and the Normen were at a table at the far end. Pulling up a chair, he offered, "Good evenin', all!" The Normen looked only slightly better than Nesneratha did that morning, except they were smiling while they belched, and they reeked of the stable.

Lewatollma cleared her throat and began, "Nesneratha has decided we will leave early tomorrow morning. Everyone should retire early tonight and get a good night's rest. We will all meet downstairs for a morning meal, then depart."

"I should let Lord an' Lady Donatina know we're leavin'. I'll get the guard ta send 'em a message."

Gorim pulled out his money bag and shook it out upside-down, yielding a single copper coin. Frowning, he turned to Hamlin and asked, "Got any coin left, cousin?"

"Not any," Hamlin responded then added, "We's all set ta go home, nuttin' left ta do 'cept sleep."

Lewatollma shook her head disapprovingly, then turned to Eramus. "How about you, Eramus? Are you destitute as well?"

"Destitute? What's that?"

"Out of money."

"I have 'nuff for ma room an' food. I should 'ave sumpin' left over when we leave. Does ya have any yerself?"

"I have one gold piece, six silver, and two copper of my own. I still have the three extra gold pieces for our return journey; I was planning to use that to buy some hay and oats for the horses. I will also obtain some food for the journey: jerky, apples, and milled corn. Plus, anything that catches my eye. Does anyone have a special request for food?"

Taking a chance, Gorim proposed, "Ale?"

"That does not even merit a response," Lewatollma scoffed.

Eramus chimed in, saying, "How 'bout some kerrits? They keeps good an' it can be a treat fer the horses."

"Excellent suggestion," Lewatollma remarked. She looked around the table for any more suggestions, but everyone was silent. "Well, good enough for now. I am getting some supper."

"I'll be joinin' ya, Lewatollma," Eramus stated. Looking at the Normen, he asked, "What about ya two? Gorim? Hamlin?"

"Methinks I kin get some stale bread for a copper," Gorim speculated.

"Oh, for star's sake!" Lewatollma cried out in exasperation. "I will pay for both of your meals."

The Normen broke into broad, grateful grins. "See 'Ammie, ya should chase Lewa instead of that hard, old Nessie. She has a heart 'o gold."

Scolding Gorim, Hamlin responded, "I kain't do that, cousin! Eramus wants her fer hisself. Ain't ya seen 'im followin' 'er like a puppy, sighin', callin' her name in his sleep, lookin' at 'er like she wert the prettiest lass he ever sawed?" Hamlin paused, folded his arms, then finished, "Wouldn't be right!"

Blushing, Eramus hid his face in his hands. Lewatollma covered her mouth with her hand to conceal her smile. Eventually, she got herself under control, stood, and hollered across the room at the proprietor, "Can we get some supper!"

HARES END

Finally, all was arranged, and the time had come to depart Miricel. They all agreed to travel together as far as possible. Lewatollma and Nesneratha planned to travel north with the Normen to their winter encampment, a place they called Fishers Port. Despite his coaxing, Eramus could obtain no detailed information about their encampment. Not even Normen were helpful. When Eramus seemed to be finally making progress interrogating Gorim or Hamlin, a single look from Nesneratha instantly silenced them.

Since the night he and Nesneratha talked on their way back to the inn, she had become very cool toward Eramus. Not mean — she no longer insulted or taunted him — but all conversations had become terse and to the point. She also kept Lewatollma occupied to minimize the time he and Lewatollma spent together. Nesneratha's warning was repeated frequently, not in words, but by every look and action.

The Normen had no care for horses and were content to sit in the wagon or walk. So, that morning, they were sent off with gifts from Lord and Lady Donatina and several days' supply of food for all. Again, Lord Donatina exacted a promise from Eramus that he must return and stay as their guest.

Without great ceremony and with a curt, "We leave now," from Nesneratha, they departed east along the same road that brought them to Miricel under a sullen gray sky. They ascended in relative silence with the women in the lead, slowly making their way back up the hillside via the switchbacks until they arrived on level ground. Eramus looked back at Miricel one last time as a flood of emotions welled inside him: the rescue and flight from the ghouls, the gracious reception from the Donatinas, and the Grandames. He wanted to share these with Lewatollma, but Nesneratha had put her in the lead and placed herself between them.

Several hours out of Miricel, they met the armed detail sent out by the Grandames returning to Miricel. Nesneratha gestured for Eramus to leave the road and allow them to pass. Lewatollma and Nesneratha dismounted as the horsemen rode silently by, followed by a wagon stacked with coffins. They covered their heads with their hoods and made odd gestures as they passed. Bringing their hands together in front of their chests, with two fingers — the forefinger upon the wrist and the second finger upon the palm — they bowed their heads until the entire procession passed. Gorim, Hamlin, and Eramus stood until they passed as well. Gorim seemed genuinely saddened and muttered to himself, "Sorry we was too late, lads."

The wagons were followed by a large contingent of cavalry soldiers all clad in battle gear. One of them broke ranks and trotted to the horsemen in front, briefly conversing with what was probably the officer in charge. After a brief interchange, the man rode over to Eramus and his companions and dismounted. Not until he had removed his helmet did they recognize Sergeant Aster. "Ah, Emil...er...Sergeant Aster, sir," Eramus recovered.

"I have just a moment to bid you all farewell. This is not how I planned it, but you have already taken your leave of Miricel and there is no time for a proper thanks. I owe my life to you all, but most especially to you, Nesneratha."

A sly smile began to form on Nesneratha's face, but before she could open her mouth and let slip a sarcastic remark, Emil dropped to one knee in front of her, took her hand, and reverently planted a kiss on it. He swiftly rose and donned his helmet. Facing them, he drew his sword and saluted them, saying, "Adieu, my friends, neither your friendship nor your courage will I ever forget. If our paths ever meet again at the crossroads of peril, perhaps I may return as great a favor as you have shown me!" Then he mounted his steed and rejoined the formation.

Nesneratha stood there in shock, staring at her hand. Everyone's eyes turned to look at the rare sight of a speechless Nesneratha. They silently watched the formation until they disappeared. Nesneratha dropped her hand and said almost inaudibly, "Time to go." She walked silently to her mount and rode off, taking the lead.

Hamlin turned to Gorim and Eramus, saying, "Oh, that were a fine piece a courtly work, that were. I'm goin' ta havta remember that!"

Later that afternoon, they passed the ill-fated West Road that led north. A newly planted sign was posted bearing a warning, and several trees were felled to block the way.

"What does it say, Lewatollma?" Eramus called out loudly.

"Danger. Ghouls. Closed per order of the Grandames," Nesneratha replied, cutting off Lewatollma before she could speak.

They rode until late, stopping just before dark to make camp and prepare a simple meal. There was little in the way of conversation except for how to proceed and the Normen singing their raucous songs and reminiscing about their inebriated antics at the inn.

Early the next day, they came to a fork in the road leading northeast. Nesneratha and Lewatollma stopped and had a heated argument in their native tongue. Nesneratha was visibly angry, but Lewatollma seemed calm and determined.

"What be this about, Nessie?" Hamlin asked, sliding off the back of the wagon.

"This is the quickest route to Fishers Port and where we should all leave Eramus to continue on his way to Hares End. But we are not all in agreement!" Nesneratha shouted angrily, shooting Lewatollma a disapproving look.

"You can take the Normen and go, but I would like to travel a little farther with Eramus," Lewatollma stated. "I can catch up with you later. Surely, that should not bother someone who left her friend alone in the woods while she went exploring on her own?" There was a trace of bitterness in Lewatollma's voice that was not lost on Nesneratha.

"You know what this is about, Lewatollma, and you are a fool to encourage it! Do not say I did not warn you," Nesneratha shot back in a low and angry voice.

"You are a fine one to give a warning, never having heeded one yourself," Lewatollma answered caustically.

"Bah! Hamlin! Gorim! Are you coming with me or not?" Nesneratha barked.

Gorim jumped off the wagon and the two Normen gathered their backpacks.

"Take care, lad!" Hamlin said to Eramus.

"Aye, take care," Gorim chimed in.

"I'll be fine," Eramus said and then in a lower voice, added, "Ya be careful too, Nesneratha seems very angry," and he gave them a wink.

"Fear not, lad. I know how ta deal with Nessie-girl. If'n she won't calm down, I'll just tie her ta a tree till she does," Hamlin replied with a wink of his own.

Nesneratha spurred her horse forward, and the Normen broke into a run to catch up to her.

"I will catch up to you in two days!" Lewatollma called after them. The Normen waved back but Nesneratha's only response was to pull her hood up over her head after she gave Lewatollma one last angry look.

"Well, that unpleasantness is concluded. Shall we continue on our way, Eramus?" Lewatollma asked, her voice completely void of any agitation, doubt, or regret.

"We be only two days from Hares End an' I'm starting ta look forward ta gettin' home," Eramus enthused.

"Excellent! Before you start, let me tie my horse to the back of the wagon so I can ride up front with you." Lewatollma trotted her horse to the back of the wagon, dismounted, and lashed him to one of the metal rings on the sideboards, then transferred the heaviest of her gear into the back of the wagon. She climbed up front with Eramus and sat gently on the wooden seat.

"Ready?" Eramus asked. Lewatollma nodded and he urged the pair forward down the road toward Hares End. He tried to remember all the things he wanted to talk to her about over the last few days, but he couldn't remember one. He was simply content to have her beside him.

"I'm glad ya decided ta come along with me," he finally said, smiling broadly at her. He looked into her soft brown eyes and his heart melted. The wagon bounced upward abruptly as he hit a rock and despite the springs mounted in the seat, they both landed hard.

"Ah! Please drive more carefully, Eramus. I do not know how much more abuse my backside will tolerate," Lewatollma scolded as she shifted in her seat, trying to get comfortable again.

They drove on until evening chatting idly, reliving their recent experiences, and sharing their insights and observations.

At camp that night, they built a small fire and enjoyed a simple warm meal. Eramus began talking of Hares End and how much Lewatollma would enjoy meeting everyone. She listened patiently, but finally, she felt she had to say something.

"Eramus, I never said I was going to Hares End with you, only that I would accompany you a little longer."

Eramus looked at her across the fire in surprise. "But I thought..." he started.

"No, Eramus, I have business elsewhere. You know this. Our meeting was happenstance, and I count it my privilege to have met you, but the time of our parting is near. Do not make this any harder than it already is. You have been a faithful friend, and I will miss you, but it is ending."

"I wantcha ta meet ma village, ta see Little Miriam, ma house an' the rabbits."

"Tomorrow we part, Eramus. I suggest we get our rest. We both have a long day ahead of us."

Eramus grew loud. "No, ya got ta come ta Hares End! I want the people ta see a real Nawiman an' not think I've lost ma mind wanderin' out in the woods. Withoutcha, who will believe me tales? Now listen, ya can take another day an' come with me ta Hares End, then catch up with Nesneratha. Who cares if ya be a day late?" Without giving her a chance to respond, he concluded, "So, it's settled. We'll get goin' early an' ya can spend the night an' leave the next day. You'll be fine. So, let's get ta sleep. Good night, Lewatollma."

When Lewatollma failed to respond, Eramus felt like he had convinced her. She retired as he fidgeted about the camp for a short while, and then he too went to bed. He felt bad for being so pushy and loud, but he was afraid to admit to himself that he might lose her. He rolled the blanket around him tightly and fell asleep while making his plans for tomorrow. A feast, a dance, a celebration in her honor for saving him and his village. Yes, tomorrow would be a grand day. He would make it up to her this way. His last thoughts were of Lewatollma sitting in the place of honor in the lodge with him seated beside her.

Lewatollma gazed into the starry night, her senses picking up on activity within the little camp. She could hear the horses nearby, occasionally snorting and shifting their feet. But it was Eramus she was intent on, and she waited for the slow, rhythmic breathing that would tell her he was deeply asleep. He was there now, but she waited a little while longer to be sure.

Reflecting on the past, she thought of how she had met Eramus, drawn from her trek by that anguished scream to find him propped up against a tree surrounded by wolves. How he foolishly went to the young Lady Donatina's rescue with only a hand sickle. A smile spread across her face as she remembered how he flattered her with his eyes; the young men at home never seemed that interested in her or any women for that matter. It was a new, strange feeling to be treated like this, so different from her people. It possessed a special charm of its own, and she found it somewhat intoxicating. She had grown to like Eramus, despite his limited education; he was a good friend, open with his feelings, selfless, and always eager to be of service. She struggled with the fact she cared for him as more than just a friend. She had taken his sorrows into her heart and yearned to be with him, to support and comfort him. Something drew her to him in a way she was at a loss to describe.

But just as Eramus had to complete his mission, Lewatollma had business of her own to attend to, and it was not at Hares End. Nor could she postpone it any longer. Winter would be here all too soon, making travel difficult. Deep inside her, she would have liked to go with him, but as a spectator, not a spectacle. She sat up and looked over at the slumbering lump across the fire from her. She wasn't completely at ease with leaving him like this, but he had made it too awkward to just ride off. Besides, he just might follow her. She had ridden with him this extra day just to quell his fears, and now it seemed a bit underhanded to slip off into the night without saying goodbye. She wondered what she could leave to let him know she cared for him, something that Eramus could understand.

Then she remembered what Eramus had said when Arnette had given him a lock of her hair. Drawing her dagger, she reached back into her long hair and isolated a section from the back that wouldn't be missed. The sharp blade cut loose a small section of her long straight hair without any effort. She worked it into a friendship knot but had no ribbon to tie it with. She pondered for a moment and then cut off a short length of her bodice lacing to secure it. Quietly, she got up and put her parting gift on the seat of the cart where Eramus would find it.

She gathered up her blanket roll and backpack, then moved noiselessly to the horses. She patted her steed and spoke softly to assure him. She untied the reins from the sideboard of the wagon and led him away. At the edge of the camp, she looked back at Eramus and said softly, "Farewell, Eramus of Hares End. Think well of me and do not be angry. If circumstances had been different, I think we could have forged a wonderful relationship. I will always remember our time together fondly."

Turning away, she led the horse down the road a considerable distance before securing the bedroll on his back. Her mind was now occupied with the task at hand. She looked quickly at the stars for orientation, then stepped gingerly into the saddle and departed at a trot into the night.

––––––––––––––––––––

Eramus rolled over and stretched his aching muscles. Sleeping on the ground was getting to be less of an adventure and more of a pain, he mused to himself. He was hungry and it spurred him to get a move on. He stood up, facing the early morning sun, which was much farther above the horizon than he expected.

"Lewatollma, why didn't ya get me up sooner? With an early start, we could've made…" he started to say as he turned to face her. Searching the campsite, he found himself alone. Calling out her name loudly, just once, he listened to it die in the still morning air. Then he noticed her horse was gone. Fear, then anger, flooded over him but they were quickly replaced by guilt. It was his fault. He shouldn't have tried to order her around. What could he have been thinking? He felt bad earlier but had never apologized, for he had believed there would be time later — and now it was too late. Just as mysteriously as she appeared that night to save him, she was gone.

All kinds of thoughts started to crowd his mind, but he brushed them aside. He just wanted to leave. *Forget breakfast*, he thought, having suddenly lost all appetite. He shook his blanket off and tossed it into the back of the cart. He retrieved the horses and hitched them to the wagon. As he was running the reins back to the seat, he saw something there. He picked it up carefully and looked it over, feeling the softness of her fine hair. He carefully put it into his bag of treasures and pulled the drawstring tight. Climbing up into the wagon, he surveyed the area one last time.

"Goodbye, Lewatollma, thankee fer everythin' an'—," he sighed, "—I'm sorry." His head hung for a moment, then he drew a deep breath, and snapping the reins, he urged the team onward. With luck, he would be back home before nightfall.

As he bounced along, his thoughts turned to Hares End and home. He found quite a few of them that made his heart swell with joy. To be surrounded by his friends. How pleased the Ruling Hand would be with his success. Sleeping in his bed and not on the ground. Safe in his little village — no ghouls, no wolves. He recalled his sweet little niece's smile, and it warmed the cockles of his heart and brought a broad smile to his face. It would be so wonderful to hug Sheron and Little Miriam. Suddenly, he had an overwhelming need to be back home. Snapping the reins hard, he urged the horses to pick up the pace.

The wagon wobbled as it made its way across the uneven ground. In the distance, he could hear the Emmering roaring noisily on its way to the sea. The falls and rapids that cascaded into the gorge ran for more than ten miles. Their origin was Ravens Ford, a large open place where the river wandered across a swampy plain. Above Ravens Ford, the river hid inside a deep valley where it moved swiftly. Somewhere up that valley, in the hills to the north of the river, was a little village that Eramus called home.

"Mom," she gasped breathlessly. "Mom!" Her little frame heaved as she drew in another breath. "It's—" and she swallowed hard, "—Uncle Eram!" she managed with a final breath. Grabbing her mother's skirt, she tried to pull her toward the door. "Mom, hurry!"

"Miriam, let me finish!" Sheron answered impatiently as she took the small loaf she was kneading and rolled it into an oiled cloth. She dropped their meal into a wooden box near the hearth and wiped her hands on her skirt. Grabbing Miriam by the wrist, she flew out the door toward the village commons.

Already a crowd had begun to gather about Eramus, who sat perched upon the wagon silently smiling amid a torrent of questions. He smiled and waved to Sheron as she ran into the throng, pushing her way to the front, Little Miriam in tow.

"Here, gimme that sweet little niece," he said, extending his arms toward her. He pulled her up into his lap and gave her a great hug. "Oh, I've missed ya! Have ya been good for yer mother?"

She shyly nodded yes.

"Do ya want ta see what I 'ave in the wagon?"

She nodded yes again.

"Well, ya can't unless ya give me a kiss right here," he said, gesturing to his cheek with a stubby finger.

She gave him a little peck on the cheek.

"Is that all!" he protested. "I brought all this an' all ya can do is give me a little peck! That simply won't do! I want full payment an' nuttin' less!"

Miriam looked at her mother for help, but Sheron only responded with a goofy face scrunched up with her lips puckered exaggeratedly. Little Miriam fidgeted nervously for a moment, then threw her arms around his neck and gave him a big, wet, noisy kiss.

"Ah, now that's better! Well, let's take a look, eh?" He lifted her by the arms and set her down on the ground. Then hopping out of his seat, he began to loosen the ropes holding the canvas in place. In the distance, the Ruling Hand approached. Eramus picked up

Little Miriam and cradled her in one arm while he continued to remove the ropes.

The crowd finally fell silent as Sherman and the other village elders approached.

"Welcome back, Eram," Sherman said, his face nearly swallowed up in a broad grin. Ed placed his hand on Eramus's shoulder and gave it a friendly squeeze. Everyone's face was all smiles, except Orson, who stood back with his arms folded, his face chiseled out of stony skepticism.

"Well, what is yer report, Eram?" Sherman asked.

Taking Little Miriam's hand, he whispered in her ear to grab on tight to the canvas and together they pulled back the cover to reveal his cargo. Everyone's eyes popped and the sea of faces with crescent smiles turned into full moons of open-mouthed wonderment.

"Corn an' wheat, enough ta last a full year," Eramus announced loudly. "An' more than just food." He smiled, giving Sherman a wink. Excited voices fired questions at Eramus, and a dozen conversations erupted at once. The children danced up and down and the dogs started barking.

Above all this racket, a stern voice called out, "At what price, Eram?" The tone was harsh and accusatory. "What devil's bargain did ya make, farmer, fer such a treasure?" Orson stepped forward to face Eramus. Four young women pushed closer, feeling their fate was bound up in this as well. Sherman started to speak but Eramus held up his hand and said, "That be a fair question an' I'll answer it."

He looked around to make sure he had everyone's attention, but he needn't have. "I'll tell ya now the conditions that I came by this food but—" he said, and he paused for effect, "—I'll take it all back if everyone ain't agreeable ta the deal!"

The group grew suddenly somber as they waited for Eramus's reply. "None of this came out'a trade fer yer daughters — they'll have ta find their own husbands." At this, three of the young girls hugged each other, greatly relieved. The fourth looked down, kicked the dirt, and frowned. "It was a reward ta me fer saving someone's life an' I want Hares End ta have it. Does that meet with yer approval, Orson?"

Orson looked blankly at Eramus, not sure what to say. He licked his lips and looked furtively about him as everyone looked eagerly in his direction. "Well, yeah, sure...I can agree ta that, but what do ya want? Are ya just gonna give all this away? Or do ya want one of my daughters?"

Eramus laughed at him. "Since when do we bargain amongst ourselves? We've always shared what we had an' nuttin's changed as fer as I'm concerned. What I have I share freely with all...even you, Orson," he said, adding the last part quietly so only Orson would hear.

"So, what say ya', Hares End, do ya' accept my gift?"

A unanimous cheer of "Yea" rang out.

"Well, then, let's get this unloaded an' put away!" Eramus yelled, throwing his arms into the air. Sherman began barking orders to the others, and a line of men and women quickly formed leading from the wagon to the storage barn. Artur and another young boy jumped into the wagon and brought the sacks of grain forward, passing them gingerly to Sherman, who was first in line.

"Not that one, Artur," Eramus interrupted. "That's seed for next year. Set it aside for Jimmy."

"What about this, Eram?" the other boy asked, his eyes filled with curiosity. "It doesn't feel like corn!"

"Naw, it's not food at all. That be stuff I got special as gifts fer everyone," Eramus answered.

The boy's eyes widened with excitement, and down the chain the words "gifts for everyone!" echoed in awe. Soon the wagon was emptied, and the village once again gathered around Eramus and bombarded him with more questions.

"Who did ya save? Where? When? How? What's in the sack?" He looked into their faces and shook his head.

"I haven't had nothin' much ta eat today," he began, "an' I'll be danged if I'm gonna tell a long story on an empty stomach! Whatever happened ta hospitality?"

The men and women looked at each other for a moment, then a flurry of invitations to dinner came flying forward, desperately vying for Eramus's favor to be the first to hear what happened. Offers of bread, pie, and various goodies were tossed out like bids at an auction, each claiming to be better than the others.

Sherman finally cried out above the din, "Will all of ya' shut up!" The crowd cowered back at Sherman's raised voice. "We'll all meet in the lodge tonight. Everyone will bring food ta share. Eram will be the guest of honor at a feast. Then he can tell us all about his journey. I don't want ya ta wear him out telling it over an' over one at a time. The Rulin' Hand has proclaimed it! Now beat it! We start at dusk!"

They dispersed to their homes, chatting excitedly as they went. Eramus chuckled to himself. "I see ya is still in control at Hares End." He smiled with a twinkle in his eye.

"Fer a while yet, I 'spose," Sherman drawled, scratching his head. The wind caught the few strands of hair he had left and rearranged them arbitrarily on the top of his head. He turned to Eramus and placed a hand on his shoulder. "Well done, Eram. I don't know what else ta say — there aren't words big enough ta praise ya," he trailed off. "See ya in the lodge," he added, giving him two final thumps on the shoulder before letting his arm slide away. He ambled off toward his own home, slowly at first but then shifting into a trot, and he disappeared into the dusk.

Suddenly, Eramus found he was alone with the horses and the wagon. He led the horses and positioned the wagon outside the barn, then removed the leather straps that tethered them to the wagon. Taking them by the bridle, he guided them one by one and secured them to a post. Eramus clambered up the makeshift ladder and kicked down some dried grass from the loft. He slowly made his way back down and kicked the hay into a pile near the post.

"Night, ole gals," he added softly, patting them gently on the neck.

Eramus walked outside into the rapidly cooling evening air. The first star began to twinkle weakly in the east. It was then he noticed Sheron and Miriam standing silently in the courtyard just outside. Sheron smiled and came to him, giving him a great hug and he reciprocated by hugging her tightly and lifting her off the ground.

"Oh, it's so good to see ya again, Sheron. You'll not believe what I bin through!"

She laughed and said, "Welcome back, Eram," and again squeezed him long and hard, relieved that he was back. A tear escaped and she wiped it quickly away with her hand so he wouldn't see.

"Come," she said, taking his hand, "keep me an' Miriam company while I fix sumpin' fer yer dinner."

He dropped her hand and put his arm around her shoulder, and together they made for her home with Little Miriam skipping alongside. Eramus's gaze turned northward, and he couldn't help but wonder where his friends were, the rowdy Norman cousins, the devilish Nesneratha. But most of all, he wondered about Lewatollma. It had been less than a day and he found himself desperately missing her and kicking himself for being a fool.

He abruptly returned to the present when Sheron's elbow jabbed him softly in the ribs. "Hey, are ya listening ta me?"

"What? Oh, I'm sorry, Sheron, I was just, uh, um..." and he trailed off, not knowing how to continue.

"No, I'm sorry, ya must be tired. Ya just come in an' sit down an' rest while I work. Yer home now."

Am I? he wondered and couldn't resist looking northward one last time before ducking through the short doorway into his sister-in-law's home.

The center of the lodge was cleared away and a cheerful, crackling fire ringed by stones held the center place. Good food was abundant, inasmuch as food ever was abundant at Hares End. Eramus was given an honorary seat among the Ruling Hand along with his pick of victuals.

From the elevated stand, he told his story and gave as much detail as he could recall. Some scoffed, saying it was all too fantastic, and he was challenged to provide proof of his claims. Eramus defended himself by showing his scar, the ghoulish blade, and Arnette's lock of hair.

These silenced most, but his feelings were a little hurt when they dismissed his account of the pointy-eared women from a distant land as pure nonsense. Yet he could not bring himself to show Lewatollma's gift to anyone — it was something he could not bear to be ridiculed about. So, he dismissed the skeptics with a shrug as they laughed and said, "Are ya sure ya didn't hit yer head as well when ya fell from that tree!"

The evening was one of song and dance, all designed to entertain Eramus and celebrate the village's collective survival. Even Orson made a pretty speech praising and apologizing to Eramus. Near the close of the feast, Eramus passed out the gifts he obtained in Miricel: metal fishhooks, arrowheads, combs, sewing needles, tops for the children, cloth, thread, buttons, and seeds — simple gifts, but more precious than jewels or gold to the struggling inhabitants of Hares End. All marveled at their excellence and Eramus's wisdom in ensuring Hares End's continuing struggle against nature.

Slowly, the villagers bid Eramus thanks and goodnight. The families with children left first, exhausted little bodies slumped across their shoulders or under their arms. The young women began to dance around the fire, to the sound of Alma's panpipe.

Eramus was weary and he took a seat beside Sheron, who sat leaning upon the outside wall with Miriam curled up in her lap fast asleep.

Looking sideways at Eramus, she whispered to him, "I believe in yer women from fer away, Eram. But I think there's more ta it than yer tellin'."

His arms were folded, and he looked at her through narrowed eyes. "Oh? An' what would ya know?" he inquired with a laugh.

"Ya can laugh if ya wish, Eram, but I've known ya a long time. I can see y'ave been swept away by this mysterious an' beautiful woman! Don't try ta deny it, it's the same look in ya eyes when ya fell so deeply in love with ma sister."

Eramus was afraid to look back. The thought of Miriam caused him pain, a pain that he kept finding over and over again, one that just wouldn't go away. And now guilt swept over him as well.

"I suppose ya think me unfaithful ta abandon Miriam an' have feelings fer another woman," he said dejectedly.

"I think it's bin a long time. Long enough for ya ta forget an' move on. So, if I must accuse ya of anything, it's mourning far longer than needful. Even I have left Miriam behind, an' I expect no less from ya."

"It's all so confusing. But what nonsense, I'll never see her again!"

"No, neither of us will ever see Miriam again," she sighed and unconsciously stroked Little Miriam's hair.

"No, not Miriam, the other one, the Nawiman. Ahhh! I'm just screwing meself up!"

"Tell me her name," she said, nudging him gently with her shoulder.

"It's Lewatollma," he answered without thinking.

"What an unusual name!"

"In her tongue, it means a new star."

"What's she like?"

"Oh, Sheron, she's like an angel, soft brown eyes, long straight brown hair to match her eyes. An' she's kind an' she's good an' gentle, so loving an' peaceful. She's a lot like Miriam in that way, a gentle an' graceful air, but strong in spirit, too. An' smart, way smarter 'n me, but modest, too. And she's as tall an'..."

Sheron's laughing interrupted Eramus.

"What's so funny?" he asked.

"Oh, Eram, ya have it bad," she replied, and she laughed softly again. Eramus stopped for a moment then laughed as well.

"I guess yer right, that is pretty bad, huh." They sat in silence leaning against each other for a few moments. "Would ya like ta see a lock of her hair?" he finally asked in a hushed whisper.

She nodded yes against his shoulder. Eramus carefully retrieved it and placed it in Sheron's hand. She ran her fingertips across it gently.

"So fine," she sighed and handed it back to Eramus. Together they watched the girls dancing about, twirling now in unison to the pipe's soft melody, then joining hands in a circle turning left, then right, then breaking apart and twirling on their own.

"I've bin thinkin' about us, Eram. That perhaps we could, ya know, be together. Not so much fer me, but fer Little Miriam's sake. We are friends, ain't we? Perhaps the three of us would be less lonely together. I think it could be a very good thing. Ya love Little Miriam as much as I do, I can feel it. I'd choose ya over anyone else here at Hares End ta care fer her. I know I'm nine years older than ya an' likely not giving ya children but—"

"Sheron, I can't think about that right now. I..." Eramus's voice trailed off.

"Sorry. I said too much," she apologized softly. They both fell silent but after a few minutes, Sheron said, "But just remember if ya never find yer mysterious maiden agin, there be other options. Miriam an' me is just one a many ya could pick."

She gazed thoughtfully into the dying fire. Suddenly, she sat up straight and looked into his face. "I 'ave one last thing ta say: you've a good heart, Eramus. Trust it an' follow it. If ya do, I believe you'll never go wrong."

Sheron scooped up Little Miriam into her arms and left for home. Eramus watched in silence as she departed, but in his mind, the thoughts turned over and over. So many possibilities. Duty, desire, and curiosity all competed for his attention. It had been a big day, and he was tired. So, gazing into the hypnotic flames, he let himself drift off to sleep, where he dreamed not of Nawiman maidens, nor adventure, nor ghouls or men of any sort, but rabbits.

CHANGING WINDS

"Change is a two-edged sword; wield it prudently."

– Grandame Arnette Donatina

Leaving Hares End turned out to be much simpler than Eramus expected. The team of horses and wagon had to be returned, of course. There was a standing invitation to stay with the Donatinas. One fewer mouth to feed at the little village would be readily accepted by the Ruling Hand — not that food was a concern any longer. When he announced his departure and rationale, the village accepted it without argument and bid him good luck. Even Sheron was supportive. She and Little Miriam were his only real excuse to stay, but in reality, all was well enough for them and Miricel was not so far away if he was needed.

But it was when he was on his way and found himself whistling a merry tune that he realized something had changed in him as well. That the farm and village were not as important to him anymore came as a bit of a surprise. The desire to travel supplanted that.

He planned to spend time in Miricel learning all he could. The world, it turned out, was much bigger than he had imagined, and suddenly he had so many questions that needed to be answered. The Donatinas welcomed him, and it was decided he would spend the winter with them and return to Hares End in the spring. That winter, the Donatina girls taught him to read and write and he was almost as capable as the third-oldest daughter. They were days to be cherished. The laughter and warmth of the girls was something not well-known in Hares End, and it made him feel young, alive, and incredibly happy.

He returned in the spring as promised and helped get the crops planted. He brought with him tools that he had acquired through the friendly farmers he had met in Miricel. These tools sped up the entire planting process and enabled them to plant and maintain larger fields. The weather was good, and the new seed and associated planting techniques amazed them all. By mid-summer, Eramus felt his work was done and he returned to Miricel, again staying with the Donatina family after promising the Ruling Hand he would return in time for harvest. Eramus gave Sheron his home to live in, allowing Sheron's old home to give a larger family more room.

Come fall, the harvest was bountiful, and the work went swiftly. They now had sufficient production to trade for other items and the village grew. So, for three years, Eramus traveled back and forth to Hares End. But each trip, his stay at Hares End was shorter, and the time came when he realized he needn't worry about his old village, and he could make Miricel his permanent residence.

At the Donatina's, he was like a part of the family, and he genuinely enjoyed his time with them. But things were changing around him. Arnette married and had a child of her own and the second-oldest daughter was preparing for marriage. The girls grew up strong and beautiful. They had taught him well and now only Lord and Lady Donatina could advance his learning — when they had the time. Eramus realized he had changed as well, but something inside him became restless and he knew that soon, he must leave this family as well.

The time had come for him to stand on his own, and he hired on as a drover to transport crops and goods from fields to storage or nearby villages. With this income, he acquired a horse and became quite a good rider. And so, it was in a short time he found himself with a new home and a new teacher to advance his learning, all paid for through his labors. Because he traveled outside the city, he armed himself and became trained in the use of sword, knife, and bow.

On a pleasant autumn day, Eramus found himself riding through the streets of the town outside of Miricel when a strange discussion caught his ear. The words were atypical of the residents and the sentence structure was rather formal. This piqued his interest, and he dismounted and followed the sound to an alley where two young men were trying to barter with two of the local riffraff.

"What be this business about?" said Eramus, interrupting the exchange. At his entrance, the two locals backed away slowly and slipped out the back.

A young man in a brown cape turned to Eramus and explained, "We were trying to obtain sufficient supplies for our journey and these men led us here to make the exchange."

"More likely, they would have relieved you of your gold and slit your throats," Eramus scoffed.

"Oh, I think not," his companion said, throwing back his hood to reveal a set of pointed ears.

Eramus looked at the two men carefully. They were the first Nawiman men he had ever seen, and suddenly, certain memories flooded back. "Well, it has been a while since I have been in the company of the Emallinawima."

Their ears perked up and their eyebrows rose in surprise. They shot each other a questioning glance. One of them stepped forward, saying, "You seem to have us at a disadvantage, sir. You know of us, but we do not know you."

"I once traveled with a pair of your kind several years ago. Lewatollma and Nesneratha were their names."

A smile spread across their faces, and they nodded to each other. "Then you must be Eramus of Hares End."

Eramus executed a bow and grandly said, "The very same."

"What a singular pleasure to meet you! I am Mosinum and this is Carteledo. Lewatollma has told us all about you and your adventures as we journeyed here."

"Is Lewatollma here in Miricel?" Eramus inquired.

"Oh, yes. She is our Minsemus — that is to say, our expedition leader. What a surprise it will be for her to hear we met you in person."

"Why don't I help you obtain your supplies from a more reputable merchant, then we can surprise Minsemus Lewatollma together."

"How kind of you! That would make our task so much simpler. Our efforts thus far have been less than productive, and I am certain she would want to see you again."

"Well then, what do you need?" Eramus inquired as he gestured to the street.

Lewatollma waited amid the red and gold leaves beneath a large maple near the edge of town. The tree was still sporting a few final leaves, enough to provide mottled shade from the afternoon sun. She had been reviewing her mission parameters mentally while the denduine went for supplies. She hoped her confidence in them had not been foolishly placed. This was her first leadership assignment, and she was following all the training she had received, including developing those assigned to her charge. Miricel was a reasonably civilized town and as long as one stayed clear of the taverns, the dangers were minimal — but not entirely non-existent. She hoped her guidance was sufficient to get them off to a good start without having to elaborate on every detail.

She heaved a sigh of relief when she spied them rounding the corner with horses laden with the required supplies. A third man was with them holding the reins of two more horses, one of which was not carrying supplies. She wrinkled her brow. Her instructions were for three horses, not four. She prayed she would not have to resort to remedial math lectures later today. The third man was well-dressed and carrying a blade at his side, not a typical merchant and certainly no stable boy. Yet he seemed familiar.

As the denduine approached, Mosinum delivered a greeting, "Minsemus Lewatollma, three horses and requisite supplies as requested. Forgive us, but we have encountered a most unusual person of interest who assisted us greatly and wished to meet you."

Eramus bowed and spoke gently. "Minsemus Lewatollma. It is an immense pleasure to be in your company once again."

Lewatollma's face lit up in surprise and she gasped, shocked by his appearance and precise grammar, "Oh! Eramus! I did not recognize you! How grand you look! No longer a farmer, I see! So refined and polished, you have the bearing of an educated gentleman." Smiling broadly, she laughed and continued, "You have caught me completely by surprise. How wonderful it is to see you again!"

"You, however, have not changed one iota. Still as straight, strong, gracious, and beautiful as when I last saw you years ago. I see you have exchanged your brown cloak for a tan one. An indication of your new title, I presume?"

"Yes. A temporary assignment. I see you have met my denduine. They are here to accompany me as we explore the territory west of Miricel."

"Where is that old thorn in my side Nesneratha?" Eramus quipped.

Lewatollma smiled wryly. "Assigned elsewhere at present. Eramus, come join us for a meal; we would be honored to have you accompany us."

"At the Sudsy Tankard?" Eramus asked, smiling.

"Decidedly not! We are going to patronize one of the outdoor establishments where we can eat in relative peace and keep an eye on our transportation." Extending her elbow, she continued, "Come now, you must relate all that has transpired since we were last together."

Soon they were enjoying a simple meal on a wooden platform beneath the shelter of a porch. Though the day was pleasant enough, very few tables were occupied. The harvest was in full swing and nearly everyone in the community was occupied in labor or trade related thereto. There was much conversation and relating of old tales. Eramus entertained the denduine with his version of the antagonistic Nesneratha, carefully omitting her indiscretion at the Sudsy Tankard. He also related in detail the rescue of Arnette and Emil from the ghouls. Lewatollma was surprised, as she had never heard the delicate details of the affair. When asked about it, Nesneratha simply answered the question with a shrug and "Just an ordinary rescue; we cut some ropes and ran."

At length, Lewatollma dismissed the denduine to feed and ready the horses for their journey. Once she and Eramus were alone, Lewatollma became somber and in her unique, gentle way began to discuss all that was left unsaid up to that point.

"Eramus, that night I left you, I never intended to hurt..."

Eramus cut her off. "No, it is I who should apologize. I was trying to force your hand, and it was wrong of me to do so. I have replayed that scene differently in my mind over a dozen times, and in none of them could I ever justify my actions. I was too smitten with you to see clearly. Oh, but how I wish you could have seen the celebration at Hares End that night. It would have warmed your heart. If it were not for you, I would never have made it back with that food, so in a great measure, it was you who was responsible for saving my village. I am sad you were not there to be honored properly."

"I also wish things had ended differently, Eramus. Our parting gave me no peace either. Yet here we are back together again, and it is like nothing has changed. I never expressed my feelings to you because of the impossibility of our situation. Nesneratha was right to try to keep us apart. I lacked the perspective and maturity to see outside myself. I am just too young and too easily confused." She sighed deeply and then took Eramus by the hand. "Having said that, it feels so wonderful to be here with you."

"I thought I had put all this behind me as well, Lewatollma," Eramus admitted. "But as soon as I saw you, all those feelings came flooding back. I feel so much warmth and peace being in your presence." Raising her hand, he kissed it and said, "You are still that beautiful, gentle angel that I want to spend my time with."

Blushing, she broke free and resting on her elbows, cradled her head in her hands. "What are we to do, Eramus? I cannot abandon my duty or my people. I cannot stay here with you — it would break both my family's heart and mine if I did not return, and..." Her eyes began to well up with tears, which she swiftly swept away to avoid leaving any trace that might betray her innermost feelings to the denduine.

"Then let's just enjoy the time we have together," Eramus suggested. "No promises to each other. No expectations except to enjoy each day. Let me accompany you on this trip. We have chaperons and I have advanced my horsemanship skills and trained in the use of weaponry. I have no attachments here. A few goodbyes and I will be free to go. Besides, I can help you break in these two neophytes properly."

Lewatollma said nothing, but her logic and emotions battled each other; her brow furrowed, and her lips were firmly set together.

"I can see you're struggling with this, so don't answer me now. Think it over and discuss it with the denduine. When are you planning to leave and how long will you be gone?"

"We will leave tomorrow, after breakfast, and return in three weeks."

"Good. I will be here tomorrow morning, packed and ready. If you decide that I can join you, meet me here. If you are not here, then I will go on with my normal life and perhaps I shall see you when you return. If it is too much for you, then I should stay behind, and you should use this time to find your own answers."

Lewatollma nodded in agreement. She and Eramus rose from the table and observed the denduine across the street struggling with the straps securing the gear and supplies. Lewatollma suddenly stepped close to Eramus and brushed her left cheek against his, whispering, "Until we meet again, Eramus." She pulled quickly away and started in on the denduine, "No, no, that will not do at all..."

Eramus shook his head and smiled as he mounted his horse and headed home.

The next morning, Eramus arrived early at the rendezvous point and broke fast there. He completed his meal and rechecked his horse and backpack. He was beginning to think Lewatollma had decided to leave him behind when Carteledo came down the street struggling to control his horse. Eramus watched as he mishandled the reins and awkwardly coaxed his ride over to where Eramus stood.

"Eramus of Hares End, Minsemus Lewatollma has accepted your gracious offer to accompany us. If you follow me, we will begin."

"Carteledo, if I may offer some advice. You and the horse are partners, but not equal partners. Be firm with the reins. You are in control. If the horse senses his rider does not know where he is going, he will decide for the both of you. Also, use a firm, commanding voice. The horse will not respond to reasoning or rhetorical arguments."

"Thank you. Perhaps you can illustrate on the way back. The five-minute lecture I received was informative but was seriously lacking in practical example."

With a little guidance, Eramus was able to help Carteledo improve his technique and give him more confidence in managing his mount. They met Lewatollma near the narrow suspension bridge that spanned the Neramer.

"Eramus, thank you for joining us. I will be taking the lead, and you shall take the rear. We will be leading our horses across the bridge one at a time." The latter instruction was for the benefit of the denduine, for Eramus knew that the horses must be led, for they would not willingly venture out onto the narrow bridge that tended to sway side to side easily. On the other side of the river, they all mounted and headed west into the wilderness.

The trip was uneventful and the first few days Lewatollma spent teaching Carteledo and Mosinum cartographic skills and what characteristics of the land should be recorded and why. Eventually, they were sent out on short journeys together to discover the origins of small streams or the constitution of rock formations. These periods of respite allowed Eramus and Lewatollma to talk while he assisted with her duties. The days were full and busy, and the evenings were usually nothing more than a quick meal and sleep. The weather was fair for this time of year, but it grew steadily cloudier.

One evening after dinner, Eramus strolled to the top of a nearby hill. He scanned the horizon to the south, examining the vast expanses beyond. Then something caught his eye. Far in the distance, he could see light, a faint blue glow. As the daylight dwindled and the darkness deepened, the soft glow transitioned from a small patch to fill most of the southern horizon.

Coming up from behind, Lewatollma placed her hand on his shoulder, reminding him, "We start early tomorrow; everyone should bed down for the night."

Eramus pointed to the phosphorescence along the horizon.

"Ah, it is the Blue Desert, Eramus."

"I have heard of it but have never seen it until now. They say the land is cursed. People who travel there rarely come back and those who do die horribly. Why do you think that is, Lewatollma?"

Sighing, she explained, "There is poison out there. You cannot see it or smell it or taste it, but it is present everywhere in that region. If you expose yourself for too long, it will kill you."

"How long is too long?"

"The poison is not of the same potency everywhere. Do you see the brighter spots along the horizon?"

"Yes."

"That is because it is more concentrated in those areas. Traveling through most of the desert, it might take a few days to become sick, but in those areas, an hour may be sufficient."

Tugging his sleeve, she said, "Come along, you should rest. You need not worry about the Blue Desert; we will not be going there."

Eramus gazed at the great Blue Desert one last time, then yielded to Lewatollma's kind persuasion.

About two weeks into the venture, Lewatollma sent the denduine off northward on a short expedition, giving them instructions to meet back at the camp in two days. Lewatollma and Eramus turned south and headed toward the bluffs on the north bank of the Emmering. As they rode south, the clouds gathered, and a bitter northwesterly wind rose to bring solid cloud cover with it. Dark fell early, so they dismounted and made camp.

Pulling her cloak closed tightly, Lewatollma observed, "The weather is changing quickly. It will be cold tonight." She looked at the sky, gray clouds in motion. Eramus stood beside her, gazing skyward. His instincts told him rain was coming. Cold, wet weather was not welcome at any time of year, but less so while the grain was still drying in the field. Eramus frowned.

"The corn," he mumbled to himself. For the first time in many years, his mind turned to Hares End.

"We had better sup before the weather turns bad."

"Right," mumbled Eramus, "I'll start a fire."

"We will not have time to cook anything tonight."

"Okay. Do you think the denduine will be all right?"

"If they remember their training, they will," Lewatollma answered casually and rummaged through their foodstuff for a quick meal. They ate in silence, dried fish jerky and some apples

Eramus had found along the way. The daylight dwindled rapidly. Eramus grabbed a fistful of dry grass to clean his hands then and pulled out his bedroll. He spread it out over a pile of leaves he had hastily kicked together, then retrieved the waterproof cover. He sat down to start taking off his boots as Lewatollma walked over to him, her sleeping roll under her arm. She spread her blanket overlapping Eram's. He looked at her quizzically.

"What are you doing?"

"We can stay warmer if we sleep next to each other."

"Okay," Eramus said cautiously, as he finished removing his boots. He pulled off his coat and rolled it up to use as a pillow. Then he took his boots and rolled them into the foot of the rain cover and scurried under the blanket. He turned his back to Lewatollma as she prepared herself for sleep. She climbed in beside him, curled up around his back, and snuggled in closely. Eramus drifted off to sleep, listening to her rhythmic breathing and the wind in the trees.

He awoke later that night to something tickling his nose. Brushing some of Lewatollma's long hair out of his face, he stared up into a clear, star-sprinkled sky. Lewatollma was curled up in his arms resting her head on his shoulder, her leg thrown over his. He was surprised to find his arm around her. The wind blew a few strands of her hair into his face again. He pushed them back, brushing her face lightly as he did. She stirred, snuggled in closer, and sighed.

Eramus pulled the blankets and rain cover closer with his free hand. For some reason, he thought of Lady Donatina's cat. He remembered how it jumped into his lap and made itself at home, just as if it had always belonged there. So, it was with Lewatollma. Eramus yawned, closed his eyes, and began to dream.

He saw Miriam, her dress blowing in a gentle breeze. She was standing in the open pasture east of Hares End, the green grass halfway up her calves. Her face was slightly distressed, and her eyes were pleading. She pointed down the slope toward the river. Eramus turned his gaze in that direction. The pasture dropped off into unnatural darkness that disturbed him. Miriam called out to Eramus, "Save her!" He started walking down the hill toward the darkness, searching for the person Miriam was speaking about. He spotted her there sitting in the darkness, her face in her hands crying like a lost child.

As Eramus approached her, the darkness grew thick around him, chilling his soul and filling him with a sense of dread. He turned back to look at Miriam. She was still pointing, saying loudly, "It's all right. You can do it!" Encouraged, he approached the girl, who was now a woman. He was surprised to see she had pointed ears. He called out to her, "Take my hand!" but she did not respond. *Didn't she want to be saved, he wondered?* He looked back at Miriam. She spoke emphatically. "Go to her, Eram!" He turned his attention back to the woman, who had grown older — her dark hair started to sport a few silvery threads and it had lost its youthful luster. Eramus moved right in front of her. "Take my hand and I will help you out of here," he pleaded. She sobbed an almost inaudible, "I cannot!" Eramus sensed she was somehow emotionally overwhelmed, so he scooped her gently up into his arms and headed back to Miriam, who was smiling brightly. Eramus stayed focused on Miriam as he made his way out of the darkness. Miriam blew him a kiss and waved goodbye then walked into the grass, which had suddenly become quite deep.

"Wait for me!" Eramus cried out but Miriam did not stop. "My love!" he shouted.

"Here am I," the woman in his arms said. Eramus looked down at her but all he could see was dazzling, brilliant light in the form of a woman.

Eram's eyes snapped open and he sat bolt upright. He was breathing heavily as if he had exerted himself. The dream was still vividly clear to him. He looked down at his arms, half expecting to see the woman still there. He looked up into the pre-dawn sky, the last of the stars fading slowly.

"Ah, you are awake!" Lewatollma commented. "We seem to have avoided the rain. This will make breaking camp easy, so rise, have some food, and let us be on our way."

Eramus got up and mumbled, "I had a dream."

"I hope it was not about me, because you looked very upset just now," she laughed.

They rode in silence that morning, reaching the bluffs about midday. Lewatollma dismounted and made her way to the top while Eramus tethered the horses. She gazed about, and then suddenly dropped to one knee in the tall grass. She turned and came running carefully down from the bluff. Halfway, she stopped and motioned to Eramus to join her. Lewatollma made her way back up and blended, nearly invisible, into the tall grass. As Eramus neared the top, Lewatollma was crouching in the tall grass. She turned back to see Eramus come puffing up the hillside.

"Stay low and be quiet," she said in a hushed voice. Eramus dropped to his hands and knees and scrambled up beside her. Lewatollma pointed across the great cliffs carved by the Emmering to the plains southward. "Do you see that cloud of dust?" Eramus spotted it now. It almost blended in with the late-season grasses, which were turning brown after the long, sweltering summer. It extended for a great distance along the far bank of the Emmering, in front of the tree-covered rolling hills. Within the cloud, he spied horse-drawn wagons and men in formation. He tried to count them, but the number was impossible to determine while obscured by the dust cloud. He looked to the front where many horsemen led the way.

"Who are they and where did they come from?"

"Soulanders, Eramus, from far south."

"From the Blue Desert?"

"Nothing survives in the Blue Desert, Eramus. No, they have come a great distance, south of the Blue Desert. The drought has lowered the water level of the river, giving them a route around the poisoned lands; otherwise, they would not have been able to survive crossing the desert."

"What does all this mean, Lewatollma?"

"War," she said, frowning. "Take a good long look and remember what you have seen here."

Eramus looked at her. He probably never would have forgotten such a sight, but he had to ask, "Why?"

She was silent. After a long moment, she took his elbow and said, "Let us return to the horses." They turned and stayed low until after they were well below the hill's crest.

Lewatollma began adjusting her mount's saddle, tightening it as if she expected to do some hard riding. "Eramus, do you remember how to get back to Miricel?"

"Of course, just follow the Neramer's west bank northward. But why?"

Lewatollma finished with her horse and began adjusting Eramus's. "Because you are riding as fast as you can to Miricel to warn them about the Soulander army that is approaching."

He pursed his lips for a moment, then cocked his head and said, "You mean *we*, right? *We* are going to Miricel," he corrected, placing great emphasis on "we."

"No, Eramus, we must split up. Someone must warn the Normen and since I am the more experienced rider, I should go. Besides, you would get lost in the northern wilderness, whereas I know the way. I will find the denduine along the way. They will return the way they came via Miricel since they cannot possibly keep up with me. I will then cross the Neramer upstream and go through the forest north of Miricel until I catch the West Road, then cut eastward to Fishers Port."

"Why can't we ride together to Miricel and then go tell the Normen?"

"By taking separate routes, I can save almost three days' riding time."

"But..."

"Eramus, stop it!" she lashed out harshly, still tightening the straps. She turned to face him, her countenance angry and stern. "Just get on your horse!" Standing there, he regarded her critically, hurt by her sharp tone. She finished with the fittings, strode quickly to him, grabbed his arm, and pulled him toward his mount.

"I don't want to get separated from you, you're devilishly hard to find!" he complained. He hoisted himself into the saddle and settled in, then turned toward her and tried to catch her eye, but she had her back to him. Pulling her hair together and securing it under her hood, she then boosted herself into her saddle.

She looked at him and said, "Ride hard. Ride fast. Stay out of sight along the bluff. If the Soulanders see you, they may hasten their march or attempt a preemptive attack." They locked eyes and she said in a tone that chilled him, "The lives of many people are now in your care, Eramus." She maneuvered her steed to his side and reaching across, brushed her left cheek against his and in a softer voice added, "Be careful, Eramus." She turned her horse, directing him into the ravine. Leaning forward, she jabbed her heels into the beast and shot forward.

Eramus followed suit. The ravine's winding turns and thick brush prevented any great speed. Nevertheless, Eramus could scarcely keep up with her. He followed as long as he could, but as soon as she reached the grasslands, she lashed the horse with the reins and sent him into full stride. Eramus watched her disappear amid the low rolling hills, her cloak flowing out behind her. He sighed and wondered if he would ever see her again.

Slowing his ride, he crossed the stream that cut the ravine. Spurring his mare forward, he climbed the embankment and turned east toward the Neramer. He pushed the horse as fast as he could safely ride her. In his mind, he could see the great army pushing east. They would have to cross the Emmering at some point, but where? The cliffs along the Emmering's northern shore would not allow a great army to pass. They would have to go east past Miricel. Quite a distance east in fact, almost as far as...suddenly, Lewatollma's words took on greater significance and a chill ran down his spine. Eramus spurred the horse on faster.

The afternoon sun was warm for this time of year. Eramus walked his steed across the narrow bridge spanning the Neramer. He was hot, tired, dirty, and hungry. He contemplated stopping to eat, but he found his hunger kept him alert. He only stopped twice for a short break, water for him and the mare, and to re-tighten the riding gear.

When he came to the bridge, he led the horse across, talking quietly to soothe her, promising long rest and grain. Once clear of the bridge, Eramus mounted and took the horse up the road leading to the southwest gate. He rode hard past the merchants who squabbled with their customers over "fair trade value" for their wares. Some children waved and laughed. A man yelled something at him when Eramus came racing by too close. They knew nothing of the news he bore, and the great weight that fell upon his heart to bear it.

He could see the gate now; outside stood two guards. They moved to block his entry as Eramus reined the mare to a halt.

"I am Eramus of Hares End." He caught his breath before continuing, "I have urgent news, let me pass. I need to speak with Lord Donatina." He had decided to tell him first, primarily because the lord would believe Eramus and would know whom to tell next.

"What is your business with the lord?" a voice cried from above. The captain of the watch leaned from his perch to get a good look at the dirty, sweaty horseman. Eramus announced himself loudly a second time. A second man joined the captain above. He looked at Eramus and yelled, "Hello, Eramus! What news do you have that you would enter Miricel in such a filthy state?"

Eramus recognized that mocking tone — it was the lord's son, Aaron. "Bad news, I fear. Please take me to your father."

"As soon as you bathe and change clothes, you dirty dog!" The guards chuckled at this insult.

"Don't delay me! Take me to your father now!" Eramus yelled back.

"Where is your pointy-eared consort, Eramus? Has she left you for a better-looking jackass?" Aaron pulled the tips of his ears up with his hands. The guards burst out laughing and Aaron joined them.

Beginning to lose his patience, Eramus gritted his teeth. He could forgive Aaron for teasing him, but it angered him to hear Lewatollma being insulted. He searched for appropriate words and as soon as the laughing subsided enough for Eramus to be heard, he replied, "She is on her way to the Normen to warn them of the approaching Soulander army, while you keep vital news waiting outside the gate!" The laughter ended abruptly. Turning, the captain spoke a few words to Aaron, who then sped away. The captain leaned over the edge to see the men below. Waving his arms, he yelled down, "Let him pass! Let him pass!"

The guards stepped aside and Eramus rode through the narrow entrance. On the other side, he saw Aaron bolt from a doorway and duck into the stable.

"Two fresh horses, now! By the captain's order!" Voices shouted out orders from within the stable and there was a considerable commotion. Eramus heard the soldiers talking in hushed voices, most of the words indistinct except the word "Soulander" — and it fell upon the air like a curse from their mouths. Eramus dismounted and walked slowly toward the stable, leading his mare. Aaron appeared leading the two white horses, a stable boy at his heels. He gave one to Eramus and muttered, "Eramus, I'm sorry."

"Where's your father?" Eramus interrupted.

"At the citadel."

Eramus handed the reins of his exhausted mare to the stable boy and said, "She has been ridden hard since early yesterday. Take good care of her." Eramus and Aaron mounted up. "Let's go!" said Eramus. Aaron spurred his steed forward with Eramus close behind. The clattering of horses' hooves on stone echoed off the mighty walls of Miricel.

When they arrived, Eramus took the horse's reins from Aaron, who dismounted and walked briskly into the citadel. Eramus waited outside the citadel under a nearly barren tree when Aaron appeared with his father. The lord's jaw was firmly set, and his face creased with worry. Eramus felt sorry for the man. They strode quickly toward each other and embraced briefly.

The lord pushed away from the embrace, his hands still on Eram's shoulders. He looked into his eyes, asking, "Is it true, Eramus? Are the Soulanders on the march?"

"Yes, Lord Donatina, a large army is on the southern shore of the Emmering heading east." A deep, mournful moan escaped the lord and for a moment, he despaired. Taking a deep breath, he recovered.

"Aaron," the lord called over his shoulder, "hasten to General Ephramus. Let him know the Soulanders are on the march. Tell him I will meet him at the High Seat."

"Yes, pa-pa!" Aaron ran to his horse and disappeared amid a noisy clatter to the military headquarters. Lord Donatina turned to Eramus.

"We must inform the Grandames, but I want our commander of forces to be present."

The three men entered the council chambers of the Grandames. Eramus felt very self-conscious. He was filthy, steeped in his own fetid odor mingled with equine stench. In the field, there wasn't much one could do, but here in the city, it seemed a vile travesty.

Lord Donatina began, "Grandames, Eramus has come with urgent news. Please forgive his appearance, as he has ridden fast and hard, but the news he bears is time critical." The lord motioned for Eramus to start.

"Forgive me, great ladies, I'm sorry to bring such bad news. But two days' ride west of Miricel, we spotted the Soulander army moving east along the south bank of the Emmering."

"You say *we* — who was with you?" asked the matriarch.

"Lewatollma, the lady who helped rescue Lord Donatina's daughter."

"Was it an army or just a scouting party?"

"No, it was an army, M'Lady — an exceptionally large army. Horsemen in the lead and foot soldiers in formation at least eight abreast and fifty deep. There might've been fourteen of these formations. But I cannot be sure, as there was a lot of dust. Behind the men, there were lots of wagons. Overall, the entire caravan was about two and a half miles long."

The Grandames looked at each other and quietly exchanged words. The matriarch nodded in agreement.

"General Ephramus, what is your recommendation?" she queried, her voice straining.

"We should establish a defensive force at Ravens Ford and hold them there. If they get a foothold on this side of the Emmering, we will be hard-pressed to contain them."

A brief, hushed discussion ensued among the Grandames, heads nodding in agreement.

"General Ephramus, assemble your forces and take whatever steps are necessary to prevent the Soulanders from entering our territories. We grant you authority to activate reserves and conscript young men. We shall immediately issue an order to grant you access to all food reserves and equipment. The assets of the city will be at your disposal. Please keep us apprised of all your activities and plans. Go and Godspeed to you."

The men bowed and turned to leave.

"And Eramus," the Grandame called softly, then paused until he met her eyes, "thank you."

FLY AWAY HOME

"Do you want freedom? Do not ask for that which you are not willing to pay for in full. Freedom is not free. Its price is fixed and non-negotiable. In the markets of history, it has been, and ever will be, bought and sold in exchange for blood: yours and your oppressors."

– Unknown

Eramus stayed with Lord Donatina, tagging along as he made several stops to pass the word to members of his family and fellow reserve officers. Once they were home, the family was gathered, and the lord informed them of the situation. Lady Donatina wore a brave face and smiled, put the youngest in her lap, brought the rest to her side, and with soothing words and loving touches comforted the children.

She had learned as a child about the Soulanders and their aggression. She had heard the call to war and seen the men leaving in droves while she was quite young, and being young, was frightened and confused because she did not understand. She saw those same men return wounded both in body and mind. She had heard the wailing of wives and the crying of children who had been bereft of loved ones. Had seen their struggles in the ensuing years to shoulder grief and continue life without the aid of those men they had believed would always be at their sides.

Inside, yes, she was frightened, but this time because she understood too clearly what this meant. Her children too would learn as she had learned of the cost of war and its toll on the people around them. She feared most of all for the safety of the men in her family.

Like her mother, she too would become the source of hope and courage to sustain her family and those of her community. At this moment, she could remember so clearly her mother's smiling face and her words of encouragement and comfort. It brought a smile and a small measure of peace to her soul. She drew strength and inwardly was grateful for her example. She knew what she had to do.

The older girls took cues from their mother and ushered the younger ones away to occupy them with chores or a game to give their parents a moment alone.

Eramus also excused himself and waited outside. Frankly, he was surprised at how quickly the lord joined him, now in his uniform. The emblems on his shoulders were those of a senior field officer. He looked quite stunning even though the belt seemed to be rather snug at the waist. As they strode off, Eramus felt this was the moment to ask some questions forming in his mind.

"Where can I serve in all this?" Eramus asked.

The lord was silent for a few long moments then replied, "This is not your fight, Eramus, and there is no expectation from anyone for you to take up arms in defense of the Fair Folk."

"Hares End could be affected also."

The lord's jaw tightened briefly before he said, "You must do what you think is best for your people just as I will for mine. The time may come when we will need to stand together, so I hope you will keep in close contact."

"I have been considering leaving with the advance scouting party in the morning. I know the land and I think I could be of use there."

He nodded. "Very good. I will put in a word with the commander to ensure you are taken seriously and not viewed as some busybody. If you hope to join the scouting party, you had best go pack and gather up some supplies. I would plan on at least ten days. Food and gear will quickly become scarce here with the mobilization in full swing. I will not be leaving in the morning, perhaps not for a week or more. I have responsibilities to help prepare an army to defend our borders. Based on what you have told us, I expect this to be a protracted engagement."

Eramus grabbed his arm and swung him to face him. "I want to thank you for all you have done for me over these past few years."

He scoffed, "I could never do enough to repay you for saving my daughter."

Eramus didn't think it was all that big a deal, but he knew better than to argue with him. "There's an awful lot of uncertainty here and I don't know when we may meet again, if ever." They embraced, and Lord Donatina nodded in affirmation, putting his hand firmly on Eramus's shoulder. He then turned on his heel and left quickly. Eramus took a slow, deep breath, pushed the events of the day out of his mind, and savored the warm glow of a brilliant sunset for a moment before he too sped off for home.

Within an hour of the meeting with the Grandames, the military machinery of the Fair Folk lurched into high gear. The standing senior military officers met and made plans to send out scouts and activate a defensive force. They dispatched couriers and initiated a recall of all military reserve personnel as well as drafting young men under the age of nineteen. Though this was usually the minimum age for military service, anyone strong enough and able-bodied was pressed into service. The timing couldn't have been worse, for labor was in high demand to bring in the harvest, which would now be relegated to older men and all the women and children capable of field labor.

By nightfall, a mounted party of scouts had formed without the city walls. The armory was ablaze with light and the streets were filled with men running back and forth, orders being barked without ceasing. Wagons rolled in full of supplies and formed lines outside the armory, where gangs of men formed human chains to unload the supplies with amazing efficiency.

As promised, Lord Donatina had secured Eramus a place in the advance party and as suggested, he became part of the scouting party. Eramus was tightening his saddle on his mount and rechecking his gear when Captain Turom approached him.

"You will ride with me eastward. We will go directly to Hares End and look for enemy attempts to cross the Emmering in the valley." He paused and looked back at the rest of his party forming up. Without turning to face Eramus, he said, "I doubt we will find anything, but you never know. It's not above the Soulanders to send raiding parties to test defenses or identify places worth looting. Not that there's much worth looting that far east." He then raised his voice so all could hear. "We leave in fifteen minutes!"

Eramus wondered if it was Lord Donatina's idea to scout near Hares End; Turom did not seem all that concerned about the strategic significance of the lands that far east. He was right in one sense: the steep valley leading to the Emmering was densely wooded and the terrain was rough and rocky. On the opposite side of the Emmering, even more so; not a likely place for an army to cross. The river at that point was narrow and swift and hardly seemed a viable way to travel by boat. Inwardly, he hoped Turom would be proved wrong. Eramus then thought about Sheron and Little Miriam and the others. There were many he was fond of or respected deeply at Hares End, and his concern for them occupied his thoughts.

Turom climbed easily onto the horse and holding his fist high in the air, cried out, "Mount up!" Immediately all talk ceased, and the men complied swiftly. In all, fifty horsemen were present, and they fell into formation, ten ranks formed. Turom being the leader, the riders formed on him. The center position of each rank was occupied by a ranking officer with two men on either side of him. Eramus trotted up front and took the left end of the first rank. After the first rank formed, Turom moved ahead of the formation and turned to face them. When all were in position, he dropped his hand and barked out, "Officers, report!" The center column moved forward and formed a close rank immediately in front of him; together they saluted Turom. The captain glanced from right to left and returned their salute. "At ease!" he began and started giving them detailed orders.

They were to monitor the banks of the Emmering. Each group was assigned a particular area. They were to watch and wait, sending two horsemen to report enemy activity. The units from Ravens Ford and points west were to send one to the main army that would be forming at Ravens Ford, and the other to Miricel. Those stationed east of Ravens Ford would send word to Ravens Ford only, and from there a fresh courier would relay the information. They were told that courier stations would be established in the next day or so along the main road between Ravens Ford and Miricel, and they were to use them if they were available.

He instructed them that if a dangerously large force were to cross the Emmering, they were to send messengers, and the remainder retreat to Ravens Ford. Captain Turom gave the order to move out and the first rank followed him at a brisk pace. In turn, each rank fell in behind its leader and charged out.

After a hard two-day ride, Captain Turom's men entered Hares End late in the afternoon. As soon as they entered the edge of the village, Eramus noticed the cornfield was naught but smoldering ash.

Eramus suddenly stood up in his stirrups. "No!" he gasped, then spurred his horse forward into a gallop. Turom motioned to the men to split up and ordered them to secure the immediate area and then meet back at the center of town.

Eram's heart broke at the scene before him. The storage barn had been burned along with several of the family dwellings. In the street, the villagers had gathered, mostly old women and young children. Some sat on the ground head in hand, others huddled crying, some wandering about as if lost, but all were crying, all in anguish. Alongside the road leading to the center of town, there was a neat row of bodies lined up, side by side. Eramus slowed to a trot, his face ashen.

At the sight of Eramus, the villagers began to scream and run away in a terrible panic, but Sheron recognized him and called out loudly, "It's Eram! It's Eram!" As one, they ran to him, their cries a cacophony. Eramus dismounted and walked toward them in total shock, his eyes taking in, but not believing what he saw. First to reach him was Ed's daughter wailing, "We can't get 'im down!" repeatedly. Grabbing his hand, she forcefully pulled him toward the village center, and shaking off the confusion, he picked up his pace and joined her in a panicked run. She led him to the lodge and everyone else followed. She fell to her knees, pointing to the side of the lodge, gasping and sobbing, and she pleaded, "Please get 'im down." It was Ed. They had staked him to the side of the lodge. He had been brutally beaten and cruelly cut. A powerful feeling welled up inside Eramus and he struggled to comprehend exactly what it was, but it paralyzed him, and he could not take his eyes off Ed.

Turning to Sheron, Eramus asked, "Where is Sherman?"

"Passed on two winters ago," she replied. Now Eramus understood why it was Ed impaled up there.

Suddenly, Captain Turom and his men converged on the town center, sending everyone shrieking and scattering in all directions. This snapped Eramus out of his trance and he shouted, "They're with me!" Sheron relayed the news and beckoned them to come back and sent some of the other women to calm them.

Turom gestured to his men to get Ed down. On horseback, they could reach the stakes that pinned him. One man grabbed him around his waist and lifted him slightly while the other freed his hands. Together they ushered him gently to the ground as his daughter sobbed, "Thankee!" More wailing ensued as those women who retained a modicum of composure lifted Ed and carried him to be laid with the rest of the fallen men.

Turom barked orders to his men to round everyone up, get them seated inside the lodge, and attend to injuries. He looked at Eramus, shaking his head weakly, and muttered softly, "I am so sorry." Eramus looked at him blankly.

His gaze fell upon Sheron and when her blue eyes met his, his tears began to fall unchecked. The two ran to each other and crushed each other in a fierce embrace. She whispered soothing words to him and patted his back, letting him cry on her shoulder. Suddenly, Eramus pushed away.

"Little Miriam?" he managed to croak.

"We hid in the woods. We're both fine. Good thing we was at the edge a the village, looking fer herbs. We…"

"Where is she?" he asked.

"I sent her ta get water."

"I want to see her."

"You will, you will," she said soothingly as he fell back into her arms and wept.

Eramus started to laugh through his tears, "Look at who is comforting whom."

"Oh, Eram, I canna tell ya how good it was ta see ya ride inta town. The minute I saw ya, I felt my courage return. Oh, Little Miriam an' I have missed ya so!" she cried, and she hugged him as hard as she could.

He suddenly remembered Sheron's son. "Where's Artur?"

"I don't know, Eram. Maybe he's got away an' hid, but I ain't seen him yet. I hope he's all right."

Artur was a smart lad; he would have figured out it was safe to return by now. A disturbing thought crossed Eram's mind, but he refused to entertain it and he certainly wasn't going to share it with Sheron. "We'll find him once we get the village sorted out and help the others."

Eramus and Sheron pushed each other away suddenly as fresh cries of alarm sounded. Not as panicked as before, they stood and pointed toward a lone, cloaked individual on horseback entering from the east end of town. Eramus wiped his eyes to see more clearly. A Nawiman?!

One of Turom's men drew his sword and advanced toward the rider, who drew back her hood, revealing long, dark hair, and held out both arms showing empty palms. Eramus stared in disbelief; it was Lewatollma! There was a brief, but quiet exchange between the soldier and her, then she dismounted. She took in the surroundings and her countenance fell into a stern but concerned look. She looked pleasantly surprised to see Eramus here and approached him. Lewatollma made the formal sweeping gesture of greeting and called him by name.

"Lewatollma, what are you doing here?" he queried.

Sheron's eyes widened in surprise upon hearing Lewatollma's name.

"Checking on you, of course," she replied. "Our last parting was rather hurried, and it felt incomplete. I only went this way because the Normen insisted on coming along, and the only road capable of admitting a wagon led to Hares End. I felt it would be appropriate if I checked in on your village, that I might be able to ease your mind when we met again at Miricel. Alas..." she trailed off, looking suddenly sad, refusing to state the obvious.

"What's this about Normen?"

"Two wagon loads of them, outfitted for battle. They are probably no more than an hour away. I felt it my duty to warn the village, so I rode on ahead," Lewatollma said with a "you know what Normen can be like" look. She then noticed Sheron was staring at her open-mouthed. She turned to her and smiled, saying, "Eramus, you should introduce me to this lady."

"Oh, sorry! Lewatollma, this is Sheron, my sister-in-law. Sheron, this is Lewatollma," Eramus fumbled awkwardly.

"Little Miriam's mother!" Lewatollma joyfully exclaimed. "Eramus has mentioned that Little Miriam is his favorite niece..." She stopped mid-sentence, her face frozen in a look of mild horror, her breath abated showing her realization that Little Miriam may not have survived.

Just then, a little girl came up from behind Sheron, blurting out, "Who's this, Mommy?"

"Miriam, this is Lewatollma," Sheron said softly. The little girl gasped in surprise. Smiling, Lewatollma resumed breathing.

Lewatollma appeared to sense an awkward situation was developing, so turning to Eramus, she asked, "What can I do to help?"

"I assumed they were all dead, but could you check?" Eramus asked, motioning to the line of bodies. Continuing, he said, "Maybe you can help them."

"Of course, I will see what I can do." Lewatollma turned and strode toward the assembled bodies.

Turom interrupted, "We need everyone in the lodge. We need to find out what happened here. This information may prevent further loss of life. I need to get messengers going. This is a bad affair, Eramus. Please, everyone, join us!" he finished. Getting behind Eramus, Sheron, and Miriam, he herded them in the direction of the lodge. Other soldiers were doing likewise. One was trying unsuccessfully to drag Ed's daughter away from her father's body, so he tossed her over his shoulder and carried her. Lewatollma waited for the streets to be cleared before she examined the line of bodies.

Inside the lodge, a semblance of calm was forming. Children were quieted and given water to drink and some of the soldiers' bread and dried meat to pacify them. Methodically, Captain Turom asked them one at a time to stand or at least sit up and relate what they knew. Picking on the calmest folk first, he began to gently interrogate them. Stories varied wildly in terms of what and how many; the only things they agreed on were that many had been taken and that all their food stores were gone. From the descriptions given, he had no doubt it was the Soulanders.

In the midst of this, Lewatollma strode through the door carrying Ed in her arms. "This one is still alive — but just barely.

He needs to be warmed immediately and given some water — but only a few drops at a time so he does not aspirate it." Seeing only puzzled looks, Lewatollma remembered where she was, so she clarified, "...so he does not breathe it in and drown." Finding out Ed was alive completely derailed Turom's line of questioning as the room exploded into a dozen different conversations.

Turom's chin dropped to his chest in resigned despair. At that moment, one of the soldiers motioned for Eramus, Turom, and the other soldiers to come outside.

"I have scouted around and found out where they went," he explained. "The tracks are south of here, cutting through the fields and woods south of the main road — probably to avoid being seen. It appears they may be headed back toward Ravens Ford."

"They attacked just before dawn," Turom began, "so they have a good five to six-hour lead on us. From all that I can gather there, there must be at least twelve, and as many as twenty of them." Shaking his head, he continued, "There are not enough of us to mount any kind of rescue. I fear they are lost."

Eramus jumped in, "Lewatollma said there were two wagons of armed Normen less than an hour away. They could do it." The soldiers looked unimpressed. It was evident they did not have a very high opinion of Normen or their military prowess. "I have seen these men in action, and I tell you they can hold their own."

"I have got to get messengers out right away and I don't dare send more than one man to help them," Turom said. "Besides, the Normen will be too late."

One of the other soldiers spoke up: "Sir, they have to move prisoners and a fully loaded wagon through rough terrain — surely, that will slow them down. If these Normen are traveling in wagons, they will be fresh and rested. I think this could work to our advantage."

Eramus watched Captain Turom's mind weighing this new idea. He looked up. "Very well then, here is the plan. Smith, you accompany the Normen and rescue the hostages, and if possible, the food. Engage if you must, but the rescue of the villagers is the priority. If some of the Soulanders slip through, so be it. Let's hope the brigade at Ravens Ford will intercept them. Tenise and Obedon, you head for Ravens Ford and let them know what has happened and our rescue plan." The two messengers saluted smartly and ran to their horses.

Eramus turned to Turom. "What do you want me to do?"

Turom looked at him sternly. "Assume leadership of this village. Get everything organized and prepare to evacuate Hares End in an orderly manner. You will have my full support."

Eramus opened his mouth to object, then closed it as he reflected on all that happened, all that remained after the raid, and all that must happen to sustain his village. It quickly overwhelmed him, but Turom was right: It would not be possible for the village to sustain itself through the approaching winter — not enough shelter, not enough food, not enough backs to bear the burden. Eramus worried this would be the end of his village, that it would be lost forever.

Captain Turom seemed to sense his thoughts and tried to comfort him. "It need not be permanent. Once this whole Soulander business is over, you can rebuild. I think this spot might become a strategic outpost. Perhaps some folk stifled by Miricel might make this their new home. Fields and farmland expanded; this could be a wonderful place to live."

"What would you be saying if it was Miricel that had to be evacuated?" Eramus countered.

Turom, ever the soldier, replied, "I would put my feelings aside and do what was best for my people. The time to sort out feelings will come later."

The distant sound of hooves and creaking wagons caught their attention. Rounding the corner and entering the little village, two wagons rolled into view.

"Normen," Eramus stated.

Pointing, Turom ordered, "Smith, get that rescue underway!"

Smith snapped to attention, and saluting, replied, "Yes, sir!" Without waiting for a return salute, he dashed out to meet them. Too far away to hear clearly, Turom and Eramus watched silently. Smith motioned the Normen to gather around. He waited till they all got out of the wagons, then he laid out the plan. Intent faces were drinking in his every word and nodding heads punctuated each time he paused seeking affirmation. At last, he seemed to finish.

The Normen stroked their beards and briefly discussed the whole plan among themselves. One of them strode up to Smith —

a man Eramus instantly recognized as Gorim — and extended his hand and shook Smith's. Smith pointed out the direction where the Soulanders' tracks began and with a shout, the Normen grabbed their weapons and as a mob ran off in the direction indicated, leaving Smith in mid-sentence. Caught by surprise, Smith just stared at them rapidly leaving their leader behind. He slapped his forehead with his palm and ran hard back into the village. As he passed Eramus and Turom, he shouted, "That didn't take much convincing!" He quickly mounted his horse and galloped after them.

"No formation, no order, no leader," Turom scoffed, shaking his head. "But I will give them this: They are an enthusiastic lot."

"You have no idea, Captain," Eramus said, smiling. Eramus was also surprised that a number of the Normen carried bows. He assumed they only used axes. The two men returned to the lodge.

Inside, Lewatollma was attempting to get Ed cared for so she could check the other men, but the women just stood there in shock. Partly because of the day's horrendous events, and partly because it was a miracle that Ed was still alive. Lewatollma looked around for a spark of rationality. She singled out one villager, calling out in her best commanding tone, "Sheron, get two or three blankets!" Sheron nodded, and physically shaking them out of their stupor, enlisted two other women to help.

Suddenly changing the tone of her voice to calm and gentle, she caught Little Miriam's eye and cooed, "Miriam, could you please bring water?" Little Miriam bolted away immediately. Reverting her voice again to commanding authority, she ordered, "Someone take him from me and get him situated!" Ed's daughter immediately took him from her arms. The others were beginning to come around and they cleared a spot for him. "Warm him with your bodies and elevate his feet," she commanded. The women looked at her in dismay. Sensing she was asking them to violate some moral code, Lewatollma shifted her voice to a more pleading, compassionate form. "Do you want him to live?" she asked, looking each woman in the eye. She could see the conflict in all their eyes. She started to consider doing it herself, wondering if they would attack her if she tried.

Ed's daughter prevailed when she tearfully pleaded, "Please? Help me save ma father!" They responded to her instantly, moving to help. Miriam ran back into the lodge with a small pail of water. Lewatollma took this opportunity to leave and check to see if any others could be saved. As she turned to leave, she heard Miriam whisper to Ed's daughter, "That's Lewatollma!" The whisper spread across the room like wildfire, igniting awed exclamations as it went. It initially shocked Lewatollma, and she felt herself begin to blush with embarrassment. Shaking her head briefly to clear it and reminding herself to set it aside, she pressed on to the task at hand.

She met Sheron and her helpers just outside and stopped them. "Wrap the blankets around him and those who are warming him. Try to get him off the ground. Do you have any straw or the like?"

"No straw or corn shocks — it was all burned," one bemoaned, the rest nodding in sad agreement.

One of the other women spoke up. "But we kin send the children ta gather dry grass from the fields!"

"An excellent idea!" Lewatollma added, praising her. Moving closer and touching Sheron on the shoulder, Lewatollma said, "When you can, please come to assist me out here." Sheron nodded, then they all ducked inside.

The other men were long dead. Most had died from severe internal injuries caused by sword thrusts. They all suffered multiple wounds on their arms and faces, so they must have died resisting. Farmers against soldiers — it could not have been a protracted battle. She closed the eyelids of those still staring skyward. She felt a tear run down her face as she did so, so she let the rest fall, mourning the death of men she did not know but who were known to Eramus. She wondered if there were relations of his laid out here and she silently prayed it was not so. She sat there kneeling and silently wept.

After a few minutes, she ceased and wiped the tears from her face with the back of her hand. She sat there a few moments longer, composing herself and checking off in her mind what else needed to be done. In a few short hours, the sun would be setting, and a chilly autumn evening would follow. Food and shelter, she decided, would be the next priorities.

Lewatollma heard footsteps behind her. She rose and turned to find Sheron approaching.

"Who were these men?" Lewatollma asked gently, gesturing.

"Husbands an' fathers all," Sheron replied. A second later, she broke down and fell into Lewatollma's arms, sobbing. Lewatollma held her silently, trying not to let herself be caught up in this tempest of emotion. With her head pressed against Lewatollma's chest, Sheron sobbed through the tears, "We're doomed! There be no men ta care fer us! Most of our homes burned ta the ground! There's no food! What will we do?"

Lewatollma did not have an immediate answer, so she just let her grieve and held her close. It struck Lewatollma suddenly that it was not just the death of a few men — it was the death of an entire village. She didn't mean for it to happen, but it overwhelmed her so suddenly that she joined Sheron in her bitter lament and let the tears spill again, but not silently as before.

Eramus and Captain Turom were inventorying everything that remained to evaluate the survival needs of the village. They decided everyone should stay the night in the lodge, where they could be protected and hopefully comfort and warm each other. Between them, they could provide two meager meals to the village, excluding the Normen, out of their supplies. In the Normen's wagons, there was food, but not enough for more than a day or two. Based on what Eramus knew of the Normen's appetite, maybe less. They found a couple of kettles that the Soulanders missed during the pillaging. Perhaps a warm meal could be prepared to comfort the survivors through the cold night. When they finished conversing, Captain Turom looked about and said the obvious: "Not good!" In his plans, Turom could not count on recovering prisoners or the food; he had to assume the worst case.

That evening, Eramus announced to everyone he was taking over village leadership until Ed could resume his duties. Turom's men served a warm meal, and everyone settled in for the night. Sheron came up behind Eramus and took him by the arm. "I 'aven't seen Artur, 'ave you?" she whispered.

"No. But I think he's okay. The fact that they took the able-bodied villagers tells me they are valuable to them. Artur is smart; maybe he will escape and find his way back. If not, I have high confidence that the Normen will be able to rescue everyone." Her face was creased with worry so he took her in his arms to comfort her. "Now don't you fret about things you can't control. It's been a rough day; you should take Little Miriam and rest."

"I ave a spot all set up, come be wit us. We be right there," she said, pointing to the back corner of the lodge.

"Sure. Right after I check on Lewatollma."

Looking around, Eramus could not spot her, so he stepped outside the lodge. He found her leaning against the lodge wall, hood up, arms folded, mindlessly staring at the ground.

"Hey," Eramus began as he touched her shoulder, "come on inside."

"Do you think I should? These poor people have endured a traumatic day, and I am not sure a stranger would be welcome."

"Nonsense. Come sleep next to me, Little Miriam, and Sheron."

"Are you sure this will not create a problem? When I tried to get the villagers to use their bodies to warm Ed, they seemed offended. How will they react to me sleeping beside you?"

"Everyone is all huddled anyway. I don't think it will be a problem." Eramus took her by the hand and led her inside. They found Sheron sitting against the outside wall, rocking her daughter in her arms, singing quietly. She smiled upon seeing Eramus and patted the ground beside her, indicating where he should rest.

"May I join you?" Lewatollma asked Sheron.

"Acourse. Asides, I'd feel better knowin' ya was safe with us."

As Eramus and Lewatollma lay down next to Sheron, Little Miriam stirred and squirmed out of her mother's arms, saying, "I wanna sleep nexta uncle an the pretty lady."

Sheron was about to scold her daughter when Lewatollma spoke up, saying, "It would be my pleasure." She extended her arms and Little Miriam scrambled across Eramus and snuggled in between them.

Smiling, Lewatollma whispered to Little Miriam, "Besides, I would feel safer sleeping next to a brave little girl." Miriam smiled in response as Lewatollma drew her in close and covered them both with her cloak. Little Miriam's demeanor suddenly changed and Lewatollma noticed a tear rolling down her cheek.

"What is wrong, Miriam?" Lewatollma quietly asked.

"Do ya think me brother will ever be back?"

Smoothing Miriam's light brown hair, Lewatollma smiled faintly and offered, "I do not know for sure, but this I can promise you; the Normen are fierce fighters and if anyone can rescue your people, it will be them. But no more tears for now, just snuggle up close and let us keep each other warm and sleep, dreaming sweet dreams." Rocking Miriam gently, Lewatollma began to softly hum a tune she had heard her mother sing to her when she was a child.

Sheron lay down next to Eramus and climbed into his arms, resting her head on his shoulder. She threw her arm around him and clung tightly. Looking across at Lewatollma, Eramus met her eyes. With his free hand, he reached out, found hers, and gently caressed it. It had been a troubling day, and he was grateful that Lewatollma was near and giving him a small measure of comfort.

The night passed in relative peace except for the occasional muffled sob and sniffle. The next day, they were greeted by a chilly dawn, but the sun shone boldly through a cloudless sky. Ed was still alive, and his color was much improved.

Breakfast was meager. Afterward, the women began to take it upon themselves to care for each other and the children. Small tasks were assigned to every child to occupy their time and keep their thoughts as far as possible from the events of the day before.

Eramus and Turom talked through all the viable options at their disposal to relocate the village. Turom knew Miricel would take them in without question, and he felt that would be the best option despite the long journey. There were other villages to the north as well, but most struggled to survive and Eramus was uncertain as to their reaction to suddenly having to feed and shelter women and children — all too old or too young to share the burden of the demanding work required for survival.

Sheron and Miriam could go to Piney Grove and live with her son, but Eramus was uncertain about any other family connections to other villages. In all his time at Hares End, he recalled very few visits in either direction with relations. Still, it should be something each family should consider.

Late that morning, the air was shattered by Normen singing a rousing but completely inappropriate drinking song as they strutted into town. The villagers ran out to meet them and shouts of joy sounded out as families were reunited, Artur and Sheron not the least. Last of all, the wagon rolled into the town full of food and stolen property, and behind it, a string of horses.

Smith rode up to Turom, dismounted, and grinning broadly, he saluted. "Report!" Turom barked.

"Rescue a complete success, sir. All hostages recovered, all food and property recovered!"

"Well done." Turom smiled as he returned the salute. "How did it go?" he asked.

"It was a massacre, sir. What Eramus told you was a gross understatement of the Normen's capabilities."

Turom and Smith looked at Eramus, who shrugged and said, "I only saw two of them in action."

Smith continued excitedly, "We caught up with them just before sunset. They were indeed moving slowly. The Normen scouted out before us, and we had not been detected. We decided to circle them in the south using the river's noise as cover, then lie in wait for them up ahead. We secreted ourselves on both sides of the road and took up positions to cover the entire length of the caravan. It was nearly dark when we sprang the trap. It was over in seconds! I have never seen such stealth or ferocity..."

Turom cut him off with a wave of his hand, indicating he got the picture.

"We also captured all their weapons and most of their horses, sir," Smith finished, bringing the excitement in his voice back to a more dignified tone.

"This is good, Eramus; it greatly expands our options for evacuating Hares End."

"You still think we need to evacuate?" Eramus asked.

"Yes. The Soulanders are still out there and when they need more supplies, where do you think they will come looking for them? There is also the possibility another party, a larger party, may be sent to discover what happened to the first. Until we have driven them out completely, this village cannot be secured. As their campaign progresses, they will send out larger raiding parties.

They may even decide to occupy this entire area, move their families up here, and take over. We don't have enough forces to protect the whole land north of the Emmering, and to date, we have relied on the natural boundaries to protect us, but now it seems that is not enough. The question was never about whether to do it, only how and when. With a good supply of food and the return of younger, more capable people, we can relocate in a more organized manner."

Three hours later, Turom's messengers returned, arriving back much sooner than expected. Courier stations had indeed been established and they let them relay the message. Reciprocally, they received the latest intelligence on Soulander activity along the front and the status of their forces. After a brief respite, Turom sent them northward along the road to alert the other communities. Based on the proximity and willingness of the other villages to spread the word, Turom expected the men back by nightfall.

Later that day, Ed opened his eyes and called for a meeting. Eramus and Turom took this opportunity to apprise all the men of the peril of remaining and the need to evacuate. They all sadly agreed. It would not take a second raid to convince them. Turom explained that the Normen would protect them and escort them someplace safe. But he and his men would be leaving to continue scouting.

The word spread rapidly of the plans to have everyone leave Hares End. Later, after leaving the council with Captain Turom,

Sheron found Eramus and sought to confirm the rumor. "Eram, is it true we'll be leavin' Hares End?"

"Yes, it is simply not safe here until the Soulanders are driven back south of the Emmering."

Wringing her hands, she continued, "Where will we go?"

"You could go be with Erin in Piney Grove. I'm sure he will take care of you, Artur, and Little Miriam. But to be honest, I think Miricel will be safer. I have friends there who could help you find work and get settled."

Looking down, she admitted, "I donna wanna leave ma home, but I unnerstand the danger." Then taking his hands in hers, she continued, "Eram, please stay with us. Join me an Lil' Miriam. Take me to wife and let's be a family. I know I 'ave said this afore and I let you go yer own way cause I knew ya'd do the right thing an I'd no right ta ask ya. I figured I could stand on me own, but now everythin's changed." Letting his hands go and placing her hands on his shoulders, she tearfully continued, "And Eram, I'm afraid. Really afraid. An not jest fer me, but for Lil' Miriam, too. I need ya. We need ya. Please, Eram, please?" With this last plea, she buried her head in his chest and wept.

Eramus pulled her close and stroked her hair to comfort her, saying, "I know this is a hard thing, Sheron, and it breaks my heart too to see all the work everyone put in to make Hares End a proper village. I never thought the Soulanders would have advanced this far so soon. You're right, everything's changing and changing faster than ever in ways we never expected."

Gently taking her by her upper arms, he pushed her back and lifted her chin to gaze into her face. "Sheron, get to Miricel and ask for Lord and Lady Donatina. Tell them I sent you and let them know you're my kin. They will help you. I have a place there and you can live there for now. I'd feel so much better knowing you and Little Miriam are safe. Please go there, for me?"

"Aright, we'll go, but when will ya be joinin' us?"

"I have a commitment to help scout the area presently, and I don't know what will happen after that or how long I'll be gone. It could be quite some time. For now, get settled in Miricel. Maybe after this war is over, you can move back here or perhaps you'll like Miricel and stay there."

Wiping her face dry, Sheron conceded, "Okay, we'll go, but promise me you'll come asoon as ya kin?"

"I can't promise you anything for certain. Just go quickly and be safe."

Sheron gave him a long, final hug and whispered in his ear, "Don't ferget us." Turning, she left to join the others in the lodge.

Coming from his left, Lewatollma came up beside Eramus. "What was that all about, Eramus?" she asked softly.

"Sheron wants me to marry her and care for her and Little Miriam."

Lewatollma looked down, while a brief battle of emotions played across her face, then turned to Eramus, smiled, and said, "I think you would be an excellent husband and father. You are well established and would be able to provide for all their needs. What did you tell her?"

"To go to Miricel, see the Donatinas, and get established with their help."

"That is wise counsel. Are you going with them?"

"No."

"Will you be joining them later?"

"I don't know. I'm feeling conflicted. I should be taking care of my kin but..." He turned to face Lewatollma and continued, "I want something else." Taking her by the hand, he tenderly kissed it and confessed, "I have feelings for you, Lewatollma. You're the one I want to be with for the rest of my life."

"I have feelings for you as well, but ours is an impossible situation and I fear we are just tormenting ourselves by hoping for something that can never be. Perhaps caring for Sheron and Miriam is the right and best thing you can do. You should give it serious consideration."

"Yet, here we are, together again. Why is that, Lewatollma?"

Wrapping her arms around him, she rested her head on his shoulder and shrugged, offering, "We are fools. It is the only plausible explanation."

In the dwindling daylight, Eramus gave Lewatollma a brief tour of Hares End. Finishing at the hill overlooking the warrens, they stood together in the dry grass and witnessed the retreat of day and the triumph of night in all its glory. There was no further discussion of plans or possibilities. As the evening cooled, they returned to the lodge.

RAVENS FORD

"Ravens Ford has strategic significance in that it is the only way to easily pass northward across the Emmering for hundreds of miles in either direction. While level, it is a wet, marshy plain many miles in length and nearly a mile wide. Many small tributaries enter from the east, divide, and meander over the plain, forming hundreds of constantly changing, intertwining, shallow channels. At the west end, they rejoin and become rapids that plunge into a deeply cut canyon. From there, the Emmering widens, rolls slowly west, then turns south. Its north border is an impassable, steep bluff several hundred feet high. It is along the top of this bluff that the city of Miricel sits unassailable from the south and protected by the deep gorge cut by the Neramer on the west."

– excerpt from Miricel Defense Plan

At dawn, Turom began to organize and outfit his scouting party. The activities attracted the attention of Hamlin and Gorim, who volunteered their services, completely ignoring Captain Turom's objections. Their determination to stay with Eramus was unbreakable, so they too became a part of the scouting party.

Somehow, between Eramus's pleading and the Normen's goading, Lewatollma reluctantly agreed to join them.

After bagging up some supplies, the eight of them departed into the southern end of the woods that morning. Since the Normen were traveling on foot and were able to more easily move through the thick forest, they took the lead with Turom close behind.

The next two days, they made their way scouting out the land north of the Emmering but found no traces of Soulander activity. Eventually, the woods became less dense, and they could all move on horseback except the Normen, who jogged alongside them.

Eramus and Lewatollma were constant companions both day and night, often falling to the rear to speak privately. Eventually, the forest yielded to grassy plain, and the river dropped below sight as the party followed the edge of a steep bluff.

Upon the edge of the bluff, Captain Turom looked where the mighty Emmering River was divided into a hundred rivulets across the vast floodplain. It was dotted with sandbars and small clumps of trees on little islands. From the northeast, a small stream came down to lose itself in the Emmering. Eramus and Lewatollma rode up beside him.

"Looks like a hard place to cross," noted Eramus.

"Yes, but if you are careful," he replied and his hand traced a route in the air, "you can cross with only getting your feet wet. Many of the sandbars are very solid and easy to travel. If the Soulanders try to bring a huge army north, this is where they will have to cross. The drought has lowered the water level considerably, making it easier to cross. Probably the reason they chose to invade now." They gazed briefly across the shimmering plain. Pointing down into the floodplain, Turom informed, "We'll set up camp along that stream. There are still a couple of hours of good light yet."

The company rode their horses, descending the long slope where the flatland transitioned to the floodplain scores of feet below. Turom motioned to everyone to move toward the stream. They crossed the shallow stream and tethered their horses to a log abandoned long ago by floods. Next, they began making camp in a small, protected area near an embankment carved out by the stream.

Hamlin and Gorim were eager to start dinner after the long day's trek. They had been envisioning a duck dinner since Turom's men shot two en route. Gorim asked, "Cap'n, sir, kin we make a wee cooking fire? Roast duck sounds mighty fine tonight!"

"Yes, but keep it low. We don't want to attract any attention."

"Aye, sir, we will. Me n' Hammy will make a roastin' pit, we'll just find some good stones ta line it." They clapped each other on the back and with watering mouths, made off looking for suitable-sized stones.

"Oh, attention everyone!" Turom announced. "Travel in groups and stay close in case there is trouble and keep the noise to a minimum." Everyone nodded in agreement.

"Gorim! Hamlin! Wait, I'll help," said Eramus, and he bolted off to join them. Tenise and Obedon dug a pit near the bank where it would be well out of sight. Smith and Lewatollma began gathering driftwood from nearby for the fire. Captain Turom walked up to Tenise and spoke quietly.

"Stay alert. Just because we haven't seen any Soulanders yet doesn't mean they aren't near. If there are any scouting parties still reconnoitering the area, they will most likely come this way to rejoin their forces."

Tenise smiled, saying, "Aye, sir, I'll keep my eyes open," and patting his hilt continued, "and my arms at the ready."

"Good man." Turom smiled back, squeezing Tenise's shoulder. "Tell the rest."

Tenise nodded in acknowledgment and moved to join the others. Turom looked at the Normen and the farmer, who had already wandered too far away to suit his tastes. He hoisted his crossbow higher and headed off to join them in a trot. He covered the ground quickly to join the three men, who were espousing the virtues of roast fowl along with Eramus throwing in his opinion about what would complement the meal. Turom came up close, hushing them, and was beginning to chide them about wandering off too far when a scream and the sound of clanging metal caused them all to turn suddenly toward camp.

They saw Lewatollma, Tenise, Obedon, and Smith surrounded by seven Soulander scouts. It was Tenise's scream they had heard, and he was falling to one knee hugging his sides. Lewatollma grabbed him by the collar and pulled him back out of the fray.

Eramus drew his sword and bolted toward his companions with the Normen right behind him. It seemed like time stopped and the distance between them was infinite. He saw Smith and Obedon felled by spear thrusts, their slumping bodies hacked and callously kicked aside.

The Soulanders did not seem sure what to do about the unarmed Lewatollma. The scouts looked at their leader, who pointed to his neck and then, pointing his sword toward Eramus, gestured for the remainder to attack. There were only thirty-five feet between Eramus and Lewatollma. The Soulander scout closest to her grabbed her by the arm and pushed her roughly to her knees.

Thirty feet. He put his foot on her leg, near the knee, and pulled her head back sharply by the hair. Lewatollma threw her arms backward to catch herself and her eyes widened in terrified surprise.

Twenty-five feet. The other Soulander touched his sword to her neck, then raised the blade high above his head.

Twenty feet. The Soulander was staring at Lewatollma's neck, preparing to strike the lethal blow.

Fifteen feet and five Soulander scouts separated Eramus from Lewatollma. Gorim and Hamlin were at Eram's side, axes in hand. Sudden panic filled Eram's breast as he thought: *I'm not going to make it*. His vision began to blur. But Captain Turom's eyes were clear as he let loose a bolt. The impact drove Lewatollma's executioner backward. The sword slipped from his grip as he grasped the shaft protruding from his chest.

The three men crashed through the Soulander scout line, the two Normen using the flat of their ax blades swung from the center outward to create a gap for Eramus. He stepped through, raising his blade high, made directly for the Soulander holding Lewatollma. Momentarily shocked, the Soulander recovered, then drew his knife and raising it high, began to plunge it downward toward Lewatollma's breast. Just inches above her face, Eram's blade flashed and caught the Soulander's arm near the wrist. Howling in pain and frustration, the Soulander jumped back from Lewatollma, his right hand dangling uselessly by a shattered bone and a few tendons, and went for his sword, scarcely drawing it in time to meet Eram's first blow. Swinging his sword double-handed over his head, Eramus knocked the blade out of his opponent's hand. The momentum of Eramus's attack sent the Soulander tumbling onto his back. Putting one foot on his chest, Eramus turned his sword downward using both hands and savagely drove his blade point . into the warrior's neck just above the collarbone.

Looking up, he saw three more Soulanders splashing their way downstream toward them. Eramus looked back to find Gorim and Hamlin facing the enemy, with just the three of them forming a small semi-circle around Lewatollma and Tenise. Eramus stepped backward to close ranks with them.

"Lewatollma, are you all right?" Eramus asked without looking back. He thought he heard a faint yes. Eight Soulanders growled quietly amongst themselves as they closed upon the remnants of Captain Turom's party. Turom landed close to Gorim as he sprang from his elevated position down to join the three men. He grabbed Obedon's sword and fell in beside Gorim. Hamlin spat at Turom, "Ya should've stayed back an' used yer bow!"

"I used both my bolts the best I could, but they were all I had," Turom panted.

The Soulanders encircled the little band and began to advance, but they stopped suddenly just a few short feet away. Eramus was puzzled as they looked distracted, but why? Then he, too, felt the earth tremble.

A mighty host was descending from the northwest, turning south toward the ford. In the front, a wave of pounding hooves churned the dust and caused the ground to quake. The main cavalry of the Fair Folk, fitted with their red battle leathers, approached.

Turom smiled and announced, "Our army is here!"

"The Fair Folk! The Fair folk!" cheered Gorim and Hamlin. Their exultant cries resounded in the air. The Soulanders frowned and pressed forward, snarling. It appeared they felt they had plenty of time to finish off this pocket of rabble before rejoining their forces.

Seizing the advantage, Gorim and Hamlin stepped out suddenly in a renewed attack. Hamlin caught a Soulander, who was looking over his shoulder, unawares, splitting him open from the collarbone to the colon with a single lightning swing of his ax. He tumbled backward with a grisly scream. Gorim blocked the spear thrust from another foe, forcing the shaft down into the ground with his left arm while using his right to smash the Soulander's face with the blunt end of his ax.

The air was again filled with the sound of metal biting into metal as the contest for their lives resumed, oblivious to the charge of the horse brigade heading their way. Grunts, curses, and the moaning of the wounded added to the din.

Eramus shielded himself from attack, using the flat of his blade to absorb the blows. A Soulander was swinging a short sword double-handed over his head, pummeling him with strong, rapid blows. He was breathing heavily through his fiercely clenched teeth, and Eramus could smell his fetid breath and feel his long dirty locks brush his arm as they rocked with each swing.

A dozen cavalrymen crested the ridge and charged down the long incline onto the plain. Upon reaching the bottom, they began their charge leaning low, their swords pointed earthward and to the rear in close quarters attack formation. Spreading out, they surrounded the Soulander party, trapping them between themselves and Captain Turom's company. It was only when the sound of the splashing of hooves pounding across the stream rose above the battle noise, that the Soulanders realized they had been flanked.

Surrender was not a virtue known to Soulanders. Raising their swords high, they screamed a hellish war cry, and like crazed savages, they lunged at their attackers. Gorim and Hamlin threw themselves into the fray, spilling as much Soulander blood as the cavalry would leave them. As the last Soulander fell, the Normen leaned on their axes for a few moments, caught their breath, then inspected each Soulander and hacked off the heads of any who were even remotely alive.

Eramus looked for Lewatollma. She was at Tenise's side using her hands to apply pressure to his wound. "Captain," she cried out, "he is still alive, but seriously wounded!"

The riders dismounted and one came forward, saluting and addressing Turom. "Sir, we should evacuate. There may be more scouts out here. We saw the scouting party that attacked you moving downstream earlier, and we were moving in to intercept, but we did not know you were here. You are most fortunate, indeed."

"What about the wounded?" asked Turom.

"We need to move now. We'll have to take a chance and move them on horseback. How many wounded, Captain?"

"Just one," Turom said grimly.

"Make that two, Sergeant!" called out one of the cavalrymen who was kneeling beside Smith.

"Avery, Corrin! You are the fastest riders — mount up! The rest of you, tie the wounded to their backs so they can get them to the medics!" Acting quickly, the soldiers put Smith and Tenise behind the riders and tied them securely with ropes. The moment they were done, they slapped the horses' flanks, sending Avery and Corrin racing away at a gallop. Two others carried Obedon and placed him across his saddle, securing him by his waist belt to the saddle's horn. Another man freed the wounded men's horses and strung them behind his horse. Everyone mounted their horses except for the two Normen who, determined to avoid riding double on horseback, were already slogging their way back up to the level plain.

Things had happened so quickly. Eramus tried to catch Lewatollma's eye, but she had her hood drawn over her head and was already moving her mount forward out of the floodplain. Eramus looked over the campsite, where the Soulander corpses lay strewn about. A chill seized him. A vision haunted him and would not abate: a wide-eyed, frightened face with a blade at her throat.

Taking a quick inventory of his men and horses, the sergeant signaled with a wave of his hand, and they all departed. The sound of snorting steeds and pounding hooves drifted off into the distance, and soon a peaceful quiet settled over the area. The sounds of water gurgling along its way were the only backdrop to the macabre scene.

A large black bird glided down to the sandbar. Nervously, it circled the bodies, watching cautiously for signs of movement. Soon another swooped down, while others took up position in nearby bushes and trees. Boldly, the first hopped forward, cocked a pitch-black eye at the nearest corpse, and stared unblinking for several seconds. Taking wing, it alighted on the dead man's chest and tore away a piece of loose muscle from his severed arm.

Throwing back its head, it gobbled the flesh down greedily. Two more glided in, black and silent, to join him.

The ebony carrion birds approached, their heads bobbing back and forth with each step. Today, a few gathered to dine. In the days to come, a numberless host would congregate and gorge themselves on the great feast laid out for them, here in this place of carnage that men had named in their honor.

THE FORGE

There is something sacred lost from a person when they slay another. A beautiful, childlike, and innocent part of them dies along with their victim.

– from Lewatollma's "Lament of Life"

Eramus was dancing with Miriam, holding both hands outstretched, spinning. He looked up to see her smiling at him. In her hair was a flower wreath he made for her. A great green field of grass spread to the horizon in all directions, the cloudless sky a brilliant blue. Miriam broke free from his one hand and reached out to a woman standing alone nearby. She entreated her to join them. They all clasped hands in a great circle and danced for a while, then Miriam broke free and took Eramus and the other woman by the wrists. Miriam smiled kindly at Eramus, then brought his hand and the hand of the other woman together and as their fingers touched, Eramus awoke.

"Miriam!" he croaked in a hoarse whisper as he sat up. The crackling of the nearby fire drowned out his weak cry. He blinked and looked around him. The morning was gray and damp. The day's first light was only just now pushing back the still night. Around him he saw the Normen tossing and turning, fighting off the chill autumn air. Lewatollma sat beside the fire, her cloak draped over her shoulders, her face concealed by its hood. She turned at Eram's rustling and inquired, "Sleep well?" Without waiting for his reply, she continued, "I did not!" and tossed a stick into the fire.

He gathered his blanket around his shoulders and moved to sit beside her.

"I should not be here. I should never have come here, Eramus. What happened yesterday was stupid, so very stupid! We almost got ourselves killed!" She spat out the words angrily and pulled her cloak closed, exposing just one delicate hand clutching the material between her breast and throat.

"Why did I let you talk me into this? I should have left Hares End and returned home without you! What was I thinking? Have I taken leave of my good judgment, to get involved in this insane bloodlust?" Her eyes were dark and angry, and she glared at Eramus.

"Don't be angry at Eram, lass," Gorim added, sitting up. "Yer still alive, not even a scratch on ya. It's just battle fear. It happens ta all a us. You'll get over it soon enough."

"I am not afraid!" she replied hotly.

"Right, an' I'm a fish!" Gorim answered sarcastically. They locked eyes for a long moment in a contest of wills, but the truth was on Gorim's side and Lewatollma retreated and looked away.

"So, I was right, eh? Heh! Give the farmer a break, girl, he's crazy fer ya, can't ya see? He can't help hisself. He wants ya around all the time. Not his fault the stupid Soulanders come up here makin' trouble raidin' his village an' such. He's jus' doin' what any man would do. Ya should be happy he wants ya so bad. Why don't ya go give him a big kiss an' stop yer fightin?"

Lewatollma quickly got up and left. Eramus glared hard at Gorim.

"What?" Gorim said, answering Eram's stare with his own. "Too early in the morning fer the truth? Don't set well on an empty stomach, eh?"

"I don't think you're helping much. Maybe the truth would be a little more palatable if we all had some food!"

"Food? Where's food?" Hamlin sat up suddenly. His hair was a wild tangle, a leaf poking out of his beard.

"'Ammy, there's no food! Go back ta sleep." The wild-haired Norman groaned and slumped back down onto the ground.

Eramus rose and went to find Lewatollma. The morning fog hid her from him, but he finally discovered her standing at the edge of camp staring northward. He slowed to a walk and moved cautiously to her side. He didn't dare look at her face. Her gaze remained fixed on the mists shrouding the forests beyond. Eramus glanced sideways; her arms were folded, not a sign that she was very receptive. He decided against putting his arm around her.

"What will you do now, Eram?"

"I haven't given it much thought. So much has happened lately, I just try to do my best as the moment presents itself."

"I have no business here. I must leave, and soon."

"I can't leave, not just yet. I must make sure that Hares End will be safe from the Soulanders. I am sorry to have placed you in such danger, and that idiot Gorim's right, I can't bear to be away from you. But if you stay in the camp, away from the battle, you'll be safe. Won't you please stay a while longer, until I can settle my debts here with the Fair Folk? Then we can leave together, and we'll go wherever you want."

"How long do you expect me to wait? Until they drop your maimed or dead body at my feet?"

"No! No more soldiering for me. I'll stay away from the battle. There must be something I can do to help, besides asking endless questions."

"This is all very bad business, Eramus. Do not expect me to linger here too long."

They both stared into the forest watching the mists become golden with the rising sun.

"Are you still angry with me?"

She sighed before saying, "No, just badly shaken from yesterday." She shook her head and looked earthward. "Poor Oberon, he died protecting me and there is nothing I can do to repay him!" Her hands went to her eyes and pushed away the tears. She turned and placed both her hands on Eramus's chest before burying her face there. Eramus put his arms around her.

"I think he would be gratified to know that we are here today to enjoy this beautiful sunrise."

Lewatollma turned her face eastward into the golden dawn.

"His sacrifice was not fruitless; it means life goes on for us," she softly intoned.

They watched the daybreak as the camp began to come to life.

"Speaking of life going on, are you hungry? I am."

"Eramus, only you could think about food during a moment of such deep personal reflection. Do you possess any driving force in your life that transcends the physical that is essential to keep your spirit alive?"

He pondered the question for a moment, searching his soul for an answer. At the time he didn't realize it, but the answer was right there in his arms.

Eramus volunteered to help build the fort. There had never been Soulander attacks of this magnitude in the past. Their forces would labor for a season and the battles would rage across the entirety of Ravens ford, but when the weather turned cold or the river rose, they simply retreated back to their own lands. This time, instead of tents and temporary shelters, stone buildings and an extensive support infrastructure was being established. Multiple bridges were being erected. He soon found himself, shovel in hand, digging a deep ditch and throwing up a protective embankment with several other men. Lewatollma wandered the camp, taking in the activity of everyone preparing to defend themselves against future hostilities.

Eventually, she found herself overlooking Ravens Ford. She moved to the west side of the tower, away from the muddy road where the weary and wounded trudged past the tense and anxious in a seemingly endless parade. The sight and sounds of the brutal conflict at the river's edge sickened her. She wandered along the edge of the steep embankment, away from the fighting. Stepping carefully, she descended to a lower ledge. To take her mind off the conflict, she focused on the Soulander encampment in the distance.

A large group of wagons approached from the west, bringing supplies. The Soulander camp bustled with activity. Teams of oxen hauled logs and pallets of fieldstone into staging areas for construction. Temporary shelters were being replaced with permanent structures. She could easily discern several barracks, a hospital, a kitchen with a messing area, and a slaughterhouse with adjoining holding pens. The fact that all the dwellings had one or more stone chimneys rising ahead of the walls told Lewatollma that the Soulanders were determined to see this campaign through the winter and probably much longer.

They were also busy building bridges to link the sandbars and islands that separated them from their goal. A network of multiple paths across the floodplain was beginning to take shape, clearly a prelude to a multi-pronged attack. Today the daily tally of wounded was half a dozen with just a few deaths. Once the Soulanders completed the bridges and began their full assault, those numbers would increase twenty-fold.

To her surprise, a tear ran down her cheek. She captured it with her finger and stared at it in disbelief. Once, Eramus had asked her if anything had ever put a shadow on her heart and at the time, she could think of nothing. There was nothing to which she could relate in her life. But now the idea of all these men killing and maiming each other, the anguish and suffering of the wounded, the bereavement of families deprived of a father, brother, son, or husband, hatred ignited to smolder in the breast of generations to come was overwhelming.

Melancholy seized her breast. How naive she had been. He was right, what a blissful, unspoiled life she had as a child; a stranger to suffering and grief! But now she was witness to a tragedy unfolding before her very eyes and worse yet, she was a part of it. For the first time since leaving home, she truly wished she had never left.

She couldn't fathom what would drive men to wreak such violence and destruction upon one another. What did the Soulanders need so desperately that they would travel great distances and kill others for it? She knew that over the ages, the prevailing southerly winds slowly shifted the poison from the Blue Desert to encroach upon their territory. They just needed fertile land and a safe place to live, but taking it by force was not the answer. There was so much land all around, why wouldn't the Fair Folk negotiate? Surely, something agreeable could be arranged and this senseless violence avoided. What would either side gain from bloodshed? What did all this prove? It all seemed madness to her.

"Go home," her voice called out faintly, carrying a note of sadness. "There is nothing here worth the price you will have to pay." She covered her eyes to blot out this depressing vision and suppress her tears.

A stirring in the thick underbrush below the ridge ended her inward reflections and brought reality back into sharp focus. She started to peer over the edge when suddenly, Soulander soldiers began to swarm over the embankment on both sides of where she was standing. She recoiled from them reflexively and almost lost her balance. The dense brush behind her cut off her escape; she was surrounded! Her head snapped left then right in rapid succession. Almost two dozen of them appeared out of the brush. They must have hidden during the night and then used the underbrush to conceal their approach, taking advantage of the tower's blind spot to avoid detection.

"Soulander attack!" she screamed in the direction of the tower. She could hear the alarm call sounding to her left — at least she was able to warn the men above. The raiding party glared at her, then charged up the hill except for two men with their short swords drawn, heading straight at her. Her last encounter with the Soulanders was vividly etched in her mind. They had shown no mercy before, and she expected none now. Neither was there any neutrality in this conflict. The first time, she was caught unawares thinking that an unarmed woman would be safe, and it nearly cost her life.

Suddenly, she recalled her mother and the last words she said to her: *Come home safe to me*. Now she exercised logic to overcome her instinctual nature of kindness and trust in civility. This time, she surrendered to her defensive training.

The melancholy that had overpowered her earlier was suddenly replaced by a surge of powerful, aggressive passion. Crouching, she shed her cloak and drew her dagger. Her eyes fixed on the nearest Soulander as her muscles coiled and her feet instinctively made themselves sure against the ground. With unbelievable speed, she exploded into the astonished warrior, her blade slashing upward, slitting his larynx and jugular deeply to the ear. Lewatollma bounded off her victim onto the back of the other Soulander. She rammed the long knife into his brain through the ear opening, then sprang away.

She landed gracefully in the same instant the first Soulander dropped to his knees, his hands trying in vain to abate the blood pulsing from his neck. The second crumpled to the ground, his entire body convulsing. Lewatollma was in a crouching position, muscles tensed, knife at the ready, and watched the two Soulanders' lives ebb away. The first fell forward onto his side and fixed her gaze with his dying eyes. He tried to breathe out a final curse, but only a gurgling sound and bright red froth came out of his mouth. She watched as his pupils dilated and his soul fled. She stared intently at the two lifeless forms, oblivious to the battle raging nearby.

The Fair Folk had engaged and defeated the remainder of the Soulanders' brazen attempt to reach the signal tower. Then they rushed down the hill toward Lewatollma. As the adrenaline rush that fueled her began to subside, Lewatollma's hands started to tremble and she teetered backward, falling softly onto her rump. She looked down at her blood-slick hands, shaking uncontrollably, and raggedly drew a great lung full of air. Her mouth dropped open and a long, horrible, piercing scream rang out. The soldiers coming to her aid stopped in their tracks and heads everywhere turned to see the source of such an anguished wail.

She reached behind her and seized her long hair in one hand and chopped it off near the shoulders with the bloody blade. Falling forward onto her hands and knees, a great mass of hair in her fist, she began again a lamentation of terrible anguish.

The soldiers near the tower were speaking in hushed tones when Eramus walked into the signal tower area. He had heard the commotion from a distance and was curious about the fuss. He was about to ask what had happened when he heard someone say, "It's a young woman." His blood ran cold, and he pushed his way through the men, calling out, "Lewatollma? Lewatollma!"

He looked about and saw several soldiers standing around three bodies. One soldier spotted Eramus and called out, "Over here!"

Eramus ran, his worst fears welling up from deep within. When he arrived, she was piling mud on top of her hacked-off hair, babbling in some unrecognizable tongue. He got down on his knees near her and called her by name. She did not respond but began to wail again and started to stab the earth with her blade. Eramus kept trying to get her attention, but without success. Finally, he grabbed hold of her dagger-wielding arm and pried the blade out of her fist. He then cupped her chin in his palm and raised her head.

"Lewatollma, it's me, Eramus," he said as gently as he could. There was no recognition in her wild eyes. Pulling her close, he tried to soothe her by saying, "Lewatollma, it's over, you're safe now." The babbling was now mixed with sobbing, but her body grew considerably less tense in Eramus's arms.

One of the soldiers behind Eramus said, "Get her out of here. This area is not secure." Then he barked orders to the other men, directing them to fan out along the ridge and search for more signs of the enemy. Additional men came running down the hill to strengthen the guard force.

Eramus turned her slightly and getting on one foot, sat her up on his knee. He shifted his weight, picked up Lewatollma, and carried her up the hill. Her head hung limply, cradled in Eramus's elbow. She looked back to see the dead Soulanders' eyes glaring at her. Her own eyes welled with tears, and she began to cry in earnest. Eramus pulled her closer, bringing her head onto his shoulder.

The camp doctor examined Lewatollma but could find no physical injury. Still, Eramus was deeply concerned and brought her to where he and the Normen had made a crude shelter from the elements. Eramus attended to her constantly. He cleaned her up, washing off mud and gore as well as he could. He was particularly saddened by the loss of her beautiful, long hair, something he had considered one of her best features. He didn't know what to make of the situation; the normally self-assured and lively woman was suddenly withdrawn and lifeless. He brought her food and water, but she refused them. Eramus slept beside her and held her in his arms through the chilly nights. During the day, he stopped by to check on her while helping to construct the fort. Her condition remained unchanged.

For three days, she would not speak, even though Eramus tried to coax her into a conversation. He even tried to reach her with a complete recital of his recipes for preparing kerrits. On the fourth night, Eramus noticed her cheeks were growing pale and she seemed constantly cold despite the extra blankets he wrapped her in. After trying unsuccessfully to force some food into her mouth, Eramus lay down beside her. Stroking her arms briskly with his hands, he tried to warm his silent and unresponsive friend.

"This is all my fault. I should never have asked you to come to this cursed place. You were almost killed by those hostile scouts and now this. Lewatollma, I am so sorry!" The tears began to blur his eyes, but he fought them back, for there was more he needed to say.

"Please come back to me, Lewatollma. I can't bear to have another soul I've loved die in my arms." He turned her so he could see her face. In the dark, he could barely make out that her eyes were open. Gently, his fingers caressed her face. He pushed her hair back, combing it as well as his clumsy fingers would allow. Shoving what was left of her dark hair over and past her ears, he put his face against hers, so his mouth was just a mere inch from her ear. He pressed his cheek against hers and rubbed it gently against her soft, cool skin.

"Don't leave me, not like this. How could someone as strong and courageous as you just fade away? When I first saw you in my fevered and disoriented state, I believed you were an angel. But after being with you, traveling the wilderness, spending nights around crackling fires, listening to your dulcet voice, I know you are. Listen to me! There must be something in your life worth living for. You only need to find it. Search deep in your wounded heart; that's where it's hiding. I thought I was dead until I met you. I believed that I was just waiting for my time. But it was you who helped me find that dim spark buried in my tired old heart — a spark called love. And you fanned that tiny ember, fueled it with your smile and gracious bearing so casually. And you were my friend, always. No matter how insufferable I was, you never failed me.

"Do you remember that night you found me down along the stream, sleepless and depressed? I considered you to be naive and foolish, but the reality is you were unfettered by sorrow, childlike and pure. I was the one who was a fool. I wish I could give that innocence back to you, I do. The past is fixed; there is nothing that can ever change it. But I will tell you this: Just as the past is the prisoner of time, time is the liberator of broken hearts. I learned this from you, and I want to thank you for that wonderful gift. It was there all the time, but you helped me see it. I shared my tragic past with you, and you were so right — a burden shared is only half as heavy. Share with me, Lewatollma. Let me return that gift to you as someone who desperately wants to be your friend and — as someone who loves you."

Then he embraced her and let the tears quietly flow. Slowly, a hand began to move in the dark. It rose cautiously and began to arch over the back of that grieving man. When just a fraction of an inch away, it paused, as if unsure it should continue. It hovered there while a great battle raged in the secret chambers of her heart. Hope wrestled against despair and trust grappled with doubt. Haltingly, her hand found its way down and her arm encircled Eramus and gently, almost imperceptibly, returned his embrace.

Eramus pulled back his head to gaze into her face. For the first time since that fateful afternoon, those dark eyes did not avoid him, nor were her features emotionless. Eramus kissed away the tears that trickled down her gaunt face.

"I am cold," she whispered.

Pulling away, he rose and wrapped her snugly in the blankets, then carried her close to the fire. He sat her down against the log that was their makeshift bench. Eramus stirred the fire and added more wood, sending the flames high into the night. Fetching his dinner pot, he set it on a stone near the fire's edge. His evening meal hadn't been touched except for what he tried to put into Lewatollma's mouth, and the spoon was still sitting there. He grabbed the waterskin from its perch and an extra blanket, then settled in behind Lewatollma and wrapped them together. He pulled her into his arms and cradled her against his shoulder. He brought the waterskin to her mouth, and she took a long, slow drink.

He leaned over slightly and stirred the gruel that was beginning to steam on one side of the pot. He fed her and they sat together silently before the fire. Stroking her hair and rocking her gently, he tenderly watched over her as she drifted off to sleep.

Lewatollma awoke gazing up into a sky filled with peaceful sheep grazing on a pasture of bright blue. Reflecting on the night before, she remembered how good the warmth of the fire felt on her face and the strange comfort of being held close in Eram's arms. So many feelings had stirred within her breast last night, and she was uncertain of many of them or what they meant. She recalled pushing away the blackest of those thoughts and replacing them with thoughts of home. She had closed her eyes and visualized her mother's face. Although she knew it was Eramus holding her, she allowed herself to dream she was in her mother's arms. Arms that had held her so many times as a child. Embracing a flood of warm memories, she had floated away her sorrows and fancied herself in a boat rocking gently in a harbor of love. It was those thoughts that brought a measure of peace, allowing her to slumber.

For now, the darkness in her soul had gone, but she was at a complete loss as to who she was. She was no longer the same; something had died within her along with the men she had killed. Their faces. That image was burned into her mind, and she struggled to banish it. *Time to think of something else,* she reasoned. She forced herself to sit up and found she was alone. The sun had risen long ago. There was a small pot of something sitting on the rocks beside a fire, which had now turned to a few coals amid a bed of ash.

Rising, she inspected the pot. Although it was greasy, Norman fare, she was ravenous and gave the actual content no further thought. It was still warm, and she devoured it quickly. Her body felt stiff, and she knew she needed to move. She had been prone too long, but how long? She could not be certain. She looked all around to observe that much had changed. She stretched her aching limbs and moved into the now-bustling fort.

Lewatollma wandered the hastily constructed fort overlooking Ravens Ford. She found herself at the stables outside the blacksmith's shop. She spied a water trough and approached it. Gripping the edge with both hands, she slowly pushed her head into the chilly water. She held it under for as long as she could, then finally pulled it out, taking in air with a harsh gasp. The water dripped all about as she looked at her distorted reflection. *What have I become?* she wondered. Her thoughts were interrupted by a hulking man wearing a heavy leather apron. In his hand, he wielded a dull red horseshoe with a pair of tongs.

"There are better places to clean up than that trough."

Startled, she jumped back and mumbled, "I am sorry."

The smithy stepped forward and plunged the iron into the water, which hissed and bubbled angrily. Lewatollma was wiping the water from her face and pulling her hair forward, wringing it out.

"That water isn't very clean. If you want to clean up, I can arrange something for you. The men aren't using the baths this time of day and my brother is in charge. He's a good man. He'll make sure no one bothers ya. You can have yer bath in safety and privacy. He can even have some hot water and soap for ya."

Lewatollma just stared at him. Although a huge man, he had a kindly face, his cheeks were round, and he had a pleasant expression. Lewatollma gazed into his face but said nothing. She just stood there dripping wet and shivering. The smithy pulled his work out of the trough and walked back to his shop. Lewatollma followed him with her eyes as he walked through the open door. Soon his hammer rang out with a rhythmic *ting-ting-ta-ting*. Lewatollma unconsciously stumbled toward the noise. She didn't know why she followed; she was just drawn there. From the doorway, she watched him work the forge bellows with one hand while arranging the coals with a poker in the other. Sparks flew into the air, and she could feel the blast of heat. Standing back, he wiped the sweat from his brow with the back of his forearm.

He saw her out of the corner of his eye silhouetted against the bright light outside. Her shivering had now changed to pronounced trembling. The smithy frowned, and his face reflected genuine concern. Then he asked her, "Are ya all right, miss?" But she still did not reply. Shaking his head, he stepped away from his work and grabbed a horse blanket from off the edge of a holding pen. Giving it a great shake, he knocked loose the dust and bits of straw from it, then he wrapped it around the miserable woman, adjusting it so it covered her head. Putting his arm behind her back, he guided her over to a wooden crate to one side of the forge.

"You sit right here and get dried off before ya get yourself sick. Whatever is wrong, not taking care of yerrself won't make it right."

He gently pushed her down onto the crate. She watched him return to his craft. Unconscious of time, she just watched him pump the bellows and hammer on the great anvil. She stared into the glowing coals, looking for something, but could not find it. An hour passed away in silence. Stopping for a break, he reached over and pulled a dipper from a pail of clean water and took a deep drink. He refilled the dipper and offered it to her. Accepting the metal dipper from him, she took a small sip and then watched him return to work.

A man came in through the door leading a draft horse by a rope halter. The great beast snorted and fidgeted as it entered the smith's shop.

"Hey, Robert, do ya have time to look at this animal's foot?" the man shouted out over the clamor of the hammer and anvil.

"Sure," the smith answered, shoving the iron piece back into the coals. "What seems to be the problem, Tom?"

"Aw, he lost a shoe and must a picked up a stone or sumpin'. We had him out pullin' stumps and noticed him favorin' his left front."

The smith went to the right side and tried to get the foot up to have a look. The horse started to dance around and fidget.

"Come on, boy, let me have a look; I'll make it right for ya," the smith tried to coax the beast, but it snorted and moved away.

"You're going to have to hold him still, Tom, or I'm not going to be able to help," Robert told him.

"I'm trying, but he's jittery and I don't think he likes me much anyway."

Lewatollma watched the men struggle with the beast for half a minute. The poor thing was in pain and frightened, something to which she could relate.

"Here, let me." Letting the blanket slip off onto the box, she rose and went to the animal's head, and taking the halter, she looked into his eyes. She talked softly to him and stroked his muzzle. Soon the horse quieted and let the smithy examine his hoof.

"Well, look at that," Tom said in amazement. "That's quite a helper ya got there, Robert. She has a real way with the beasts." He smiled as he scratched his head.

"Bring me those pliers," the smith said and motioned to his tools hanging on the wall. "There is still part of a nail here." Tom complied and the smith removed the troublesome piece of metal from the hoof.

"There, that's better, let me clean out that hoof a bit and get a new shoe on him, then he should be ready to go, Tom." The men chattered while Robert gathered up his knives and files. The smith cleaned and filed the great hoof, then found a shoe about the right size and shaped it in his forge to suit the horse. In no time, the job was done and putting her cheek against his muzzle, Lewatollma bid the animal goodbye.

Robert watched the woman carefully. She followed the horse to the doorway and watched silently as he was led away.

"Thankee for the help, miss. Old Tom is right, you have a way." Lewatollma neither moved nor responded. He turned to tend his forge. Working the bellows, he sent a great spray of sparks into the air. Looking back, he saw Lewatollma staring at him.

"Ya know, I could use a helper in here. I get half a dozen horses every day. But holding the beasts is only part of the job. I'll need water and wood carried, the holding stalls cleaned, and a hundred other tasks. It's not traditionally a woman's job, but I'm offerin' it to ya anyway 'cause ya have a gift. Even if ya can't do everythin', it'd be that much less I would have to do m'self. If ya work hard for me, I'll spot ya yer mess chit. What do ya say then, are ya game?"

Lewatollma chewed on her lower lip for a moment, then asked in a quiet voice, "You do not care that I am a stranger?"

"As long as yer hard-working, I don't care what ya are," he said plainly. She nodded in agreement. "Good," he said, "be here an hour after sunup."

Smiling faintly, Lewatollma gently said, "You have been very kind to me and I thank you." Turning, she exited the building and wandered away.

Before returning to the forge, he shook his head and expressed his concerns out loud, "There's something very wrong there." He wondered who she was and what she was doing here at camp. She was preoccupied, but with what? Had she lost a loved one so early in the conflict? Was it fear? Or was it just the horror of it all? Maybe it was all of those things. But whatever the circumstances, she was lost and looking for something, of that much he was certain. He had seen the empty, hurting eyes of lost souls before.

RETURN

"Far to the north of the eastern farming villages lies a vast lake called Coldmere. Its waters are deep and icy. If you were to ask the Normen, they would say it is bottomless. The weather can be capricious. Sudden storms can arise with fierce winds and torrential rain, when just a few hours before, the water was as smooth as glass. The few brave souls who venture out to fish never lose sight of the shore, for fear of never returning home again."

– Lord Pascal Toussant Donatina

Lewatollma enjoyed working at the blacksmith's shop. As they had put it earlier, she "had a way" with animals. They were open and plain to read, which she found healing to her soul in her service to those who had no voice. Her nature was one of gentleness and patience, something the animals could sense instantly. The work at times was demanding and dirty. Robert presented her with a set of coveralls — a curious combination of pants with a shirt front, but no back. It was a little larger than she would have liked, but perfect for cleaning stalls and other grimy chores. She exchanged her cloak for coveralls while she worked, leaving the coveralls behind at the end of the day hung neatly on a peg on the wall.

Things were at relative peace during those times, working during the day and joining Eramus and the Normen at night for a meal and a little conversation before they dropped off quickly to sleep. Eramus was employed building a picket that cordoned off the entrance to Ravens Ford and construction within the fort. The Normen cut trees and fashioned platforms, towers, and various structures for the fort. Eramus spent his time digging deep footings for the picket as well as barricades and trenches. The cool autumn nights were pleasant, and the days were still warm when the sun shone down upon them.

The peace, though, was not to last. One evening, the night was broken by the howling of Soulanders attempting to breach the picket and force their way into the fort. All that night, the battle raged on and although they were well to the rear of the battle, the sound pierced the night and was inescapable.

Lewatollma barely slept, reacting to every sudden outburst. Her eyes shot open, and her mind puzzled about the meaning and origin of each sound until she could convince herself she was in no danger. As if that weren't enough, nightmares plagued her, replaying horrifying moments in excruciating detail. Several times, she awoke shaking and breathing raggedly, laboring to assure herself it was only a dream and to regain control.

Shortly before dawn, the Soulanders retreated, and the fort settled into a near-normal pattern of life.

Dutifully, Lewatollma arrived for work at the appointed time. Robert was already hard at work, but in addition to the usual complement of work animals, a pile of weapons had formed outside: bent and broken blades, armor dented and pierced. With morbid fascination, she stepped closer and picked up one of the broken swords. She carefully examined the edge, which was nicked throughout from striking something sharp, most likely another blade. It was dull in other places, the edge flattened and useless. The tip had been snapped off and it was altogether filthy. Upon closer examination, she found bits of cloth, hair, and small chunks of flesh caught up in the nicks.

Shuddering, she let it drop back into the pile with a loud clang. Turning, she nearly walked into Robert.

"We'll get to those later. First, let's get these animals ready. Start bringin' 'em in, girl."

Opening the pen, she grabbed the reins of a strong, lean mare that was avoiding the use of her front left leg. Gently, she lifted the leg and inspected the hoof. Unsurprisingly, she found a piece of metal jammed underneath. She let the leg down, patting her on the neck. "We will have that out before you know it. Come along, my beauty."

Robert was continually amazed by Lewatollma's skill with the animals. It seemed as if they had known each other all their lives. The morning passed quickly, and the animals were finished after a couple of hours.

"Start bringing me the blades now — try to match up the broken parts the best ya can. Some I'll be able to re-forge; others I can use fer scrap."

Grabbing three of the least-damaged weapons, she brought them to Robert. Taking the first, he looked it over and told her,

"This only needs a good sharpening. Do ya know how to use a grinding wheel?"

"No, I do not."

"Are ya willing to learn?"

Looking at the weapon, she realized by repairing it, she was only contributing to more death and destruction. Taking a step backward, she informed Robert, "I cannot be a part of this any longer, for it is crushing my soul. I am sorry, you have been so kind to me and now I feel I must bolt like a frightened animal. I do not even know which way to turn, but I cannot stay any longer."

She turned to go but Robert spoke up, stopping her. "Yer the one I've heard stories about, aren't ya? The woman caught in a sneak attack who killed two Soulanders." Shaking his head, he continued, "Terrible thing, war is. No place fer a woman, no, not at all. The whole thing sickens me, I can hardly imagine what it's done to ya, but clearly nothing good. Ya do what ya must to keep your soul — you'll not get another."

Looking back over her shoulder, she mouthed a thank-you and slowly walked away.

Using the back of his arm, Eramus swept the sweat from his face before plunging the shovel into the red clay of the pit he and twenty-two other men were turning into a bulwark. Hearing someone call his name, he looked up to find Lewatollma standing on the edge of the pit. Wringing her hands, she looked about anxiously, her face a mixture of fear and confusion.

Without even looking directly at him, she addressed him in a halting voice, "Eramus, I cannot stay any longer."

"Lewatollma, if you could just..."

Turning to face him, she screamed, "No!" She recovered, and her voice changed and suddenly sounded hollow and desperate. "Eramus, I am dying here! I can feel it in my very soul. Every cry of mourning or anguish penetrates my heart like a jagged blade!" The tears began streaming down her face as she lifted her hands in front of her eyes. "And with these hands, my very own hands, I have been a partaker of this madness!" Her mouth hung open for a long moment, but she could not articulate the words to adequately express her anguish. Drawing in a shaky breath, she turned abruptly and hurried away.

"Wait!" he cried as he jammed the shovel into the dirt and clambered out. Running, he caught up with her. "I'm coming with you. If you will pack up our camp, I will go get our horses."

She shook her head softly. "There is nothing here I wish to retain, and I wish I could leave these horrific images in my mind here, but they are part of me now. Like a bitter, painful wound that will not heal." She paused to wipe her face dry before continuing, "Get the horses. I will meet you at our camp."

It was all Eramus could do to persuade her to wait until the morning to leave, but departing without bidding Hamlin and Gorim farewell turned out to be the winning point. They enjoyed one final meal with them and discussed each other's plans. The Normen had decided to stay. The work was good and there was nothing to do in the long, cold winter of the north country. They had become important resources in the harvesting of timber and construction. Gorim was smitten by one of the nurses, who beyond all understanding, seemed to care for him as well. The endless bounty of the mess hall was Hamlin's love, so they both were content to remain.

The villagers from Hares End had been trickling in, arriving with small bands of Normen for protection. Sheron had not yet arrived and Eramus worried for her and Little Miriam. But it was also possible she moved to Piney Grove to be with her son, so Eramus laid that concern to rest and focused on Lewatollma.

That night, another fierce battle raged, keeping Lewatollma in a state of fitful sleep; she started at every loud noise or cried out in disturbing dreams. As soon as the sun touched the horizon, Lewatollma and Eramus were on their way north. He tried to involve her in conversation, but she was sullen and refused to engage with him.

They rode all day, stopping only briefly for the horses' benefit and a small bite of food. The nights were damp and cold, so they huddled for warmth, but sleep was nearly impossible. Often Lewatollma would weep, cry out, or moan pitifully. Eramus did his best to comfort her by pulling her close and holding her.

Once, she suddenly sat up screaming at the top of her lungs, then leaped to her feet and paced around frantically. When Eramus came up behind her and tried to put his arm around her to calm her, she reacted violently, throwing him easily to the ground, knocking the wind out of him. In the dark, he could see her glaring at him, knife in hand. For a long moment, she just stood there breathing heavily. Finally, she managed a tearful, "Don't!" then turned and wandered off into the woods. It was several minutes before Eramus regained his wind, then he climbed back into his bedroll. In the distance, he could hear her softly weep but he stayed put, reasoning that if she needed him, she knew where to find him.

The next morning, he found her curled up in a ball next to him, wrapped tightly in her cloak. Quietly as he could, he got up and rummaged through his backpack for breakfast. When he turned, she was right behind him, cloak drawn tightly around her, hood up.

"Some breakfast?" he asked as he offered her some food.

"No," she replied quietly, then retrieved her saddle, went to her horse and began preparing to ride. Five minutes later, she mounted and started away. Eramus quickly did the same.

Two long days' ride brought them within sight of Coldmere's shores, where they followed the road until they reached Fishers Port. The last day was one of a chilling, gray drizzle that kept them in perpetual twilight, making Lewatollma's mood seem even bleaker. The blazing lights of the settlement were a welcome sight as Eramus and Lewatollma rode slowly in on the evening of the last day. Lewatollma departed to report to her captain, assuring Eramus she would have both a warm bed and food. He was disappointed that she did not even brush cheeks with him, but he kept it to himself and hoped for better days. Eramus made his way to an inn, where his money from Miricel went far in getting him a nice dinner and a comfy bed.

Lewatollma's meeting with Captain Emunihus was brief. She summarized all that happened since she left just over a week ago. Emunihus asked her to surrender her blade, then informed her there would be a hearing in the next few days and she was to remain in her cabin at all times except to mess, perform ablutions, and report when summoned.

Nothing in this surprised her; it was identical to the process Nesneratha related regarding her hearing. What surprised her was that she managed to give her report without breaking down and crying. Soaked to the skin, she felt numb and very tired. Despite having promised Eramus she would eat, she found no appetite within her, so she made straight for bed.

Her cabin, which she shared with another woman, was small. Her roommate was out on a survey mission and was due to return before winter had set in hard. Doffing her clothes and miskinir, she pulled a warm sleeping outfit from her drawer and put it on. Then she climbed into the top bunk, rolled herself up in the blanket, and closed her eyes, trying not to think of anything. The exhaustion, warmth of her bed, and stillness around her swept her quickly away into a deep, dreamless sleep.

The next morning, she arose, changed into a fresh outfit, and made her way quietly to the officers' mess. There were few there and she quickly grabbed a few things, put them on her tray, and made her way to a small table in an alcove, far from everyone else.

"Well, if it is not my dear friend Lewatollma," Nesneratha quipped, placing her tray daintily on the table and sitting directly across from her. Looking up, she began, "And how are you this..." Her question was cut off by a startled gasp. "Your hair! What has happened!"

"Nothing good," Lewatollma replied dismally while picking at her breakfast. Dropping her spoon in disgust, she pushed the tray to one side. Nesneratha put her hand atop her friend's and leaned forward to try to catch her eye. But Lewatollma avoided looking directly at her. Finally, she cupped Lewatollma's chin in her hand and forced her to look at her. Nesneratha searched her face and was shocked by what she found.

"Oh, my dear Lewatollma, a part of you has died! I can see it! Why did this happen to such a gentle soul as you?" Nesneratha's eyes welled with tears as she dashed around the table to embrace her friend. Nesneratha took her gently into her arms and held her close. Then she whispered into her ear, "Whoever did this to you will feel my wrath and my blade. I swear!"

"There is nothing to avenge, Nesneratha. I am the offender. I spilled two men's blood and now I am undone! I am so lost and confused that I cannot find my true feelings any longer. I am empty and numb. I want to go home and be with my mother. I wish I could crawl back into her womb and start my life over again!"

"I am here for you, my dear one. Anytime you need or want to have companionship, come see me."

"I am on restriction until after the hearing, and honestly, I am not in the mood for companionship." Lewatollma pushed her away to see her face.

"I have a kindness to ask of you, though, one you may disapprove of, so bear with my request. Would you please go into town, find Eramus, and let him know I am well, but it may be some time before I can meet with him again?"

Nesneratha's eyes flashed angrily. "Eramus! He is here?!" she erupted, hiding neither her disapproval nor her contempt. "If he has had a part in your undoing, I will destroy him! I had warned him — warned you both, in fact — of the foolishness of cultivating a relationship, but now I will hold him fully accountable! He shall—
"

Lewatollma silenced her by putting her finger to Nesneratha's lips. "Do not confuse my choices for his. Perhaps we both were foolish, perhaps it is just how circumstance has played out in our lives but if not for Eramus, you would be crying over my cadaver today instead. Promise me you will be kind to him or promise me you will stay away from him. He has borne suffering through this as well, so I feel it unjust for you to heap your wrath upon his hurt, and I care for him too much to send you to him with revenge in your heart."

"Lewatollma, what have you done?" Nesneratha begged as she took both of her hands in hers. "Do you not comprehend the folly of this relationship? You and Eramus can never be one — your parents, our society, will never permit it! Allow me to convince him to return home or let me drive him away, for both of your sakes, please, Lewatollma?"

Squeezing her hands tightly, Lewatollma persisted, "Do you promise?"

"How can I allow myself to be a participant in what can only yield heartache and suffering for my friend?"

"Will you deliver my message? That is all I ask, with your oath to be gentle and kind."

Nesneratha dropped her head and shook it woefully. "Very well, I promise. But I object to your course of action."

Lewatollma took her into her arms. "Objection noted. Thank you. I must return to my room now. Will you meet me here for dinner with his reply?"

"If I find him, yes," Nesneratha agreed reluctantly. "I have duties I must attend to first that limit me to the ship. Later today I will go to look for him." Lewatollma rose, took her tray and deposited it with the other dirty trays, and departed the mess solemnly.

Nesneratha watched her leave and then returned to her seat to stare at her food. After a while, she took the fork in hand and began to tap rapidly on the edge of her tray while looking thoughtfully into space. Suddenly, she viciously speared a bit of food from her plate and held it before her eyes. "Eramus," she muttered, then snatched the food off the fork with her teeth and chewed it slowly, deliberately.

Eramus pulled his jacket close around as he wandered out toward the docks where Lewatollma's ship was berthed. He had waited here earlier that morning but had seen no sign of her. That morning, several Nawiman milled about conducting business, and two large Nawimans stood guard at the gangway. He returned to the inn's meager dining area and waited, hoping she might join him for lunch. The time for lunch came and went without a trace of his friend. He left and walked the length of the town, poking his head into the shops, inns, and taverns. Canvassing one side of the street, then reversing his course, he perused the other side.

Now he leaned against a post mindlessly looking out at the lake, the sun behind him sinking beyond the trees. He heaved a heavy sigh and turned back toward the inn. He watched his feet plod through the muddy street as he made his way slowly back. Ahead of him, someone was headed directly his way. He stepped aside to avoid colliding, but the stranger, a Nawiman, hood up and walking purposefully, changed course as well, directly toward him. Eramus stopped and tried to see who it was. His heart leaped, and he started briskly toward her, smiling with relief. When he was but five paces away, she pulled back her hood, stopping Eramus in his tracks. It was not Lewatollma, and his last encounter with this particular person had not been entirely civil or pleasant.

Nesneratha stopped directly in front of him and with a forced smile asked, "Eramus, might I have a word with you?"

Eramus considered saying, *If you're going to kill me, be quick about it*, but decided to use a more cautious approach. "I was about to return to the inn for dinner."

"That is most generous of you! It would be so much more comfortable inside. I would be delighted to accompany you!" She held out her arm for him to take. Her smile was quite artificial and to Eramus's thinking, ominous.

Cautiously, he extended his elbow and let her put her arm in his, then silently led her to the inn. Once inside, he selected a small table near the crackling fireplace and signaled Gangby, the innkeeper. Nesneratha sat across from him, smiling, hands folded on the table. The innkeeper approached, wiping his hands on his filthy apron.

Beaming a great smile, he asked, "What'll it be, good sir?"

"What have you put on for dinner tonight, Gangby?" Eramus asked.

"Oh, tonight ya be in fine luck, sir, we 'ave roast goose wi' taters an' cabbage."

Eramus glanced at Nesneratha, who then smiled at Gangby, saying, "That sounds wonderful! How thoughtful of you to prepare such a magnificent feast. We are most fortunate indeed!"

"Well, then, I'll be fixin' yer platter right quick! What will ye be drinkin'? Ale?"

"Yes, two ales, please," Nesneratha jumped in before Eramus could respond. He leaned back in his seat and regarded her with unmasked concern as Gangby sailed away.

"You're frightening me, Nesneratha. First, you are uncharacteristically nice, then you order an ale, which I seem to recall you despise! What is it you're up to?"

"The ale — despite its horrid taste — is safer to drink than the water and..." She paused to draw a deep breath through her nose. "I am being nice because Lewatollma made me promise to be kind to you," she responded with the same forced smile. "As to what I am up to, Lewatollma asked me to tell you she is well, but it may be some time before she can meet with you again."

Eramus heaved a sigh. "I'm glad she's well. She had me worried."

Nesneratha scoffed. "I did not say she was well. I only said she asked me to tell you she was well." Nesneratha folded her arms across her chest and the blissful facade evaporated instantly. "She is, in fact, not well. She is depressed, not eating, on restriction, and suffering from some deep emotional trauma. She told me little of what happened, but what little she did relate was disturbing." Her eyes narrowed as she leaned forward, and with a cold, piercing stare, she spoke carefully in a quiet, but menacing tone. "I also suspect you had some part in this disaster. What have you done, Eramus?"

At that moment, Gangby set down two tankards of ale before them. Leaning back, Nesneratha folded her hands in her lap, turned, and gave the innkeeper a great smile. Gangby returned the smile, nodded, and turned toward the kitchen. No sooner than he had turned his back, the icy stare resumed.

"Well? What do you have to say for yourself, Eramus?"

"I didn't do anything to Lewatollma. We were attacked by Soulanders!"

"And where did this happen?"

"Ravens Ford."

"Why was she there?"

"She was with me, Hamlin, and Gorim. We were scouting the area along the Emmering with a few soldiers when we left Hares End."

"Soldiers?"

"Yes. After Hares End was attacked..."

"Attacked?! Did you take her knowingly into danger? Did she go willingly into a potential conflict with such a pathetically small party? Whose idea was that?!"

Eramus reflected for a moment on how hard he had to work to convince her to join them, then he dropped his eyes to avoid looking at his inquisitor.

"Let me guess," Nesneratha continued. "You and..." and she leaned in, lowering her voice to a near-whisper and spat out, "...two bone-headed Normen..." Then returning to her previous position and volume, she continued, "…cajoled her into accompanying you on this insane excursion."

Eramus did not respond.

"If you had let her alone and not courted her as I counseled you…"

"Threatened, actually," Eramus muttered.

"…this never would have happened! Do not think I do this on some jealous or mean-spirited whim! You two can never be together. The only possible outcome is heartbreak, pain, and misery for both of you." She leaned toward him, took his hands in hers, and with a soft, gentle voice pleaded, "If you love her, Eramus, if you truly care about her happiness, forget about her and return to your home. Please?" Eramus looked her in the eye but remained quietly resolute.

After a long moment, Nesneratha continued, "Do you want me to beg? Is that what you want from me? To see me grovel. To see me prostrate myself before you? Because for Lewatollma, I would." She then got down on her knees and with genuine tears asked again, "Please, Eramus, go. For both your sakes?"

Eramus shook loose from her grip and said firmly, "It will work out. We will be fine and happy. You wait and see."

Nesneratha let her head fall against the table with a dull thud. She raised it slightly and banged it against the table twice more. She sat there silently for a few more moments, then rocked back on her haunches and wiped the tears from her face with her sleeve. Heaving a heavy sigh, she arose, took a deep breath, straightened her clothes, and started slowly away. But after two steps, she stopped, pivoted quickly, grabbed the mug of ale off the table, and gulping noisily, drained it. The mug came down hard on the table, a breathy "Ahhh!" escaping her mouth. Then flipping her hood up, she turned and left.

Gangby arrived with a platter of mouth-watering food and set it down as if it were a masterpiece. Eramus watched through the steam rising from the half goose, cubed potatoes, and mounds of cabbage, as Nesneratha departed.

"Will she be joining ya, sir?"

"No, she will not," Eramus replied slowly.

"That be too bad. She were a tidy lass wi' a fetchin' smile. Ahh, don't worry, lad, there be more ducks in the pond," Gangby commiserated, putting his hand on Eramus's shoulder as a sort of consoling gesture, while simultaneously extending the other hand palm-up for payment.

Eramus took three coins from his purse and dropped them into the plump, callused hand of the innkeeper, then muttered, "Not like that one, I hope!"

LOST AND FOUND

"I have acquaintances who have experienced trauma that alters their psyche. I have waited patiently for their former selves to return, but the truth is, it is gone. They have changed and to continue a relationship requires us to accept that change as well."

– Nesneratha

Nesneratha found Lewatollma sitting in the mess with her back to everyone. Setting her tray down lightly, she sat opposite her.

"Have you eaten already?" Nesneratha inquired.

"No, I have not."

"Have you eaten anything today?"

"A little."

"*Very* little, I suspect. Go get yourself a tray and stop moping," Nesneratha responded, then popped a piece of raw vegetable into her mouth and began slowly chewing.

"I am not hungry, Nesneratha."

Finishing her mouthful, she wagged her fork at Lewatollma, saying, "You know you must have sustenance."

"Very well." Lewatollma sighed, picked a bit of food off Nesneratha's tray, and popped it into her mouth. She quickly chewed and swallowed it. "There. Happy?"

"No. You will need much more than that. Go get yourself a tray — or do you want me to get you one, set you in my lap, and feed you by hand?"

"You seem to be unable or unwilling to accept that I am not hungry."

"No, I understand it perfectly. I also understand you are depressed, feeling sorry for yourself, and pouting like a denduin ordered to mop the floor while everyone else is doing something exciting. Perhaps some good news will perk up your appetite. I found Eramus a short while ago. In fact, I have come here directly from meeting with him."

"And?"

"And I will tell you the rest after you get some food and start eating." Nesneratha smiled back.

"You think you are clever," she sneered.

"No, I know I am clever. I also know you are not leaving here until you eat. As I see it, you have three choices: Feed yourself, have me feed you, or be escorted to the doctor, where I will report your self-destructive behavior — and you know where that will lead."

Angrily, Lewatollma pushed her chair away from the table and went to the galley. Upon returning, she slammed down her tray, plopped into her chair, and began to eat.

This behavior, atypical of Lewatollma, caused Nesneratha deep concern. Several questions and conjectures crossed her mind, but she decided not to express them aloud, so she began as promised.

"I met with Eramus at Gangby's inn and relayed your message in its entirety. He seemed relieved to know you were well. I then informed him of your actual state, asked him a few questions, and then left. It was a truly short exchange."

"You were kind?"

"Yes — well, mostly — but I did not varnish the truth. Nor did I withhold my opinion. I also begged him on my knees to leave and forget about you." Choking up, she continued, "I poured out my whole heart, but he did not give my plea the least consideration." Taking a deep breath, she cleared her throat. Regaining composure, she continued, "You can visit him and discuss it further after your hearing — provided you are not put on restriction. At least you have time to consider your actions until the hearing is over."

"The hearing was earlier this afternoon. In terms of probation, I am restricted to Fishers Port and am not allowed off the vessel from sundown to sunup. I have also received extra duty as a disciplinary measure."

"Why so severe?"

"It would seem that meddling in the affairs of the indigenous population is not looked upon favorably." Then she rattled off the charges without the least bit of emotion. "Encouraging and participating in armed conflict, reckless confrontation resulting in loss of life, fraternizing with a native, dereliction of duty, disobeying a direct order, conduct unbecoming an officer, and several other lesser charges consequential to the former infractions."

"They did not bring any charges against us for our involvement with the ghouls. Why so harsh now?"

"In and of itself, that incident was not of grave concern. Our only real offense was limited fraternization, and in consideration for improving relations, that was dismissed and all we received was a verbal reprimand. In light of this second event, I have, and I quote, 'demonstrated a pattern of disregard for rules intended to ensure the safety of personnel, harmonious interaction with indigenous cultures, and conduct reflecting positively on Emallinawiman society.' All of this I can accept without argument, but there is one final punitive measure that remains. I am to ensure Eramus returns home."

"It is the right thing to do, Lewatollma."

Her demeanor darkened visibly, and in a low, angry voice she stated, "Nothing would make you happier, would it? To see Eramus humiliated. Oh, how sweet a moment you would be savoring. Your disdain for him being justified and gratified. Perhaps you would like to throw some decayed vegetables at him as well when they cart him away!"

Nesneratha rose, placed both her hands on the table, leaned forward, and with a stern look, replied, "He. Saved. My. Life. The only thing I disapprove of is this relationship you have cultivated — it is madness! You know how this will end! You have only yourself to blame. You had so many opportunities to end it, but would you heed my counsel? No, you let your emotions sweep you away. Did you have fun stringing him along? Did it gratify your vanity? It was so easy, was it not? What a disgraceful display..."

Nesneratha had unwittingly fanned the smoldering anger of her friend, and it suddenly burst into a conflagration of uncontrolled fury, catching Nesneratha completely by surprise. Lewatollma's lightning reflexes and superior motor control allowed her to execute it in one blindingly swift motion. She swept Nesneratha's arms from beneath her with one hand, grabbed her by the hair of her head with the other, and slammed her face violently into her plate. Then she rose, turned, and strode unhurriedly out of the mess hall, avoiding eye contact the entire way, barely able to contain herself.

Alone in her room, she grabbed the edge of the upper bunk with both hands and leaned her head against it. She reflected on what she had just done and struggled to understand why she responded with such venomous violence. She recalled what Nesneratha said and the outcome of the hearing. She wondered how Eramus was doing, and how she could make herself do what must be done. These events and questions began to swarm in her mind, and she became overwhelmed with unrelenting stabs of anxiety, guilt, sorrow, and love — one after another, or all at once — she could not tell. Grabbing the blanket off her bed, she wrapped it around herself and sat on the floor.

Hugging her knees to her chest, she shut her eyes and rocked slowly to quiet her mind. The toll of this war of emotions began to manifest itself outwardly and she began to tremble uncontrollably. Terrible images flashed through her mind: a man cursing her noiselessly through blood-smeared snarling lips, sticky blood covering her hands, spattered on her clothes and face. Her head yanked back, and cold steel pressed upon her throat, a frightened and anguished face as life ebbed from a sword wound to the chest.

"No! It is too much!" she screamed, then sank her teeth into her arm fiercely and held fast for many minutes until the only thing she could feel was her throbbing arm. Releasing her arm, she fell back against the wall, panting in ragged breaths. Conjuring up images of her mother, she soothed herself remembering her warmth, her scent, a kiss upon her cheek, her hair being lovingly stroked, and let it lull her to sleep.

The harsh banging of a fist on her door obscenely ended her slumber. Wrestling with the blanket that ensnared her, she broke free and answered the door. An irritated spetcinmal regarded her coldly, informed her she was late for duty, then strode quickly away.

Gathering her wits, she quickly doffed yesterday's outfit and put on a fresh one-piece work suit. Smoothing her hair, she dashed out the door. She reported to the officer of the mess, who looked her over in disgust, scoffed, then said, "The entire messing area floor needs to be swept and mopped, but wash all the tables first, including the pedestals and feet. Carry — do not drag — the tables to one side of the room, and clean half the floor. Carry — do not drag — the tables to the other side of the room and clean the rest of the floor. Redistribute the tables as they are now but do not drag them. Be quick about it. The next meal will be served in a little less than an hour. Do you understand?"

"Yes, sir."

"Report to me when you are finished. Now move it!"

Lewatollma retrieved a rag and a bucket of warm, soapy water and set to work. Coming to the table she shared with Nesneratha last night, she found several small blood splatters and blushed deeply with shame. She did not realize how much she injured her arm until she picked up the first table and painfully carried it out of the way. Mopping proved equally painful. Passing a reflective surface, she caught a look at herself. Wild hair sticking out at obscene angles and a dirty, tear-stained face. Wetting the end of her sleeve with saliva, she cleaned her face, then tried in vain to smooth down her hair.

She finished the floor just as the first few crewmen appeared. The officer of the mess assigned her to assist the steward in setting out food and stacking trays and utensils. When people finished eating, she had to retrieve dirty dishes and clean them.

Near the middle of the shift, she heard Nesneratha's voice from a table near the back. Looking around quickly, she chanced to leave her post to go and apologize to her. Nesneratha was bent over a bowl of soup and did not look up when she approached.

"I am so sorry, Nesneratha. I do not know what came over me last night, and..."

Another female crewmember interrupted as she sat across from Nesneratha saying, "Good morning, Nesneratha. Why did you cut your hair?"

Lewatollma had not noticed, but she had indeed cut her hair to shoulder length.

Without looking up from her soup, Nesneratha replied, "I am mourning the death of a friend."

Gasping, the woman across from her said, "I had not heard of anyone passing away. Who was it?"

"Well, she is not dead in the mortal sense. Her body is still around, but her beautiful, gentle soul has perished," Nesneratha replied, then looked up and glanced at Lewatollma.

Both the crewmember and Lewatollma gasped. Nesneratha's nose was badly swollen, dark bruises had formed below her eyes spreading across to her left cheekbone, and her lower left eyelid was swollen, as was her split upper lip.

"What happened?!" the woman across from her blurted out.

"I would rather not talk about it."

Lewatollma left immediately to return to her post, her stomach in knots. She spent the rest of the shift silent, eyes down, keeping to herself.

Shortly after she returned to her quarters, a sharp knock sounded on her door. She opened it to find two strapping crewmen.

In a curt and coldly unemotional tone, she was told the executive officer had summoned her to his office.

"May I have a moment to put on my uniform?" she inquired.

"Yes. But be quick about it."

Attempting to close the door, she found it blocked by a boot. Looking up, all she found was a stern face. The crewman turned his back to the door, but his heel was firmly planted in the doorway. Lewatollma grabbed a fresh uniform and changed behind the door, well out of sight. She was steered to Commander Prasillus's ready room with an escort close on each side.

The door was open when they arrived, and they entered immediately. The crewman on her left said, "Sir, Minminuma Lewatollma as requested."

Leaning back in his chair, Prasillus said, "Thank you. You are dismissed but remain posted outside and please close the door behind you." To the left of his desk sat the doctor, an older woman, Juwimla — her grandchildren were Lewatollma's age. Doctor was one of the few positions occupied by someone so senior in age to the crew. She sat serenely with her legs crossed at the ankle and her hands folded in her lap.

"Minminuma Lewatollma, you are acquainted with a fellow crewman Under-Lieutenant Nesneratha — I believe you served with her on your first scouting mission?" Prasillus asked calmly.

"Yes, sir."

"Did you know she was seriously injured yesterday?"

"Yes, sir."

"Witnesses say she was most likely assaulted by a fellow officer. She has, however, declined to name that individual and was not interested in pressing charges. A most peculiar situation, do you not think?" Prasillus paused, giving her ample time to respond. Waiting several seconds without an answer, he continued, "Since you are a close associate of hers, I felt that perhaps you could help us better understand these circumstances."

Lewatollma swallowed hard before responding, "It does not surprise me she would defer charges when seriously offended by someone close to her. She may present an insolent and callous facade, but in truth, she is a caring and devoted friend. What I did to her was inexcusable." And with that admission, Lewatollma's tears began to spill freely down her face.

The doctor shifted in her seat and then softly asked, "Lewatollma, will you tell us what led to this unfortunate incident?"

Turning to face Juwimla, she stammered, "Since Ravens Ford, I have not been the same — I am undone."

Gently, kindly, the doctor spoke. "I have read the proceedings from your hearing, but I would like to hear how you perceive this has affected you."

"The hearing does not cover everything that happened to me there, just the parts relevant to violations of code and protocol." Lewatollma paused and bit her lip to gain a measure of control before continuing. Gazing into space, she continued, "I was nearly beheaded by a Soulander. He placed the blade on my neck to ensure an accurate, fatal blow." Her hands moved involuntarily to her throat. "I can still feel it. I watched him lift his sword high above his head and..." She shuddered and the memory of the horror disfigured her countenance. "Have you ever seen someone struck in the chest with a projectile; the sickening sound it makes as it pierces flesh and shatters bone, and heard their agonizing cries? Ever held a person in your arms while he bled to death and not been able to do anything except watch? Or slit a man's throat, have him curse you with his eye as he perishes, and find your hands slick with his blood?"

Lewatollma looked at the doctor, then the executive officer. "I cannot get these images out of my mind, the nightmares, the sudden panic that grips me unbidden and..." She paused to take a deliberate breath before finishing. "...the sudden, violent impulses that come out of nowhere. I struck Eramus hard enough to knock him senseless and I stood over him with my knife in hand — I might have killed him. Eramus, who saved me from the brink of despair when I had given up. When I would not eat or drink, became listless, and just shut out everything, he brought me back with his care and concern."

As if in pain, Lewatollma began hugging her stomach. "Then poor Nesneratha, she forced me to eat and then she..." Again, she stopped, and shaking her head, continued, "...did nothing worthy of what I inflicted on her, but I became enraged, and it was over before I realized what I had done.

"Now I cannot eat without becoming ill and I dare not sleep lest I find myself in the grip of night terrors."

Juwimla turned to Prasillus, asking, "A word in private with you, sir, if I may?"

He nodded and summoned the guards and gestured for them to take Lewatollma out, informing them to await further orders.

"And get her a chair," added the doctor.

The guards escorted Lewatollma outside to the hall and gave her a chair, but before she reached it, she dropped to her hands and knees and began to retch. When the sickness subsided, she climbed into the chair, hugging her knees to her chest and burying her head in them.

Several minutes later, the doctor exited the office, stood in front of Lewatollma, and took her hand. "Come with me, dear." Gently, she raised her and taking her kindly by the arm, led her away.

Lewatollma launched a barrage of questions at her. "Where are you taking me? Confinement? Am I under arrest? Have I been stripped of my rank?"

Chuckling, the doctor replied, "A delightful place, no, no, and no. You have been through some horrific events recently and it has overwhelmed your natural ability to process and make sense of it all. What you need is rest, quiet, and gentle nourishment."

"What about my duties and responsibilities?"

"I have convinced Prasillus to place you on medical furlough, so you do not have to worry about those things for a time."

"For how long?"

Stopping, she turned to face her and sternly told her, "You are under my care now and you will be following my orders. Is that understood?"

Lewatollma nodded.

"Good, because nothing upsets me more than a patient who will not cooperate when I am doing my best to help them. Now I warn you — defy me and I will send you back to Prasillus, who, I assure you, had in mind a far different remedy. You should know there is no set time for recovery. I — not you — will determine when you will resume your duties. So, my first standing order is this: You will not talk, ask, or think about when you will return to duty. Is that clear?"

"Yes."

"Also, do not fret about your friend Nesneratha. I patched her up well. Straightened her nose, stitched her lip, and though she looks awful at present, she suffered no permanent damage. In a month or so, there will be no indication that anything had ever happened."

"When I saw what I had done to her, it twisted my stomach into a knot. She will never forgive me, I fear."

"Oh, in time I am sure she will. But that is not a priority now. So, the second standing order: You stay focused on your healing, and you are not to worry about anyone or anything else. Our next order of business is to get you packed, so let us stop by your quarters and get your essentials, but not your uniforms."

Lewatollma's voice was fearful. "I will not be staying on the ship? Where am I going?"

Scoffing, the doctor continued, "How are you going to rest with an ever-present reminder of your responsibilities? Besides, this place is far too depressing. You will love this little place we have set up off the lake. It is a quiet little cabin away from town with an absolutely delightful Norman woman to care for you. Once spring arrives, you can take walks in the woods, be in the garden, or sit on the beach — just the place to heal a wounded mind."

Lewatollma looked at her skeptically. The doctor stopped and turned to face her.

"Third standing order: Trust me. I have seventy-three years of experience. I know what I am doing."

Several days had passed since Eramus met with Nesneratha, and he had neither seen nor heard from her or Lewatollma. It was only by chance he heard Nesneratha's voice in the crowd — there was no mistaking her biting sarcasm. Summoning his courage, he located her and tapped her on the shoulder. She whirled about suddenly and spat out, "What!"

"Nesne...what happened to your face!"

Crossing her arms, she glared at Eramus. "Lewatollma 'happened' to my face!" Again, sarcasm.

"You two fought?"

"No, we did not fight. She simply slammed my face into her dinner plate." Nesneratha propped up her chin with her hand thoughtfully. "What were we talking about? Let me think. Oh, now I remember, it was about you," she ended loudly, jabbing her finger into his chest.

"Me? What about me?"

"Oh, much the same as we discussed at Gangby's inn. That you should return home, and she should forget about you."

"And then she attacked you?"

"Yes, suddenly and viciously."

Eramus stood silently and his face became one of deep concern. Quietly, he responded, "She attacked me, too. I was trying to calm her after she woke up screaming one night. She hurled me onto the ground and then stood over me with her dagger drawn. Just like you said, suddenly and viciously. This is not like Lewatollma at all. I'm very worried about her."

Nesneratha cast off the sarcasm, softening somewhat. "At least we agree on one thing."

"Where is she now?"

"I have not seen her, nor have I attempted to see her since."

"Does anyone know where she is?"

"I have not asked. But I did notice two days later that her name was removed from the duty roster."

"What does that mean?"

Nesneratha shrugged. "It could mean one of many things."

"Will you please find out what is happening and let me know?"

Nesneratha suddenly became petulant. "No! I will not, you daft farmer! Can you not see that you have played a significant part in this tragedy? That you precipitated this disaster by courting her? You seduced her and led her away from her culture and reason! I warned you! Why did you not believe me? I have known her for years! What made you think you knew her better than I did? Do you see my hair? Do you know what this means in my society?"

"No."

"It is a sign of mourning for the loss of someone we loved."

"She's dead?!" Eramus gasped.

"No. But everything gentle, beautiful, and decent about her is!" Nesneratha drew her blade and brought it close to Eramus's neck. Putting her face close to his and speaking menacingly, she growled, "Leave! Go back to Ravens Ford or Miricel or anywhere far from here and never return."

A commanding voice vehemently called out Nesneratha's name. Sheathing her blade, she shook an accusing finger in his face and commanded, "Never speak to me again!" Turning on her heel, she moved quickly to respond to the officer who summoned her.

Eramus watched as the man who called her out proceeded to reprimand her quite loudly. Then he observed something he had never seen before. He flicked the tip of her ear with his finger. Nesneratha flinched and blushed deeply then glared at Eramus angrily.

Eramus wandered back to Gangby's, took a seat near the fireplace, and brooded.

It was shortly thereafter that Nesneratha inquired about Lewatollma. Not that she had any intention to update Eramus, but out of concern for her friend. She held no ill will toward her, and in fact, she mourned that Lewatollma had experienced such a psyche-damaging event. Although Nesneratha displayed a callous demeanor, she actually had a kind and generous heart; her love for Lewatollma had not diminished in the least.

After the swelling in her face disappeared, she requested an audience with the executive officer, Commander Prasillus. Several days later, he invited her in and offered her a chair.

"How may I help you, Under-Lieutenant Nesneratha?"

"I am concerned for my friend, Minminuma Lewatollma, sir. I noticed her name was removed from the duty roster and that she had vacated her assigned cabin. I have been unable to locate her aboard the ship and I am concerned for her general welfare."

The commander studied her briefly before asking, "You are a close friend?"

"Yes, sir. We shared a dormitory at the academy as well as being together on this mission."

"Did you know she confessed to me regarding the assault on your person?"

Without pausing or blinking, Nesneratha responded, "I did not."

"It is really not policy to share information about other crew members, so I must inquire — why are you asking and what are your intentions?"

Taking a deep breath and clasping her hands in her lap, she explained, "I know she suffered significant trauma because she shared with me some, but not all, of the details. In my efforts to help her, I encouraged her to break off a relationship with one of the indigenous townsfolk. I offered to approach this individual personally on her behalf. My visit to him may have precipitated her unfortunate and violent reaction.

"My hopes are to visit her and let her know I am not holding a grudge, that I still care for her and want to continue our friendship. I believe this visit might give her an opportunity to seek forgiveness and remove some of the guilt she may be carrying needlessly. I want to help her to recover her kind and loving nature."

Leaning back in his seat, Prasillus said, "I applaud your desire and efforts to maintain harmony with the crew. I personally do not see any reason you could not visit her, but I have released her to Doctor Juwimla, and you will need her permission. I advise you to counsel with her. You may let her know I have no objection. Is there anything else you wish to discuss?"

"No, sir."

"Then you are dismissed."

Rising, she bowed slightly and said, "I thank you for your time, sir."

Prasillus acknowledged with a nod of his head as he proceeded to shuffle a stack of papers.

Lewatollma had recently finished breakfast and was upstairs brushing her hair out when someone entered via the cottage door. She heard two women talking; one of whom was definitely Juwimla, but the other was soft-spoken and simply responded to questions with one-word answers. Looking over her meager wardrobe, she selected a bright, flowery, full-length skirt and a red blouse that almost matched some of the colors in her skirt. As the days had begun to grow cold, she felt it was no sin to sacrifice fashion in favor of comfort.

"Lewatollma, you have a visitor," Juwimla called up the stairs from the parlor.

"I will be down shortly. Please invite my visitor to make herself comfortable."

Passing the mirror, she caught her reflection and paused, turning to the right, then to the left. Wrinkling her nose, she muttered, "That does not work at all!" She doffed the red blouse and found a short-sleeved white blouse. Slipping it on quickly, she then selected a comfortable, light-colored sweater and put it on as she descended the stairs.

Her visitor was on the settee with her back to Lewatollma. Rounding the edge of the settee, she smiled and opened her mouth to utter a greeting but came to a sudden stop as Nesneratha turned to smile at her. Nesneratha's lip had only a trace of swelling and her nose appeared slightly larger than usual, but her face still bore bruises, mostly yellow, with a few spots of purple.

Lewatollma cringed at the sight and a wave of shame rose suddenly from her soul and broke across her features. Being overwhelmed, embarrassed, and frightened left her speechless.

Breaking the awkward silence, Juwimla said, "Well, I am going to make some tea," as she left the room.

Nesneratha patted the cushion beside her, saying, "Come sit with me, dear."

Lewatollma slowly moved to sit on the opposite end of the settee, folded her hands between her legs, and stared despondently at the wooden floor.

"I have been worried about you, dear, but I should not have been — look at this beautiful and spacious cottage! Do you enjoy it here, Lewatollma?"

Lewatollma did not respond, nor did she move or even blink.

"It must be nice to relax and enjoy time away from the ship. So, how do you spend your days, dear?"

Lewatollma remained silent and motionless.

Not one for being patient, Nesneratha got up and sat down in Lewatollma's lap. Taking her friend's face between her hands, she raised her head to look deeply into her soft brown eyes, which were glistening with the beginning of tears. With genuine tenderness, Nesneratha offered, "I was insensitive to provoke you while you were in such a fragile state. I know I can be sarcastic at times, but I do love you. Can you forgive me?"

Taking her friend's hands in hers and returning her gaze, Lewatollma started tearfully, confessing, "I am so sorry, Nesneratha. There was no excuse for my incivility. You should have pressed charges; it was an unforgivable act of malice."

Pulling her to her breast, Nesneratha embraced Lewatollma and kissed her head. "I accept your apology, dear one; I hope you will accept mine."

"I do," Lewatollma sobbed.

In the kitchen, Juwimla was resting against the counter, a cup of tea in her hand. After taking a sip, she smiled and whispered to herself, "Well done, both of you."

WITHOUT LOVE

"Love between two people is not something that is highly valued in our society. But my parents defied that norm and they set a precedent. Putting aside all *social expectations, they let their hearts guide them.*"

– Minushua

After more than two weeks of questioning every Nawiman he could find in hopes of locating Lewatollma, Eramus began to be discouraged. In addition, he carried the burden of worry for her wellbeing. No one knew anything and if there was even a spark of recognition of her name, they would turn away, refusing to speak. Even approaching the guards at the ship mooring and asking to see her captain in his most authoritative tone produced only mocking laughter.

The only thing he could be sure of was she hadn't left. The activity around the ship seemed to be a predictable routine. If they were preparing to leave, it would be obvious. With winter coming on, they would be unable to leave once the lake froze over and they would be obliged to wait until spring for it to release their vessel.

Eram's money was dwindling rapidly, and he would not be able to afford to stay at Gangby's much more than another month. After some inquiries, Eramus found work as a teamster — a job he fell into easily since Normen were not all that fond of horses. With the Soulanders firmly entrenched at Ravens Ford, a significant buildup of Fair Folk, both military and civilian, occupied the newly established fort. Hence, there was a nearly continuous need for supplies and all manners of merchandise. The complete round trip took over a week — weather cooperating — four days down, two days of rest for the team, then three days back with an empty wagon.

A few days' rest and he could set out again. These short trips were ideal in Eramus's mind, as nothing much would change during his short absence. Upon returning, he would spend the better part of the day at Gangby's inn listening to the latest news and making occasional queries about Lewatollma and Nawiman's activities.

The winter settled in hard and bitter. Sometimes a week would pass with insignificant levels of activity due to the brutal wind that drove the snow in a blinding fury and caused the temperatures to drop sharply. When the snow lay deep and the weather permitted, the cargo was drawn on sleds, adding a day to the journey. It was later that winter when he ran into Sheron at the fort. He was looking for a place to stay when he spotted her looking through the wares at one of the merchant stalls that sprang up inside the fort.

"Sheron! Sheron!" he called out to her as he ran in her direction. Turning, she stared blankly at him until she recognized him, then her face exploded in a great smile. Extending her arms, she welcomed him with a loving embrace.

"Oh, Eram, it's so good ta see ya! I'm glad ta see you're okay with this war going on an' all. When I got here, I couldn't find ya anywhere an' so many men 'ave been killed, I began to fret! But I met a Norman who tole me ya left wit Lewatollma, so I figured ya was alright, but I didn't know fer sure." Then she hugged him with all her might, whispering in his ear, "I's so glad ta know yer alive," and afterward, she kissed his cheek.

"It's good to see you, too, Sheron, but I'm surprised to find you here; why didn't you go to Miricel like I suggested?"

Smiling, she answered modestly, "Oh, I'm not gonna burden anyone, not e'en ma own son, let alone strangers. I've found I kin make me own way. Gotta job working fer the medics, tendin' the sick an' injured. It gives me an' Miriam a place ta live an' we kin get food at the mess. Me herbal skills earn me extra pay on top a' that. Ya doesn't have ta worry 'bout us, we's doin' jes' fine on our own." Looking around him, she queried, "So, where is she — yer lovely friend?"

Frowning, he responded, "I don't exactly know. I've been looking, but no one seems to want to help me. I don't understand why, except maybe they don't want me being with her because I'm not a Nawiman." Shrugging, he continued, "But I haven't given up. Her ship is still here, so she must be, too. So, which of the Normen told you I left?"

"A friend a one a the nurses, Gorim."

"Oh, yeah, someone said Gorim took a fancy to one of the nurses and she seemed to fancy him, too." He laughed then moved on to a new topic, "So, Sheron, I'll be in town for the next two days. Can we get together? I would so love to see Little Miriam! I could buy everyone a nice meal."

"That'd be wonnerful, Eram! Aside from the mess, there's not many eatin' places ta choose from, but the best one be 'The Trough,' at least fer sittin' and relaxin'. But I wants ta go early afore the drinkin' gets outa hand — ain't no place fer a child once that 'appens!"

"All right, what time should we meet?"

"Just afore dusk."

"Dusk it is then. Well, I need to find a place to bed down, unless there's room where you are?"

"You'll not be allowed in the women's bunkhouse, I's afraid, so ya'd best find yer own place." Giving him another hug, she concluded, "See ya fer dinner, Eram," and traipsed off through the snowy street. Stopping after a few steps, she turned and demurely asked, "Kin I bring a friend?"

"Of course!" Eramus answered. Sporting a big smile, she waved goodbye and disappeared into the crowded street.

"The Trough" was aptly named. The floors were muddy and littered with crumbs and table scraps. The building was hastily erected, and the wind whistled through the cracks in the walls. By Eram's estimation, this establishment made the Sudsy Tankard look like a palace. He thought only briefly about what Lewatollma would have to say about this place.

Eramus got there early and found a table close to the pot belly stove located in the center of the room. Ordering himself some wassail, he waited patiently for his sister-in-law slowly sipping his drink, letting it warm him.

When Sheron had asked to bring a friend, he assumed it would be one of the nurses or a woman from the barracks. When she walked in arm in arm with a brawny, hulking man, Eramus nearly dropped his mug. His hair was pulled back in a short ponytail, and he was clean-shaven. Sporting a red plaid shirt, black suspenders, dungarees, and heavy boots, he was an imposing figure. Eramus could feel the floor move when he walked. Dancing alongside him was Little Miriam, all smiles, wearing a pretty, new dress.

Sheron spotted him and waved, and they strolled over to his table. Barely regaining his wits, Eramus stood up and greeted Sheron with a warm embrace, then picked up Miriam, hugged her tightly, and kissed her cheek. After he set her down, she sat in the chair to the right of her uncle. Reaching across, Eramus shook the hand of Sheron's friend. His grip was incredibly strong and Eramus winced at the pain.

"You sit here beside me, Hammy," Miriam interrupted, patting the chair to her left, "so's I can sits next ta ya an' Uncle Eram."

At the mention of "Hammy," something familiar about this man suddenly popped into his head and Eramus examined the man more closely. This time, he noticed his hair was dark copper and his green eyes twinkled gleefully. "Hamlin?!" Eramus exclaimed out loud.

"'ello, Eram, good ta see ya agin'," Hamlin responded warmly with a great smile.

Laughing, Eramus replied, "I didn't even recognize you, man! How did you meet Sheron?"

Smiling, Sheron explained, "His cousin introduced us. We've bin seein' each other fer the past five months."

Eramus sat back in his chair, struggling to take this all in, his eyes moving from Hamlin to Sheron and back again.

Miriam grew quickly tired of the silence and sighed, asking, "Kin we eat now? I's hungry."

"Me too!" added Hamlin. Putting two fingers to his mouth, he blasted out an eardrum-shattering whistle and motioned for the proprietor to come over. Eramus ordered wassail for everyone while they waited to be served. Dinner was potatoes, cabbage, turnips, and heavily seasoned, boiled venison.

The conversation turned to everyone catching up on everything that happened since they last met. There were smiles, laughter, and a general good feeling amongst their party. When the serious drinking crowd began to amble in, Sheron shot Hamlin a look and motioned with a nod toward Eramus.

"Eram, join me at the bar an' I'll buy ya a drink." Out of courtesy, Eramus got up and they went to the wobbly board that was the bar. "Don't lean too 'ard on that, it ain't very sturdy," Hamlin warned. "Two ales!" he shouted at the bartender. Turning to Eramus, he began, "Sheron an' I really like each other, an' since ya is her only fam'ly, she says I needs ta git yer permission before I kin, uh, ya know uh…"

"Marry her?" Eramus suggested.

"Yeah, that. So, what does ya say, Eram, kin I?"

"Are you going to take good care of her and Little Miriam?" Eramus inquired.

"Oh, yeah! I's already doin' that. Do ya like the dress I got yer niece?"

"Yes, it's beautiful."

"I think she's the purtiest lil' girl in the fort," Hamlin boasted, smiling at her. "An' I got yer sister new boots an' a good coat, too. I's buildin' a cabin, should be done by spring. That's where we's all gonna live once we git hitched."

The bartender set down two mugs of ale in front of them and stared at Hamlin, waiting for him to pay up. Hamlin reached into his pocket, took out two coppers, and placing them in the bartender's hand, smiled saying, "Thankee much."

Eramus lofted his mug, saying, "I give you and her my blessing. Let's drink to a happy union!"

Raising his mug, Hamlin added, "Thankee, Eram, I promise I'll make 'em happy."

As they started to enjoy their ales, Eramus commented, "I thought you were madly in love with Nesneratha."

"I fancied her fer a spell, but always I knew she thinked I wer' disgustin'." Smiling devilishly, Hamlin added, "But she wert a lot a fun ta tease! Oh, she'd tie herself in knots tryin' ta hold back, gettin' so mad, she couldn't e'en speak an' then her face'd turn red right ta the tips a' her pointy ears." Hamlin let loose a boisterous laugh, slapped his knee, and beamed, then shaking his head, continued, "Oh, them was fun times. Praps I wert wrong ta tease 'er like that, but I's jes' couldn't resist." Pausing to take another long sip, he then quietly mused, "Ya knows, I ain't seen 'er since I left Fishers Port, 'ave you?"

"Oh, I've bumped into her a couple of times, but we never spoke for very long. She did not care for me being near Lewatollma and both times she made it abundantly clear I should go away."

"So, has ya bin courtin' Lewatollma?"

"Well, you know what happened to her here at Ravens Ford, and even after she recovered from the initial shock, she refused to stay, so we rode back to Fishers Port, and I've not seen her since."

"So, what has ya bin doin'?"

"I'm staying at Gangby's and when I ran out of money, I got this job ferrying freight back and forth to the fort. I'm usually here a couple of times a month. This was the first time I ran into Sheron — didn't even know she was here, to be honest."

After they finished their drinks, Hamlin clapped Eramus hard on the back and motioned with his head toward the women. Returning to the table, Hamlin gave Sheron a big smile, nodding in the affirmative. Reaching over, Sheron took Eramus by the hand and gently patting it, told him, "I thinks we's gonna be all right."

"I think so too," Eramus replied.

Hamlin, Sheron, and Miriam said their goodbyes and after another round of hugs, they departed.

Eramus sat there for quite some time pondering what had just happened. In his heart, he knew Hamlin would love Little Miriam when he said she was the prettiest little girl in the fort with so much pride and love in his voice. Sheron's smile and the sparkle in her eyes were all the confirmation Eramus needed from her. His heart felt so much lighter now that he knew Sheron would be taken care of. Now if he could only find Lewatollma.

An ugly argument began building in intensity with people starting to take sides, so Eramus reasoned now would be a good time to leave. Finding the proprietor, he settled his debt and ventured out into the cold. Taking his time, he savored the end of the day and the quiet, deep blue still of the night.

Slowly, the unforgiving cold relented and spring chiseled its way out of the ice. While it was a great relief from the cold and snow, the warming weather and accompanying rain changed the roads into troughs of mire, making the journey back and forth to Ravens Ford slow and insufferably messy.

Opportunities to visit Sheron, Miriam, and Hamlin became the highlights of his trips to Ravens Ford. Hamlin completed his cabin early that spring. It was bigger and grander than anything Hares End had ever known, and Sheron was thrilled. Eramus was able to attend the simple wedding but was unable to stay for the celebration that lasted another three days.

With the warmer weather, Eramus spent less time at Gangby's and strolled about Fishers Port nosing about for news. He had been up and down the little town's streets so many times that he could name every establishment, its owner, and the names of the regular clientele. "Time to go somewhere else," he muttered and headed out of town on a well-beaten path near the lake.

Even though the sun shone brightly and all of nature celebrated the return of spring, Eramus was in a gloomy mood. Hands thrust in his pockets, he strolled solemnly down the trail. It aimlessly followed the lake and meandered now and then briefly into the woods.

He was quite alone, which in his current mood suited him fine. The only person he saw was a woman gathering flowers in a basket, far in the distance in an isolated field amid towering trees. He passed several cottages and followed the trail until it became obvious it was fading fast into nothing more than a wild animal path before he turned and headed back.

Keeping his eyes downcast, he watched the trail and his feet, fretfully ambling back toward Gangby's. Almost too late did he see the flower woman and stepped aside, muttering an apology, which she also proffered. Three steps later, he realized her voice seemed familiar. Turning, he saw a woman in a simple yellow dress trimmed in brown regarding him curiously. She had her hair up in a braid that was common among Norman women, yet somehow, she seemed familiar, so he asked, "Do I know you?"

"Eramus!" she exclaimed, launching herself at him and crushing him with her embrace.

"Lewatollma?"

She only laughed and cried happily on his shoulder in response.

Juwimla pulled back and slid her Onnum into her shirt. Pensively, she regarded Lewatollma. "I sensed something new in you today. You were distracted, not fully committing yourself to share. Tell me, what is it?"

Despite Lewatollma's best efforts to hide it, the old doctor was too experienced and too sensitive to miss even the subtlest of feelings. Dread filled her, but she felt compelled to be honest notwithstanding what may follow.

"Eramus and I are reunited."

Without any negative reaction, Juwimla remarked, "How interesting! How did this come about?"

"We met by chance on the lakeside trail. We almost did not recognize each other. It was a completely fortuitous meeting. I promise, it was not planned or sought after — we just found each other." Looking down, Lewatollma paused, then quietly asked, "Are you going to chastise me for not following orders and prolonging a relationship we all know must end?"

Smiling benevolently, the doctor replied, "No. I trust you will do the right thing when the time comes. You need to sort out all your experiences here. The things you have seen and done, the people you have met, the strangeness, the terror and excitement, the good, the bad, and everything in between." Then patting her hand kindly, she added, "It just takes time."

Shaking her head, Lewatollma added, "In all the years of training in preparation for this — the self-defense training, survival skills, language, and customs, I do not recall being warned about kindness, tender affection, and devotion. I was entirely unprepared for this and now this man has found his way into my heart. I deeply desire to reciprocate, and I revel in this intoxicating flood of emotion. I do not wish it to cease. Just thinking it might end, incapacitates me with profound emptiness. Knowing it will injure him equally makes it even more painful. What am I to do?"

"Today? Nothing."

"Should I continue to meet with him?"

"If you wish."

"That does not help me."

"Why are you asking me? Are you not capable of making your own decisions? Furthermore, I refuse to be the source of someone's lifelong regret of taking someone else's advice instead of solving their own problem.

"Do you not realize the true purpose of this journey is to discover for yourself who you are, what you can do, and what you can become? To develop and become confident in your abilities as well as discover and recognize the bounds of your frailties? Do you truly think you are the first denduin to become home-sick, love-sick, or traumatized?

"This is your day, your time, and your life — no one else's — yours! Rise to the occasion. Own it and embrace it. The sooner you do, the sooner you will be at peace with yourself and the world. Anyone who cannot do so will never take a meaningful place in society. You ponder that," she concluded, shaking her finger at Lewatollma.

An awkward silence filled the room. Finally, Juwimla broke it. "I would like to meet Eramus. Arrange a time when we can all be together. Soon, please. As a matter of fact, just have him be present when I return in three days."

"Are you sure that is wise?"

Juwimla chuckled, "Refer to standing order number three."

Sitting right next to Lewatollma did not bother Eramus at all. In fact, the past few days, they frequently had sat together talking or walked arm in arm and it was sheer delight. But something about an old woman watching them unsettled him. Finally, he overcame his petty fears and put his arm around Lewatollma's shoulder and she leaned into him in response. Evidently, she had no concerns, so why should he?

"I have been looking forward to this time with the three of us together. Eramus, could you start by telling me how you and Lewatollma met?"

The story unfolded while Lewatollma smiled, laughed, and interjected small details Eramus overlooked. But when he mentioned her arrival at Hares End with the Normen, she pulled away and became sullen. When the words *Ravens Ford* left his mouth, she got up and began to pace. Finally, wringing her hands, she interrupted, "I have tried to forget all of this — I cannot bear to hear it. May we speak of other things?"

The doctor motioned to Eramus to stop. Addressing Lewatollma, she said, "You are excused to leave. Find something calming to do. We will come to find you when we are done."

Nodding slightly, Lewatollma left. Not until the door was closed and her shadow passed by the window did the doctor continue. "It is important that I hear this, Eramus. It may hold a clue to her recovery. Please try to remember every detail that you can. Even seemingly insignificant things may be important."

"Will she ever be the same Lewatollma I knew?"

"No, she will not."

Eramus's head dropped in despair and Juwimla gave him a moment to accept this fact before continuing.

"That, however, is not necessarily to be mourned. Life is an unending series of events — good and bad — that will inevitably initiate change. Living in the past is pointless. You cannot go back to alter anything and the opportunity to embrace new experiences and allow them to become a part of you is only natural; to act otherwise will only hinder personal growth.

"Just be aware that it could require years for her to reconcile some of these experiences, and there may be some pain she will have to bear for the rest of her life. You will need to be patient, sensitive, and understanding. That being said, I have seen positive changes in her since you were reunited. You may be exactly the friend she needs at this present time.

"I assure you, all the beautiful characteristics she once possessed are still present. Encourage her to bring them forth again but avoid discussing past trauma unless she initiates it — and then, only listen.

"But listen to me ramble on like an old woman. Please continue."

After relating his version of the tragedy that marred Lewatollma, he thought to ask a question of his own. "Is Lewatollma in trouble?"

"Yes, she is." the good doctor replied simply.

"I feel responsible for getting her into this mess. How much trouble?"

"Plenty. But do not fret. She is currently under my care and when I finish with her, I will make recommendations to her executive officer to have some of the charges dropped or lessened."

"I ran into Nesneratha last fall. I can scarcely believe Lewatollma did that to her. She was rather harsh to me, but I came away understanding that she is a devoted friend to Lewatollma and takes Lewatollma's pain personally. Seems I have a lot to repair. She made it crystal clear I should leave, at knifepoint no less, and never think of Lewatollma again.

"But how do you forget the most compassionate, sensitive, kind, and loving person you have ever met? Not to mention beautiful, intelligent, and noble. I have completely lost my heart to her. What should I do?"

"Well, there is still some time before we will depart Fishers Port. It would seem you and Lewatollma have much to discuss and to decide before that time arrives. Based on my experience, I seriously doubt you will be allowed to travel with us."

"Could you talk to the captain and convince him to let me come?"

Juwimla started to laugh but quickly cut herself off. "My dear young friend, you do not comprehend the many problems associated with this situation. It is not simply a matter of buying a ticket, packing your bags, and hopping on board. Lewatollma is the one who can best explain this to you as a friend and as someone who cares about you. Talk to her about it. Speaking of which, where is she? I would have thought she would have returned by now."

Getting up, Eramus said, "Thank you for your time and patience, Juwimla. I need to be moving on anyway. Please give her my regards."

Taking a path near the shore, Lewatollma quickly put distance between herself and what she could only describe as the flogging of her soul. Eramus had unlocked the chain restraining the memories that now filled her mind with relentless torment.

"I have to break away from this," she said aloud. Glancing toward the lake, she spied a little cove. Leaving the path, she made her way through the brush to a large boulder set on the edge of the lake. The water was crystal-clear and was easily four feet deep. Lewatollma stripped down to her miskinir. Stepping carefully, she approached the water's edge. Springing from the boulder, she entered the lake in a shallow dive.

She was a powerful swimmer, propelling herself beneath the placid water until she could no longer hold her breath. She surfaced twenty yards from shore. When she broke the surface, she gasped, "Coldmere! It should be called Icemeer! Wooo!" She shook off a shudder and swam rapidly to another boulder fifty yards from shore. The exertion warmed her, and she focused on her breathing and stroke. She tagged it and dove underwater in a half circle and pushed herself away from the boulder with her feet. She continued underwater as long as possible then surfaced, finishing with a powerful backstroke until she tagged the boulder on shore.

Again, she reversed and swam back out into the lake. This she repeated three times. Halfway on the last return leg, she turned onto her back and floated quietly, breathing laboriously and feeling her heart pound. Closing her eyes, she found her mind empty except for the exhilarating thrill of her workout. She had found a measure of peace, a feeling of refreshment, and her senses joyously alive. She paddled slowly back, occasionally pulling herself along with a backstroke.

She climbed back onto the boulder, wrung out her hair, and stretched out on her back on the warm stone, enjoying the sun's golden rays. Her miskinir dried quickly, and she turned herself over once to let the backside dry. When she turned, she moved so her head was down near the water. Resting her chin upon her hands, she gazed into the lake. With her mind clear, she observed what she had missed earlier — small fish darting about the bottom, a water-strider, gentle ripples reflecting the sunlight, a crayfish poking around the decaying leaves of last fall. Out farther, a red-striped terrapin pulled itself upon a rock and basked.

At this moment, all was well in the world, and with a soft sigh, she closed her eyes and dozed for a few minutes. Rustling leaves and water lapping upon the shore serenaded her.

She awoke when a crow perched in a nearby tree began a raucous cawing, soon joined by his companions. Lewatollma arose and dressed. Not willing to return just yet, she cut across the path to a small pasture and picked a small bouquet. Sticking her nose deep into the handful of flowers, she inhaled the fragrance and sighed pleasantly.

When she looked up, she saw Eramus walking back to town, head down. She bounded across the clearing and jogged up beside him.

"Eramus, how did everything go between you and the doctor?" she asked sweetly.

"Well enough. I hope what I told her will help. I would love to sit and talk with you. Would you join me for dinner in town?"

"I apologize, Eramus, but I am not allowed to go into Fishers Port at this time. I am restricted to this area near the cabin for the foreseeable future. But please come and visit me when you can."

Lewatollma approached Eramus and embraced him, brushing her left cheek against his. Taking his hand, she smiled kindly at him and added, "Come visit me soon — I have missed my friend." She then turned down the path and ambled to the cottage.

The two met frequently and Eramus felt she was returning to her old self for the most part. He tried to engage her several times about returning home with her, but she just changed the subject. Late in the summer, the doctor released her back to duty, and she disappeared once again from his life. As before, inquiries were ignored, and guards laughed. He even considered trying to find Nesneratha, but he couldn't bring himself to face her. Not only out of fear, but guilt as well.

Falling back into his old routine of running freight, listening to gossip at the inn, and wandering around town, Eramus filled the lonely hours as well as he could. Summer ended and fall began to encroach upon the blissful warmth of summer. The activity about the Nawiman ship doubled. The time of departure seemed imminent.

One bitter day as Eramus was returning to Gangby's, he saw Lewatollma approaching followed by a pair of Normen. Eramus smiled to see her, but Lewatollma, with her cloak wrapped close and her hood covering her head, looked stern. While yet two paces away, she halted and said, "It is time to say goodbye, Eramus." She spoke softly, avoiding his eyes, looking askance at the waters beyond Fishers Port.

"What are you saying? You just got here!" Eramus asked, looking at her quizzically.

"I am saying goodbye and so should you." She nodded to the Normen, who came forward and took up position on either side of him. Eramus quickly looked over the pair critically. They simply returned his looks with a smile.

"Aren't ya goin' ta say goodbye ta yer friend afore she leaves?" the lanky one on his left asked.

"But I'm going with you, Lewatollma," Eramus sputtered. He moved to step closer to her, but strong arms held him back.

"No, you are not," she sighed, shaking her head slowly. Eramus tried to fix her gaze, but she looked away toward the great waters and said, "There is nothing more to say, except farewell, Eramus of Hares End. I shall always remember you." She then turned on her heel, threw her shoulders back, and strode away, her head held erect.

"Lewatollma?" Eramus managed to gasp. Then, drawing a deep breath, he called her name as loudly as he could. She neither turned nor broke stride. The last he saw of her, she disappeared in the throng of men working busily on the docks near the great Nawiman vessel.

"Come on, farmer, let's be off." The other Norman spoke cheerfully. "We 'ave yer things from Gangby's an' a horse awaitin'." They spun Eramus around, locked their arms into his elbows, and escorted him away.

"What? Where are you taking me?" Eramus said, looking at his new companions.

"We're takin' a little trip," one of them said.

"To Miricel," finished the other, smiling broadly, like it was a joke.

"Now your friend says ya can be difficult atimes," the first continued.

"So, be a good lad an' don't make us take ya home trussed up like a marketplace turkey," said the other with a smile, squeezing Eramus's arm firmly to make his point. Eramus ceased to resist, physically at least, but a terrible pain burned in his heart. He looked over his shoulder for one last glimpse of Lewatollma, but it was in vain.

He returned to look at the ground before him and shook his head in disbelief. In a barely audible whisper, he muttered to himself, "This can't be happening. This can't be happening."

Lewatollma pulled her cloak closer; the autumn chill seemed to penetrate despite her efforts. She began to organize her thoughts in preparation for the journey, certain the trip home would fill the void left by Eramus. Eramus. She would have to work hard to abstain from thinking of that name. A name that would bring a flood of vivid memories...and something else. She blinked hard, dismissing the idea. Putting her hand inside her cloak, she clutched her Onnum tightly: stability, focus, clarity, she rehearsed to herself. She didn't have time right now for this, for a long journey lay ahead, and she must be clear-headed if she was to help navigate home. She turned her thoughts to the others instead of herself. This brought the focus she needed. She stopped looking inward and finally opened her eyes and searched for her captain.

The docks were bustling with activity. Supplies and specimens were being organized and inventoried. She made her way past great wooden crates sealed up and marked with Nawiman glyphs: salted fish, plant and mineral samples, dried apples, honey, and grain. She turned into the brisk breeze coming off Coldmere and worked her way toward the gangway leading to the ship. As she approached the entrance, she pulled back her hood and threw her cloak off her shoulder to display her face to the guard at the entrance. He acknowledged her with a slight nod and stepped aside to allow her aboard. She climbed the short incline, turned left, and proceeded up another set of steps to the upper level of the ship. The guard outside the staging room delayed her momentarily, while he glanced at the first officer, who nodded his approval to allow her entrance.

She stood at the edge of a group near the wall and waited for her turn to approach the captain. Several spetcinmal were having a quiet discussion about loading, balancing the weight, and whether everything they wanted could be loaded as planned. Lewatollma turned to look at the maps on the wall. The surveyors had made detailed drawings of the region they explored. She followed the blue line, which was the Emmering River, westward and studied the detailed map of Miricel, and noted with satisfaction the accuracy of the rendition of her contribution to the geo-survey.

Her mind almost began to recollect the details of the journey, but she stopped herself and looked north to study the way across the great gap that divided the Fair Folk in Miricel from their Northern brethren.

The region was annotated by Timmenora, a woman she was acquainted with from before their journey, who was a resident of her village.

Home. Suddenly, feelings of warmth and serenity swelled within her and for the first time today, she smiled. Home. Soon they would return. Her hands moved unconsciously to her breast and lay on top of her Onnum. She closed her eyes and could see the shining sun and smell the sweet air of her native land, her mother, and the gift of Corminimorel. She opened her eyes slowly, savoring those pleasant memories.

Her gaze drifted away from the map back to the large table, where the captain was now conferring with the first officer. They spoke in low tones and once, they both looked over at her before continuing their discussion.

Finally, the captain dismissed his first officer and motioned for Lewatollma to approach. She came to his side. Without looking at her, he said, "Have you completed everything that you were assigned to do from your hearing?"

"Yes, sir."

Looking askance, he inquired, "And the fellow who followed you here?"

"On his way home under the escort of two Normen."

"Very good. I have decided to take the additional cargo into one of the lower deck crew quarters. I want you to reassign berthing for the spetcinmal and the command crew. You may have to make use of the smaller rooms for the officers, to compensate for the loss of the converted shared berthing. We must be ready to depart in three weeks. Minminuma Lewatollma, are you able to fulfill this assignment?"

"I will fulfill my assignment," she replied crisply and without delay.

The captain turned to look her deeply in the eyes. "And your command duties — are you able to fulfill those?"

"Yes, sir," she quickly answered.

Her captain studied her face as if he was looking for something deep inside. He held her gaze and continued, "Many things have happened to you here, indeed to all of us, but you are young, and this is your first duty far from home. These experiences can have a profound influence on a denduin, and many return home forever changed." Walking over to the table, he leafed through the lading records. "We have collected, cataloged, and stored many things from our exploration. Have you inventoried your experiences and feelings? Have you categorized and stored them away in their proper place?"

Lewatollma swallowed hard; she now understood she was being tested by her captain for command crew worthiness.

"Many things have happened, and in truth, not all of them are understood. But all are put away until an appropriate time when..." She paused as she sought, then found the right word. "...reconciliation can be found." She turned to look directly at him.

He locked her eyes with his stare and she sensed him searching her soul for the truth. Not that she could lie to him, but sometimes one could lie to oneself. In those few moments, he passed judgment and announced, "Very good, Minminuma Lewatollma, attend to your present assignment and see the executive officer for your command crew duty schedule." He motioned for his first officer to return and dismissed Lewatollma with a curt nod.

Lewatollma felt encouraged at her commander's approval for duty. As she strode out of the ready room, she began to consider the task at hand. Although the crewmen generally did not complain, it may be challenging to convince some of the more senior officers to accept lesser quarters.

As a novice on this mission, she noted that some officers felt the assigned duties were beneath their dignity, but she saw this as a test of greater responsibilities for a navigator, for she reasoned this was merely navigating in a different element. With a lightning mental process, she began to list what information she would need: crew size, rank structure, bunking compatibility, and personalities of potential malcontents. Smiling, she threw herself into the task.

Eramus rode between the two Normen, who were singing raucous songs and laughing. He did not share in their good humor.

"Come on, lad! You be better off at home than traveling all o'er creation with them silly Nawimans!"

"What I can't believe..." Eramus paused. "...is that you two would be so happy to take a stupid farmer far away from your own homes."

"You needn't worry, lad. We be well paid!" The other Norman shot his partner a shut-your-mouth-you-idiot look.

"She paid you to take me away?!" Eramus exclaimed in disbelief. "She paid you!" he said, repeating it to himself several times, trying to come to grips with it. He rode in silence for another hour. Finally, he composed himself enough to ask, "How much?"

"What?" they asked.

"How much?" Eramus repeated. "How much did she pay you?"

"Three silver pieces each. Fair Folk coin, mind ya, the good stuff!" His partner shot him another disapproving look and just shook his head.

The ensuing weeks busied Lewatollma overseeing berthing and room accommodations for the crew. Additionally, she had to work the docks, cataloging crates and inventorying foodstuff for the journey home. The vessel was being loaded with its final stores and practice drills were conducted to ready the crew for departure.

After a period of intense preparation, the captain announced a departure date. On the appointed day, the officers lined the deck as they released the ship's moorings. Friends who were close to the crew lined the docks and bid them a fond farewell, smiling, cheering, and waving kerchiefs. Lewatollma searched the crowd for a familiar face but found none. She was disappointed yet comforted that Eramus was not there. It was a shame he was so stubborn; this would have been a much sweeter goodbye than being hauled away by Normen.

Once out of earshot of Fishers Port, the crew resumed their duties. Soon they were sailing smoothly into the lake. The first week was especially busy finalizing details and sorting out paperwork. Once far from land, the crew began removing the exterior wood and casting it overboard. The masts were felled, ropes and the sails committed to the deep. Beneath the facade, a sleek and elegant craft began to emerge. It had taken months to render the disguise and some of the crew complained bitterly about tearing it apart. Yet it was a necessity to prevent the indigenous folk from being curious about technology they couldn't possibly understand.

Cloaks, robes, boots, and other trappings were removed and stored. The crew donned one-piece work outfits and special deck shoes. Insignias indicated rank and the technical members wore different color outfits to distinguish them from the officers.

Lewatollma spent much of her time on the bridge getting and passing out assignments, running errands, and coordinating activities leading up to the next juncture in their journey.

At the beginning of the second week into their journey, the first officer approached the captain and whispered in his ear at some length. The captain nodded and Lewatollma overheard him say, "I am not surprised." The captain motioned for her to approach and addressed Lewatollma plainly, "Minminuma Lewatollma, please attend to the situation in the briefing room." Lewatollma nodded in acknowledgment and strode off to address the problem at hand.

It was probably another officer-tech spat. She ran through the list of crewmembers in her mind, calculating the probabilities of who was at the center of the issue. The most likely candidate was Temerranma, but she did not see her escalating to the point where a junior officer might be asked to intervene. She shrugged and told herself, *This should be easy.*

As she turned the corner, she was surprised to see two guards outside the door. *More serious than I expected*, she thought. When she opened the door to find Eramus sitting at the small table in the corner of the room, her mouth dropped open in shock. When Eramus saw her face, he beamed as if his heart was bursting with joy, but Lewatollma looked like hers nearly stopped. Open-mouthed, she stared at him in stunned silence. Finally, she managed, "How did you...who helped you...when did you...Eramus! What are you doing here?!"

"Why don't you come in and shut the door," Eramus offered. She continued to stand there, her hand still on the door handle, staring in unbelief. Eramus got up and led her by the arm to a seat, pushing the door closed behind him. "I was hoping you would be glad to see me, but I guess I caught you by surprise."

"Surprise does not even begin to describe what I feel right now, Eramus!" Sitting down, she rested her elbows on the table and put her forehead in her hands, staring down. They sat in silence for a few minutes.

Suddenly, Eramus perked up. "You're wearing your hair up! I loved your long hair; I hope you let it grow out. It made you look so beautiful. Hey, where's your cloak? I liked the brown one best because it matched your eyes, and it made you appear mysterious and magical. Forgive me if I say so, but blue is not your color." He paused momentarily, waiting for her to respond. Sensing no immediate reply, he continued, "Oh, I have something for you." He reached into his pocket and produced six silver pieces, which he dropped one at a time under Lewatollma's downturned face. She slowly looked up at him, the realization dawning on her face.

Eramus savored the moment. "The expression on your face was worth twice that much."

"That is not funny, Eramus," she said sternly, dropping her hands. Eramus stopped grinning and brought his face closer to hers. Taking on a more serious demeanor, he said, "I still can't believe you paid them to take me back to Miricel!"

"Well, believe this!" Rising, she barked a command in her strange tongue and the two guards entered. Pointing at Eramus, she motioned to them to follow her. One guard at each side, Eramus was guided down the hall, to a door leading outside. Passing along the side, she led them to the stern.

"Hey, what happened to the sails?" Eramus asked.

Pointing off to a distant horizon, she informed him, "Fishers Port is that way!" Snapping her fingers, she motioned to the guards to toss him overboard, which they did promptly. Eramus yelled when he hit the cold water, "I can't swim!"

"One hand at a time, pull yourself forward. Kicking your feet helps," Lewatollma suggested.

Spurting water and thrashing wildly, he repeated, "I can't swim!"

"You are doing it wrong, try harder," she encouraged. He went under for a moment but surfaced quickly, spewing water and fighting to breathe.

Pointing again, she informed him, "That way!" The lake swallowed him again, but this time, it took slightly longer for him to get back to the surface. He managed two gasps of air before he sank the third time.

Lewatollma stood there, hands on her hips shaking her head in dismay. After about twenty seconds, she gave up. "Oh, pull him out and revive him!" she said dismally. One of the men slipped off his boots and belt, then dove in. The other grabbed a rope and waited. Soon, the first guard reappeared with Eramus under his arm. The rope was thrown, fastened, and Eramus was pulled out of the water. The guard laid him on his side and slapped him hard on the back. Eramus spurted water from his mouth and nose, then began coughing and gasping for air. Removing the rope, the guard threw one end over the railing and helped his companion back on board.

Lewatollma dismissed the guards and flopped down to sit beside Eramus. Pushing his wet hair out of his face, she moaned, "What am I going to do with you?"

Eramus was confined to a small area. Small enough that he could touch the opposite walls without stretching very hard. Once, he tested the door and found it was not locked. Peeking outside, he found a rather large man in a red uniform staring back. The guard slammed the door shut in his face, ending any hopes he may have had about escaping.

They gave him a blanket and strangers brought him some food on occasion. Without any furniture, he was obliged to sit on the floor. On the second day, his food was delivered by a face he knew and feared. Nesneratha handed him a plate and shut the door behind her, leaning against it with folded arms. From his spot on the floor, she seemed a menacing figure.

"I heard a rumor that we had a stowaway. Curiosity got the better of me and I just had to see for myself. Lo and behold, it is none other than Eramus of Hares End."

"You're not here to kill me, are you?"

Laughing, Nesneratha answered, "Oh, it is far too late for that! Besides, would that be any way to treat a guest? No, Eramus, we are too far into our journey to turn around and take you back, so you will be returning with us."

"How much trouble am I in?"

"Well, given you are not a citizen, our laws do not apply to you, nor can you be realistically expected to obey laws of which you are ignorant. So, from a legal standpoint, you will not be held accountable for any transgression of our rules and regulations. However, I would like to point out that you have placed yourself in a most troubling situation; the severity of which you have no inkling, but in time will become painfully manifest to you. So, I am not here to vex you because you will be vexed copiously by your own choices. I am surprised they did not simply toss you overboard when they found you."

"They did," Eramus glumly admitted. "By Lewatollma's orders no less. But I guess she felt bad because I couldn't swim. She had the red shirts pull me out and revive me."

"Oh, how I wish I could have witnessed that," Nesneratha lamented.

"How long will it take to get home?"

"Months. But fear not, this closet will not be your permanent berthing. Lewatollma is probably working out that detail right now. I am sorry you had to be confined like this, but we have been very busy and do not have time to properly accommodate you. As a matter of fact, I must leave you to attend to pressing duties of my own."

"Wait! Is Lewatollma in trouble, too?"

Laughing heartily, Nesneratha left. Eramus could hear her continue to laugh as she went down the hall.

Lewatollma was rushing about with a long list of tasks to accomplish and a very short time to complete them. In addition to her regular duties, she now had to find a bed for Eramus in an already crowded ship with a crew murmuring about cramped living conditions. Eramus's discovery couldn't have happened at a worse time. He was safe and fed; that was the best she could offer for now.

Then there was the embarrassment of explaining to the captain the entire stowaway incident. He let her off easy, though, just a verbal reprimand for throwing a person off the ship without the captain's express approval. But he also assigned her an additional task to review the loading protocols and look for improvements. He suggested Eramus should be involved since he possessed valuable insight.

She had thought that she had her emotions under control, but Eramus upended her attempt at self-mastery. Now she was set back to the beginning and had to start all over but with Eramus in the picture. The jumble of opposing emotions kept her tossing and turning at night.

"Why, Eramus? Why could you not have accepted and respected my decision?" she bemoaned aloud to herself. Suddenly, she realized she had walked past the hallway she had meant to turn at. Turning, she silently chided herself for getting wrapped up in her personal problems instead of attending to duty.

Hearing someone call her name, she looked up to see Nesneratha excitedly approaching her.

"Lewatollma! You will never guess who I ran into today!"

By her tone of voice, Lewatollma already knew the answer, but out of courtesy, she replied nonchalantly, "Who, dear?"

"A dear, old friend of yours. Guess! You will not believe it but do guess!"

Lewatollma did not care for being toyed with, especially by Nesneratha, who knew exactly how to get under her skin.

Groaning, she answered with unmasked dismay, "I surmise you found Eramus."

"Eramus it was," she gaily exclaimed.

"I had him locked away. How did you find him?"

"Well, the rumor was that a stowaway was found. And you know me, being so insatiably curious, I started poking around. As luck would have it, I overheard someone saying she had to deliver food to a stowaway. So, I took the opportunity to be helpful and offered to deliver it myself. And surprise of surprises, there was Eramus!"

"I suppose this is your opportunity to gloat and remind me that this is one of the serious consequences you warned me about?"

"Me?! Never! I just thought you would be ecstatic to find out your beloved was here to fawn over. You know, spend hours just gazing into his eyes and being swept away with giddy infatuation. Oh, so romantic!" Nesneratha hugged her friend's arm and laid her head on her shoulder, sighing deeply.

"You can stop now, Nesneratha. You have made your point, and I am going to ask you politely to please cease. I would prefer to not lose control and slam your face into one of these bulkheads. I am reasonably sure they are much harder than a plate of food. It would be a shame to have to repair your nose again after it had healed so beautifully."

"Oh, but he is so dreamy with that wavy hair and those cute, round ears..."

Lewatollma grabbed her by the shirt front, put her forearm onto Nesneratha's neck, and pinned her to the bulkhead, warning her through clenched teeth, "I am serious! Stop!"

After the mirth on Nesneratha's face dissolved, Lewatollma released her. She then straightened Nesneratha's uniform and embraced her, whispering, "If you are my friend, I will need your strength and compassion to get through this ordeal. I thought I had completely severed my ties to Eramus, but he is stubborn, persistent, and much more intelligent than I ever suspected. I paid two Normen to take him back to Miricel, but he offered them more money and effectively outbid me. Then somehow, he got past all our loading protocols to get on board undetected." Breaking down, she began to weep on Nesneratha's shoulder, sobbing, "I swear to you, I tried! I really tried!"

Nesneratha finally returned her embrace. "Oh, my dear Lewatollma, I apologize. I sometimes let myself get carried away with sarcasm. I know you both are going to suffer because of this, so I now pledge to be the dutiful friend and care for you as I ought."

"Thank you, Nesneratha. I too am sorry. I think you are beginning to see how stressful this is for me. I must get going. I am already behind in my work, and I still have not found a place for Eramus to sleep," Lewatollma added.

"I have completed all my assignments. Is there any way I can assist? Let me make amends by helping you." Pushing away, she smiled at Lewatollma, hooked arms with her, and started back down the passageway. "I have an idea for berthing Eramus. Put him with the techs and create a triple rotation for hot bunking."

"They are already on triple rotation."

"Put up another hammock."

"Possibly. But I have a better idea. You can share your bed with him, Nesneratha."

Shuddering, Nesneratha responded, "I can picture nothing more horrifying than awakening next to Eramus."

"Oh, it is not so bad," Lewatollma let slip without thinking.

Nesneratha looked at her in shock. Then she began to smile. "Ah, you were teasing! You had me frightened for a moment. Very good, I usually catch on to such absurdities immediately." Nesneratha looked across at Lewatollma's face, expecting a grin. But she did not find one. "You were joking, right? Lewatollma? This is a joke. Please tell me this is a joke. Lewatollma? Lewatollma? Oh, Lewatollma!"

SECRET OF THE EMALLINAWIMA

"We often deceive ourselves by thinking that nothing can surprise us. We map out the future considering every possible complex interaction to comfort and assure ourselves that we are in control — the master of our situation. Inevitably, something will occur which never entered our consciousness and the overwhelming improbability of it sends us reeling."

– Sheralutra

When the door swung open, Eramus shielded his eyes from the harsh light shining into his dark chamber. Much to his relief, it was Lewatollma. She held out her hand and simply said, "I wish to show you something."

Eagerly, he took her hand, got up, and exited the box he had been in for three days straight. He wanted to hug her. Not because he loved her, which he did, but because he was relieved and grateful to be let out. Reflecting on the circumstances, he probably would have hugged Nesneratha if she had freed him.

Lewatollma walked alongside Eramus, leading him toward the outside of the great ship. She seemed pensive and looked across at him, saying in her "Listen up, farmer, this is important" voice, "Eramus, there are no words in your tongue to explain what will happen next, nor is there anything I can say to prepare you. I have brought you here to see for yourself in the hope you will gain understanding through your powers of observation." They turned a corner and ascended a short ramp to an elevated room that gave a view of the endless water outside through a large transparent window.

"What is this place?" he inquired.

"This is the observation deck."

Eramus approached the window and stroked its smooth surface with the back of his hand.

"Glass," he said, pointing to the window and tapping it gently with his knuckles. "I have seen this before in the magnificent citadel of the Fair Folk. They use it to let in light to their dwellings or to see out. Which I never really understood because you could always go outside if you wanted to see outside. I mean what is the point of going inside if you wanted to see the outside?"

Ignoring his rambling, she replied, "It is like glass, in that it can be seen through, but made of a different substance and many times stronger." Eramus leaned closer to examine it further. He stared intently and tapped it a little harder.

"There are no bubbles in this piece, and it is much larger than any I have seen in Miricel." He turned to Lewatollma, squinting slightly, and met her gaze. "Is this why the Fair Folk despise your kind so much? Because your craftsmen are superior to theirs?" She made no reply except to stare out into the great blue waters. "The

Fair Folk do not seem to be the kind to be jealous...but what would a stupid farmer know?"

The corners of her mouth turned upward momentarily but she kept her gaze fixed on the distant horizon. She was intent on something, anticipating something. She called to him, "Eramus, come stand near me." He moved closer and joined her in staring out the large aperture. He was beginning to wonder what was so important about looking at the endless blue waters that they had recently crossed. A few birds flew past in the distance, geese perhaps, but too far away to tell for certain. Moments passed in silence.

Lewatollma drew a deep breath and let it out in a short, barely audible sigh. She then broke the silence and in a distant voice said, "Eramus of Hares End, you are a mystery to me despite all the experiences we have shared. I should know you by now, but in this one thing, you are like a stranger to me. Why do you wish to come with me now? I have told you that we will journey far and most probably never again return to see your native lands. Will you not miss walking amid the murmuring pines? Or look at the night sky figures or share a story and song with your fellow men? Or dine on kerrits smothered in butter and honey? You are not one of my kind and are a stranger among us. You do not speak our language. Surely, you have seen how you are treated in the presence of my companions. How can you ignore this? How can you leave your home, your beloved fields? Will you not miss kneeling in the spring-warmed earth, and seizing a fist full of your mother element, breathing in its rich goodness and rejoicing to see it bring forth fruit and foliage?"

She turned slightly to look at him through the corner of one eye. He did not turn to meet her gaze, and he never saw the little tear she blinked away. She took stock of his facial features. He was stern and silent, hands clasped behind his back. He worked his jaw, as he often did when thinking deeply, moving his teeth against each other lightly. She looked hard to find regret or sorrow there on his visage, but to her surprise (and it's hard to surprise a Nawiman), he began to beam. "You say you do not know me, but you do. A stranger could not know my sweetest memories. These are things shared only by friends — heart to heart. Do you wonder how I can leave all these things behind? Well, simply put — I'm not." She turned full aside and gave him a quizzical look. He paused, then continued, "They will always be here..." He motioned to his chest. "...and here," he said, his finger tapping his temple.

"I haven't told you about the day we parted at Fishers Port. That was when I made up my mind to go with you. I knew you would not stay — something far away was calling you, indeed had been calling you for quite some time, so I did not even ask. I knew by your eyes, those all-telling eyes." He smiled at her. "I knew long ago that Fishers Port was not your home — your speech and gesture betrayed that. But until that day — until that moment you said farewell, turned on your heel, and strode bravely away — I did not know what I was going to do. I was ushered away in the opposite direction, but my heart pained me." He grunted a short laugh.

"Hmph. I even put my hand on my chest, the pain was so real. I turned to see you one last time and hoped to see you looking back at me. You were stoic to the end, but I was not surprised.

"I have come to expect no less from you. But it was at that moment I knew that I could not bear to be anywhere without you. Any world without you would be hollow and empty. After renegotiating with the Normen, I engaged them to devise a way to steal aboard the ship. So, we rigged a container for me to stow away in.

"But do not think this was all my doing, my pointy-eared companion. You infected me with the spirit of adventure, and I know of no cure save to rush headlong into its waiting arms. So, tell me, how could I not follow where you go? What an excellent adventure to journey far away with the mysterious Nawiman race! Not even the know-it-all Fair Folk will be more learned than I about your kind, so there's my claim to fame, eh?"

She turned to him, both eyes full of tears, to say, "Do you not realize you will be a nemrean, an outsider, never fully accepted by my society? Do you know what difficulties await you? You should be afraid, shivering in your boots, not swooning like some romantic poet! You poor, stupid farmer!" she laugh-sobbed, wiping her eyes with her small finger and flicking the salty tears at his feet.

Eramus locked his gaze on her, saying, "I have never forgotten anything you have ever told me. Never! And what if it is love or foolishness or even both — they're mine! It's all I have, save these few rags I wear. And I'll be damned if I will part with something that makes my heart beat stronger, puts a spring in my step or a song on my lips! I have seen so much in the last few seasons, that my life before seemed small and meaningless.

"Above all, I have learned that life is a precious gift and every moment a present waiting to be unwrapped and appreciated with childlike awe! And speaking of what you have told me, I distinctly recall a certain Nawiman telling me about how great it was to have faithful friends. Well, here I am. I did not waver at Ravens Ford when I pulled you from the clutches of those murderous Soulanders, and I will not waver now!"

She sobbed twice more after his terse retort. An awkward silence ensued. After a few seconds, he softly mumbled, "I am sorry to be so abrupt with you. I never meant to hurt your feelings...and I am ashamed...to have brought you to tears. This is not how I hoped our friendship would...could..." He did not find the words to finish his sentence, so he turned back to the shimmering sea. An awkward silence passed for an uncomfortable period of time.

"I should apologize," she began. "It is not my place to question your motives. You have, of your own free will, selected a course — I promise now to honor your decision. It was just that a profound melancholy overcame me thinking that you might never see your home again. I was caught up in putting myself in your place; I could never turn my back on my native soil."

He reached out and put his arm around her slight frame, pulled her to his shoulder, and softly said, "There is no sorrow, no regret in my decision, so be happy for me, for I am filled with great pride and peace to stand here with my friend, Lewatollma. Don't be sad anymore."

She reached across with her free arm, put it around his back, and pulled him to her breast with a gentle squeeze. She lightly brushed first her left cheek against his and then her right against his other cheek. Then reaching down, she gathered his hands and brought them together with her hands to clasp her amulet. They stood facing each other and she looked deep into his eyes, enfolding his hands firmly around the amulet, and leaned her forehead against his.

At that moment, an incredible feeling of warmth, wellbeing, and peace flooded over Eramus. The feeling was strong and all-consuming. Suddenly, he could not feel the floor beneath him and lost all sense of presence around him. The experience was surreal; he felt he was in communion with the universe, but that he himself was nothing but a thought floating freely through a warm void. She released his hands and dropped the amulet back to its familiar place around her neck. Suddenly, the room reappeared around them. She brushed her right cheek, then her left against his, gently hugged him, and pulled away.

"Wha-what was that?" he managed in a voice full of amazement, not breaking from her entrancing gaze.

"We call it Corminimorel. It is a special joining of people's minds where thoughts, ideas, and feelings can be shared. You may have noticed Nesneratha and I engaged in this while we journeyed."

It took a minute or two, but Eramus finally regained his senses and came to stand beside her. They stood watching the rhythm of water infinitely repeating its pattern of reflected sunlight. Eramus was confused, and he thought, *I am just a stupid farmer*. Magic still captivated his imagination, and this last experience was no exception. He tried to imagine how she did it, but he could only draw a blank; this was far beyond his understanding. Even after all the times he had witnessed her working magic, the only common factor was her amulet. This time, she had him touch it, and for the first time in his life, he felt magic power. His simple musings were interrupted by Lewatollma releasing a deep sigh. A few more minutes of water-gazing brought Eramus back to his original question: "Lewatollma, what were you going to show me?"

"You will see in just a few more minutes." She grabbed his elbow and drew him near the window as a faraway *ting-ting-ting* sound came from behind them. There was a low hum building in intensity as time progressed. This unsettled Eramus, but not as much as the deep shudder that suddenly penetrated the entire ship. He could have sworn the ship was moving, but not in the usual sense. He felt the floor shift and he looked around and behind him, wondering what was going on.

At that moment, the ship lurched upward. Grasping the sill of the window to keep his feet, Eramus looked outside to see the water below them boiling. It was violently frothy, pockets formed by splashes of water dripping off the bottom of the vessel. Eramus was frozen in place, his eyes riveted on the scene below. Lewatollma looked across and noticed his face had lost color, so she tightened her grip on his arm and steadied herself. The ship sat motionless a dozen or so feet above the surface, which had begun to settle back to normal.

"Eramus…" His head snapped to look at his companion. "…I am glad you are here with me." She smiled slightly and gently squeezed his arm. She cocked her head slightly, looked at his pale-excited-panicked face, and asked, "Are you feeling well?" He motioned yes, then no, then yes, as he looked out the window. At first, he didn't comprehend what he was seeing.

The great expanse of water prevented Eramus from perceiving true speed and distance, but when they broke through the scattered cloud cover, he realized he was above the clouds and moving at an incredible velocity. He uttered a low moan that came straight from his gut and his knees began to shake. He was frozen in place as he saw what he thought was an immense sea become a lake with discernible shores. Great forests became mats of green and rivers, silvery threads reflecting the late afternoon sun.

"Look, Eramus — the Blue Desert," she said, and her finger pointed to a brownish patch far below that stretched to the horizon southward. The ship began moving eastward and Eramus watched the land speed away below him and the sky around the ship grow a deepening shade of blue like an accelerated night was falling. His knees gave out and Lewatollma let him slip gently to the floor. Grasping the edge of the window, he peered anxiously outside.

His heart raced and he found himself gasping for air as the horizon became fuzzy, beginning to take on a definite curvature. He looked up to see brilliant pinpoints set in inky blackness. He looked down to see his world appear as a white-flecked blue and brown ball shrinking from view. His heart was in his throat and a paralyzing fear seized him. He swallowed hard and in a trembling voice, much like that of a frightened child, he asked Lewatollma, "Where are we going?"

He looked up at her gazing into the inky sky. She was clasping her Onnum with one hand, holding it tightly to the center of her chest. Lewatollma's eyes had become dark and unfathomable, but her face was one of serenity. She looked upon the trembling farmer and stroked the back of his head to try to reassure him. A tear of joy trickled from one eye as she answered, "Home."

If you enjoyed what you read, please post a review online. Your input is greatly appreciated!

Eram's journey continues...

THE NEMREAN GAMBIT

2025

The following is a bonus sneak peek at the first chapter.

TRANSIT

"Many assume that the Emallinawima developed space travel on their own, but the truth is they were introduced to it inadvertently by another race. The crash landing of an extraterrestrial vehicle awakened them to the possibility of traveling beyond their planet. The occupant perished but enough of the craft survived for them to reverse engineer key technologies to enable trans-atmospheric and orbital flight. One hundred and sixty years later, they were master explorers of their solar system. Three hundred and twenty-seven more years would elapse before they discovered how to transit using the Psy."

- Introduction to Space Exploration, 3rd Edition

It took Eramus a while to recover from the revelation he lived on a planet and that it was round. He struggled to process the fact it was just one of innumerable planets orbiting innumerable stars, and people lived on some of the planets and could travel between them.

He was separated from his clothes and cleaned with some incredibly pungent liquid. His nails were manicured, and his hair was cut and then given a pair of tight-fitting black garments called miskinir.

He would later learn they were black because they were impregnated with activated charcoal. Supposedly it absorbed and neutralized body order, and he was told to leave them on for the duration of the trip. He was issued several one-piece yellow work outfits, a pair of boots, and work gloves. Then, he shuffled back to Lewatollma.

Before he could say a thing, Lewatollma started in on him, "Now, Eramus, you need to understand that only a few of us know your language, and we will not be able to accompany you continuously to translate. The burden falls upon you to learn our tongue. If you are stuck and I'm available to help you, I gladly will.

"Lewatollma, one question before you send me away."

"Yes, what is it?"

"Why did you get a nice blue uniform, and I got this hideous yellow one?

It didn't take Eramus very long to learn the layout of the ship– at least those parts to which he had access. He discovered the ship was multiple ships connected to a central hub referred to as the command center. The ship he departed on was one of many that had been sent to different parts of his world. Except for the command deck–an area he was forbidden to enter–the other ships were identical. You just had to read the distinguishing markings to keep your bearings – markings that were a complete and utter mystery to him.

Lewatollma explained that everyone worked on a ship and that he was no exception. Based on his minimal skills, he was assigned to assist in the kitchen. Not that he had ever seen a kitchen like this before. The head cook was a grumpy, bad-tempered, and foul-mouthed individual: nothing at all like the others he knew. He yelled, threw things, and cursed. This did not help Eramus pick up the language.

In the few moments he could spend with Lewatollma, he asked her to explain some of the phrases that the cook bantered about. Some of them caused Lewatollma to blush; some caused her to blanch. She hastily ended their time together, shaking her head and sending him away.

Apparently, many of these phrases were considered inappropriate for use in civil conversation. So, he sought out an expert in these matters with whom he just happened to be acquainted: Nesneratha. She was delighted to translate and was highly entertained by any new and unusual vulgarity he brought to her. She patiently explained the meanings and gave him insight into the origin, context, and relevance of these colorful metaphors. She also coached him on how to respond to such abuse in kind, reveling in the extensive use of her sophisticated vocabulary. She made him practice proper inflection and enunciation and taught him some simple sentence constructs.

One repartee she worked on for several days with him, ensuring the hand gestures, tone, and delivery were perfect. Even though Nesneratha seemed genuinely kind and helpful, in truth, she had not changed one whit. The day after he delivered the long-rehearsed curse, he noticed the crew smile when they saw him. He

III

assumed it was a sign of respect because he had stood up to the cook. However, a week later, one of the junior officers informed him what he actually said was, "I am a singularly grotesque off-worlder," and even though it was true, he would be well advised to refrain from using it. If Lewatollma knew, she never made mention of it. But then, she had long ago stopped apologizing for Nesneratha.

After just three weeks working in the kitchen, he had obtained a working knowledge of every imprecation, slander, innuendo, insult, or blasphemy formed in their tongue. Plus, the words for bake, pot, bowl, water, cut, cup, dice, boil, knife, ladle, simmer, fork, steam, and a few other simple words known to every child aged three and up.

He was assigned to sleep with the spetcimals—also referred to as technicians or techs for short, who also just happened to wear yellow work suits. In the barracks, he shared a bunk with two other men. Because they worked in shifts, he had sole use of the bunk for about seven straight hours. He quickly learned that if you overslept, a crewman would climb right in and snuggle up to you in his miskinir. He found this somewhat disturbing. Waking up in the embrace of another man was sufficiently unsettling, that after three incidents, he was completely cured of oversleeping.

The tech's duties were, well, technical. They cooked, repaired, cleaned, and in general made sure the ship functioned. Most of them specialized in very complex tasks. One not-so-complex specialty Eramus encountered frequently was the security forces.

These included the very same men who held him prisoner on the lake and threw him overboard. He was determined not to hold a grudge–they did, after all, save him before he drowned.

Most of them were broad-shouldered and heavily muscled. Maybe this was just an illusion, for they never wore loose clothing or cloaks, just a skintight red outfit that seemed to brazenly advertise their peak physical condition. Clearly, the message was: I can stop you, and I will do it without the least bit of remorse or mercy. If he encountered one blocking his way, he quickly learned the best and simplest recourse was to go in a different direction.

His kitchen experience made it much easier to understand their mutterings. Additionally, he became well acquainted with several more important shipboard phrases like 'Where are you going?' 'This area is off-limits.' 'Leave immediately before I *action verb* your *anatomical reference.*' Very seldom did Eramus have a prolonged conversation with them. A stern look and crossed arms often made a verbal exchange completely unnecessary.

One of Erams' huge frustrations was that the officers and techs were separated. Different sleeping areas. Different dining areas. Different communal areas. Both Lewatollma and Nesneratha had a private room shared with just one other officer. And they each had their own bed! Which they did not have to share! Ever!

Meetings with Lewatollma were brief and usually conducted in a hallway or a recessed doorway. The sight of a senior officer meant the meeting was over. She would just walk away without a word. Officers and technicians were forbidden to mingle. Eramus never

asked about the propriety of off-worlders and officers fraternizing–
he didn't want to know, nor did he care. He thought he would be
welcomed and given guest status, but in the pecking order of the
ship, off-worlders, or nemreans in their tongue, fell somewhere
below the techs and only barely above the trash.

The journey home to their planet, Herebris IV, would take eight
months. Lewatollma had a particularly important job, and she was
addressed formally as Minminuma Lewatollma. There were a
dozen or so of these Minminuma, and somehow, it was their job to
get the ship from his world to theirs. The exact details were vague
and involved words for which there was no equivalent in his
vocabulary.

Fortunately, the men he bunked with took a liking to him and
helped him learn to speak a fair bit of their tongue, which was
called Emallinawiman, but they mostly used the shorter term
Nawiman. Most of the learning time was spent pointing to some
object or pantomiming some action and listening carefully to their
responses. He and they would then repeat them until he could
pronounce them correctly. They would then join them together to
form simple sentences. The bunk is warm. He snores loudly. Lunch
was awful.

It was tedious and painstakingly slow work, especially in the
beginning. His bunkmates were rewarded with stories of Eram's
adventures in his home world, which they called Pernaus III. The
techs were never allowed to get very far from their ship while on
the planet. They had only glimpsed their surroundings and were

eager to hear such details as he could provide. His stories became the diversion of choice for them and soon the bunk area was packed to the ceiling with attentive crew members. Often, he would have to act out and gesture wildly to make himself understood. He frequently had them laughing raucously or profoundly puzzled as they tried to decipher his performance.

A complaint was registered by someone who, though keenly interested in the stories, had to sleep. So, Eram's storytelling was moved into one of the common areas where he would not disturb those who needed their rest and had the added benefit of accommodating a larger audience. The stories spread by word of mouth among the techs, and soon, it became common knowledge among the crew that the "singularly grotesque off-worlder" was a refreshing source of entertainment. He was the only entertainment; non-work hours were normally occupied by cleaning and reading manuals.

Slowly his language skills improved, his accent became more natural, and his vocabulary expanded. He looked forward to the day when he could fully relate the salacious details of a certain person's indiscretions at the Sudsy Tankard—he had decided that would be his grand finale. First, because he wanted to relate the tale in unmistakable terms, and second, he might need to escape quickly from her. Often, he was asked to repeat certain of the crew's favorite stories, and over time he recalled more details, so no two renditions were exactly alike.

On occasion, a junior officer would look in and sometimes stand in the doorway intently listening while pretending to be disinterested. Then, there were a couple of officers until the passageway outside the commons area was crowded. Eramus suggested they be invited in, but the techs told him they were not allowed in officer's areas and vice-versa. Everyone seemed to be happy standing in the passageway until the captain came through one day and found his way blocked. It only took several words in his booming voice to scatter the officers and put all the techs on alert.

The captain—the only person who could roam where he pleased—walked in, looked around, and, seeing no real mischief, told them to carry on but to keep the door closed in the future. It tickled the techs that they had something the officers did not. Yet a good story begs to be told, and so while in the business of fixing or cleaning, the techs shared stories with some of the officers.

It was a good deal of time later that a lot of excitement and preparation began to occupy the crew's spare time. Things were fastened down and stored securely. Drills were conducted to ready the crew to 'make fast' during transit. What was being transited, Eramus had no clue. It was just another meaningless word to him, like microgravity, vacuum, magnetohydrodynamics, and barycenter, which fell into the category of 'too hard to explain.'

During these drills—held seemingly at random—every crew member was to find a place to brace himself and remain perfectly still. The signal was a red light that flooded the compartment and passageway along with three blasts of a piercing tone which ensured even sleeping crew members knew. During this period the ship became eerily quiet until another three blasts of sound and the lights extinguished.

After one such drill, which seemed much longer than usual because Eramus had wedged himself into a doorway in a painfully uncomfortable position, which made it seem longer, he was on his way to work when he heard a commanding voice.

"Clear the way."

Eramus ducked into a doorway and folded his arms. What he saw shocked him. Several officers were being aided down the ladder from the command center, handed down as if they could no longer move under their own power. Once in the passageway, another officer put a supporting arm around them and slowly helped them down the hall. Their faces were pale and gaunt, with eyes glazed and vacant. Their hair was matted onto their heads, and they were dripping perspiration, their shirts dark with sweat.

One of them stumbled, coming down the ladder and someone caught her as she fell backward. The officer was practically carrying her, her feet shuffled, and her legs wobbled. Lewatollma!? Eramus stepped forward.

"Can I help?"

"Yes. Please!" the officer replied, straining.

Eramus took her free arm, slung it around his neck, and placed his arm around her waist.

"Are you Okay?" he softly asked.

Lewatollma slowly looked up to see Eramus. After a couple of seconds, she tried to smile, but then her head dropped back down. Eramus realized he was in a part of the ship he had never visited before–the officers' quarters. They stopped in front of what must have been her room and slid the door back. Her room consisted of two low bunks, a small desk, a chair, several storage compartments, and barely enough room to walk. Somehow, he was disappointed; he had imagined something grander.

"Which one is yours, dear?" the officer asked her.

"Top," she responded weakly.

"Get her legs," the officer ordered, and together, they carefully got her in and placed her on her side. The officer grabbed two blankets from a shelf and threw one at Eramus. She snapped hers open and covered Lewatollma, tucking her in snugly.

"Well?" the officer barked. Eramus shook out his blanket and handed it to her. This one she used to cover her head as well as tucking it in all around.

"Out!" she ordered, but Eramus hesitated and asked.

"What happened? Will she be alright?"

"Of course, she will! Some rest, some food and she will be back to work in a few days."

It was at this point the officer recognized him and recalled his connection to Lewatollma. Some of the circulated stories included accounts of how she and Eramus met and their adventures, and she knew that it was exactly the kind of epic bilge the techs loved.

X

"I suppose you want to stay, watch over her, and attend to her needs?" the officer asked softly.

"I would," Eramus answered.

"Well, you cannot!" she barked. "Her roommate will be here any minute, and I will not permit a Nemrean hanging about in the female officers' quarters. Now clear out!"

After this incident, the drills mercifully ceased but were replaced by other rehearsals and training in the preparation and manning of trans-atmospheric craft. The TAC would be the means of leaving the ship and getting back on solid ground. This was not the reverse of what he experienced when he left his home world. He found out the trip down would be much rougher and contain an element of danger. But despite any anxiety the crew may have had about the TAC, an air of excitement and joyful anticipation filled the ship.

With the transit completed, Lewatollma had much more time to spend with Eramus. She spent a lot of time telling him about her parents, the friends she left behind, and her world in general. She especially warned him that her father may not take to his presence very well. Eramus was not phased. Meeting your love's father was always awkward. But he had survived it once before, so he felt confident he could survive this one as well.

Nesneratha, on the other hand, was extraordinarily busy. Her duties revolved around returning home. There was to be a ceremony of sorts after landing, and there would be a grand reunion of friends and family. Nesneratha, however, had to return to the ship, and it would be several more months before her shipboard duties were complete.

Lewatollma explained that Nesneratha would be returning to space soon, whereas she was going to teach until she received her citizenship. After that, she would marry and raise a family.

"How long will that be?" Eramus asked.

"Five years. But it will pass quickly."

"Then we can marry?"

"Who I marry is my father's decision. So, you must obtain his permission," she sighed.

"I take it he is not fond of nemreans?"

"Only Nemreans who want to marry his daughter. I am a lord's daughter and a Minminuma. I expect he takes a great deal of pride in that, so there will be significant resistance to my marrying a nemrean. He and my mother probably have someone picked out already to be my mate. A formal betrothal will not occur till a few months before I receive my citizenship."

"I can't be the only Nemrean to marry a Nawiman. What have others in our situation done?"

"Eramus, I have never read or heard about such a union. They simply are not done. You must prepare yourself for the very real possibility that it may not happen. This is why I was so upset when you showed up on my ship. I do not want to hurt or disappoint you; you mean so much to me. But I feel it would have been kinder to leave you on Pernaus III than to strand you here heartbroken, a

XII

stranger among people, whom, as you have already discovered, do not look favorably on nemreans.

"Eramus, it would be difficult for you to court me because of my status. There will be considerable competition from men my father would feel are far more deserving – men of nobility and achievement. What do you have to offer?"

"I did save your life," he said hopefully.

"For which you will receive my family's heartfelt gratitude and be forever in their debt. But it by itself, will not be enough, I fear."

She grabbed his hand.

"I must tell you something hurtful, Eramus. You would not be accepted by even the lowest Nawiman commoner as a mate. Many in this society will never marry because they are considered physically or mentally imperfect. No one will mix their bloodlines with them for fear of introducing defects into their progeny."

She looked carefully around to see who was nearby and then leaned in.

"They call them ewam. I do not like to use the term myself. I consider it very rude to judge someone about something over which they have no control. But you are considered ewam. Do you begin to see the impossibility of our marriage?"

"Are you abandoning me?"

"I would never abandon a friend, but I might be separated from you against my will. Once married, I will be consumed with the task of raising and teaching my children. Families are very insulated from everyone except blood relatives. It would be an insult to my husband for you to visit me and you know how sticky we are about honor! A duel would most certainly be the result. I have enough blood on my hands already, it would crush me to add more.

"I wish the circumstances were different. I should have had this talk with you long ago before we even left your home world. I was wrong to withhold this from you. Can you forgive me?"

"You don't need to apologize to me any more than you need to apologize for Nesneratha. Fate brought us together; fate will see us through. Besides, I have seen us married in my dreams."

"Eramus, dreams are not reality, just wishful thinking and hopes spun by our minds in the depth of sleep."

"Most dreams are as you say, but there are others that are glimpses into the future. Puzzling, at times, in their symbolism, but I can recall them in vivid detail. So, they must be important. Haven't you ever had a dream like that?"

"I have not, Eramus."

"Hmmm, must be a nemrean thing," he laughed. "I'm sticking to my plan. I will convince your father and propose to you in four and a half years. Any more questions?"

"You will have to become a citizen, too."

"I have five years. How hard can it be?"

A NOTE FROM THE AUTHOR

The idea for this book began decades ago when our family was immersed in anime. One anime didn't sit right with me because of the huge disparity between the ages of the two romantically involved characters: He was 18, she was 600. I don't know why that bothered me so much because I am, in fact, married to an older woman (but not 582 years older).

Such was the inspiration for Eramus, the first part of a series. Initially, I had some very distinct ideas about the plot, setting, and characters and I wrote several chapters out of sequence. In the following years, I worked on filling in the blanks, evolving cultures, language, and plot as well as seeing the path that would allow the story to continue beyond the original scope. In retrospect, this is the hard way to write a book. But working full-time with a host of other responsibilities did not give a lot of creative writing time. At the time of this publishing, the second part is over ninety percent complete. I promise it won't take two more decades.

ACKNOWLEDGMENTS

Many thanks to GetCovers for the cover artwork and promotional materials. Big thanks to Michael Waitz of Sticks and Stones Editing. Not only for his editing skills, but the encouragement and sage advice he provided throughout. To Mikael Carlson, for his belief that this story was worthy of print and navigated me through the labyrinthine world of publishing.

I would be remiss if I didn't acknowledge Mark Howard, whose example motivated me to become serious about finishing and publishing my book. Mark, you helped me see the end was in sight and convinced me that I could reach it.

I want to thank all those who read my drafts and provided feedback, including my three daughters, but especially Barbara, who provided extensive, unbiased, and sometimes upsetting feedback. Thank you, Barb, for being brutally honest.

But most of all, I want to thank my dear wife and friend, Pamela, who also read and reread it. And put up with me being away from her. And my whining and fretting. And when it was all over, still loved me.

ABOUT THE AUTHOR

Guillaume Charron is many things: outdoorsman, husband, nature-lover, father, pastor, grandfather, poet, great-grandfather, gardener, US Air Force veteran, computer programmer, and writer. Living quietly in Ohio, USA, he dreams of becoming an author, hoping to turn fictional writing into a third career to keep him busy until he actually retires...or the zombie apocalypse happens...whichever comes first.